KEEPER OF THE LIGHT

by
Patty Metzer

Keeper of the Light
by Patty Metzer

Second Edition
1997

This is a work of fiction. The events described are imaginary and
the characters are fictitious and not intended to represent specific
persons. Even when settings are referred to by their real names,
the incidents portrayed there are entirely fictitious. The reader
should not infer that the events ever actually happened.

All Scripture quotations are taken from
The King James Version of the Bible.

ISBN 1-885904-09-6

Cover design by Richard Allen Schaefer

PRINTED IN THE UNITED STATES OF AMERICA
BY
FOCUS PUBLISHING INCORPORATED
1375 Washington Avenue South
Bemidji, Minnesota 56601

Dedicated
to my family

Brian
Adam, Jenny and Katlyn
as together we have learned to be
keepers of the Light.

My thanks to

Jan Haley
for trusting the Lord's guidance
and for challenging me to dig deeper.
God will be faithful to complete
the work He began
through this book.

Prologue

Cape Cod , Massachusetts
October 1797

The shoreline was smothered in a veil of gray mist, forsaken completely as storm clouds overwhelmed the sunrise. An eerie silence came with the unseen dawn. No signs of life could be seen. Suddenly the storm broke loose, releasing its power. Brilliant, white light tore through the veil of gray followed by a long, low rumble of thunder in the distance. Ocean waves were churned into a restless cauldron.

Another flash of lightning snaked its finger at the shrouded child, who rocked pitifully back and forth where she was crouched in waist-high grass on top of the bank. The first drops of icy rain brought no change in the pattern of her movement, back and forth. Back and forth she rocked, oblivious to the violent storm.

When the rain increased, so did the ache inside of her. All through the night, she had tried desperately to forget the nightmare which had chased her miles north of home to this barren stretch of coastline. But the images would not depart, neither would the tight feeling that choked her every breath, stealing away the words which she longed to cry out.

Deadly streaks sliced through the clouds again, causing her to stare upward until rain and tears mingled together upon her pale face. Anger ripped through the stormy sky, hurtling across the sea to throw itself at her in a strong blast of wind.

To feel the same kind of anger might release her from the nightmare, but she was too utterly alone and exhausted to be that angry.

Back and forth, back and forth. Though the cold seeped through her thin clothing, down deep into her body, it still could not quite reach to where she hurt the most - her heart. Nothing else would ever touch her there...not now that her mother was dead. Now that they were both gone.

Another explosion, another long rumble of thunder.

She squeezed her eyes shut, hid her face against her knees. The storm moved closer, pressing down on her until she had to stop rocking. Nowhere would be safe now. Nowhere to hide. Back and forth. Back and forth.

A violent crash nearby startled her into looking up again. Her next breath was caught back in alarm. What was that dark bundle lying on the sand, left behind by the last terrible wave? She stood slowly and, lifting her skirt, began to wind a wayward path through the thick grass.

When the animal whimpered, the girl hurried those last few steps to the water's edge where she bent her small frame and sat in the damp sand beside the creature, gathering it tenderly into the folds of her shawl. It was barely alive, but she would not abandon it as she had been abandoned. As soon as she claimed her intentions, the next wave retreated from them, pulling out to sea.

After a moment, she, too, retreated, tracing the path of footprints back to her hiding place, cradling the puppy with one arm while she struggled up the steep bank, stumbling over tufts of sea grass along the way. She wasn't sure if the pain of the past hours lessened or if it only moved deeper inside of her. All she knew was that she no longer felt alone.

As she lowered herself and her protected bundle into the grass, she looked eastward, past miles of nothing but sand and scrub-oak. Silhouetted between sky and sea was a pinpoint of light. Highland Light.....It was true then, the light burned brightest in the midst of a storm.

Provincetown, Cape Cod
February 1802

It was daylight and he was free from the hated chains. For once, he could run through sunshine and chase seagulls. He could poke his nose into barrels of fresh fish and play tug of war with the ropes still tied up at the moorings. His sharp eyes missed nothing as he walked confidently along, stopping now and then to sniff at the more interesting distractions in his path. People moved aside to let him pass before they sent curious looks in the direction from which he came, wondering why he should be out alone. He was never alone.

Each movement caused the dog's black coat to shine with good health and suppressed energy. Perhaps he would have preferred to be with the girl, but he had stolen this opportunity for freedom knowing she would eventually come to find him. When she did, he would go back willingly. The bond between them was so strong, he could endure anything - even the chains.

Though her heart pounded erratically, she crept forward still, slipping between piles of crates and barrels, around coils of rope as thick as her arm. Another ship had come in from Boston. Its cargo, both human and otherwise, littered the docks. She had to find him quickly, before someone saw her.

With hands clutching the ends of her tattered shawl, she squeezed behind a huge crate, hidden from all eyes as she pressed herself deeply into the shadows. Where was he? She scanned the noisy dock again, listening intently. Because she was hemmed in on all sides by crude tones, the unexpected sound of a woman laughing captured her immediate attention. It was not difficult to find that woman. She stood just at the top of the gangway on the newly arrived ship, next to a man who looked very much like her. Though the woman's rich, black cape was certainly noticeable, it was still not as arresting as what the young man wore. His coat stirred memories in the girl's mind of a similar coat worn by a man she had known, long ago.

Tears suddenly blurred her sight of the couple on the ship, but she blinked them away. He was very tall. She was taller than average, too. They looked around eagerly as if excited about having reached Provincetown. There was something gentle in the way he set a hand on her arm to guide her over the rough plank walkway.

That same gentleness showed itself when they got to the end and the woman pressed a delicately gloved hand over her heart, faltering a moment. He asked her something, to which she shook her head and offered a smile in return. With somewhat more protectiveness, he set an arm across her shoulders, escorting her away from the bustle surrounding the ship. His steps were accommodating, the woman's were accepting and the dog's- - -.

She held her breath, heart pounding harder than ever to see that her dog meant to follow them. It was impossible to call him back. Instead, she was forced from the relative safety of the shadows, into bright daylight. People moved aside to let her pass, looking around with puzzled expressions until they saw why she was among them like this. Her desperately slow pursuit of the black dog caused some to laugh in a cruel way. Others threw jeering comments at her back which she ignored by slumping even deeper into the rags she wore. Her head was lowered in pitiful defense against their insults.

The strangers walked on, talking quietly, observing every new sight of the harbor town. As the mud-slick road began to rise away from the sea, the man measured his steps even more carefully. The silent parade took on a slower pace, bringing the dog almost to the man's heels and the girl's anxiety to a new height. Why did he have to trail behind the two of them as if he had some purpose for doing so? If he got caught, he would get her in trouble again. She hurried her steps at the thought.

When the young man stopped just outside the general store, the dog did, too. He sat a few feet away, watching them intently, his head held at a curious angle. Before it was lost, the girl took her chance and rushed forward. One small hand sank into the dog's thick fur until it closed around the chain collar. Though he was much stronger, the fear she felt overpowered his momentary disobedience and she was able to pull him away, into a narrow space between the store and the dilapidated building next door.

For a few moments, she squatted beside him, shaking in reaction to what had nearly happened. As if he felt sorry now for causing her such worry, the dog licked at her cold hands, begging forgiveness. Their eyes met..... When he sensed she would not be angry, he wagged his tail in delight. The predictable reaction brought a smile to the girl's face, but the smile did not last. They weren't out of danger yet.

Because it wasn't safe to leave, they stayed in that cool, shadowed space, crouched together in watchful silence.

What seemed a long time later, she saw the reason for her fear storm toward their hiding place. His rage was obvious to those who stopped to witness it. No one stopped long, though. More crucially, no one stopped *him*.

She bit down on her lip, held her breath, waited...

But he only moved past them, unaware how close he was to his prey.

A weakness spread through her legs, causing her to sink down onto both knees beside the dog and bury her face against his strength. Usually, he growled at the man. Today, he had remained tensely silent, keeping their secret, instinctively protecting her as he had done many times in the past five years.

Sunlight was starting to seep between the buildings. They would have moved then except that the strangers came out from the store and paused on the steps, talking to the owner. Both dog and girl watched the couple with new interest. They were close enough now to see them more clearly. In a town filled with strangers, these two seemed different somehow. Maybe it was the simple fact that they were so friendly. Or maybe it was the way this young, strong man in his navy coat with the brass buttons seemed not to be a stranger to the Cape at all.

The girl's heart somersaulted to hear him mention Highland Light. She knew then.....She knew that he was to be the keeper of the light.

Chapter One

Why was it that he found no pleasure in the way brilliant August sunshine tripped playfully over each wave? Or in watching the restless wind dance across stubborn blades of sea-green beach grass which seemed to want no part in the game?

Anyone seeing him frown on such a splendid, brand-new day would surely be hard-pressed to think why. But then they wouldn't know how ill Lydia was. Colin looked down upon the cedar-shingled roof of the brick house, feeling a surge of urgency to turn away from his daydreaming and get back to that wide, breezy room on the top floor.

Yet he allowed his contemplative gaze to wander the great expanse of blue Atlantic Ocean once more, almost as if he sought from her the answers to his silent, unanswerable questions. Coming here to Highland Light couldn't have been a mistake. It just couldn't have.

With practiced ease, he turned and made his way quickly down the narrow, twisting steps to the base of the gleaming white lighthouse tower, then out into a fresh summer morning. The force of the wind had ceased to take him by surprise. Nearly every day was like that, blown and tossed by the same unseen hand which delivered waves to Cape Cod's sandy shores. Sometimes the delivery was fiercely angry. Sometimes rhythmically dull. Today, it was neither. Today the sea seemed restless, a perfect complement to Colin's own mood.

He had changed in the last six months. A wiser look could be seen behind his eyes. One couldn't exactly call them brown. They were, instead, more of a tawny color liberally flecked with gold, especially when he was in good humor. But there were times, when he was truly angry, that his eyes darkened to a vibrant, snapping deep chestnut.

His hair was that same chestnut color. Thick and wavy, kept shorter than was popular with most men, simply because he preferred it that way. He also preferred to be clean-shaven.

Lydia had told him a number of times that he was a very handsome young man, in a rugged, completely masculine way. Too handsome to spend his life at a remote lighthouse. After all, she said, he should rather enjoy the feminine attention he had received in Boston. Colin, of course, knew she was only teasing him. She alone, of anyone, understood the reasons he was here.

Wind lifted the hair away from his strong, high forehead as he rounded the corner of the house. Highland Light had been built five years ago, in 1797, with its most impressive side facing out to sea. Colin thought he would surely have done the same. Life was meant to be lived that way. Head on. Face to face rather than forever turned away from the challenges which beat at the front door.

Sweat ran in annoying, little rivulets down his broad back from the effort he made to reach the bedroom at the top of the stairs. For once, he didn't stop to admire the well-appointed order of their home. Its starkness had been softened here and there by Lydia. Braided rugs. Flowering plants. Rows of books. Thick coats of mellow cream-colored paint. Both of them had worked hard since coming to Highland Light.

Colin walked past all of it now, blinded by concern and compassion. Good manners bade him knock on her half-open door. "Come in, MacRae." Her quietly teasing tone somewhat eased his frown before he walked in. Lydia had already set her book, pages down, upon the bed. "You can't have gotten so much done in ten minutes."

"And why not?" He lowered himself onto the edge of the mattress beside her. Cheery streams of sunshine flowed through tall, narrow windows on the east wall. Lydia's soft touch could be found here, too, in the hand-stitched muslin curtains and the colorful quilt upon the brass bed.

There was a definite weariness in her brown eyes. Her skin, always fair, was pale now, unnaturally sallow. When Colin frowned, she reached for his hand, unaware of how white hers looked next to his tanned strength. "Will you stop sulking. I haven't seen you so downhearted since you were ten and that beast of a dog of yours managed to get his nose full of porcupine quills."

"He wasn't a beast, Lydia. You only say that because he got paw prints on your new pink dancing dress." Colin felt relief seeping in as they joked with one another. Maybe this time, she would be up and about in a few days.

Lydia settled herself against the pillows with a barely audible sigh. "Most sisters would have gotten you horse-whipped for making them miss the dance."

"Well," Colin squeezed her hand, "you aren't like 'most sisters'. Besides, you never really liked Guthrie Williams anyway." She laughed a little in a weak way. Just those few minutes of talking had sapped her energy. Colin watched as she closed her eyes. Her hair, the same full chestnut as his, lay dull and limp past her shoulders. One would never guess now that she was only thirty years old. "Do you want me to get a doctor, Sis?"

Her eyes flew open in alarm. "Of course not! Goodness, Colin. I've been sick before."

"Not like this." His sober words laid a blanket of unspoken tension between them. The doctors in Boston had warned them this would happen. Lydia had been fighting sickness since she was a young girl when rheumatic fever had weakened her heart. "I shouldn't have let you come," Colin now sighed out his greatest source of guilt. "Do you want me to take you back to Boston?"

Though Lydia ignored this last statement with all the air of an indignant older sister, the act didn't fool him for one second. "What I want is for you to go to Provincetown and get some help out here. Look at yourself, Colin! You're about ready to drop. Running here and there. Taking care of the light. Doing my chores plus your own. I won't have -."

He silenced her anxious words by placing a single finger over her lips. They both smiled then, realizing how useless it was for them to be arguing the same point twice in one morning. "I've got to see to the animals. May I get you anything?" Her eyebrows shot up expressively as if to say he knew perfectly well that what she wanted most was for him to give in.

Colin stood to his full height, creating a strangely contrasted image of manliness in his sister's feminine room. "Read your book, Lydia. I'll be back later to check on you."

She watched his strong, familiar steps until he was at the door. "Hey, MacRae!" Colin turned back with curiosity...especially when he saw the tears which softened Lydia's eyes. "Thank you."

He was too touched to do more than nod his head before he left.

All the buildings at Highland, including the barn for the animals, were especially sturdy, having been built of thick planks which some-one had salvaged from shipwrecked vessels.

At one time, there must have been forest on this northern end of Cape Cod. Now, there wasn't a real tree within a mile of the light. There were plenty of scrub-oak and pitch pine, but nothing bigger around than his arm. It was curious how things grew so near the ground, spreading out rather than up. Perhaps it was in deference to the ceaseless winds.

Colin made short work of milking the cow, making sure she and the handful of laying hens were fed. When he first arrived at High-land, he made the mistake of letting Bess wander on her own. He had eventually found her standing knee-deep in one of the fresh-water pools some distance from home, her tail swishing away the occasional fly which dared land on her back.

Since then, Bess got her own pail of water and a smart, fenced yard to wander in to her heart's content. There was a horse at High-land, too, though the word "horse" was most likely stretching the truth. Justice - as the previous owner had named him - was a lazy shadow to even the smallest horse in his father's stable.

There seemed much here to contrast with Boston, many more reasons for Colin to believe he had made the right choice in coming. Highland was more surely his home than Boston could ever be.

He stepped out of the barn and lifted his gaze skyward, immedi-ately taken aback by the awareness that he didn't miss Boston. He never had, not once since coming here. Perchance he had secretly wished to miss it, for that would add meaning to the part of his life thus far invested there. But he was, above all, an honest man. This place was home to him. And Boston - Boston was the mold from which he had broken free.

That was one of Max's sayings, "breaking the mold." While most young men Colin's age were beginning to accept, even welcome, a father's influence upon their lives, the same was not true for Colin. If there was a mentor in his life, it wasn't his father at all, but Max. Max who had lived to ride the ocean, to be master of a ship claiming the wind's power, harnessing what was vibrant and ever-changing about the sea. Max who had tried to argue him into being a sea captain, but who listened patiently to Colin's reasons for becoming a lighthouse keeper. Those days of learning seemed so long ago.

He abruptly pulled himself back to the present. There was work to be done.

The rest of Colin's day was spent making short visits to Lydia in the midst of his other work. She was a gem, never once complaining or demanding some small thing he had forgotten. In the evening, he carried her down to the parlor. They talked awhile, not about anything in particular. A comfortable silence came as the hours stretched on. Lydia was asleep before darkness fell.

Another week passed with each day following the same pattern of work and worry, except that Colin eventually began listening to his sister's heartfelt plea. His duties at Highland were a full time job in themselves. Trying to keep the house going at the same time appeared more and more to be a battle he could not win.

At night, Colin fell into bed utterly exhausted, too tired even to sleep. It was during those hours in his own simply furnished room that he would stare out the window, watching the beam of security which the lighthouse sent out over the water. Not for the first time, he felt moments of fear, moments of not being sure he had actually placed his complete trust in God's promises.

This place should remind him each and every day that God was his rock, his shield, his high tower in times of trouble. "Trust in Him at all times," the Psalmist had written, "pour out your heart before Him; God is a refuge for us." Hadn't he come to Highland in order to know God more fully? There was a clear promise for him throughout the Bible that God was near.

More and more often, Colin found that his prayers on those nights were not a silent study of God's promises, but desperate wrestlings that Lydia should live. He would rise in the morning, determined to find her much better. But it seemed she never was.

Colin awakened slowly at dawn on the twentieth day of August. It was an unusually warm day. As always, his first job was to turn out the lamps at the top of the tower. Far out to sea, he recognized the indistinct shape of a ship his light had guided during the night.

He did think of it that way, as being his light. Some unexplainable bond had melded man and object together until it was impossible to separate where one ended and the other began. So much of what Colin felt deep inside was reflected in Highland Light. Perhaps that was ultimately what had made him accept this new post in the first place, desolate as it was.

This day, he knew he would give in to his sister. He would travel the miles to Provincetown. By nightfall, someone new, someone foreign to his light, might be standing where he was now, on the ocean-side of the glass-encased room at the top of the tower. Someone who didn't know what it really meant...

Slowly, Colin gathered his thoughts into a tight ball which fit uncomfortably in the new place he was now forced to make in his life. Lydia would be awake. He had much to do before he could set out on his journey.

Chapter Two

In the hours it took Colin to reach Provincetown, his thoughts continually rushed back to the lighthouse. What was Lydia doing? Had she fallen perhaps or would she need some small thing he had forgotten? It was impossible for him to keep from wondering how she was doing on her own.

With each thought, he pushed the worn, bone-thin old horse as hard as he dared. Justice didn't realize it yet, but his master had a pocketful of coin to spend on a replacement. The extra expense was easily rationalized. They needed a more reliable horse at the light, one who could pull its fair share. Justice had struggled today just to move the wagon along the eight mile stretch of road. Even the urgency of the hands upon the reins now, as their destination came into view, brought only a monotonous, rolling gait.

A dozen heads turned in curiosity to see the stranger who was coming to town. Colin wasn't surprised. When he and Lydia first arrived on the Cape, they had spent barely an hour in the port city. It was much more likely, he thought, that these people would recognize the Boston furniture which had been loaded on the wagon. For that very reason, he gave them quick, polite nods of greeting. Some nodded back.

Provincetown was a unique place, caught somehow between infancy and the more respectable position of established adulthood. Yet, for all its rugged appearance, it also embraced an air of pride. Coming from Boston - which held a veritable wealth of achievements in architecture, commerce, and social amenities alone - Colin appreciated Provincetown's sense of pride. It was a simple pride, really, the kind one knew was not a result of "putting on airs".

The harbor was their single claim to notability. Nowhere else on the bay side of the Cape was there a more natural place for the fishing boats to gather at the end of the day. Calm, rock-free waters cradled every tired boat and crew which wandered in. Maybe it was the same for people. Maybe tired, searching people found their way here, too. Yes, Provincetown was a good place to live.

As Colin drove through the wide street, he couldn't help but see the negative to such goodness. Actually, it surrounded him on every side. SAND! The entire town was literally sitting on sand. Whoever built the first house here must have been an optimistic person to think he could best the combined tides of ocean and sand.

Everywhere he looked today, Colin saw painfully obvious signs of the silent war. Boardwalks separated street from store with conveniently spaced top boards to remind the clinging sand it was not welcome inside and must fall through the cracks.

Thick shutters lay open now, but seemed to say they were ready in an instant to fly shut should the enemy wind send in ranks of blown sand. If it really was a war between sand and settler, Colin thought, Provincetown was unfairly flanked. Sand dunes swelled up on all three inland sides of the town. Just now, though, they were washed a harmless pale tan by the sun and were no real threat at all.

Closer to the harbor, some of the square houses had been built on sturdy pilings. Not to keep their feet dry, but to keep their skirts from dragging in the dust. Colin unconsciously smiled at comparing such ramshackle buildings with maidens on an afternoon walk. Wouldn't Lydia have a good laugh at hearing his thoughts?

He pulled Justice to a stop outside the weather-beaten general store where he had purchased supplies six months ago. Of course, he didn't have to pull very hard. Neither did he bother securing the horse to the post; Justice would most likely never notice if he spent a month of Sundays in the same place.

"Hello, theahe!" A friendly, booming voice turned his attention to the open doors of the store. "You the lighthouse keepah out ta Highland, ain't ya?"

Colin walked up the steps to grasp the man's outstretched hand. "Yes, I am. Colin MacRae. And you're Jolly Troy."

Age-faded blue eyes in a deeply wrinkled face clearly showed Jolly Troy was pleased Colin had remembered his name. The older man, bent to a small five feet-two inches by years of hard work, pumped Colin's hand with enthusiasm. "Expected ya long befoahe now. Been doin' good out theahe?"

"Not too bad, thanks." Colin set both arms around his chest, not realizing the gesture made his own muscular, six foot-four inch frame look all the larger.

Jolly Troy's eyes widened a bit. No one could miss that this young man was city folk and from Boston besides. The uniform probably had something to do with it. As far as Jolly knew, the last keeper at Highland had never worn one. It was impressive, alright. A navy blue coat set off by gleaming brass buttons. The young fella must have polished them that very day. One look at his strong jaw and Jolly knew it wasn't for vanity's sake that Colin MacRae had worn the uniform. It was for duty's sake. And duty was something too few men cared about now-a-days. "Can't 'membeah, but ya said you was Scots, aye? Should know with a name such as MacAhe and that look 'bout ya."

Colin showed even white teeth when he smiled. His "looks" could have easily been French, but Jolly must have seen something there. "And what might that be?"

"Ahhh." Jolly winked at the same time as he turned and led his captive audience of one into the merchandise-crowded store. "Why, it be the touch o' the sea. Ain't but a good Scotsman has got a wind-lashed tan 'bout him and that theahe deteahmined light in youah eyes." The old man had, by then, taken up his usual post behind the counter set in the middle of the huge space. Only one couldn't tell it was huge because it was packed floor to ceiling with goods of every description. The air smelled of smoked fish and the ocean and tobacco...and, oddly enough, roses.

"Provincetown seems busy today." The casual observance on Colin's part brought forth a week's worth of explanations from Jolly Troy. In the middle of it all, Colin handed him a list of things they needed at the light. Jolly, in turn and quite without interruption, gave the list to a pint-sized boy who appeared from some unseen hiding place. The delegation of responsibilities didn't really surprise Colin. There was indeed a time in old age when a man could fully expect to hand over the real work and, in doing thus, settle back to enjoy life's easier side.

It was a full fifteen minutes before Colin was able to squeeze in a few words without seeming very rude. "Mr. Troy -."

"Ahhh!" There was a wave of a hand to go with the wink this time. "Call me 'Jolly'. Why, I'm too old ta be 'Misteah' anybody."

"Okay," Colin agreed with another easy grin. "Jolly it is, then. I'm in need of a better horse out at the light. Do you have any idea where I could find one?"

Jolly's bushy, white eyebrows rose upward into a matching shock of hair which seemed very thick for one so advanced in years. "Well now...might be the liveahy would have one oah two ta choose. Talk ta Michael. He'll fix ya up."

"And where is the livery?" Deciphering Jolly's speech was getting easier with time.

"Liveahy is at the end o' this heahe walk. Tuahn left. Can't miss the smell taday." Jolly laughed at his own joke. "Ya want I should have Timmy load the wagon foah ya?"

Colin caught sight of the boy scurrying about. "No, thank you. I'll load it when I get back. I won't be gone long." He knew Timmy had heard when the boy flashed him a grateful, lopsided smile.

True to Jolly's word, the afternoon smell of the livery was impossible to miss. Of all the businesses he passed, it was the least active. And no wonder. Even Michael had stationed himself out-of-doors to repair a harness.

Colin was able to make a good purchase. Offering Justice to the man as a free bonus probably helped complete the deal. In poor Michael's eyes, Justice still had a few months "work" in him. Some desperate bloke might even come along and offer good money for such a "docile" horse.

The new horse was anything but docile. He was a giant of a Belgian draft, the healthiest shade of bay brown and in need of a much better name than "Hoahse". Michael didn't pronounce his "r's" either. Colin had learned it was a Cape Cod trait.

By the time man and horse had returned to the general store, it was decided: Samson. There could be no better name for him. Young Timmy was suitably impressed. He barely came up to Samson's withers and that even with standing on the top step leading into the store.

Now that he had acquired the horse, there was only one thing left to do. While they loaded the wagon, Colin contemplated, rather moodily, the best way of finding a housekeeper. Even Timmy, as young as he was, recognized the expression of concentrated frustration which had taken over the light keeper's earlier good humor.

The last bag of salt was hoisted onto the flour barrel behind the wagon's seat. As if on cue, Jolly appeared on the steps. "It be puttin' up time. Youah sisteah may want moahe salt ta do the cannin'."

The opening seemed too timely for Colin to miss. He leaned his forearms on the buckboard. The muscles beneath his white shirt stood out clearly now that he had removed his coat. "My sister isn't well, Jolly." Colin could read unspoken sympathy in the blue eyes which returned his look. "One of the reasons I came today was to find someone who would go back with me. Someone who could help with the house and take care of Lydia."

"Well, now," Jolly reached a hand to his chin as if he was rubbing a full beard, though that must have been long ago, for only a few stray gray whiskers remained now. "Don't know as if -."

"It's a young, strong giahl you be needin' then?" The man who spoke so unexpectedly stepped out from the doorway of Jolly Troy's store, eyeing Colin with piqued interest.

Almost in the same instant, Jolly sent Colin a cautious glance, the kind of look that caused Colin to stand warily as the stranger came close. He didn't exactly like how ill-kempt and surly the man appeared, but he wouldn't be hiring him as a housekeeper. "Yes." Colin used his best authoritative voice, though he guessed several years separated them. "I do need someone strong. There's a lot to do at Highland." Was that a gleam of opportunity he saw on the man's face?

"Name's Everette Koch." He held out a grimy hand which Colin had no choice but to shake civilly. "How long you be needin' this heahe help?"

Colin backed up the man's assumptions a few steps. "Do you know of someone?"

"Suahe do."

"Now wait theahe, Koch." Jolly was quick to interfere. "You can't be thinkin' ta send -."

"An' why not?" Koch was on the defensive immediately. A hard look crossed his face. "You know anybody else heahe could do betteah? She be young an' strong, just like he want."

Colin waited for Jolly to continue the argument, but the older man simply shook his head. "No. Ain't nobody else I cen think o' would go."

As if the matter were decided between the two of them, Everette Koch gave a pleased nod. "I'll tell heah ta come in ten minutes, then." He took off too quickly for Colin to stop him with more questions.

But that excuse didn't get Jolly off the hook. Colin folded both arms across his chest again, unconsciously emphasizing the broadness of his shoulders. "And what was all that about?"

Jolly shrugged his bent shoulders indistinctly. " 'Bout you gettin' youah new housekeepeah, I guess."

"You mean there's but one woman in this whole town who can do the job?"

While his question may have sounded normal enough, it was the tone behind it which betrayed impatience.

"This heahe ain't' youah Boston, Misteah MacAhe. Theahe be twenty men ta one lady. 'Sides - ," Jolly had the good sense to add a diplomatic air to his voice. "Mahy 'Liz'beth's gal ain't' a - woman. She only be sixteen, no moahe than seventeen, I'd say. Got heahself a name of bein' a hahd woahkeah."

Colin couldn't just ignore the hesitancy he heard in the other man's little speech "So, what's wrong with her?"

There was a long pause.

"Well? Speak up," Colin urged firmly. "I'd like to know before she gets here."

With the advantage of wisdom on his side, Jolly decided it would be best if Colin MacRae found out for himself. "Timmy!" The boy - who had been listening from just inside the store's entry - poked his head out, but no more. "You hop up in the wagon theahe an' take Misteah MacAhe ta the Koch place." Jolly met Colin's questioning eyes. "Save the lass a long, hot walk, won't it?"

Colin's expression wasn't exactly readable. "I suppose it would. You aren't going to tell me anything about her, are you Jolly?"

"Don't guess as if it be my place." He looked on as Colin and Timmy climbed into the wagon. " 'Membeah, Colin...Youah sisteah."

It was the oddest thing for him to say, especially since they were acquainted but an hour ago. Colin slapped the reins firmly across Samson's back and the wagon moved forward. Maybe there was still a way for him to find more information. After all, Timmy was only a boy. An eager, friendly boy.

"Thanks for your help, Timmy."

"Yes, Siah." Timmy grinned up at the larger-than-life man beside him, feeling important for being given such a job as this. He hoped some of his pals would see him riding in the keeper's wagon.

"How old are you? Nearly a man, I'd say."

Timmy nearly burst the buttons on his homespun shirt the way his chest swelled out with pride. The boy's black eyes danced beneath his curly black hair. "Twelve, Siah. Had me a biahthday month 'go."

"You must know a lot about Provincetown." Colin glanced down at his passenger. "Where is it we're headed now? What part of town?"

That was an easy question. "Shank-Painteah Swamp." His eagerness somehow glamorized the ugly name.

"This Everette Koch, is he a good man? I suppose he owns one of those fishing boats down there." Though Colin eyed the few vessels left at dock on such a gorgeous day, he was still alert to the frown on Timmy's youthful brow.

"Misteah Koch don't have no boat."

"Really? Where does he work then?"

"Don't woahk, I guess. Neveah heahd o' him woahkin', least ways. The Dummy, she woahks."

Colin's hands gripped the reins so tightly his fingers turned white at the knuckles. The Dummy? How could Jolly have thought he would hire a simple-minded girl? A deep frown cut into Colin's brow, causing Timmy to try to right the damage. "She woahks hahd, Misteah MacAhe. Moahe'n ten o' most. Seen heah out late, sellin' them bait bags." None of what he said seemed to relieve the frown. Timmy hated that silent mood and tried again. "Most o' my gang thinks it's Koch what makes the Dummy the way she be."

"Doesn't she have a name?"

"Don't know o' one 'cept -."

"Okay." Colin broke in before he had to hear that horrid name again. They were getting into the older part of Provincetown now, though perhaps that was no excuse for the run-down, overgrown shabbiness of Shank-Painter Swamp. There was little time to ask questions. "What do you mean 'the way she is'?"

"Well," Timmy wanted to think this one over. He couldn't outright lie. Not to a man as big as Colin MacRae. "She don't neveah lift heah head. Scahed of heah own shadaw. Folks what say she be dead-dog ugly!" Colin's head snapped in his direction with a disapproving look and Timmy bit down hard on his lower lip, not willing to say anything further. He knew when to keep quiet. Now was one of those times.

Colin found Everette Koch's house on his own, though he questioned his better judgment at calling it a house. Everette Koch wasn't a tall man, by any means, but standing as he was in front of the house his head came level with the roof line. There was a guarded look on his face at seeing Colin pull up, "You'ahe not changin' youah mind, ahe ya?"

"My mind," Colin said as he got down, "was never made up in the first place. I'd like to talk with your daughter, please. Maybe she won't even want to be a housekeeper."

Everette Koch dug his hands into the pockets of his faded brown coat. "My step-daughteah. An' she does what I tell heah ta do."

"I'd still like to meet her."

"She be gettin' heah things tagetheahe." Koch's eyes took on a serious look. "You say it be a few weeks oah months?"

"I'm not sure how long." Colin tried not to be annoyed. "Look, Mr. Koch. Is she up to doing this? There's a lot of work at Highland and my -."

"She cen do it. Ya'll pay heah a wage, o' couahse."

Colin chose to nod in answer to the abrupt question. He was afraid if he spoke it would be to teach Everette Koch a lesson in politeness.

"I'll let heah go foah a six month time. Half wages in advance."

"Mister Koch -."

"She woahks heahe! Do ya think I would just lose heah wage? No!" Everette would have gone on, too, except that a deep-throated growl came from the darkness of the house's interior.

Colin's eyes widened perceptibly. He glanced back at Timmy and was surprised to see that the boy had already scooted off the seat and was making a move in the direction of the store.

By the time he looked back, Everette had also moved, away from the door. A dog - bigger than any Colin had ever seen, and blacker than the darkest night - stepped out into the sunshine. Behind this shaggy monster came the girl.

Despite the day's heat, her head was covered by a ragged shawl. One hand held the ends together while the other gripped the handle of a worn carpetbag which could hardly have been any flatter had it held nothing at all.

The immediate reaction Colin felt was shock. This bit of a waif was to be his housekeeper? Everette's gruff voice interrupted his thoughts. "Chain 'im up! Told ya that befoahe!"

If there was one thing Everette Koch was afraid of in life it seemed to be this dog. Colin could hear it in his tone. When the girl moved to the side of the house, the dog followed, sitting obediently while her small hands hooked his collar to the chain which lay in the sand.

Colin saw intelligence in the dog's unusual green-gold eyes. The two of them studied one another. A feeling grew within Colin that the dog was judging him somehow, measuring him.

"Well?" Koch snapped out the word impatiently. "It's a long way back ta Highland."

The reminder wasn't necessary. Colin knew his decision had to be made in the next brief minutes. As he moved up to the girl, he silently prayed, "God let me know for sure." Outloud, he simply said, "Hello." Only a slight nod told him she had heard. Timmy was right then, she wouldn't raise her head. Colin looked down at the dog, wondering why he had been allowed so close, for it was clear the girl was under fierce protection. "What's your dog's name?"

"Don't botheah none. She can't talk." Everette ended his words by sending a stream of dark spittle into the sand at his feet.

Colin frowned deeply, fighting to keep his next words from sounding harsh, but he had to know. "Is there anything else wrong with her?"

"Ain't nothin'!" Koch took up his defensive stance again and the great dog tensed, giving that same low growl. Everette cast a murderous look at the animal. "Told ya she woahks hahd, won't give ya no back-talk!" The joke was cruel, thoughtlessly so.

As Colin rubbed a hand over the back of his neck, he saw that a small crowd had gathered, mostly women and children. He ran his gaze over them, recognizing emotions which ranged from complete indifference to blatant curiosity. One woman - an elderly, gray haired matron - looked sympathetic. He turned to face her. "Do you know this girl?"

The woman stepped out from her place in the crowd. "Yes, I know her."

It wasn't only the educated speech which drew Colin to trust her. She seemed to want to help. "What's her name?"

"Kaytra...Kaytra Lange. She's sixteen. Her mother, Mary Elizabeth Lange, was a friend of mine."

"And where is she now, Kaytra's mother?"

"Dead these past five years."

Was it only his imagination or did the girl beside him somehow shrink deeper into the folds of her thick, woolen clothes?

"That's the last time Kaytra spoke." The woman held her head a bit higher as she went on. "It's true, what Koch said. She'll work hard for you."

Colin looked again at some of the other women, but they all lowered their eyes. Had they only gathered, then, to see the town outcast? Something deep inside him wondered why he felt as if he should accept Everette Koch's offer. Was it sympathy? Perhaps a growing desperation to complete his business and get back to Lydia?

He stared down at the girl called Kaytra. "Do you want to come to Highland Light?"

"Couahse she does." Everette suddenly moved up to her, ignoring the black dog's bared teeth, to grab her arm and start pulling her toward the wagon. "You get in that theahe wagon now. Go on."

When Kaytra stumbled a little and Koch righted her with a savage jerk, the dog lunged past Colin to the very limit of the chain, but it wasn't enough. "Wait a minute, Koch." The gentleman in Colin simply wouldn't let him look on in silence. "If I do take her, it's for a week's trial period."

"No way! " Koch stopped in his tracks. "Six months! I could hiahe heah out foah a yeah if I'd a mind to."

And Colin would lose his chance at getting the only available person. His long strides carried him to the wagon. Once he had his jacket, Colin pulled the leather pouch from the breast pocket. "Alright, Mr. Koch. I'll agree to keep her for six months."

Koch eagerly eyed the money Colin was holding out to him. It wouldn't do to take it too quickly, though, so he waited.

Colin bit back his anger. "What's wrong? That's a good wage."

"She eahns moahe heahe."

Colin added a few coins to the pile, anxious to quit this foul man's company. "There. The rest will go to Miss Lange."

Everette released his hold on the girl. "Go on, then." He gave her a shove toward the wagon, forcing Kaytra to catch herself on the boards with one hand. "I've youah woahd, keepeah? Six month?"

"Yes." Colin answered through a clenched jaw, shaking Everette's hand to seal the unwritten contract. The other man had a very pleased expression on his face as he watched Colin walk around to the back of the wagon.

Kaytra had placed her bag there and was preparing to climb up into the one empty spot among the supplies, but Colin wouldn't have it. "You should ride up front." She barely shook her covered head. "It's too rough back here."

Everette felt free to offer his advice. "She's used ta walkin'. I'd -."

"She won't walk! It's eight miles!" Colin's tone was just on the right side of harshness. In his anger at Koch, he took firm hold of the girl's arm, leading her to the front.

Behind them, the dog began barking again, straining with every muscle to protect Kaytra. His jaws snapped. His bark changed to a growl. He lunged forward. Just as the boards which held the chain in place were ripped from the rotting wood, Colin whirled around. If not for Kaytra putting herself in front of him, the beast would have surely taken him to the ground in one leap. Instead, the girl had only to hold out a hand and the dog was under control.

She knelt down then, half-hiding her face in the blue-black fur.

Colin released the breath lodged in his throat. Even as he did, as he witnessed the display of affection between Kaytra and her dog, he felt a stirring inside, prompting him to speak his thoughts out loud. "You don't want to leave the dog here, do you?"

Once again, her only answer was a slight shaking of her head.

Everette immediately saw another stroke of luck present itself at his doorstep. "Take 'im, then. But I'll need ta get anotheah."

Of course, more money! Colin fairly ripped his pouch open, dumping out several larger coins so Koch wouldn't again have the chance to say it wasn't enough.

It was only natural to assume Samson wouldn't take kindly to having the dog in the front. Colin spent a reluctant few minutes rearranging the load in back to make room for another passenger only to find that the girl climbed up to be with her dog. His eyes sought out the elderly woman he had talked with before. Her silent look seemed to tell him just to leave things as they were. Certainly Everette Koch wasn't giving it a second thought. He had already disappeared into the old wooden shack, money in hand.

Colin sat stiffly on the front seat guiding Samson along the wide streets which would lead him back to Jolly Troy's general store. The old man was standing at the door as if he had been there all along, waiting for him to return. "Ya got heah, I see."

With one lithe leap, Colin was down on the ground. "Yes. I got her. And the dog, too. You could have told me she couldn't talk."

Jolly shrugged his shoulders in a way which was more wise than uncaring. "Don't need moahe 'n a good back an' good sense ta keep house."

"Well, I'll need more. Soap for instance."

Jolly smiled broadly as he sensed Colin's good judgment taking over. "Soap it be, then. An' a few yahds o' cloth. Child ain't got but the clothes on heah back, it seem. Come in, Colin. We'll get ya all set."

Chapter Three

It was early evening when the weary travelers arrived at Highland Light. Colin could remember the first time he had looked upon Highland as it stood now, at peace with the world. Strong. Sheltering. He could remember that first gentle change from gray-blue afternoon to a sky awash with sunset colors. And beneath the bright orange and red and purple, the constantly moving sea reflecting what it saw.

Was Kaytra seeing any of it the same way, with a sense of awe? He drew Samson to a halt beside the back of the house. Even the big horse had found the trip over miles of loose sand a difficult one.

There was much to do in unloading the supplies, but Colin wanted to check on Lydia first. He stopped briefly next to the place where Kaytra sat. "I'm going up to see my sister. I'll be back shortly." She kept her head averted from his eyes, giving him a nod.

With a renewed sense of energy, Colin hurried into the house, taking the steps two at a time. "Lydia! I'm back!" He didn't bother with the polite knock this time. She smiled up at him sleepily as he burst into the room. "How are you?"

"Fine, silly."

He knelt by the bed, studying her face, seeing no change. Part of him had dreaded finding her worse because of his long absence. "I suppose you've done nothing but sleep all day."

Her eyes brightened at his brotherly teasing. "And what else could I do? You left strict orders I wasn't to move a muscle. Did you find someone?" For her, it was the most important question. Later, she could hear about the rest of his day.

"I did." Colin rubbed her cool hand between his warm, larger ones. "I hope you like her."

Lydia pushed herself upright upon the pillows. "Oh, I'm sure I will. But you haven't kept her waiting downstairs all by herself, have you?" Her time alone had been spent picturing their new housekeeper, forming and then discarding most every image her mind had conjured up. "Do go and get her, Colin. Is she old or young? What does she look like? Is -."

"She's young." Colin laughed at her enthusiastic questions. "Don't go getting too excited now or I shall say tomorrow is soon enough for you to meet her."

"Oh, don't you dare!" When his charming smile told her he wouldn't, Lydia smiled back with relief. "I've been hoping she would be young. Someone I can talk with. Really get to know. It does get very quiet here. Having a woman my own age will be nice."

Why hadn't he sensed that she was lonely? He should have. "She's a bit younger than that, Sis."

"Younger? Oh, but that doesn't matter, Colin. It will be like having a younger sister, I suppose. Is she pretty? Tell me what she looks like."

Colin's hesitation brought a questioning look to Lydia's eyes. He had practiced describing Kaytra Lange to Lydia. Yet all those words seemed wrong now. "I don't know what she looks like."

"But you said she -. Oh, Colin, didn't you bring her back with you?"

"Lydia." He moved up onto the bed, soothing her with a calm tone and a firm grip on both of her hands. "I did bring her. She's downstairs. I don't know what she looks like because - well, she must be painfully shy. She's kept her head completely covered from the moment I first saw her and she hasn't raised her eyes."

"Oh, my." There was a note of disbelief mingled with Lydia's sympathy.

"I wouldn't have hired her except that there seems to be a shortage of women in Provincetown and there wasn't anyone else." Colin felt his sister relax a little. "She's only sixteen, Lydia. And - she can't talk."

A moment's silence hung between brother and sister. Lydia seemed to be absorbing what he had told her. The sympathy deepened, of course, just as he had expected it would. What he didn't expect was to see tears come into her eyes. "But that's awful, Colin. And her parents still let her come?"

"Her step-father did."

A troubled frown creased Lydia's brow. "There's more to her story, isn't there? Please, Colin! Tell me all of it before I meet her. I want to know."

Colin stayed with his sister longer than he had planned, yet that still didn't prepare him for what he saw as he came down the stairs. The back door was propped open with a small barrel. Fully half of what had been in the wagon was now sitting in the middle of the kitchen floor. Even before he reached the last step, the girl appeared from outside, carrying a sack of flour which weighed no less than thirty pounds.

"What are you doing?" Colin hurried across the room, startling her by the disapproval in his tone.

She jerked upright and, just for an instant, raised her head. By the time he reached her, she was practically shrinking away, head hung low.

If it wasn't for the sack, he guessed she would have run. Colin grabbed the flour from her. "I didn't expect you to unload the wagon." This time, his words were gentler. He tilted his own head at an odd angle, trying to get another glimpse of her face. Something was unusual about her, but he wasn't sure what. She had hidden herself so quickly. "These things are far too heavy for you."

She shook her head back and forth rather emphatically as if really wanting to make him understand she didn't mind the work.

When he turned to set the flour down, she slipped silently out the door. Colin followed more slowly. The first thing he noticed was Samson's empty harness. "What did you do with the horse?" She pointed to the barn, making him want to ask how such a pint-sized girl had managed to get the huge animal to do what she wanted. But those were things she couldn't tell him without words.

A quick glance at the contents of the wagon showed Colin that she had separated it into piles. The house pile was already inside. There was one stack waiting to go into the light and another for the barn. Colin studied the girl's bent head for a long while. No one had exaggerated in saying she would work hard. When he saw that she meant to lift a sack of corn for the chickens, he knew it was up to him to set limits. "Leave that, please. I'll do it."

Kaytra pulled her hand away, holding more tightly to the shawl which covered her head. A sudden gust of wind revealed strands of light hair, but Colin couldn't say for sure what color. He shifted his gaze toward the edge of the bank which led down to shore. The black dog ran freely with the wind, so unlike the chained animal of before that it was a wonder to behold. "Does your dog have a name?" Colin glanced down at the girl again. No. "We'll have to let Lydia think of something then." He knew he had to make sure Kaytra knew the truth before she met his sister. "She's sick. Did your step-father tell you?" No.

The silent communication was going to take some getting used to. Maybe it wouldn't be so bad either, if she would look at him, if she would let him see her eyes. "Why don't you go start supper. If you can't find what you need, just let me know."

She went back into the house, moving in a way which Colin realized was humble, yet strangely supple at the same time. To him, it seemed as if she glided across the yard and up the steps.

Of course, she never did come to him. In the half-hour it took Colin to put the rest of the things away and to make sure Samson was bedded down, Kaytra had nearly finished making the meal he requested. Unknown to her, he stood just inside the back door, watching her move about the kitchen as if she hadn't just seen it for the first time in her life. As soon as she sensed him there, she pulled the shawl up from where it had fallen to her shoulders in order cover her blonde hair.

Colin's eyes narrowed in a serious expression. Still, he was unsure of what those brief glimpses of her meant. The pieces refused to be fit together. He moved into the room then, stopping to wash his hands at the basin on the far counter.

The house supplies had all but disappeared. He had to wonder how she found the time to discover where everything went, put the supplies away and still make supper. A scratching noise at the door made both of them look in that direction. Colin grabbed up a towel for his hands before going to let the dog inside. Instinctively, he knew the girl wouldn't have done so without his approval.

Her dog seemed even larger inside the house. Colin watched him take a sweeping survey of the room before moving over to Kaytra as a sign of devotion. It couldn't have been to seek security. A dog that size didn't need security. In fact, it seemed to Colin that it was a matter of the dog making sure she was all right.

"I don't mind if he's in the house. We had lots of dogs at home in Boston." Colin kept his voice even as he moved up to the dog. When he was within arm's reach, he squatted down, holding out one hand which the dog sniffed inquisitively. It wasn't until Colin saw the slight wagging of his tail, that he patted him on the head. One friendship made. The other, it seemed, would take more time.

Although Kaytra had continued to busy herself with the meal, Colin sensed she was very much aware of the interaction between the dog and himself. Indeed, he would guess there wasn't much of anything which slipped by her. With another thoughtful look at her bent head, he pulled out one of the chairs by the wide pine table.

Other than the tray which was obviously for Lydia, there was only one place set. Colin frowned at that and would have asked why, but Kaytra had finished fixing Lydia's plate and now slid it ever so slightly toward him. He stood at once, knowing she meant for him to take it upstairs. "Come with me. Lydia wants to meet you."

If he had given her a choice, he wasn't sure she would have followed him to Lydia's room. His sister was waiting for them and none too patiently either. "Well! There you are. I was about to call down." Her eyes strayed toward Kaytra. "Hello, Miss Lange. Or - may I please call you Kaytra? I'd much rather. It is such a pretty name."

There was a slight nod of the down-bent head beneath the ragged shawl.

Colin gave his sister an encouraging smile as he set the tray of food upon her lap. "Look, Lydia. It's not eggs!"

Lydia's gay laugh rippled like sunshine. "Oh, how heavenly! Cheese!" Kaytra had managed a delicate cheese sauce to serve over slices of the fresh, tender bread Colin had brought from the store. Over the top of this, she had crumbled the tiniest bit of smoked fish from the larder, just enough to add flavor and texture. For dessert, a sliver of pound cake from a tin hidden on one of the shelves and a generous scoop of strawberry preserves on top "But this is marvelous, Kaytra! And fresh tea. You shall spoil me for sure."

Colin thought it the most impossible act for his sister to be spoiled about anything, but didn't say so. Instead, he cast a curious glance at Kaytra. She must be sweltering in those layers and layers of clothes. Jolly had probably been right to say she was wearing all she had. Yet even those clothes were so ill-fitting as to make her appear impoverished.

It wasn't that they were unclean. Quite the opposite, really. The colors were indistinct from repeated washings. Gray skirt. A short jacket which at one time must have been brown and now looked rather mottled. He couldn't even begin to guess what color her blouses were. Worn leather shoes peeked from beneath the skirt. Lydia had noticed every detail, too. Colin could tell by the look on his sister's face. Her sense of fashion had generated a strong rush of sympathy for this ill-kempt girl. Colin tried to distract her. "Kaytra brought her dog, and he's in desperate need of a name."

"Oh? Do call for him, MacRae. No good dog should be without a name."

The sudden whistle Colin gave caused Kaytra to jerk in fright. For a second, he caught her lifting her head, then she looked away. Not down, just away.

When the big dog thundered upstairs in answer to the whistle, Lydia's eyes became wide with surprise. "My goodness! He's huge!"

"Isn't he, though." Colin squatted down as he had before and the dog came to him, nuzzling the outstretched hand. "He'd certainly keep your feet warm at night."

"If he didn't break the bed first!" Lydia chuckled. All the excitement brought color to her pale cheeks. "Do you remember how Father always said the bigger the dog the smarter the dog? Is this one very wise?"

Colin looked up at Kaytra. "What of it, Kaytra? Is your dog smart?"

Even Lydia recognized the subtle challenge in her brother's voice. She motioned for him to leave the poor girl be, but he only ignored her.

"Well?"

Kaytra nodded. Not slightly as before, but quick and firm, almost as if she, too, realized the question was a personal challenge.

Colin threw his sister a pleased look.

"Well, then." Lydia, of course, tried to smooth over the awkward moment. "He should have a very grand name. Like - Napoleon or Alexander."

"He's a dog, Sis. Not a general."

Lydia shushed him with a wave of her hand. "How about - King something?"

"How about Rex," Colin suggested. "That means king."

"Rex?" Lydia tried out the new name while staring quizzically at the black dog. His eyes were alert, waiting. "I think he likes it. Rex it shall be then. If -." She glanced at Kaytra. "If that's alright with you, Kaytra. He is your dog."

There was a nod, but Colin couldn't say it was an agreeable one, especially when the girl suddenly turned and slipped out of the room. Rex followed her.

When they were alone again, Lydia raised sad eyes to her brother's face. "Oh, Colin...I do think I've hurt her feelings."

"I don't think so." He walked nearer to her and patted her hand. "She probably isn't used to being around people. I told you what Timmy said. Maybe we shouldn't expect too much from her at first, at least as far as communicating goes."

"Yet maybe -." Lydia was looking thoughtful again. "Maybe she's like that because no one cares enough to communicate with her. When you made her answer, did you see how she reacted with a little more emotion?"

"Anger, you mean." Colin half smiled.

"Anger is an emotion."

"So it is. And hunger is one, too. I'm starved, Sis." He placed a quick kiss on her forehead. "I'll be back up later."

A pretty pout rounded Lydia's lips. "Can't I come down tonight? Please, Colin?"

He would have argued that she had already had enough excitement for one day, but she looked too hopeful. "Alright, I'll come get you."

Colin sat in his usual chair at the table, waiting as Kaytra brought his meal. More of the smoked fish. Fried potatoes ladled with the rest of the cheese sauce. Fresh bread. Jam. Milk. She walked away after the last dish was set down. "Aren't you eating?" His query sounded troubled. Kaytra shook her head. "Why not?" How stupid. It wasn't a question she could answer with a yes or no. "Did you eat already?" No. "Are you hungry?" There wasn't any response. Colin's frown deepened as he bowed his head to ask a blessing.

He wasn't comfortable eating while she cleaned the kitchen. "The food is very good, Kaytra. I'm not much of a cook myself." Her back was turned to him. "We've a big garden outside. And of course you saw the laying hens. Lydia hasn't had much more than eggs to eat lately."

Colin twirled his half-empty glass of milk around in tight circles with one hand. "Are you upset because we named the dog Rex?" No. She was pouring water into a dishpan. "You could at least take your jacket off and make a person think you'll stay longer than an hour." Whether because she was warm or because he said it so firmly, the jacket did come off.

Minus its thick bulk, Colin was surprised to see how much smaller she looked. A plain length of rope was looped around her waist to hold up the skirt. He had seen poorly dressed people before, beggars on the streets in Boston, but this wasn't Boston. Kaytra Lange was under his roof now. As much as he was able, he would try to erase the impossibly cruel conditions it seemed Everette Koch had enforced - if Kaytra would let him. "Don't you want to take off the shawl? It must be hard to work with it hanging around like that." Kaytra's back had become ramrod stiff, her hands perfectly still. Was she weighing his words, wondering if this, too, was a command? For her own good, he made it so she didn't have to wonder. "Take off the shawl, Kaytra."

Her compliance was so slow as to be laced with anger. She brushed the shawl onto her shoulders and from there placed it with her jacket on the counter away from where she would wash dishes. Colin felt no sense of victory. In truth, he was somewhat bewildered. Kaytra's hair, though tangled and loose about her shoulders, was a pale, goldenrod color. He instinctively felt that Timmy's "dead-dog-ugly" description wouldn't suit her. Maybe she was plain, but certainly not homely.

She pushed back the sleeves of her blouse just a little and began scrubbing the first pile of dishes. Colin hadn't washed them for a couple of days. "I'm sorry about the mess. You don't have to get it all done in one night, you know. In fact, you could spare my pride by making it take longer."

His attempt at lightening the tension failed miserably. It was almost a relief when Rex went to the door and whined to be let out. Colin watched the dog run across the yard. It was good he felt so comfortable here.

Kaytra was another story...

"I'm going to go fill the lamps. You might want to check on Lydia in a while." He didn't bother to look back before he left.

"What is she doing now, Colin?" Lydia barely let him step into her room before she asked the question.

"I don't know what she's doing, Lydia. I just came down from the tower." His words were carefully distinct as if he were explaining something to a child. Lydia knew when he spoke that way he wasn't in one of his better moods. "I heard her rummaging in the pantry on my way up. Maybe she's putting away the supplies."

"Surely you didn't ask her to do that tonight!"

"I surely didn't." Colin clenched and unclenched his fists where they were firmly held at his sides. He was trying very hard not to lose his patience.

Lydia smiled rather weakly at the censoring look he gave her. It was one of those times when he made her think she was twenty-five and he was thirty instead of the other way around. "Oh, Colin. Please don't be that way." She held up her arms. "Carry me down and we'll all three have a nice cup of tea together."

Kaytra wasn't in the pantry when they came downstairs, but was back at the dishpan. "Kaytra," Colin spoke loudly so he knew she heard. "Lydia would like some tea. Set three cups, please." In the parlor, he settled Lydia in her usual spot, on the settee where she could look out the windows and see the ocean. After he covered Lydia's legs with a lap robe, he went into the kitchen to help.

The kettle was already hot on the back of the cast iron stove. Heat rose in waves from the black monster, making it unbearable to stand very close. "Are those mugs clean?" Colin edged past Kaytra to get them at the same time that she reached out to do likewise. Instead, his hand went to capture her wrist. "My God!," It was a whispered exclamation, a crying out to the Lord in sudden anxiety. "What happened to you?"

She tried to pull away, but he was too shocked by the ugly bruises he saw marring the length of her arm to let her go. Colin knew before he saw her hide the other arm behind her back that it, too, had been beaten.

He felt his heart pound violently against his chest. His free hand easily forced her chin up until he could see her face. For one long moment before she tore herself away from him and turned to hide, his eyes met hers....

"Colin?" Lydia called out from the other room, obviously concerned by the quietness she heard. "Colin?"

"Just a - a minute, Lydia," he answered. Kaytra was weakly leaning both arms upon the counter. Even though he didn't touch her again, he could feel her whole body shaking. "Are you all right?"

Her nod was too slow in coming, too unsure.

Colin rubbed a hand across his eyes, but nothing could erase the image of her battered, black and blue face.

"Why don't you go find Rex. Go for a walk - along the bank. I'll tell Lydia that you needed to get out for - for some air." At first, it seemed that she would choose to stay, then she suddenly turned and fled out the back door. The thought came to Colin, too late, that she would think he had sent her away because the sight of her was too horrible, too utterly dreadful for anyone to have to endure.

The only one at Highland Light who slept much that night was Rex. Worn out from his many explorations and content with the good meal of leftovers Kaytra had given him, the dog curled up on the floor by her bed in the simple room upstairs which was now to be theirs.

Chapter Four

"Kaytra!..Please stay." Lydia just couldn't let the young girl walk out of the bedroom again without speaking to her. The whole day seemed to have gone the same so far and it really was becoming bothersome. As if doubting that Kaytra would stand by the door very long, Lydia pushed the lunch tray from her lap and started to swing her legs over the side of the bed. "I'd like to talk with you, please. About the house."

Adding those last words was necessary or Kaytra would indeed have bolted out the door. As it was, she only half-turned back. "I'm afraid there is so much to do. Colin - bless his heart - just didn't have time to clean things properly."

Lydia probably didn't know the half of it, Kaytra thought to herself. There was a small mountain of wash to be done, weeds tangling around themselves in the garden, dust a half-inch thick on all the furniture and -. Her private inventory was interrupted when Lydia began speaking again.

"I wish I would just get better so I could help." There was a woebegone note in her voice. Kaytra stole a furtive glance at her. She did look tired today.

Lydia sensed a slight relaxing of the tension which kept the girl apart from her. "Do you know what is the worst of all? Not being able to putsy about as I used to, fixing dainty things for the house. I could sit here and sew, of course. It is the getting of the cloth and the measuring and the deciding that uses so much energy." Was that a curious glance about the room? Lydia hurried on. "Maybe now that you are here with us, making such wonderful meals and lifting the burden of worry, I shall gain strength each and every day! Oh, I do hope so.

"Fall is my favorite time of year. I'm not at all sure what to expect of the season here at Highland. When we first came, though I've never said so to Colin, I was dreadfully disappointed. It is such a barren place. He sees it much differently, of course...Oh, be a dear and bring me the mirror and brush from the bureau."

Kaytra glided across the room to do Lydia's bidding. Her only hesitation came when she had to draw close enough to set them in her hands. But Lydia was quick to take encouragement from the fact that the girl didn't move away afterward. "My hair has no bounce anymore. It is unhealthy, really. Not at all like yours. If you have some time later today, would you help me wash it? Colin is all thumbs when it comes to doing such things. I do believe there is a brass tub somewhere. It would be nice to have a bath. You know, you must feel perfectly free to do whatever you wish as far as clothes and your toilette and such. I do want you to feel at home here."

Just as she had done the evening before, Kaytra suddenly turned and left the room. Her shoulders were set in the same injured fashion, giving Lydia the impression she had said too much. With a deep sigh, Lydia set aside the brush and mirror and settled herself back upon the bed. Her prayer of blessing before she ate included asking God for wisdom and patience. Faith could be at its strongest - as it was in Lydia's heart - yet a person must at times still pray for patience.

From where Colin stood in the top of the tower, he could see Kaytra as she worked in the garden. Already half the obnoxious weeds had been rooted out and lay in neat piles just the other side of the fence.

He didn't quite know yet how she could work so diligently and yet do so with such an appearance of litheness. Judging by the pail full of fresh milk on the counter and the breakfast she had waiting, Kaytra had been up long before him that morning. When he asked her to share the abundance of food, she did not stop to eat with him. Since then, he had seen her working at a dozen different tasks without rest.

Colin trimmed the wick on the lamp he had just finished cleaning and replaced the chimney. One more to go. There was a certain pride in seeing the circle of lamps sparkling clean. Surprisingly, the task had yet to become simply routine. He hoped it never would.

Routine. Father had said, in trying to discourage his only son from this life, that being a lighthouse keeper was the same "routine" day in and day out. Colin smiled to himself now in remembering what his answer had been. "Being a banker means the same 'routine' five days a week. I get my routine for a full seven!'"

Shaun Logan MacRae hadn't appreciated that response at all. In fact, he had mumbled a curse and stormed from the room. That had been three years ago, just before Colin left for his apprenticeship at the Boston Light.

His father had hardly mellowed since then. He still held to the idea that Colin would tire of the "boyhood adventure" and return to take his rightful place as heir to one of the largest banking firms in Boston. Not to mention that he would bring Lydia home where she belonged!

Mother, on the other hand, knew he had inherited more than his father's Scottish good looks. Jolly certainly hit the nail on the head yesterday. Determination. It was that quality which made a man a good banker. Or a good lighthouse keeper. Or a good anything for that matter as long as he "stuck by his choices" - another of Max's sayings. Colin smiled to himself.

What neither of his parents realized in their hearts, though he had told them often enough before accepting the assignment to Highland Light, was that he and Lydia were here as much to strengthen their faith as they were to find true contentment. He was coming to believe the two went hand in hand; one could not have a lasting sense of peace without finding God at the center of all things. As always when his parents came to mind, Colin prayed that some day they would open their lives to the kind of fulfillment only God could offer them.

It was hot inside the tower with the sun beating through so many panes of glass. Anxious to breathe fresh air again, Colin hurried to finish the last lamp, then went lightly down the spiral of stairs. As soon as he stepped through the narrow doorway, wind cooled the sweat from his arms and face. He took a moment to appreciate the beauty of Highland, it's peace, it's simplicity.

Only as his gaze swung toward the garden did he admit he very much wanted to know if Kaytra ever did what he was doing now. Did she stand still sometimes just to wonder about things? Colin took his thought along to the well where he drank deeply from the water he raised.

On hot days like this, it had become a habit to splash whatever water was left in the bucket over himself. As he did so today, he was nearly knocked over by a charging ball of black fur. "Rex!" Colin laughed at the playful light in the dog's eyes. Really, Rex looked no more than an overgrown pup with his pink tongue hanging out that way. "Are you thirsty?"

Rex barked, an answer Colin accepted as yes. Raising more water was easy enough. He filled the dipper once more before setting the bucket in front of Rex who practically attacked the cool water. When he sensed that someone watched them, Colin raised his eyes to where Kaytra worked in the garden, but she had her head bent low over the carrots.

On impulse, he carried the dipper to the fence. Even though it was too big for her, she wore one of Lydia's aprons over her clothes. The shawl had disappeared today. But she must still be warm. "Kaytra...Here's some water for you. It's cold." Colin was surprised to see her back stiffen. The next weed she pulled received a more vicious tug. "Oh, come on. Take a break." He held the cup out to her again.

It was a full minute before she stood. Somehow she walked over to him without lifting her head. Half the water spilled when she grabbed the handle of the dipper in a reckless way. She took no more than a sip, then poured the other half out onto the ground before setting it in Colin's hand .

He was forced to frown at her back because she was just as quickly bending over the carrots again, pulling weeds. "That was your break?" His question was disbelieving. She neither nodded her head yes, nor shook it for no. Colin turned away in frustration. He had better things to do than to try to figure her out!

It was shortly after a supper of vegetable soup with freshly baked bread that Kaytra entered Lydia's bedroom, dragging the huge brass tub behind her. Lydia sat straighter on the bed. "Oh, you found it!"

Kaytra tugged mightily to place the tub in the one corner away from the windows. When that was done, she disappeared again only to show up minutes later carrying not one, but two buckets full of steaming water. Lydia's forehead was creased with a frown. "But...Please, Kaytra. Where is Colin? He could help you carry the water."

A second trip was made and a third before Kaytra paused at all. Then it was to stand facing the bureau, wondering which drawer held clean underthings. Lydia could take no more of the silence. "It's lovely of you to do all this, Kaytra, and I appreciate it. Really, I do. But I assumed you would allow my brother to help."

"Help with what?" Colin asked as he walked into the room, curious to know what he was missing.

"With hauling the tub and the water."

His gaze traveled in the direction Lydia pointed. "Who's the bath for? Kaytra?"

"Colin!" Lydia scolded his suggestive tone.

Colin raised his eyebrows as Kaytra began jerking open drawers and pulling out bits of feminine garb. He wasn't a bit as embarrassed as Lydia. Kaytra's apron was dirty from all the work she had done. Her hair hung damp with perspiration where it had escaped the few inexpertly placed pins. "Well, she could certainly use one!"

"Colin MacRae!" When Lydia used that tone, he knew he was in trouble. The smile he gave didn't quite charm her this time. "Ohhh! Do get out! We ladies shall handle this ourselves!"

His eyes held an amusement which softened her anger. "It was only a suggestion, Sis. If she's going to stay here, she'll have to follow the house rules. Tub bath a least once a week and a good 'scrub behind the ears every day!"

Of course, there had never been such a rule set. He was making it all up. Lydia wished for once he wouldn't be so forthright. Poor Kaytra was practically cringing with shame. "Colin, you're behaving like an insensitive oaf!"

He held up both hands in self-defense. "I'm going. I'm going."

Somehow the silence he left behind was worse than the silence which had come before. Lydia bit down hard on her bottom lip as she watched the girl move across the room, arranging the nightgown and underthings on a chair. From the armoire, Kaytra took out a towel and washcloths and some of the bottles. Lilac water. Honeysuckle hair rinse... "There are some cakes of soap in that drawer." Lydia offered kindly. Kaytra got that, too.

Despite the fact that Lydia was the taller of the two by a good four inches, Kaytra seemed to have little difficulty in helping her walk over to the tub and getting her ready for the bath. Out of polite sympathy, Lydia said nothing about the ugly bruises on the young girl's arms.

Even the little glances she stole at the swollen lip and cheek were out of concern rather than curiosity. It was impossible not to notice how thin Kaytra's arms were. She had obviously been ill-treated. By the step-father? Lydia could only guess.

When asked to wash Lydia's hair, Kaytra did so with amazing gentleness and was as careful about seeing it rinsed. The bath was accomplished in near silence. Lydia was too preoccupied by thoughts of Kaytra's past to be talkative. Once Kaytra had helped her dress and get seated in a chair, she left the room.

But it wasn't for long. When she returned, she was almost hidden by the clean bedding she carried. Lydia recognized the sweet smell of the sachets stored with the blankets. "Oh, Kaytra. How thoughtful. I'm glad you are finding everything." In one agile motion, Kaytra had strip-rolled the bed and was reaching for the clean sheets. Was it only her imagination or was the girl slightly paler than before? "You must be exhausted, dear.".... "Colin said he purchased some material in Provincetown. Shall we spend the day sewing tomorrow? Do you think you would like a new skirt? Something lighter to wear?"

Lydia felt silly when she realized she was asking so many questions. But it was only because she did so want to help Kaytra, to make her feel at ease with them. A quiet voice inside of her gave the reminder that it had only been one day.

All the blankets were in place and the pillows fluffed. Once again, Kaytra was there to support Lydia in walking across the room. A sharp pang of compassion twisted within Lydia to feel the slightness of the shoulders upon which her arm was placed. With that same sense of unspoken gentleness, Kaytra pulled the covers over Lydia's weakened body. "Kaytra?" Lydia spontaneously caught her hand.

It seemed an endlessly long moment before Kaytra at last raised her eyes to meet Lydia's. As the two women studied each other, Lydia tried not to let her eyes fill with tears, but they came anyway. So did the quaver in her voice when she spoke. "Please, dear, I'd like us - to be - friends. I don't know what - you've been through, but there can be no reason - no earthly justification for it...I don't -." When a sob shattered her words, the break was enough for Kaytra to pull away. She and the roll of soiled bedding were gone before Lydia could blink the tears from her eyes.

Had she not needed to empty the tub, Kaytra might not have returned to Lydia's room until the next morning. Though she knew it was obligation which led the girl back, Lydia meant to apologize...In between loads, of course.

Kaytra was in the middle of tipping the tub over the last two buckets and Lydia in the middle of making new plans for the next day when Colin's frame filled the doorway. He took in the two of them with an interested glance. "All snug as a bug, huh Sis? I thought I'd come see if my services were needed to get you settled again."

"Oh, no, thank you." Lydia's smile looked tired, but content. "You may help Kaytra, though. She's made too many trips up and down as it is."

Colin agreed. The girl did look worn out. "Here." He stepped up to her. "Give me the buckets." It didn't surprise him that she held onto both handles with a death grip after hearing his offer. As their eyes met, he could see that hers had become dark with emotion. "Look, Kaytra," he said in a more patient tone. "Lydia was right. My remark about you needing a bath was insensitive and I'm sorry."

Other than a slight raising of one perfectly arched eyebrow, Kaytra did not react to his apology.

"Let's not start off this way."

Her expression remained the same.

When he spoke again, his voice was quieter, but more firm. "Give me the buckets...or you go back to Provincetown in the morning."

"Colin!" Lydia barely whispered his name in shock that he should make such a threat.

"Be quiet, Lydia." He spoke without taking his eyes from Kaytra who had lowered her head once more. It was best to get this over with now. She had to learn his word was final. "Do I need to repeat what I just said?"

Ever so slowly, Kaytra lifted her chin until she was staring up at him. What he had seen last night to be so unusual about her - the stunning blue-gray color of her eyes - was now the cause of a charged tension inside of him for those same eyes were so expressive they seemed to scream, "You wouldn't dare!"

Colin clenched the muscles of his jaw in a way which warned Lydia he was more than angry. He was furious. "I - will - take - you - back." Each word was forced and sharp as a knife point.

Kaytra's eyes narrowed, testing the possibility. Then an invisible shutter came down, protecting her true feelings from the man who stood before her. He was a full foot taller than she was, but this wasn't a battle of size. It was a battle of wills.

Afterward, as he listened to Lydia's carefully muffled giggles, Colin wondered how Kaytra had managed in a split second to thrust one bucket into his hand and then slip past him on winged feet, out the door, carrying the other. And all without spilling a drop of water besides! He stared at his sister until she stopped laughing.

"Well, it was funny." Her expression was still too amused. "Imagine, a bit of a girl besting my big, strong brother." One last giggle escaped.

"It wasn't funny." He had to purse his mouth into a straight line or risk all that good, sensible sternness for naught. Lydia, of course, knew him too well. The instant her eyebrows arched over her brightly lit brown eyes, he gave in, smiling with rather disgruntled humor. "Alright. So it was clever of her. But I was trying to teach her a lesson. She's too obstinate for her own good. At this rate, I'll be scrambling eggs for two patients instead of one!"

"Oh, please!" Lydia pretended to shudder. "Don't mention scrambled eggs. I was just beginning to see a real hope that I wouldn't sprout feathers after all!"

With an indulgent shake of his head, Colin turned to leave. "Good night, Lydia."

"Good night, MacRae, and do be a good sport when you go down."

Good sport! He'd like to throw a pail of water at the girl!

Well, he wouldn't really, but it was a thought. Maybe it would dampen some of the fire he had seen flashing in her eyes. Colin wasn't surprised to find Kaytra's bucket already empty and sitting in its usual place at the back door. He walked outside and emptied his onto the ground.

Barely twenty-four hours had passed since their arrival at Highland Light and he had already told Kaytra he would take her back. There was a part of him which was as bewildered by those words as Lydia had been. Yet he knew he had to establish some sense of conformity in the house. There must be some way to make Kaytra understand that, even though his rules might sound strict, they were only meant for her own good. She needed someone to set reasonable boundaries, to -. His troubled thoughts were interrupted by Rex's incessant barking.

It took a second for Colin to figure out the dog was somewhere on the other side of the house. Something about the intensity of those barks alarmed Colin, causing him to drop the bucket in his hands and hurry toward the well.

When he knew for sure Colin was coming, Rex barked one more time, then disappeared around the lighthouse tower. Colin was running by then, instinctively sure something was very wrong. He felt a surge of apprehension, which only became worse the closer he got.

A moment later, Colin was brought up short by the sight of Kaytra's limp body crumpled close to the base of the tower as if she had been clinging to it for strength. "Kaytra?" She didn't stir when he laid his hand on her shoulder. With a troubled frown, Colin turned her onto her back. "Kaytra?" Her face was pale beneath the bruises. Though an anxious Rex tried to press close, Colin held him back with one strong arm. "Kaytra?"

There was a soft, hesitant flutter of her eyelashes, then her eyes suddenly were wide open, staring in confusion.

"It's alright," Colin tried to reassure her. She moved restlessly. "Lie still for a minute until you feel stronger." Her color was coming back. "Have you eaten anything at all today?" Doubt filled every one of his words.

She turned her head, trying to look away, but Colin wouldn't let her. Not this time. He set a firm hand on the side of her face and made her look at him. "Kaytra, did you eat anything?"

After she defiantly shook her head, Colin let go. He thought that perhaps she got what she deserved, fainting dead away like that. Maybe it would scare her into eating properly. Or maybe not. As he had told Lydia a few minutes ago, Kaytra Lange was an obstinate soul.

Rex couldn't contain himself any longer. While he bathed her face and arms with his tongue, Kaytra struggled to push herself upright. Colin hid a smile as he stood and stared out at the familiar ocean scene. For a while, the only sounds came from below as waves rushed in, tumbling over and about themselves, seemingly in a hurry to spend themselves out upon the shore. A light dampness moved upward from the spray, barely touching Colin's face.

He spoke to Kaytra without turning around. "How do you think Lydia would have reacted if she was the one who found you just now?" He didn't expect an answer. It was said to make her think a little. "Lydia is a very caring person. She throws her heart wide open to everyone she meets. I won't have you hurting her, deliberately or otherwise."

The gesture of placing both arms over his chest was pure reflex. He had no idea how rigid it made him appear to Kaytra as she rose on unsteady legs. "My sister means a great deal to me; her well-being, her happiness. We depend on one another." Though he waited a moment, Colin didn't hear any response. Nor did he sense any movement from behind.

She was gone.

During the night, Colin awakened instantly alert, though he wasn't sure why. His eyes automatically went to the sea. The light's beam was still stretching its arm far into the darkness. He listened then for the sound which had disturbed his sleep at that predawn hour.

As he began distinguishing what he heard, he became even more confused. There was the steady slapping of waves upon already soaked sand, wind hollowing out in the many nest holes burrowed into the bank. Colin raised himself on one elbow, straining every nerve...A stray tern far down the shore, dried beach grass swiping at the base of the tower. He held his breath....

When the sound came again, it was from within the house.

Chapter Five

It somehow happened during Kaytra's first week at Highland that she was never around in the evening when it was time for the Bible reading. This wasn't the only habit of hers which Colin found irritating. She cleaned constantly, everything in sight, even the outhouse! She annoyed him by outguessing his needs and having things in such perfect order that it made him want to make a mess sometimes, just because. She didn't look up when he spoke to her. She didn't eat enough to keep a bird alive!

Most importantly, perhaps, she refused to let him reach past the barrier surrounding her solitary existence. It seemed not to matter whether he reached out in friendship or concern, firmness or outright demand. Every time he spoke to her, Kaytra refused him what he wanted - which was to see some sign, some small indication that there was a flesh and blood person behind the impenetrable, albeit feminine, armor.

The resentment between them grew to an explosive point. So it was that when Sunday came and she began scrubbing the kitchen floor after breakfast, Colin put his foot down, literally, right in front of her scrub brush. "We don't work around here on Sundays."

She sat back slowly, though not with an attitude of compliance. Colin was prepared. "Sunday is a day of rest. Keeping it so is showing respect for God. You are welcome to join Lydia and me as we pray and read, but you will not work. Is that understood?"

Kaytra nodded without meeting his eyes.

And as long as he was at it, he had a few other things to say. "From now on, I want you to join me for meals. I haven't seen you put more than two bites of food into yourself since you came. Lydia is beginning to worry because you're getting so thin. And starting tomorrow, you will allow her to help you sew new clothes for yourself. The things you have are practically threadbare. Besides, they don't fit you properly."

He didn't feel any better for having unburdened some of his thoughts. With one last look at her, he turned and went into the parlor. It was nine o'clock and time to make an entry in the lighthouse journal.

The nourishing meals Kaytra prepared probably had much to do with Lydia's improvement, but it could as easily have been the new mission she took upon herself in deciding that she and Kaytra would someday be friends. During those last sunny days of August, when they were under orders from Colin to complete a new outfit for Kaytra, Lydia thrived on the company, such as it was.

She talked on and on. Mostly about a book she was reading or about life back in Boston. Gradually, Kaytra had stopped hiding. Though she didn't really look directly at Lydia, there were times when their eyes met. Lydia was always amazed by the expressiveness of those blue-gray eyes. She learned to read moments of interest and thoughtfulness in them, moments of a faraway dreaming look, moments of sadness.

Lydia prayed fervently for the time to come when she felt free to ask Kaytra what had made that place of sorrow or, more importantly, what power it still held over her. That chance came quite unexpectedly, on the day the new blouse and skirt were finished. After much persuading, Kaytra gave up straightening Lydia's room to try them on.

Though she was careful not to show any reaction, Lydia's heart ached with pity at seeing yet more faded bruises upon the girl's body. Without the layers of clothes, she appeared nearly starved to death. Seeing her collar bone angled sharply beneath pale skin made Lydia even more glad that they had given the blouse a high, fitted collar.

"Here. Let me do the buttons." She did so with slightly trembling hands. "Do you know, I think I have a blue ribbon just the color of the skirt. We could weave it into your hair somehow."

Kaytra shrugged her slim shoulders a little. Next came the petticoat and skirt. It was full, but not overly so. The color was just a shade deeper than sky blue, more as if twilight were just touching it. "Oh, good. It fits perfectly. Does it feel all right?" Lydia stepped back a little to see if the length was appropriate. How tiny she looked. Almost like a china doll... "Let's brush your hair. My treat." Kaytra found herself being led to a chair.

It seemed no time at all before Lydia had gently combed out the tangles. The light golden hair was surprisingly thick and curled naturally at the ends which rested halfway down Kaytra's back. "You have such pretty hair, dear. If you were in Boston, you would be the envy of every young girl there. Sit still now."

With a couple of quick twists, Lydia had pulled some hair onto the top of Kaytra's head securing it with a simple comb and the promised blue ribbon tied into a bow. The rest of her hair was left loose. "There. Come see if you like it."

The reflection in the standing mirror showed a transformation so startling it took Kaytra a moment to remember to breathe. Her eyes instantly filled with tears as she raised a shaky hand to her mouth.

"Why, my dear!" Lydia put her arm around the girl's shoulders. "Whatever is the matter?"

Kaytra shook her head. She felt more than a bit bewildered by it all. For the very first time since she had come to Highland, she looked up into Lydia's face, fully, with all sincerity.

It took some hard searching before Lydia thought she knew what was wrong. "No one is going to take these things away from you, Kaytra. They are yours to keep forever and ever. And we shall make more. Maybe some nice dresses."

Ever so slightly, Kaytra's lips parted in the agony to speak. But all that came was a quickly drawn breath. Lydia enfolded her in comforting arms. "Oh, Kaytra. Please be happy. You deserve to be happy." When Kaytra didn't pull away this time, Lydia knew the bond had been completed. It wasn't the gift of a few clothes and a piece of ribbon. It was because someone had cared.

"My goodness. It's nearly lunchtime. Let's go down and I'll watch while you cook. Something simple, I think. Is there any cheese left?" Kaytra nodded, blinking the shimmer of tears from her eyes. "Good. We can have sandwiches and milk and -. Oh, we'll think of something!"

Lydia's something proved to be a picnic! In hardly any time, Kaytra had made a simple lunch and Lydia - against Kaytra's anxiously mimed protest - had gone outside to find her brother. Over one arm, she carried a thick, woolen blanket they could spread upon the ground.

Nothing was going to keep her from enjoying herself today. Besides, they might not get another day like this before fall. Lydia threw a smile up to the face of the warm sun. She felt so good about helping Kaytra. Perhaps she and Colin would have time yet to talk about it before lunch. Or maybe she should let it be a surprise for him. Her gaze swept the familiar line of the bank before rising to the tower. "MacRae!" A lightness went with her call. "Colin Shaun MacRae!"

It was but seconds before he stepped out onto the narrow walk which encircled the top of the tower. "Lydia! What the deuce?"

"Oh, now Colin. Don't be like that." Lydia laughed at him, shading her eyes against the sun. "Come down. We're to have a picnic!"

"Not outside!"

"But of course, silly. Where else does one have a picnic?"

For a moment, he stared at her, trying to see across the distance. Then he suddenly disappeared. Lydia was waiting for him at the door when he came rushing out of the lighthouse tower, his brow set in a grim line "Who said you could come out here?"

"I did." Lydia slipped her arm through his and began walking toward the bank. "Please don't spoil the fun by being overprotective. I feel wonderful today." She could sense his eyes upon her, weighing each word to see if they were true.

Though Lydia had improved a great deal, she still tired quite easily. Colin wasn't about to let this - this girlish whim cause a setback.

As he noted the strength in her steps, some of the tension left his body. A healthy flush colored her cheeks to match the rose dress she wore. Perhaps it would be all right for a while.

"Where shall we sit, MacRae?"

"This way." He steered her a little to the right, closer to the house. "Where is Kaytra? Why didn't she walk you out here?"

"Why, I suppose because I didn't give her the chance." Lydia put off his disapproval by handing over the blanket. He flipped it open with one strong movement. "She'll be out soon, I'm sure. But I do have a question for you before she comes." His eyes met hers curiously as he helped her sit down. "Why is it you haven't shown her anything about the light yet? It is a rule that everyone who-."

"I know the rules, Lydia." He sank down next to her, resting one arm across an upraised knee.

Lydia thought he looked so different from the young entrepreneur who had been the talk of their social circles in Boston. What would their father say to see him now, wearing a simple white shirt and brown pants? And a definite frown. She could tell Colin wasn't at all pleased to be reminded of the rules. The Federal Lighthouse Commission had a standing policy that anyone living at a lighthouse be taught how to run the light, just in case they should ever have to do it themselves. Accidents did happen.

When they had first come to Highland, Colin had painstakingly taught Lydia everything she would need to know if he should be too ill or hurt in some way that he couldn't work the light. There was no reason why Kaytra could not be taught the same. In fact, there were more reasons why she should be.

"Colin?" Lydia laid a cautious hand upon his arm, bringing him out of his private thoughts.

He tenderly covered her hand with his. "It's hard to explain, Sis."

"You don't want to teach her?"

A thoughtful shrug moved his broad shoulders. "Maybe not. It was different with you. You - know me; what I'm like, how I feel inside," his eyes drifted up to the tower, "what all of this means to me. You - cared about learning it."

"But not like you, Colin. I learned for your sake. It wasn't in me to learn for any other reason than because you asked." She saw a twinge of disappointment in his eyes. "Oh, MacRae. I do love you so. And yes, I even love Highland. But I cannot fool either one of us into thinking I'd love it here without you."

"Do you want to go back to Boston then?"

"Heavens no!" She actually sounded alarmed that he should suggest it. "You're misunderstanding what I said."

"Maybe Kaytra won't be here that long."

"But maybe she will!" Lydia was puzzled by his reaction. "Colin, it's not like you to be so - closed toward people. You must realize she's been through a difficult time. She needs -."

"She needs?" He interrupted quietly, but with a certain edge to the words. "I brought her here because of your needs, Lydia. You needed someone to help you, not the other way around."

Lydia folded her hands together in her lap and looked off to the horizon. "Are you sure that's the way it was, Colin? God works in such intricate, unfathomable ways." She shifted until she could see the strong, familiar profile of her brother's face. "I think maybe you should be asking Him to decide why Kaytra is here."

A tiny muscle worked at the corner of his jaw. "I don't know, Sis...I'm considering going down to Truro. It's only six or seven miles away. Maybe there's someone there who could -." He stopped suddenly when he heard Kaytra coming toward them. The glasses in one of the baskets she carried had clinked together, warning him in time before she overheard.

But the sound didn't warn him about the changes he saw when he turned to look at her. She was trying to hold one basket high enough away from Rex's playful attempts at getting a free sandwich. An expression - not quite a smile - crossed her face. The breeze was tugging at her hair. Simply having new clothes couldn't have made such a difference. There was something else.

"Oh, do go help her, Colin." Lydia urged him to his feet. She was not able to describe the look on his face. Nor was she able to decide if it somehow added to the dispirit which brought a cloud to her earlier happiness. Surely his response to her idea hadn't been what she expected.

Kaytra was preoccupied during the meal. Quite often during the next hour, she would stop eating to stare at the ocean. It became obvious to both Colin and Lydia that a certain fascination could be found in the way she sat there watching and - waiting? Though he didn't know why, Colin realized with perfect clarity that Kaytra was indeed waiting for something....or someone .

By the time he and Lydia were eating cookies from the basket, Kaytra had only managed half of her sandwich. "You'd better finish, Kaytra." His words seemed to fall on deaf ears. "Kaytra?"

She looked at him then, somewhat startled to find she wasn't alone.

Colin's eyes held a measure of disapproval. "Eat up. You'll be carried away by a good stiff wind the next thing we know."

As if it were a foreign thing to her, she stared down at the bread in her small hands, then just as suddenly, placed it into the basket. Without a single wasted motion, she decided that her part in the picnic was over and she packed everything away. "Kaytra." Lydia's tone revealed that she was confused. "But-...Oh, do stay and sit awhile. The house is clean. You could -."

Kaytra shook her head very hard and stiff, not meeting Lydia's eyes. As she rose and hurried to the house, brother and sister shared a questioning glance. Kaytra even ignored Rex's attempt to gain her attention. He finally gave up and lowered himself to the ground with a dejected sigh.

For Lydia, it seemed impossible to find the right words. She didn't at all understand what had just happened. "How odd."

"It wasn't odd, Lydia. It was rude." Colin helped his sister to her feet. "Very rude."

"Don't be angry, Colin."

"I'm not angry. I'm - frustrated." Colin fairly jerked the blanket off the ground as he threw out the word. "She upsets you by acting that way."

On sudden impulse, Lydia stepped close to circle his waist with one arm. "I'm not upset. Not really. I'm just -. Well, I feel sort of - helpless."

His arm came around her shoulders, pulling her into his strength and protection. They walked that way toward the house, each of them trying to sort out the past few minutes.

"If there was only some way for her to tell us what she feels and thinks. She's such a beautiful girl, Colin."

He wouldn't deny that. "Even beautiful girls need to learn a few good manners, Sis. Maybe we need to face the fact that she doesn't want our help, that she only came here to get away from Koch."

A shadow settled into Lydia's eyes. "I'm sure that must have been part of it Colin, but God did His part by making sure it was Kaytra you found that day." In pausing beside the porch railing, Lydia looked up into Colin's face, searching his expression before saying what was really on her heart. "Kaytra must be very confused, very unsure of what she wants, what to expect. Maybe, just now, she's afraid to accept the kind of help you want to give her. You can't forget, Colin, that God has ways of changing a person's heart."

"Even when they are stubborn and unwilling to change and -."

"Are you describing yourself? Or Kaytra?"

"I'm saying Kaytra is walking a fine line, Sis."

Perhaps it was more true than either of them could imagine. Lydia set her free hand on his chest, conveying how very serious her next words would be. "Please, Colin. Please don't push her off that line. She could fall harder than you might think. Promise me?"

Colin set his fingers over her hand, squeezing them in a gesture of reassurance. "All I can do is try, Lydia. I promise I'll try."

While Lydia slept that afternoon, Kaytra put on one of the big, white aprons to protect her new clothes and worked quietly at washing the windows throughout the kitchen and parlor. Then she began wiping away imaginary dust from the furniture. Once, she caught her reflection in the glass front of the clock on the wall near the door. How impossible it seemed to her that she was at Highland.

For so long now, she had given up any hope of leaving Provincetown, of escaping the pain and degradation. She stared at the face before her, wondering at the image so like the woman she could remember her mother to be until -...but those thoughts had to be put aside. Kaytra turned and wiped the cloth over the back of the settee. Beside it the big sturdy desk with its many compartments was warmed a honey color by the sunshine.

Though Kaytra could stand and admire the neat piles of papers and envelopes and pens, and how the thick, burgundy-bound journal was placed squarely upon the near corner, she had never dared to touch any of them. Colin MacRae would know if the slightest thing were out of place. He had a sharp eye. There wasn't much which escaped his attention. For that same reason, she had not dared to sneak into the lighthouse tower. If he caught her there, inside his lighthouse, he would indeed send her back to Provincetown.

The last piece she dusted in the parlor was the book shelf. There were books everywhere in the house, more than Kaytra had ever seen in one place. Her gaze ran over the volumes, looking for the one she had seen Lydia reading the day before. Several breathless moments after she saw the book, she knelt down in front of the shelf to slide it from its place. The words on the first page immediately captured her imagination away from the real world. *"...leaves sang in the very tops of the willow trees. A song of summer. Light and airy as a Vienna waltz. A song reminiscent of days when she had loved Henry. Her-."*

"Kaytra."

The sound of Colin's voice startled her so much the book fell limply to the floor and she whirled to her feet. There wasn't any color in her face. Her eyes showed fear. Did she really think he would punish her in some way for having the book in her hands? Colin frowned a little. "I'm sorry I frightened you." He stepped further toward her. "It's three o'clock. I came to record the weather in the journal."

He had seen a cornered fox once during a hunt with that same expression. It bothered him deeply. Kaytra even flinched when he leaned over to pick up the book. It felt cool in his hands. "Isn't this the one Lydia just read - again? It's one of her favorites." His brown eyes searched Kaytra's face. "You can read?" He knew it somehow, but was still surprised when Kaytra nodded her head the tiniest bit.

Colin handed the book back to her, waiting until she reluctantly took it from him. "Whatever books are in this house are yours to share, Kaytra. You don't need to be shy about reading them." He would have been blind not to notice the furtive glance she took at the desk. Or more particularly at the journal. Colin walked to it with thoughtful steps. "What I write in here isn't very interesting, I'm afraid. I record the direction and speed of the wind, any ships I have seen and what the weather is like. My daily routines." He lifted his eyes to hers again.

Surprisingly, the look of fear was gone. "Here. I'll show you." While Colin sat down in the chair by the desk and opened the book to the page he had already dated September 2nd, 1802, Kaytra hesitantly stepped toward him. "I record at nine a.m., noon, three o'clock and six o'clock everyday. This morning it was thick-a-fog. That's what you Cape Cod people call foggy." He reached for the pen and ink bottle, writing as he spoke outloud. "Three o'clock. Breezier now. Sky still clear blue. Faint sign of clouds to west. Temperature cooler than this same time yesterday."

As soon as he set the pen down, he could sense a thoughtful disappointment from Kaytra. Her arms tightly hugged the book she held. Colin tilted his head, sitting back in the chair. "What's wrong?"

She frowned a little at the question.

Not for the first time, he felt an odd sensation deep in the pit of his stomach. Before he could ask anything else, Kaytra went back to the shelf, slipped the book into its spot and took up the dusting cloth. Inside of a minute she had left the house completely.

Rex ran ahead of her, chasing the bank swallows high into the air. Every once in a while, he would look at her as if wondering why the birds wouldn't play with him. Kaytra found a stick and placed it into the over-sized basket she carried in one hand.

If they were to have steamers for supper, she would need to see some sign of them soon. She reluctantly tore her gaze away from the ocean and concentrated more on the damp sand at her feet.

It felt good to be out by herself, and during the day. Her late night walks with Rex were sometimes very lonely. With the sun shining, the world at least seemed friendlier. No, maybe that wasn't a fair thought. Lydia was good to her. Colin MacRae tried to be. Hadn't he given her the book to read? Hadn't he shown her the journal?

Once Kaytra spied the tiny holes which told her where to dig for the clams, she fell to her knees, using the blade of a knife to scoop out sand. Yes, Colin had shown her the journal, but there was something about his manner which made her think there wasn't a willingness about it. He resented her being at Highland. In spite of all his talk about Lydia needing help, he spoke a silent message that a house-keeper wasn't his first choice.

She moved on to another buried covey, thinking of Colin's entries in the journal. It was indeed breezier now, as if nature was waking from a summer nap to discover it hadn't kept up with its work and was now pushing in from the west to hold back the waves. An off-shore breeze was pleasant, even restful. Yet Kaytra much preferred the salt mistiness of an on-shore wind.

A "clear blue" sky?

She raised her eyes. It was a handful of shades and not merely blue at all. The "faint sign of clouds" was a wispy puff. Angel's wings. That's what her mother had called them. And it wasn't only "cooler", fall was calling at the door and would not wait as patiently with the next knock.

Kaytra stood slowly, brushing away the grains of sand which clung to her skirt. There were enough clams in her basket now. She could head back. The stick she had picked up before was sturdy enough to make a loud sound when she clacked it against the handle of the knife. Rex came at the signal.

Tired from chasing birds, he was content to walk beside her. It wasn't long before they were within sight of the light. A lone figure stood on the walk outside the top of the tower. Kaytra looked at Colin once, then out to sea, wondering what he saw. Perhaps the sails of a ship still too distant for her to see from shore. Or maybe he was seeing beyond that.

When she shifted the basket to her other hand, Rex licked her free fingers. The dog had taken to Colin MacRae. Where other strangers were threatened by a fierce snap of those powerful jaws, Colin MacRae found a friend. She had watched them together. It was a friendship which didn't lack respect. Rex was a good judge of people and he had sensed the goodness in Colin MacRae. But then, he hadn't been told to take a bath, either!

Remembering that humiliation brought a flush to her cheeks. Kaytra's steps slowed and finally stopped completely. There were flashes of white in the green-blue water just beyond where the waves started to rise and break over the shore. She studied the darting shapes...Bass. Wouldn't they taste good with the clams? She could fry them in a bit of butter.

In no time, she had pulled off her shoes and her stockings. The cool water came up to her ankles, then to her knees. As soon as Rex knew what she was up to, he joined her in the water. By motioning with her hand, she made him stay back. For the next few moments, she stood perfectly still, waiting for the fish to return.

The first one got away from her. The second didn't. She threw it up onto the sand. So smoothly was it done that she had half a dozen fish waiting on the sand and a seventh in her hand before she came out. Rex eyed her prize with such longing, she smiled and gave the last fish up to him.

That same smile was the one Colin saw as he walked toward her. All the way from the tower, he had been preparing to give her a lecture for rushing headlong into the water as she had. Yet now, seeing her happiness, how could he play the uncomfortable role of disciplinarian again? In truth he felt more curiosity for her strange behavior than he did annoyance.

When Kaytra caught sight of him approaching, she became withdrawn again and the smile vanished. Colin tried not to notice, tried to keep his tone pleasant. "That was quite some fishing, Kaytra. They're bass, aren't they?" For a moment it seemed as if she would consider his presence an intrusion, then she nodded her answer. "I'm surprised you kept Rex out of the fun."

They both looked down at the dog, who was lying at Kaytra's feet. One huge paw was holding down the flapping fish. Every once in a while, he nudged it with his nose to get it to stop moving, but the fish wasn't giving up easily. When it got away from him, Rex pounced on the bass, then ran a few steps with it in his mouth, stopping to look at Colin as if daring him to take it away.

Colin, who knew better than to start the game, looked over his shoulder to see that Kaytra had already retrieved her basket and knife from further back on shore. Though her skirt and apron were soaked half way up her legs, it didn't appear to bother her. Even as she glanced around for a place to clean the fish, Colin found a flat board nearly buried in the sand a few feet away which would serve the purpose quite nicely. He would even have offered to clean the fish for her, but was convinced she would refuse.

Kaytra took the board from him with an unguarded expression of thanks. Neither did she seem uneasy when he sat down by her to watch. He could tell right away that she had done it before. Her small hands worked with efficiency.

For a few minutes, Colin twisted a dried blade of sea grass in one hand. Back up in the tower, watching her had been like watching one of the ships gracefully gliding toward harbor. Did she feel safe here now? Did she feel safe enough to tell him the truth?

"It's been good to see Lydia feeling better. I am amazed some-times how determined and strong she can be." Colin watched the glim-mer of sun riding in with the next gentle wave. "Even in coming here she was strong. The doctors said she should have stayed in Boston where life was easier. Lydia never has listened very well." He almost added that Kaytra was the same, but didn't want to ruin the easiness which had settled between them. When he shifted his gaze to see how she was doing, he frowned a little. "Kaytra?"

Sometime while he talked, the knife had fallen to the sand and she was holding one hand in the other against her apron. There was a definite expression of pain on her face. Colin was beside her instantly. "Did you cut yourself? Here. Let me see."

She didn't resist when he pulled her hand away. A gash lay on the inside of her right palm. Though it wasn't very deep, her breath-ing increased and she stumbled to her feet. But Kaytra wasn't paying attention to her hand anymore. There was an ugly red stain of blood on her apron. Blood! With her hands, both of them, she tried desper-ately to rub it away.

"Kaytra?"

Though Colin reached for her out of genuine concern, she stumbled backward, tearing at the hated, blood-soaked cloth, each breath now more rapid than before. Colin caught her arms in his hands.

"Kaytra, please let me help." She shook her head in panic, still rubbing at the bloodstains until he grabbed the top of the apron and tore it from her. Against his strength, the seams quickly gave way. "There, it - it's gone." He threw the apron to the ground, watching as she was unable to keep from staring at the discarded heap.

Even after he let go of her, he continued to stare at her white face. He couldn't understand how she could have been cleaning dead fish a moment ago and now it seemed she was petrified at the sight of blood? Her actions upset him more than he cared to admit. "What's wrong, Kaytra?"

At his words, she shrank tightly into herself, inching away.

"What's wrong with you?" he repeated, in frustration this time.

Suddenly, she ran for the bank.

"Kaytra!" Colin was torn for a second between letting her go and following his instincts. Already, her blind fear and agility had carried her halfway up the bank. He had to follow.

With Rex running beside him, Colin easily caught up to her. He made her sit down right where she was on the sandy path. By then, Colin was breathing as hard as she was. Anxiously, his eyes probed her every feature, finding no reason for what had just happened. Maybe there wasn't any reason. Maybe this was like all the other times. It seemed more and more as if Kaytra's life was ordered from within. Any twist, any unexpected occurrence no matter how big or small seemed to upset her the same way.

By virtue of superior strength, Kaytra had no choice but to follow Colin when he pulled her back down the bank to shore. She stiffened when he plunged her sand-caked hand into the saltwater. "Leave it there."

He went to the apron then, tearing a strip from the bottom to be used as a bandage. Kaytra didn't look up when he tied it securely over the still bleeding cut. She was a mess. Her new clothes were wet and crusted with sand. Her hair had mostly fallen from the comb.

Colin set a hand alongside her face, forcing her to meet his questioning eyes. "When someone tries to help, you don't run away, no matter how afraid you are. Now, let's finish cleaning the fish. Then we will both go back up to the house." His eyes were gold-brown and searching. Hers a deeper blue-gray, almost amazingly lavender in the rich, late afternoon sunlight. "And then, Kaytra-," he spoke in a different way now, with less control over his emotions, "we will sit down and you will tell me what it is you're hoping to gain from this game of silence you've been playing."

Her eyes widened with an expression akin to horror. The frown which marred her brow was very real.

Colin raised one eyebrow in unwelcome suspicion. "Yes, Kaytra. I know your secret. I've heard you at night, crying out in your sleep." She moved her head slowly from side to side and pulled a few steps away. "You can talk, can't you?"

She only shook her head again, like a child bewildered at being accused of some wrongdoing which she knew nothing about. Her uninjured hand brushed weakly at the hair which the breeze was blowing across her face.

The expression on Colin's face clearly showed his own confusion. For the past week now, he had been awakened a number of times by those pitiful cries. He had stood at her bedroom door, listening in silence as the nightmares gripped her, hearing her moan words he couldn't understand. Yet now-.

Colin knew he wasn't wrong. She could talk! "I won't be lied to, Kaytra. Not again." She wouldn't know how much he hated lies. Lies had caused him more pain than he cared to remember.

Before he could say more, she swung around wildly and then, seeing what she wanted, lunged for the stick near the basket of clams. Heedless of the tide which washed at her bare feet, she scribbled out words in the sand.

Colin's impatience grew when he read them.

"*The Dummy.*"

So, she did realize what the people called her. "You aren't a Dummy. You're very smart. You only let people think you can't talk so they stay away from you!"

Kaytra's eyes flashed in desperation. She knelt again to write.

"Can not talk!"

"But I've heard you, Kaytra!" Colin spread his hands wide in a desperation equal to hers. "You have to stop this, Kaytra. You aren't a child any more."

Tears coursed down her pale cheeks.

He wouldn't allow himself to be moved by them. He wouldn't...But his tone still became hushed with compassion. "Tell me the truth, Kaytra. That's all I want."

She looked down for a long time at the stick she held in her hands before she wrote again. When she was done, she stood and left, taking with her the basket and the half-cleaned fish. Colin moved until he could look directly down at the words she had scratched into the sand.

"God knows the truth."

He read it over and over again, until finally the tide crept in to leave only empty sand once more.

Chapter Six

Unexpectedly, a visitor came to Highland Light the next day. But then that was how the Commission inspectors worked, never announcing when they would arrive to do their job. Colin greeted the wiry, balding man with his usual friendliness, while at the same time, silently thanking the Providence of God which brought him now rather than a week and a half earlier when so many jobs had been left undone because of Lydia's illness.

Elliott Martin had sharp, close-set eyes and an odd way of moving about, as if there wasn't enough time in a twenty-four hour day for him to complete the things he set out to accomplish. It was impossible to guess how old he was. Perhaps Lydia's age, certainly no younger than that. Even wearing his hat, he only stood to Colin's shoulder. As the hours wore on, it seemed to annoy him that he had to keep looking up in order to meet Colin's eyes.

His experience at Boston had taught Colin what to anticipate during the inspection. Mr. Martin would completely examine the light itself, making sure everything was in perfect working order. Any necessary repairs would be noted and a time limit set for them to be completed. After a thorough search, however, Mr. Martin found that no repairs were needed. This, too, seemed to cause some sense of resentment.

Since the house was also government property, it received the same careful scrutiny. He found little to fault them with: some painting to be done on the outside trim, a new latch for the back door and a coat of wax upon the parlor floor. Colin was secretly grateful Kaytra wasn't there to hear the list rattled off. He knew she would have begun the tasks immediately.

But Kaytra had, in fact, disappeared at the first sign of Elliott Martin's horse and buggy coming across the field of sand and scrub oak. That had been over two hours ago. In the back of his mind, Colin wondered where she could be. The day was a good deal cooler now. Gray clouds veiled the sky.

"Mr. MacRae."

He swung his gaze away from the window to where Elliott Martin sat at the kitchen table.

An array of papers and books were spread out around the inspector. There was a touch of scorn in his expression. "About this journal entry dated - August the 20th. You have a new housekeeper?"

"Yes." Colin nodded his head slightly. "It was necessary because of my sister's illness."

"Of course." It was said with enough rancor to tighten the muscles across Colin's back. "You do realize such an expense will not be covered by the Federal Lighthouse Commission?"

"I will personally pay her wages, Mr. Martin." Surely, there could be no problem with that. He was wrong.

Elliott Martin spent the next few minutes grilling Colin for details about Kaytra and, upon finding that she was a young, unmarried woman, cautioned him with the strict need to protect the reputation of the Commission.

Just moments before Colin thought he would lose his temper and tell the man to mind his own business, Lydia came gliding down the stairs.

"Oh, Colin... Mr. Martin. I do hope I'm not interrupting." Her bright smile always could charm the most stalwart gentleman. In fact, she had overheard some of what the inspector was saying and knew that her brother would be in a foul mood. The mere thought of Colin throwing the man out made Lydia smooth her hair and hurry to the rescue. "It isn't often we get company at Highland. I just couldn't stay in my room a moment longer." Colin's raised eyebrow was all the reprimand he gave as he pulled out a chair for her at the table. Lydia laid her delicate hands upon her lap. "Has Colin told you, Mr. Martin, that we both find Highland Light a unique and marvelous place?"

Elliott Martin's eyes widened perceptibly. "Indeed?"

"Oh, yes!" Lydia had won her audience. "Why, not one day is the same as the next here. And the light. It is the very best, isn't it? The FLC must be extremely proud of how well it serves not only the Cape, but all of New England. The stories of those awful shipwrecks before the lighthouse was built here are simply too horrid..."

Her praise went on. Colin smiled to himself as he began to pour three cups of coffee. Leave it to his sister to make Elliott Martin putty in her hands, but her real purpose for such dramatics, her real reason for making the effort to come downstairs, would be to tell him the story of how Kaytra came to be with them.

As Colin lifted his eyes to the kitchen window, he caught sight of a black speck just rounding the corner of the barn. Where Rex was, Kaytra couldn't be far away. He excused himself rather suddenly, leaving Lydia to entertain their guest alone for a few minutes.

No attempt was made to steal up on her. Colin just walked along quite naturally. Yet when he unexpectedly appeared inside the open doorway of the barn, Kaytra was so startled she dropped the armful of hay she was taking to Samson. She stared at Colin for only a moment before bending down to gather the hay. It wasn't easy to ignore his shadow as it moved nearer to her across the floor. If she had only heard him coming, she could have been gone. Or, at least she could have prevented him from guessing her thoughts as he did.

"So, this is where you've been hiding, for the past few minutes anyway."

His smug tone not only caused Kaytra to chew on her bottom lip, but she decided to make the job last longer than necessary. She really didn't want to face him. Not now.

Colin crossed both arms over his broad chest. "Did you think you could outlast the inspection? These things take hours. Besides which, it's nearly time we offered Mr. Martin a decent meal before he starts out on the long trip back to Provincetown."

With a display of swift grace, Kaytra rose and took the hay to Samson's stall. The horse nudged at her hands while she "arranged" it in the manger. Not wanting to appear idle, she reached for the hand brush and began grooming Samson's coat, a task for which she received two curious looks: one from Samson, who had just endured a vigorous rub down, and one from Colin, who also knew she was stalling.

"Kaytra." The first warning came quietly. "What's so hard about going inside and making a meal? Martin won't likely eat you for supper... He wouldn't dare. You'd give him indigestion." Angry blue-gray eyes flashed quickly to his face, reminding Colin of the ocean on a winter's day before the storm hit. He took a couple of steps closer. His second warning came firmly. "Put the brush down and go into the house." From the corner of his eye, he saw how her hand tightened upon the brush. "Now, Kaytra."

There was a tense moment when he thought she would throw caution to the wind and refuse. Instead, she carefully replaced the brush on its hook.

When she tried to slip past him, Colin caught her arm, keeping her there while he studied the closed expression on her face. "You don't have to like me, Kaytra, but you'd better have a good reason to hate me. Anger isn't a good reason." He walked out as silently as he had come.

Once Elliott Martin saw the "housekeeper", he jumped at the chance to delay his departure. What an interesting little thing she was and they said she couldn't talk. Very interesting.

Kaytra felt every one of his stolen glances as she tried to concentrate on cutting even slices from the loaf of bread in her hand. Colin MacRae and Elliott Martin must have discussed her at length for the man to look upon her in such a way. They were both lucky she didn't give them hardtack and beans. Indigestion indeed! The knife clattered onto the counter. If it weren't for Lydia, there wouldn't be a meal.

No. Kaytra felt a stab of conscience. That wasn't true. This was part of her responsibilities now. The plates were set on top of the table with jerky movements. How childish it had been to run away as soon as she saw Elliot Martin coming. She shouldn't distrust people so.

As she checked the potatoes and carrots boiling on the stove, Kaytra pushed a stray lock of hair from her forehead with the back of one hand. Shame filled her for the way she had let her anger run rampant. It wouldn't do any good to be angry. She flaked some bass in the fry pan to see if it was properly cooked.

Perhaps while the others ate, she could slip away to her room where no one would pay any attention to her. She finished setting the table with three places rather than four. As soon as she could, Kaytra meant to escape to some private place and sort out her feelings.

That chance never came. While Kaytra set food on the table, her eyes happened to meet Colin's. The disapproval she saw did not go unspoken. "Get a plate for yourself, Kaytra. It will round out the numbers."

Round out the numbers? This wasn't Boston! She swallowed hard at the look he sent her, then moved to find another plate and some silverware. Once she was seated, Colin prayed a simple blessing for the meal.

Kaytra would not look at him as the food was passed around. At least not until he added an extra helping of potatoes to the minuscule portion on her plate. His expression silently said she wouldn't be allowed to starve herself while a guest was present.

It seemed Elliott Martin was scheduled to go to Boston next. Lydia was quick to ask if he would be so kind as to hand-deliver some letters to the MacRae's. He readily agreed, more out of curiosity to see the famed household where this brother and sister team came from than because he held any feelings of obligation.

Conversation moved from the growing interest in the whaling industry to politics to the other lighthouses Martin had recently visited. Kaytra, with her head lowered most of the time, listened to every word without appearing to care a whit for what was said, that is until Elliott Martin happened to ask if she had been shown how to work the light.

A hesitant silence on Colin's part made Kaytra glance up at him. His eyes were fixed on his plate, but she could still see the firm set to his jaw, she could still guess that he had deliberately chosen not to show her. The realization overwhelmed her with disappointment. Once more, she lowered her eyes to stare hard at the uneaten food on her plate.

When he did speak, Colin was careful to say the right words. "I have been - considering if teaching Kaytra how to operate the light would be appropriate given the circumstances. Lydia has improved a great deal. There may not be a need to have a housekeeper for an extended period of time."

"Well," Elliott Martin seemed undecided about what to say. "You are in charge here, Mr. MacRae, and I trust you have sound judgment. In my opinion, she should be taught. If you believe she has the capacity to learn such duties, you shouldn't delay showing her."

His last remark cut deeply. Kaytra poked a carrot with her fork, trying not to cry.

If she had looked up, she would have seen how Colin's hands clenched into tight fists. "It isn't her 'capacity', Mr. Martin."

"Very well, then. Consider the advantages." Martin leaned one arm upon the table and let his gaze shift from Colin to Lydia as if he wanted to include her, too, though such a gesture completely bypassed Kaytra. "You would be able to assign her some of your tasks. The simpler ones, surely. But none the less, it would ease the amount of work for you."

Colin sat stiffly in his chair as the other man went on. If not that he was answerable to the FLC, he would have given Elliott Martin a good piece of his mind. The man was an idiot! Even Lydia seemed to be having a difficult time enduring him and Lydia was a most polite and understanding person, not given to finding fault.

Did God look down upon Kaytra just then and send Rex scratching at the door to release her from the table? Colin gladly let her leave.

In another half hour, it was reasonable to suggest that Elliott Martin should be on his way back to Provincetown or nightfall would catch him on the open road. Martin gathered his papers together while Lydia and Colin both sat down to write letters home.

Lydia's was amusing and carefully void of any mention she had been ill. Colin's letter was brief. He asked after his parent's health and happiness, told them of his sister's returning strength and how he had found help for her. At the end, he asked about Sondra, something Lydia would never have done.

Elliott Martin promised to deliver the letters as soon as he arrived in Boston. "And perhaps, Miss MacRae," he added with a long look at Lydia's pale face, "you should go and lie down now. You appear tired after this busy day."

She moved her slim shoulders indecisively and would have corrected him from calling her "Miss MacRae", but Colin was already agreeing. "You do look peaked, Sis. Will you excuse us, Mr. Martin? I'll take my sister upstairs."

"Yes, do."The older man settled his hat upon his head. "And thank you for your hospitality. I can see myself off."

Colin, who shook the man's outstretched hand in a preoccupied way, was carrying Lydia to her room before Elliott even stepped out of the door.

Unfortunately, Kaytra was working within sight of the house. It did not take Elliott Martin long to make his way to the garden. He leaned casually against the fence, watching her for a moment as he thought more about the girl's story. "Say, you wouldn't know how to rig up the buggy, would you? I'm rather in a hurry and more hands would help." Kaytra paused at her work, but didn't answer yes or no. "Colin MacRae said to ask you. He's busy with his sister now. I'm afraid she quite wore herself out."

A satisfied smirk lifted Elliott's mouth when Kaytra moved to do as he asked. He walked a few steps behind her to the barn, then stood and watched as she brought the horse to the buggy. It was Kaytra who hooked up the harness, although Martin did step in at the end to take the reins from her hands and hook them around the edge of the buggy. "Thank you, Kaytra." When she would have left, his hand whipped out to clamp around one arm.

Her startled eyes flew to his face.

Elliott grinned wickedly. "Such a pretty innocent. Or are you? I'll wager, if the truth be known of your past, people like the MacRae's wouldn't have taken you in. Am I right, Kaytra?"

Though she tried not to let him know he was hurting her, she couldn't help but tremble when his hand dug more deeply into the flesh of her arm.

"I've seen plenty of your kind, Kaytra. Young girls. Pretty ones who grow up so destitute they learn to do 'anything' just to survive.... Ahhh," he nodded in a self-gratified way. "I see you know what I mean."

Kaytra shook her head firmly, trying to pull away. But Elliott's other hand came up to touch her face. She was sickened by the expression in his eyes. Sickened and afraid.

"Come now, Kaytra." His tone was low, persuasive. "I won't hurt you."

She could feel blackness threatening to overwhelm her, but she couldn't faint. Not now.

Elliot pinned her against the buggy. "I do feel badly, of course, that you are unable to talk." His sarcasm was a sharp pain sinking into her heart. Kaytra twisted desperately to be free. "Oh, some spirit?" He tried to kiss her, but she avoided him. It was the wrong thing to do. All at once his temper exploded. His hand came up to grasp her hair. He would make her cooperate.

Without warning, without even one sound, Rex was there. His great bulk flew at the stranger, knocking both Martin and Kaytra to the ground. The horse shied away as Rex's ear-splitting barks changed to a menacing growl.

As soon as Martin released his hold, Kaytra struggled to her feet. All the breath had been knocked out of her. When he saw her safe, Rex moved in, stalking up to Elliott until there were mere inches separating them. The man's face went ashen at the sight of his huge, bared teeth.

Colin found them exactly that way when he ran up to the yard. Rex's first barks had alerted him to some trouble, but he wasn't at all prepared for this. He stopped abruptly, trying to catch his breath, letting his gaze take in the situation. Kaytra's devastated face told him the wrenching truth. "Are you all right?" She shrugged her shoulders in a helpless gesture which made him all the more infuriated with Martin.

At hearing Colin's voice, Elliott recognized this might be his only chance at escaping unscathed "Call - the - dog - off, Mr. - MacRae."

"Not yet." Colin advanced with carefully measured steps to the place where Rex had Elliott Martin pegged to the ground. The man's fear-filled eyes rounded. "Suppose you tell me how you got yourself into this?"

"Your - dog - attacked me!," Elliott spat out defensively and received a threatening growl from Rex for his tone.

Colin stood with both arms crossed. "Rex isn't my dog...he's Kaytra's." Martin began to sweat under the pressure. "It looks to me like you made yourself a deadly mistake, Mr. Martin."

The girl would have two protectors! Martin swore fiercely, though Rex didn't like that either. His front paws came down on top of Martin's chest. "Okay, okay. So maybe I did make a mistake. Just -." Elliott squirmed uncomfortably. "Just call him off!"

"Rex! Heel!"

Colin's demands were heeded too slowly for Elliott's comfort. He watched through wide eyes as the dog moved to stand by Kaytra. She had remained white and shaken in that very same spot.

"On your feet, Martin!"

Elliott was justifiably wary of the edge he heard in Colin's voice.

"You have exactly two seconds to apologize to Kaytra and get on your way."

"But MacRae! She-."

"I said, apologize!"

Elliott's shoulders stiffened in a determined huff. "I can make your job here fly right out the window, MacRae. One word to the FLC about the 'liaison' going on between you and your 'housekeeper' and you'll be barred from ever setting foot near a lighthouse again!"

Colin didn't even flinch. "One word from me and you will be barred from working anywhere in New England. When a MacRae talks, people listen. They can't afford not to." It was the truth and they both knew it. "Apologize."

The few words Martin mumbled in Kaytra's direction were hardly what Colin had in mind. He would have made him do it correctly except that the poor girl looked near to fainting.

Elliott Martin snatched his hat off the ground, then stormed away to find his horse and buggy, all the while cursing the girl and her dog and most of all Colin MacRae.

The queer sickness in Kaytra's stomach couldn't be ignored any longer. She managed to stumble only a few feet away before her legs gave out and she sank to the ground, vomiting up what little food she had eaten for lunch. She felt even worse to know that Colin MacRae saw her in such a state.

It was his strong hands which lifted her to her feet when it was over. "You look awful, Kaytra." He said the words with kindness and concern. "Let's get you back to the house." Kaytra tried to overcome the dizziness, but after only a couple of steps, Colin stopped and swung her up into his arms. She didn't want him to and she moved weakly in protest. "Just lie still or you'll be sick again."

He was somewhat alarmed at how light she felt. Lydia had told him of her suspicions that Kaytra had been nearly starved to death. Every once in a while on their way to the house, he glanced down at her pale face. He could have spared her that ugly scene with Martin if only he hadn't taken those few extra minutes with Lydia. But how could he have known Martin would do something so stupid?

As Colin easily pulled open the back door and went inside, Kaytra stirred to be let down. "Shhh, you'll wake Lydia. I'm taking you upstairs. You can lie down awhile." Colin smiled a little at the confused look in her eyes. "If I have to, I'll lock you in your room."

So quickly did she shrink in fear, he knew that it was the threat she heard rather than his teasing tone. Colin frowned deeply, but said no more until he had taken her to her bedroom and laid her upon the bed. She was still far too pale. "I wouldn't really lock you in, Kaytra."

Her eyes closed and she turned her head from him.

"Did someone do that to you before?" He surprised himself that he asked. Kaytra chose to remain silent, disturbing Colin's emotions even more. Finally, he leaned over her, placing one hand on her face so that she had to look at him. "Did they, Kaytra? Did someone lock you in a room before?"

Tears flooded her eyes. She nodded.

"And all the bruises? Did-." Colin swallowed hard. "Did they - did he beat you, too?" She hesitated too long. "Kaytra, tell me!" He whispered the words fiercely. "Was it Koch?"

There was an unmistakable message in her eyes. A plea that he not make her tell. She had endured beatings to ensure her silence.

Colin pulled away. Not so much from her, but from his own feelings and that nagging sense of frustration. Why? Why wouldn't she let him help? "You know, Kaytra," he studied her face. "Maybe you wouldn't feel so alone if you let yourself out of that silent, self-pity of yours. You're the one who's making it hard."

He walked to the door, pausing to turn around and face her again. "I want you to stay put for two hours. If you won't take care of yourself, I'll have to make you rest . Lydia has grown to depend on you a great deal. I was serious about taking you back if you don't do what I say. I won't have my sister hurt."

After he was gone, Kaytra lay upon the bed going over and over the things he had said. As much as Lydia was trying to understand, Colin was misunderstanding. Even if he knew all she had gone through, he might not feel differently. Never would he see her as more than a pathetic lump of humanity to be formed into the mold he thought she should fit into.

His housekeeper should obey and be meek. His housekeeper should have no feelings of her own except, of course, compassion toward Lydia, devotion toward serving and submission toward him.

Most of all, his housekeeper should speak, simply because his life would be easier then.

Twin tears slid down her temples onto the pillow. What hurt the most was that he thought she was choosing this hated silence. As much as she desperately wanted to speak, Kaytra was still helpless to do so. She could only accept what everyone else thought of her: that she was the town Dummy, scarred beyond repair.

More than ever now, she felt ashamed for not being the person Colin MacRae expected her to be. Coming to Highland had meant escaping one trap, only to be led into another. It had seemed easy to be lost in Provincetown, to forget she was anything more than a machine, moving from one day to the next with no feelings, no purpose.

Perhaps, she could pretend the same here. She could slip back into herself, be obedient and submissive to this second master. Kaytra flung an arm over her eyes, afraid to be that lost child once more.

Self-pity? She had no self-pity. She had only this new sad hope which somehow she must bury again in a shell of nothingness.

Chapter Seven

Lydia was not at first aware that her brother was the one who had effected the change in Kaytra and not Elliott Martin. She really couldn't say what made her begin to wonder. The longer moments of sadness perhaps...the pensive glances at the ocean...a sense of her young spirit being quenched. Truly it became worse than the first day all over again.

With much prayer and patience, Lydia tried to work around the impenetrable walls. They made more clothes for Kaytra. Two blouses, simple white ones, and a dark skirt for everyday. They planned meals together. Rather, Lydia did while Kaytra listened and nodded her agreement. They even took short walks along the bank.

Nothing seemed to bring back the signs of reaching out which Lydia had seen in Kaytra. Perhaps it would take a few steps of faith on her own part before the young woman would begin to once again desire a friendship between them.

It was not a decision made easily. Lydia had thought never to share the painful parts of her life with anyone other than Colin. Doing so now with Kaytra would mean bringing up wounds long past, but she was willing to endure the pain all over again if it helped.

"Kaytra?" They were sitting in Lydia's room a week after Elliott Martin's visit. Lydia was on the bed, propped against the pillows and Kaytra sat on a chair within arm's reach. The book Lydia had been reading while Kaytra mended one of Colin's shirts now lay upon her lap. "Kaytra, I've been wanting to - tell you something."

The strained tone in Lydia's voice was so unexpected, Kaytra looked up at her. Those brown eyes seemed very troubled. Was she having pain? Alarmed by the thought, Kaytra slipped onto the bed, letting the shirt fall to the floor.

Her concern touched a response in Lydia. "Oh, no dear. I'm quite all right. A little - hesitant perhaps." Lydia reached for one of Kaytra's slim hands. "I don't know what you will think of me once you've heard what I'm to say."

Kaytra tilted her head in an appealing way which encouraged Lydia to go on. "You see, dear...I'm sure you've just assumed that I am an old spinster. That my brother felt sorry for me and allowed me to tag along in his life, but - I am married." Lydia expected the confusion, the astonishment she saw on Kaytra's face and hurried on.

"It was not very many years ago. I met a man at one of my father's dinner engagements. Sidney Kent." A faraway look came into her eyes as she remembered. "I was twenty years old. He was twenty-eight and very handsome. Debonair. Charming. From a wealthy family in England. At first, I was too awestruck to realize that I was falling in love with him. You see, Sidney had swept me off my feet.

"He lived that way. Quickly. Impulsively. And I -." Her voice became quieter. "I had never met anyone like him. I was wildly in love with Sidney. My parents encouraged the relationship. They thought that only good could come of it. Two powerful, affluent families united by marriage. Looking back now, I can understand how they wanted the marriage as much for their own reasons as for my happiness.

"We were married that same summer. Sidney wanted children and, of course, I did, too. I wanted to make him happy any way that I could. It was a full year before we knew we were expecting a child."

Lydia took a moment to smooth the coverlet resting over her knees. She knew Kaytra was listening intently to every word, but now came the painful part. Ever so carefully, she went on telling the story. "We had a girl. A beautiful, perfect little girl. She didn't look anything like me. Blonde hair. Blue eyes. Very petite. Oh, I loved her dearly, Kaytra. The birth was difficult because of my heart. I nearly died. My strength returned slowly. But none of that really mattered to me. I was enthralled with my child, with being a mother.

"Sidney was gone often. I suppose it was natural, then, that I clung so completely to our daughter. He loved her, too, of course, in his own way. There wasn't anything he didn't bring to her. Her toddler face could hold the dearest, dimpled smile." Lydia's voice wavered as she pictured her daughter, and felt a deep ache to hold her again. It seemed that her heart could not contain such emptiness.

"When she was three, I became terribly weak. In part, it was my health, but mostly it was because I learned the truth about my - husband. He had been - unfaithful, almost from the start of our marriage. I was too blinded by love to see it.

"Colin eventually came to me with the awful truth. Not because he wished me to go through the pain of finding out, but because he was too honest to put up with the lie. It was the most difficult thing for him to do. I fell apart. Literally. My doctors insisted that I be institutionalized. Father and Mother were too embarrassed to do anything but agree. Colin stopped them. He spent the next six months with me. Day in and day out, willing me to want to live again.

"You see," her eyes shone with tears, "Sidney had taken Sondra away from me. My whole life was shattered. He felt I was an unfit mother because of the mental breakdown. It became a double loss then. The man I had loved didn't really exist. And my - my little girl - was - gone."

Five years had not even begun to diminish the pain. The sobs rose from deep within where she had tried to let the wound heal. Lydia felt herself being gathered into young, strong arms. She felt Kaytra's own tears upon her face. Any concern that Kaytra would pull even further away vanished . The only other person who had cared so unconditionally had been Colin.

Several minutes passed before Lydia moved away from Kaytra to lean back upon the pillows. She was tired, but strangely content. "Thank you, Kaytra, for listening. I feel better now that you know." Though their hands remained clasped upon the bed, Kaytra's eyes were restless, filled with a million questions. Lydia sensed her disquiet. "Oh, my dear. If only you could express all the words I see in your eyes."

Kaytra's chest rose and fell in desperate breaths, as if the past few days she had forgotten to breathe at all and now her starved body and mind were crying out to be set free. Impulsively, she leaned forward and placed a kiss upon Lydia's cheek, then as quickly she sped from the room, down the stairs and out into the dapple-gray September afternoon.

The wind came from off shore, full and damp, just as she enjoyed it most. Today however, she was too preoccupied to do more than bend her head against it as she walked to the very edge of the bank. Two white gulls soared and dived together in the chill air. A third, black and gray tipped, chased several wingbeats behind. Their calls were so much a part of the surroundings as to be lost unless one knew how to catch and hold them. It was a piercing sound, yet indelibly frail and empty.

Kaytra shivered, wrapping her arms across her body. She should have grabbed a coat, but it didn't matter - she wouldn't stay long. Her lungs filled with salty, moist air and let it out again as a heavy sigh. Poor Lydia...to have gone through so much. And Sondra.

Kaytra tried to imagine the child. Sondra would be eight years old now. Blonde hair. Blue eyes. Would she have grown to be as kind and loving as Lydia? How sad not to know. And wherever she was, did she miss her mother? Had she ever been told about Lydia? The unfairness of it all made her at once incredibly downhearted and angry.

"Why the frown, Kaytra?"

She started nervously, swinging her eyes to where Colin stood not three feet away. How long had he been there?

Long enough to see the changes of emotion upon her face. He arched his eyebrows, questioning why now, after days of nothing but blank agreement and stolid indifference, she should cast him such a purely unshielded look. "You're upset about something?"

Kaytra turned her gaze back to the vast ocean. As big as it was, she could not hope for it to hide her now. Colin had developed an increasing brusqueness toward her over the past week. He seldom spoke to her any more. If he did, it was only to say, "Stop working and rest." Had he sought her out now to tell her he would indeed take her back to Provincetown? Unknowingly, her eyes reflected the thought.

He ignored that, too. "I wonder if you have time to learn about the light now? The garden is nearly harvested."

So it was. Kaytra felt her body go tense at the slight note of resentment in his question. She knew he asked out of duty and for no other reason. Her agreement would be given the same way. If she could keep the wonder out of her eyes, hidden away, he would never know how much she had longed to learn about the light. Kaytra nodded slowly.

"Come on, then. Now is as good a time as any to start."

Kaytra followed obediently as he led her first to a post outside the tower which supported a huge brass bell. She had always imagined its joyful music ringing out over the sunshine. Maybe now she would know for sure what it sounded like.

"This is for emergencies. It can be heard a mile out from any direction. That's far enough to reach the Buckley's. They're our closest neighbors toward Truro. If it's sounded in a storm, Seth knows it's meant for the ships. I'd ring it if I suspected a wreck. Survivors would know they're close to help that way." Colin looked down to see if she was listening.

She was. Her arms were crossed over herself as she stood there in silence.

"If the bell is sounded in clear weather, Seth Buckley would be here in a few minutes. The emergency is on land then. Namely with us. He's promised to drop everything and come. It's not to be rung unless something happens to me."

He was asking if she understood, in no uncertain terms, that she wasn't to use the bell for any other purpose. Kaytra looked away from him and nodded. The solid brass bell didn't seem as jolly to her now.

Without saying anything more, Colin went to the door of the tower. His long strides carried him there before Kaytra even started to move.

It was easy for her to sense his impatience in the way he waited for her, holding the heavy, wooden door open with one hand. Inside, she waited a moment for her eyes to become adjusted to the dimness. There were only two small windows, seven feet high. Other than the strands of gray light they let in, it was dark. Not nighttime dark, but a sort of enveloping shadowiness, making one more aware of the close space.

"The stairs are kind of tricky. I can get a light." The way he said it implied the light would be for her benefit alone. Kaytra shook her head.

Indeed, the stairs were tricky. She tried to memorize them as they climbed upward. Colin went first, moving with practiced ease. Kaytra followed more slowly, trying to guess if he ever ran up and down the steps as she would do once she knew them better. She let one hand run over the rough wall. Beneath their feet, every squeak of a board, every scrape seemed anxious, as she was anxious to reach the top.

The moment she stumbled a little, Colin was reaching back for her, offering his hand for her to hold the rest of the way. When Kaytra hesitated, he took her hand anyway and closed his fingers around hers in a firm, but surprisingly gentle grip.

Arriving at the top room was like suddenly throwing open heavy curtains and finding a brand-new day. Kaytra stepped up onto the floor, immediately forgetting all else but the view which surrounded her. As she slipped away, Colin was forced to release her hand.

Could the world really be so big? Yet this was only one small part of it. Kaytra moved from the ocean side to the land side, marveling at how far she could see. After only a few seconds, the ocean drew her again. There were sails a distance out, appearing almost as birds, skimming the water. She could see where the shoals lay. Ribbons of melting sea green water moved atop them, marking the danger.

A mile to the northeast, those ribbons were wider, more distinct. The Peaked Hill Bars. So many men had died upon those sandy graves. Even now, she could imagine a grounded ship being torn apart by stormy seas. Highland Light had been built because of these shoals, but it was the waves which truly fascinated Kaytra. They were so smooth, rounded by repeated tumblings on their journey to shore. Every once in a while, one would spray white further out. Mostly though, they just rolled in, gathering force to explode suddenly as they reached their goal.

If the sun were out, she knew there would be a million sparkles bursting into the air. Today, the explosion was even more dramatic, a powerful flurry of white against the deep blue-green-gray mixed water. She would never tire of it, not when the scene was so ever-changing, so vibrant, as if someone had breathed life into a priceless painting.

Man might say he had conquered this ocean, but he never would. Such a spirit could be harnessed to carry man from one shore to the next, to further his dreams, to make him think he had accomplished a great feat, but man wasn't in control of the ocean, God was.

The thought spread warmth over her. During the past weeks, Lydia's frequent talk about God brought back feelings she hadn't known since her girlhood. Her eyes lifted to the sky. Was He there, looking down upon this extraordinary place? Did He know how it - .

"Kaytra?"

She swung around so quickly it made her dizzy. How could she have forgotten Colin MacRae was there? He had a quizzical expression on his face. And no wonder. Kaytra had revealed too much emotion. The blank look she placed into her eyes now made him frown.

For whatever reason, he chose to ignore it. "Come over here and I'll show you how to clean the lamps."

Colin's movements were precise. He explained only what he had to, almost as if he were reading a textbook. Kaytra's intense concentration wasn't a surprise to him. She did everything in that same way. What did surprise him was how exactly she mimicked each step on the lamp next to his without his having suggested she do more than listen. By the time they had worked their way around the wheel of lamps, she could have done it blindfolded.

Each lamp was then filled with oil, ready for the long night. Colin barely set the can down before Kaytra, cloth in hand, began to polish the reflecting mirror. He watched her work for a few minutes. Obviously, she wasn't aware that he could see her image in the huge mirror, for her eyes were alert and inquisitive. Colin leaned against the low window ledge encircling the room, knowing for certain now that she was enjoying her time up here.

Her reflection was blurred a bit, but he could still make out the delicate curves of her face. The soft line of her cheek. Her brightened eyes. He had been thinking she was desperately unhappy at Highland. Yet now, he saw that the opposite was true.

With graceful, circular motions, she cleaned one half of the mirror, then began doing the rest. Kaytra was a different person on the inside. So far, he had only caught glimpses of that person. Today, it seemed harder to remind himself of the barrier still standing between them. Colin straightened to his full height. "Thank you, Kaytra. Go down and check on Lydia now."

Just as as Kaytra looked up at Colin's reflection she assumed she had done something wrong. It was there in his voice, in the unbending set to his shoulders.

Her confused pause agitated Colin into moving behind her. It was odd seeing their reflections side by side. Somehow, the mirror softened his expression and heightened hers. He felt his breath catch in much the same way it had when he took her hand earlier.....The tender feeling passed when Kaytra handed him the cloth and turned to hurry away.

"Go slowly down the stairs." His hushed reminder fell on deaf ears.

Kaytra stumbled a few times, catching herself on the wall. She had stayed too long from the house. Surely, Lydia would be awake. Colin hadn't asked her to do the mirror! She shouldn't have found it so beautiful all alight with the colors of the sky. She shouldn't have made him angry! Ohhh!

Though she pushed hard against the door, it didn't budge. Kaytra blinked back the tears which rushed into her eyes, tears of weariness and disappointment and frustration. The rough wood stung her hand when she hit it so hard, but she wanted to get out. She had to get out!

Suddenly, the darkness began to close in. Panic carried her back to days when she had been locked inside a closet with not a single sliver of light, not enough air to breathe. Kaytra pounded on the door, again and again, unaware of all else except the desperate need to be safe.

Her pitiful sobs were nearing hysteria by the time Colin reached the bottom of the tower. He reacted automatically, pulling Kaytra away from the door and holding her against himself with one arm around her shaking shoulders. "Stop, Kaytra! It's not locked!" He gave the door a mighty kick with his booted foot to send it flying open. Cool air and late afternoon light flooded in.

Kaytra strained toward freedom. There wasn't any resistance when she pulled away from Colin's hold.

He stood helplessly in the doorway, watching her run to the front of the house and disappear inside. His thoughtful frown lasted long after she disappeared. Not five minutes ago, she had been relaxed, even happy. What cruel things had been done to her in the past? He didn't just want to know anymore. He needed to know.

Kaytra and Rex went for a long walk that evening. She didn't consider it right to sit in on Colin and Lydia's time for prayer and Bible study. They knew so much about God and she so little. Besides, hearing Colin read verses stirred faint whispers of her father's voice and she found it difficult to be reminded of him so often.

She pulled the shawl over her shoulders, holding the ends with both hands. Tonight her steps were slow, introspective. More than a lifetime seemed to have passed since she was that little girl, sitting at her father's knee. Listening to the deep timbre of his voice as he read to her. It wasn't so much that she remembered the verses, it was the way he made God seem so real to her. She remembered his patience in transferring his love for God into words she would know.

"Remember, Kitten. God is never far away from us..."

Kaytra stopped at the edge of the fresh water pool. He had always called her Kitten. It was his special name for her. She lowered herself onto the cushion of sand, letting it trickle through her fingers absentmindedly while Rex went off to explore.

Papa's face... his hair and hands. They were only a blur to her. She couldn't really remember what he looked like except that he had been strong. Dark, as men from France usually were. He had a gentle way about him, and he always smelled of the sea. A salty, fresh scent.

Captain Henry Lange. At four years old, she had been lifted high in his arms. They were special friends. She remembered the time he took her sailing on his big ship, how she sat beside him as he stood at the wheel. He was a happy man. He loved life. She could understand him more now that she was older. It was easier for her to piece together feelings in order to find a better picture of who he had been.

Her gaze lifted to look around. There were places where wild-flowers grew. Most had faded now. Even so, late September brought its own color to the Cape, a tapestry of richness and warmth which held those last days of life in full glory.

Had her father been that way? Holding tight to the beauty of life with a glorious, all-encompassing desire? He had been thirty-five and she just a day short of five when Mother had received news that the *Zephyr* was lost at sea. Captain Henry Lange and his crew of forty-eight were drowned.

Kaytra concentrated on the golds and rusts, the evergreens and fawn browns so that she wouldn't cry. Papa wouldn't have wanted her to cry. He had taught his Kitten about a God who was never far away. She had nearly buried those thoughts, nearly forgotten in all the endlessly dark years that somewhere there was a Light in life for her to see.

The memories brought Kaytra to her feet again. She looked back along the way she had come. The significance of Highland Light being part of her life now wasn't all perfectly clear, but she was beginning to see it. She was beginning to grasp the beauty of her new life here, to understand that perhaps God really wasn't far away. During the quiet afternoons she spent with Lydia, the older woman had shown her many verses in the Bible which told how Jesus was the Light of the world, how He would light the way for His people that they might journey upon the right path.

Just yesterday, Lydia had shown her a verse in the gospel of John, "Walk while ye have the light, lest darkness come upon you." Every time she thought about Colin taking her back to Provincetown, it was like a little bit of the light slipped away. She had to try harder to hold on to the light.

Rex came running toward her from across the sand to see if she was ready to go back. His tongue licked at the hand she held out to him. When he looked up at her that way, she wondered if he could share her thoughts. Sometimes she wanted to believe he could, for then she wouldn't feel so alone. Kaytra began walking back to the house, stopping every so often along the way to pick a few of the wild flowers.

Soft lights beamed a distant welcome from the house. As gray began stealing in to cover what remained of the day, Kaytra embraced the warm feeling those lights sent forth. Soon, Colin would be lighting the lamps in the tower. Since that morning, he had been more gentle with her than before. Something had changed between them. Maybe he would let her help this time. The hope grew in her until Kaytra ran carelessly on her way down the last rise. The fall bouquet, clutched with childlike preciousness to her breast, quivered in time to her steps, fragrant with an earthy, pungent scent.

The dog had already gone on ahead. It was he who alerted her to the trouble. Kaytra stood near the tower, poised in uncertainty. Old Bess was standing in the very middle of the garden with squashed, half-eaten cabbages at her feet, ignoring Rex's sharp barks. At first, Kaytra didn't know whether to despair or laugh. Then suddenly, she picked up her skirts and ran for the house.

As she burst inside, filled with breathless excitement, Colin and Lydia both looked up from their places in the parlor. Though they were surprised at her peculiar entrance, the sparkle in her blue-gray eyes surprised them even more.

"Why, Kaytra!" Lydia sat straighter on the settee as the girl rushed forward. "Whatever is-."

Kaytra quickly laid the gift of flowers into Lydia's arms, turning almost in the same motion to Colin, who had half risen from his chair. Her tiny hand slipped into one of his and she finished pulling him to his feet. "What is it? What's wrong?"

The amused smile on her face and appealing arch of her eyebrows seemed hardly answer enough. Colin threw a questioning look at his sister as Kaytra again pulled on his arm to get him to come with her. Lydia had no idea either, but she was rather pleased to see her new friend this way, bubbling with happiness. She shrugged her shoulders, smiling now herself .

Colin felt that impatient tug again and decided he'd better go along.

Kaytra literally ran back out of the house. With his long strides, Colin wasn't quite running to keep up. The warmth of that tiny hand in his occupied his thoughts until they rounded the corner of the house.

"Bess!" When Colin stopped abruptly, Kaytra did the same. "How did she -?" He lost the rest of his question because of the look on Kaytra's upturned face. Her lips were parted just enough to show a glimmer of white teeth. The longer he remained unmoving, the more Kaytra's smile faded.

For the second time that day, they were caught up in emotions too strong to deny. It was Rex who shattered the moment with his crazy, wild barking. Kaytra pulled away from Colin, running through the hole which the cow had broken through the fence.

What happened next bordered on the hilarious. Rex chased Bess around in circles, churning what was left of the cabbages and other vegetables into a sloppy mess. Whenever Kaytra tried from one angle to grab Bess' rope, she would slip on the sodden earth and end up sitting down with a quick thump. Colin was just as unlucky.

Amid the confusion, Rex darted from one corner to the other, barking in a purely playful way which, of course, encouraged rather than discouraged Bess. The fat, old cow didn't want to get caught. She had enjoyed her late supper snack too much.

"Kaytra, block her off to the right!" Colin shouted as he picked himself off the ground for the third time in as many minutes. Kaytra, skirts in hand, hurried to her post, until half a cabbage underfoot tripped her. Gentlemanly concern bade Colin to at least help her this time, though he couldn't quite keep from laughing as he did so. He picked her up with little effort, making sure she was steady on her feet before he let go. Kaytra's face was flushed and she was breathing hard, but she was smiling again. So was Colin. "You'd think two against one would make for pretty good odds."

Kaytra tilted her head at an appealing angle.

"Any ideas, mate?," he asked. "At this rate we'll be out here all night."

She turned to face Bess, crossing both arms over herself at the same time.

Colin laughed at the gesture. "You're picking up my bad habits."

"Oh, I hope not!" Lydia called from the fence behind them where she had been watching in amused silence. She hurried on before Colin could tell her she shouldn't be there. "You two are a mess." It was true. They were filthy. Kaytra's white blouse was now stained and a smudge covered her cheek. Colin hadn't fared much better. But they were enjoying every minute of the chase. "Why didn't you just try offering Bess a cabbage. She'd follow you anywhere for that."

"We can't get near her." Colin was too proud to jump at the idea straight off. It seemed too simple to work, anyway. Bess was as skittish as a mouse, though to compare her rolling gait to the scurry of a mouse was hardly fair.

"Just talk nice to her, Colin. It works with most girls!" When he shot her a thankless look for that remark, Lydia giggled joyfully. "Oh, do try, MacRae. Pretend she is Amanda Worthington!"

"Lydia!"

"Or Patricia!" She knew he didn't mind the teasing. Not really. "Just smile very handsomely and-."

"Be quiet, Sis." Colin was too nearly laughing to keep a straight face.

Seeing his good humor, Kaytra couldn't resist picking up the half cabbage at her feet. Before he knew it, she had taken one of his hands and plunked the mess down onto it, not forgetting to give him a challenging look at the same time.

Lydia's giggles were infectious. She admired the girl's spunk.

So did Colin. "Alright. I'll try once. If it doesn't work, it will be your turn!"

Kaytra agreed with a nod, then went to join Lydia at the fence, giving Colin lots of room to work.

As the two of them watched Colin approach Bess, Lydia laid a hand on Kaytra's shoulder in a gesture of companionship "He knows he looks terribly silly, but he doesn't mind. Thank you for the flowers, dear."

A warm smile lit Kaytra's eyes.

Finally, it felt as if Kaytra was opening up, ready to be alive again. Lydia prayed that Colin could see it, too. She had suspected for weeks now what purpose God had in bringing Kaytra to them. Whatever part she had in it, whatever things she could do, were small when compared to the changes He would work out. It was almost a view of the "impossible to realize"...But nothing was impossible with God.

"Bess! You beast!" Colin's voice drew their attention once again. The cow, with her tail swishing back and forth saucily, was running in the opposite direction from where Colin stood .

"Oh, do go help him, Kaytra." Lydia gave her a gentle push. "I think he may be ready to say we will have beef roast for supper tomorrow night!"

Chapter Eight

A storm broke during the night. Colin was up often checking on the light, watching the chaotic changing of the sea. As each flash of lightning split through the thick black sky, it illuminated a churning of raw power below, a tumult which made his heart beat faster in response. He could truly say today was one of the few times he felt glad to be standing on solid ground.

This was nature at its most spectacular, its most unpredictable. Only his light would remain the same, steady and strong, a beacon to guide any unfortunate ship riding the violent swells.

"To turn them from darkness unto light." The verse sprang into his thoughts, bringing a sense of purpose. Not only was it his responsibility to bring life-saving light to the ships, but he realized as he stood there that he had so far neglected another more important responsibility. He had neglected to share his faith with Kaytra. She needed God with a desperation he had never known before. His own salvation had come during a moment of need, yet in a way far different from what Kaytra needed.

Perhaps Kaytra's need would never be fulfilled if he failed to share what he knew. A pain came, swift and sure, into his heart to think of failing with Kaytra. "Please, Lord," he whispered. "Let it not be so. Let me show her that Your love has an awesome power in it. A gentle, awesome power."

During Colin's time of prayer on the bank, morning struggled upward from the horizon, trying in vain to quiet the storm, but clouds still hung in the sky like a heavy, gray cloak. Certainly, the light would stay on for much of this day. A gust of wind followed as he turned and made his way to the house. It was barely six-thirty, yet he opened the door to cozy warmth and the smell of fried potatoes.

Though Kaytra heard him enter, she barely looked over her shoulder at him. Colin couldn't decipher the expression in her eyes before she turned her attention to lifting a lump of bread dough into the bowl atop the counter. Rex's morning welcome was much warmer. The dog loped across the room with his tongue hanging out, his eyes bright and alert.

Colin rewarded him with a playful tussle, then went to pour himself a cup of coffee while Kaytra washed her hands. She would bring him a plate, but he really had no interest in food. At the table, with Rex lying at his feet, Colin dumped a generous measure of sugar into his cup. There was no excuse for not sharing his testimony with Kaytra. She needed to know. As Colin swallowed some of the coffee, a frown etched itself across his brow that was similar to Kaytra's frown.

The raging sounds of the storm had made it impossible for her to sleep. Any other day, she would have taken the harsh weather in stride, but today wasn't any other day. Suddenly, the plate Kaytra was holding slipped from her wet fingers and crashed loudly to the floor. For one horrified moment, she could only stare at it. Then as quickly as she could, she bent to gather the pieces into her apron. It wasn't fair! It wasn't fair that Colin should witness yet another of her childish mistakes.

Even before she lifted her head, she sensed when he came to stand over her. Her eyes were filled with apprehension, each heart beat strained. She pressed one tiny, shaking hand over her mouth.

Something darkened in Colin's eyes, but it wasn't anger this time. Still Kaytra seemed to shrink from the touch of his hands upon her arms as he guided her to her feet. "Do you really think I'll punish you for breaking the plate?" There was no positive response. "I'm not that kind of man, Kaytra."

She turned away from his probing gaze. The pieces of broken china clattered as she emptied her apron into an empty bucket. She wouldn't cry. Not now. Maybe he would go away. Maybe he-.

A hand settled on her shoulder. "Please look at me."

His height made it necessary for Kaytra to tilt her head far back before she could see his face.

"I know something is bothering you, Kaytra. Can't you tell me what it is?"

Her eyelids came down to cover an expression of dismay at the gentleness of his tone.

"Is it Lydia?"

She shook her head.

"Is it me?" Her expression of surprise caused Colin to arch his eyebrows in a suspicious way. After all, he had felt the tension his touch brought to her. "Okay. Let's say it isn't me." He wasn't convinced, of course. "But something is wrong, isn't it?"

Kaytra knew he wouldn't believe her now, even if she did shake her head. When he reached down for one of her hands, she held her breath...but he only led her into the parlor and made her sit in the chair by the desk, the place where he usually sat. Before she had time to recover any sense of balance, he set paper and pen in front of her. Every gesture he made was filled with patience. Kaytra moved her head to look up at him, but he had already turned away. "It's the only way, Kaytra. You have to start writing down whatever is bothering you."

Something inside of her recoiled. How could she write the things she was feeling?

Colin swung back slowly, catching the uncertainty. "Please? You did it once. On the beach. Remember?"

Her blue-gray eyes told him she wasn't likely to have forgotten that day.

"Try again, then," he urged softly. "However long it takes."

Kaytra, who sat with her hands clasped together upon her lap, lowered her gaze to the blank pieces of paper.

For Colin, this was the point when they must either move forward or forever stay the same. He knew which he wanted, but he wasn't sure of Kaytra's feelings. There was a slight tremble to her lips as she took in a deep breath. The lamp on the table a few feet away cast a honey gold glow over her. "You have to do it, Kaytra. I'll sit here with you all day if I have to, but you need to tell me what made you so upset a moment ago."

She didn't respond.

Colin moved to the windows then, staring out at the ocean. Though he was trying hard to be in complete control, he knew that the same kind of powerful agitation which stirred the ocean's waters also raged inside him. Beneath the outward calm, his emotions were being tossed round and round. Challenges were staring him in the face. Challenges from which he could not turn away.

The words to the verses he had read last night with Lydia came rushing back to him with perfect clarity as if God Himself was speaking them. Was He also bringing this new understanding? Colin concentrated on the inner voice....

> *"The heavens are telling the glory of God; and the firmament proclaims His handiwork. Day to day pours forth speech and night to night declares knowledge. There is no speech, nor are there words; their voice goes out through all the earth, and their words to the end of the world."*

Last night, he hadn't thought of Kaytra in that light, but now he did. Day to day since she had come to Highland, she had been speaking to them - in her own way. She had shown a strength and a knowledge which growing up a MacRae hadn't required. Colin glanced at her again. In his thoughtful silence, she had begun writing. Would it be her true feelings or merely a clipped explanation?

With a quiet sigh, he lowered himself into the upholstered chair by the settee to wait until she was done. Through the windows, he could see how the beach grass was laid low by the wind. Day had lightened the sky a little more now, defining the edges of giant thunderheads clashing together in the grayness. It was still raining, though not as fiercely as before. Rain on the Cape didn't simply fall down. Instead, it was thrown at an almost flat angle.

Colin rested his head upon the high back of the chair. He had yet to change from his plain brown shirt and pants. Or to shave. As soon as Kaytra was done...By moving his head slightly, she came into his view again. She looked so young sitting there, submissively doing as he asked. Perhaps Lydia was right. It did seem as if Kaytra was walking a fine line. God alone knew all she had gone through. God alone would be able to guide him. He closed his eyes to pray for that guidance.

"Colin...Colin, wake up."

Lydia's voice reached insistently into his sleep until he opened his eyes. It took a moment to realize that he had fallen asleep in his chair. Lydia had a definite frown on her face. Colin sat upright from his cramped position, testing stiffened muscles. "What time is it?"

"I don't know," she said impatiently, her dark green dress only accentuating the lack of color in her face. "Nine-thirty, I suppose. Where is Kaytra?"

A hesitation gripped him, "She was-."

"Writing." Lydia held out a single sheet of paper. There were lines of neat, flowing words upon it. "Did you make her do it, Colin?"

Obviously, his sister had already read the words. Colin took the paper as he stood from the chair. "Isn't she in the house?"

"No." Lydia shook her head slowly. "You'd better read it right now. I'll go call for her. Maybe she's out in the barn, milking Bess."

He frowned at the seriousness of Lydia's tone. The paper seemed to gain weight as he carried it to the light by the desk and sat down.

"Finding words to tell you what I feel is like trying to discover where the sun has gone on such a day as this. It must be there, of course, somewhere far above the thick, blinding clouds. Yet to penetrate the storm in search of the shining sun is a battle to face the unknown before finally arriving on the bright side of the day. And, once you are there, to realize it is only your soul - your most inner thoughts - which have gone the journey while you, in real life, have stayed behind, caught beneath the storm. The two must come together again. No person can live in such separate worlds. It is the most dying feeling to fall back from the warmth of your dreams into the place of reality. Today, I would dream of my father and how he loved his little girl. I would dream of his tear-clouded image imprinted upon my heart....No amount of sunshine will make that image clearer, for he died this day, twelve long years ago...The day before I

became five. The months before I could tell him, 'I love you, Papa'. The years before I could paint his portrait indelible and untouchable upon my heart. I would dream of Captain Henry Lange, except to reach such a dream today is too hard...Too completely beyond the strength which I have just now. Perhaps, someday when my place of reality and my place of dreams are not so far apart-."

It ended there. Had she not been able to finish the thought? Colin sat back in his chair feeling numbed by the depth of emotion poured into the words he had just read. Could this be the same Kaytra who had but weeks earlier been called the town dummy? If so, there was a captivating person imprisoned within those unbreechable walls.

"It's amazing, isn't it?" Lydia spoke gently from a few steps away where she had stood watching her brother's face. He raised his eyes to her, making no effort to disguise his thoughts. Lydia smiled quietly. "I never imagined she could express herself that way. Maybe it was good that you had her do it."

"I doubt if she'd agree with you." Colin set the paper on the desk very slowly. "Did you find her?"

"Rex is hanging around the tower. She might be up there." Lydia studied Colin's intent, solemn movements as he went for his coat. "Colin?" He paused, looking at her as she drew within arm's reach of him. "Do you remember the story of the butterfly?"

He became wholly still for a moment, then reached out to pull her into his arms. "Yes, Lydia, I do remember. Thank you."

She had tears in her eyes when she pulled away. "Go find her. I'll make some tea." Colin could only nod before he walked to the door.

The story of the butterfly occupied his mind as he went out into the storm. It was a story both real and make believe, a tale he and Lydia had spent days creating when they were younger. The real part was the butterfly itself...

Spring was fast becoming summer as they had chanced upon the lone cocoon in the gardens behind the MacRae mansion. How impatiently they had waited for the stirring inside to finally reveal a butterfly. It hadn't been just any butterfly either, but a rare gold color with the most beautiful markings of white and black. With breathless anticipation, they had watched the fragile wings unfold. The butterfly, unsure and delicate, had quivered upon the grass, struggling now and then to gain the strength to fly.

Lydia had finally scooped it into her hands, whispering words of encouragement. Still, the creature lay trembling, almost as if it would never overcome the weakness. "Here," Lydia had said. "You do it, Colin. You have a way of making things right. Fix it. Quickly. Before it dies."

He had accepted the butterfly into his hands as he would a gift, feeling both proud that Lydia had entrusted the unbelievable treasure to him and anxious lest he fail this time to make things right in her eyes.

Instinct told him not to smother the butterfly as tightly as Lydia had, but to let it feel the breeze beneath its wings. If it were to fly, it would be as much on the strength of the breeze as on the inner strength in those fluttering wings.

Faith told him to pray and he had, fiercely, believing God cared for even this one infant butterfly. He and Lydia sat down next to the hedge of roses by the fountain. The gay tinkle of water pouring from the cherub's pitcher was a melody he could still remember today in the darkness as he climbed the tower stairs.

The butterfly had tickled his palm, but he hadn't let go. Something wonderful had bonded between them. A measure of unspoken trust. A deeper meeting of two desires with God watching from above. When at last the butterfly beat its wings and lifted from his hand, Colin hadn't been as amazed as Lydia.

But he had been saddened, sorry that its freedom meant it would leave. Light as a feather, the treasure had glided to the nearest burgundy rose, resting there like a priceless jewel upon a velvet gown.

Then the miracle had happened...The butterfly circled the garden only to come back to Colin's outstretched hands. Lydia's eyes had been bright, her cheeks flushed with excitement. She almost reached out to touch it again, but just at that moment, the governess called out that it was time for their lessons. Colin left reluctantly, pulled along by Lydia who knew they could not disobey.

The very next morning, he and Lydia had gone back to that same spot with childlike hopes of finding the butterfly there. They were not disappointed. No one could mistake it for another. "Hold out your hand!" Lydia had urged with an excited whisper. He hadn't wanted to admit that it was he who had trembled, waiting to see if the butterfly would come to rest on his hand. How well his sister had known him, even then. "Be patient, Colin. It will come. Just you wait. It's watching you even now, I'm sure. Don't move."

There was the sound of footsteps overhead. Kaytra was in the tower. Colin slowed his steps when his thoughts returned to the butterfly.

Years had gone by since either he or Lydia had mentioned their special story, not since Lydia had nearly been put into the hospital. He had fought for her then, fought to keep from losing the dearest person in his life. The story of the butterfly had helped knit together those horribly broken pieces of Lydia's mind.

"Remember, Lydia," he had told her then, "how the butterfly came back to me that day? How it floated down onto my hand? And you said it had come to say, 'Don't ever forget me.' Remember that we made up the ending of the story, how our butterfly was there in the garden every year after that because it loved us too much to ever go away. And we would pretend it touched all of mother's roses with love and joy, peace, longsuffering, gentleness - all the fruits of the Spirit of God. Be like that butterfly for me, Lydia. Say you'll come back and won't ever go away."

It had taken months before he saw life in her eyes again. Before he could believe that she was going to be all right.

What was it now that Lydia meant for him to understand in remembering the story? That she was handing him another fragile butterfly? Had she begun to realize it would take more than her own whispered encouragements for Kaytra? Colin drew in a deep breath as if filling his lungs would suppress the rise of uncertainty within him.

Kaytra turned around with a startled expression when she heard him step up into the room. She was washing the accumulation of smoke from the windows and had evidently been at it awhile.

Though outside it was cool and rainy, inside the room the constant burning of the lamps made it uncomfortably hot. Her heavy shawl lay in a careless heap on the floor. Tendrils of hair had escaped the makeshift twist at the back of her head and clung to her damp skin. Colin wasn't sure if her heightened color came from the heat and hard work or if she was embarrassed to see him knowing he would have read what she had written.

With a practiced eye, he turned to gauge how much time was left before the lamps would need refilling. "It looks like they are burning alright. I could use some help in a couple of hours to trim the wicks and polish the chimneys. "

In turning to face her, he barely caught Kaytra's consenting nod. Their eyes locked for a brief moment before she resumed her self-appointed task. Colin took a couple of steps to where she was washing the south windows. "Kaytra, please stop for a minute." She did so, slowly and without lifting her eyes. He decided not to force her. "I've read the paper."

She didn't move a muscle, didn't let out the breath she had drawn in at his admission.

Colin rubbed the back of his neck with one hand. "I wish you would have told me before. I wish-." He grew quiet, realizing that he wasn't sure what it was he wished most of all.

She looked up with a curiously sad question in her eyes. They had taken on the deeper gray of the day outside.

"You need to find a way to heal the hurts, Kaytra. You need to let it go somehow."

Kaytra searched out the hidden meaning behind Colin's too quiet tone. Did he feel sorry for her now? Did he have pity for the little girl who had lost her father? No. It seemed more as if he were trying very hard to decide what he should say to her.

When he finally did speak, what he said came as a complete surprise. "Was your father a military captain?"

She responded automatically by shaking her head "no".

"A sea captain, then. No wonder-."

Because he wouldn't go on with the thought, she frowned and shook her head again, this time in disapproval, grabbing his arm when he would let it be left unsaid.

Frustration thrust itself to the surface of his feelings. He wanted her to talk, with words like those she had written on paper. He wanted her to trust him enough to give way, to break through the walls separating them. Dear God, he just wanted it to finally end! For all those reasons and more, Colin shrugged off her hand.

She recoiled as if he had physically struck her.

"What is it going to take, Kaytra, before you finally *want* to talk again?"

Kaytra twisted completely away until she was at the other side of the small room with her back turned toward him, facing out at the empty stretch of land and sea which lay to the north.

He knew at once, it wasn't sadness which had pushed her away. "I'm not trying to be cruel, Kaytra. I'm only trying to be honest." As he spoke, he moved up behind her. The only way for him to read her emotions was to have her look at him. She stiffened when he turned her around. The discontent in his brown eyes waged war with the despair in her blue eyes. His hold tightened. "Don't you understand, Kaytra, whatever reason stole your will to talk may just as well have taken your heart, too! It's a slow, painful death and, God help me, it seems like - like you're swallowed up in it! Nothing can change unless you want it to." Colin let his hands drop away from her, feeling the truth sink deep into his already aching heart. "I can't help you."

Her troubled eyes seemed to stare right to the core of him.

But it was true. He couldn't help her. A sigh escaped as he turned to lean against the ledge, arms stiff, broad shoulders rounded by defeat.... "It wasn't right that I brought you here."

Kaytra's hands flew up to cover her ears. She didn't want to hear him say it! She didn't want to be sent away! Not now! Tears flooded her eyes, forcing her to squeeze them shut before they spilled over. He couldn't think that it was wrong. It wasn't wrong! She -.

Colin set his own hands over hers, gently drawing them down again. Her tears only heightened what he felt inside. He brushed a few of them away with the back of his fingers. "What are we going to do, Kaytra?"

She startled him by tenderly pressing her face into the warmth of his touch. The gesture was impulsive, but it raised a new level of tension between them. They drew apart at the same time, each to face a different direction.

Long moments passed before Kaytra made any attempt to leave. At her first movement, Colin swung toward her. He couldn't let her go without knowing for sure. "You've found the secret of Highland Light, haven't you?"

Kaytra hurried to get her shawl, to leave before he stopped her. She couldn't tell him what he wanted to know.

"Kaytra?" Colin moved quickly, but not soon enough to keep her there. He watched her slip into the darkened stairway.

Chapter Nine

Kaytra awakened the next morning fully expecting October 4th to be just like any other day. She washed quickly with water from the white pitcher on her dresser, shivering all the while until she was dressed in a clean white blouse and the blue skirt. It wasn't often that she paused to study her reflection in the tiny, hand mirror, but she was seventeen today. Should she not wear her hair down anymore? Lydia wore hers down quite often, but maybe because she didn't have the energy to fuss with it too much.

After several unsuccessful tries, Kaytra managed to wrap her heavy blonde hair into a reasonably neat bun at the back of her head. She wrinkled up her nose at the image staring back at her. There wasn't a thing she could do about her face. The dark circles beneath her eyes added to the waif-like appearance she so loathed. Fiddlesticks! Who was there to impress anyway?

Her steps down to the kitchen were quiet. No one else was awake yet. Rex went ahead of her, anxious to be let out to explore the morning. Kaytra moved straight to the front door, opening it wide enough for him alone...until the wind rushed in at her and all thoughts from yesterday were forgotten. What a perfectly beautiful day! Surely, it wouldn't hurt to slip outside, just for a moment.

Before the thought could be completed, she was pulling the door closed behind her. Faint sunrise colors still lingered overhead. Beneath was a crisp blue day dotted with white cotton clouds as wispy as smoke. She wrapped her arms around herself and inhaled deeply the fragrance of morning. God felt near today, as if she could reach out and touch her hand to His.

The thought drew Kaytra's gaze to the lighthouse. She never wanted to forget how the sun, still faintly pink from it's rebirth, was bathing Highland Light from its broad white base, clear up to the circle of glass. So much promise. That's what she felt in this glorious morning. Promise.

When Rex came to tug impatiently on the bottom of her skirt, she yielded at once. She could walk just a little way, and still be back before Colin or Lydia woke up. Eager now, she followed Rex through the dew-covered grass to the edge of the bank. How wonderful to feel free like this. In Provincetown, she would never have dared to walk in daylight, with her head uncovered.

Kaytra rejected the thought at once. Today wasn't a day to be thinking about Provincetown, not with the promise of adventure drawing her further along the bank. Though Rex ran ahead, Kaytra twirled around and around, becoming dizzy as she lifted her face to the sparkle of sunshine. Everything was so different from the day before. It always felt like that after a storm. More alive somehow.

She ran forward, too, with a smile of her own. Rex was racing up and down the bank now. It took a single, playful bark from him to encourage Kaytra to do the same. Besides, there were curious, glittering spots upon the sandy beach. She had to find out what they were.

Though the bank was much steeper here, she made her way down, then ran to the nearest of the spots. Sunsqualls! Sunjellies as some Cape people called them. Kaytra eagerly knelt down beside the sea creature. She had heard of them, of course, but had never seen any.

This one was nearly ten inches in diameter, so clear it shone like a diamond each time a wave broke high enough on shore to touch it. There were others, some wine colored, as transparent as jelly. To think that yesterday's angry sea had tangled the fragile fairies with kelp and sea moss, then tossed them away.

Rex, who stood at the top of the bank, started barking again. She recognized that particular bark. It meant she needed to go - now - because he had something important to show her. Kaytra scrambled back up, leaving a winding trail of footprints in the damp sand. It was hard to keep up with his determined pace, especially as the bank began to rise. Finally, at the highest point of the clay cliffs, he stopped and turned questioning eyes to hers.

But she had no answer for him.

There was an unmistakably charred place several yards from the edge of the bank. Rising out of the blackened spot was a sturdy post as big around as a ship's mast. Rex moved forward cautiously to sniff at a broken lamp. Mooncussers! Kaytra's heart leapt wildly at the thought. Suddenly, she felt very uncomfortable and cast a sweeping glance inland. No one was about now. They wouldn't be. Only when the dark of night came.

Kaytra knew what she had to do. In one quick, trembling motion, she picked up the broken lamp and started back to Highland. Somehow, the day's innocence had been stolen from her. She hurried along the bank with a resolve to tell what she had discovered. In some places, she ran, clutching the lamp tightly to herself because she knew the evidence could not be lost.

It hadn't been her intention to stay away so long. The big light had already been turned off. She hurried up the steps to the porch, then on into the house. Her wide-eyed gaze saw at once that both Lydia and Colin were awake and sitting at the table, drinking coffee.

"Well! There you are!" Lydia sat back with obvious relief. "I was just telling Colin he should go look for you."

Still wind-blown and out of breath, Kaytra pushed the door closed. Even though Colin had barely glanced at her, she still sensed a restraint in his look. Was it because of yesterday, because -?

"We didn't know where you might have gone, Kaytra." Lydia's effort to break the tension seemed to fall short, especially when Kaytra approached them to set the broken lamp upon the table and Colin didn't even look at it.

But Kaytra knew he had to care! Suddenly, she rushed into the parlor, pulling paper and a pen from the neat cubbyholes. In a brief moment, she was back, thrusting the piece of paper into his hands, waiting restlessly while he read what she had written.

Several agonizing moments passed before he raised his eyes from the words. He stared at her with a definite wariness.

"What is it, Colin?," Lydia asked. "What does it say?"

He acted as if he hadn't heard her anxious questions. Kaytra was his sole focus. "Where did you find it? Very far away?" When she didn't answer, he stood, too. Impatience laced itself around his voice. "Well, which direction then? You can show me, can't you?"

"Colin!" There was a gentle reprimand in Lydia's tone. He sighed a little before meeting her eyes. "At least let her catch her breath. What did she write?"

"Mooncussers." He seemed just as preoccupied as he had been all morning, if not more so now with Kaytra's announcement. "Apparently, Kaytra has found a site."

Lydia shrugged her shoulders expressively. "Mooncussers? What does that mean?"

"They're men who try to draw ships into the shoals. When they burn a lamp on some high point along shore, the crew thinks it's actually a lighthouse and the deception throws them off course."

"But, that's horrible! The ship would run aground then. It would be lost on the rocks!"

Colin nodded gravely. "It's against the law. Mooncussers profit quite a bit from the salvage of even one wreck."

"Then you'll have to report them!" Lydia exclaimed. She didn't like the thought of her brother taking on such unscrupulous men alone.

"It could just be an old site, Lydia." When his vague answer didn't relieve her concern, he smiled a little. The frown which puckered her brow was familiar to him. Maybe it would be best to divert her a bit. "Do you know where the name mooncusser comes from?" She shook her head. "If there's a full moon, the lights they use don't show up as well and they curse their bad luck, hence-."

"Mooncussers!"

Colin chuckled at her. "You're gaining quite a vocabulary out here, Sis."

She brightened at his teasing mood. "Mother wouldn't like it, you know. Ground seas, bay side, back side....buggerish!" While they laughed together at the thought of their mother saying such words, Kaytra hurried into the parlor again and came back with another piece of paper to thrust into Colin's hands.

She wanted to know what ground seas meant, too. *And* buggerish. When he looked up and saw the expectancy in Kaytra's eyes, his expression changed, the smile disappeared. After yesterday, so many emotions fought within him. Being near Kaytra only made them more confusing. "You can show me where you found the lamp later." Colin let the paper drift down to the table, but didn't resume his seat. Instead, he picked up his half-empty coffee mug and took it to the basin.

It seemed a long time before Lydia broke the silence. "Come, have some breakfast, Kaytra."

Breakfast! A horrified look came over Kaytra's face. She hadn't made breakfast for them! She hurried to wash her hands. There were a few eggs in the cold pantry and bread. She needed to set more bread today. Her trembling hands jerked the apron from its hook on the wall, tying it snugly about her waist.

Bess still needed to be milked, too. Oh goodness! What was she thinking to leave at the busiest time of the day? She flew to the pantry intent on getting the things she needed to make a good breakfast.

When she came out with her arms full, Colin was gone and Lydia was sitting at the table. "Oh, Kaytra, dear, I'm sorry. I should have told you. Colin has already made us breakfast. I don't mind having eggs once in a while. Why don't you fix something for yourself, then come sit with me."

Kaytra dutifully poured herself a mug of coffee and sliced some of the remaining bread, spreading it with butter. She needed to churn the cream today, too, and wash clothes. An involuntary sigh escaped as she lowered herself into a chair across the table from Lydia.

"You sound very tired, dear." Lydia was concerned now in studying the girl's face. "Have you not been sleeping well?"

Yes, Kaytra nodded, but immediately felt guilty for the falsehood. Her gaze went to the mug she held in both hands.

The question uppermost in Lydia's mind spilled forth as if she couldn't wait any longer to say it. "Kaytra, I'd like to know more about you, to understand the feelings I see in your eyes." She paused a moment, giving Kaytra time to accept the idea. For some reason, the girl's blue-gray eyes held unshed tears. Lydia went on in a gentle tone. "I think Colin has a few extra journals in his desk. Let me get one for you to write in ."

She returned sooner than Kaytra could decide what to do. "Here, you could start with your father. He sounds fascinating, a real captain! Or maybe you could write about your mother. Was she pretty? Do you resemble her?"

Kaytra studied the pure white page.

To Lydia, her hesitation seemed endless. She had no idea of the battles raging within Kaytra's mind.

At last, the need for true companionship triumphed. Kaytra pushed aside her untouched food to pick up the pen and write. The words flowed out with a smoothness similar to her whole manner.

Lydia went to stand behind her so that she could read while Kaytra was writing....

> *"Mary Elizabeth - my mother - wasn't merely pretty. She was more than that. As lovely as a rose in full bloom. To me, she was more beautiful than a hundred royal portraits. She was - breathtaking, when she wanted to be. After Papa died, she did not want to be. Perhaps you understand?"*

Kaytra raised her eyes to Lydia's face and received a broken little nod as answer. Yes, Lydia knew what it was like. Sidney had not died, yet in a way he was dead to her. Kaytra went on....

> *"She had deep blonde hair and mysterious hazel eyes. Papa had eyes the same shade as mine. Mother was from Boston."*

She felt Lydia's amazed glance, but kept going....

> *"My father met her in Paris. They were married when Mama was nineteen. Soon afterward, I was born. I never had any brothers or sisters. I remember France a little....."*

Kaytra paused thoughtfully, wondering how to put childlike impressions into adult words....

"....like one would remember a favorite story; not so much each chapter or the words written upon each page, but the feelings you had while experiencing them. France is like a fairytale to me, all enchanted visions, softened around the edges as if I see them through the lightest fog. It is only unbearable that there was not a 'happy-ever-after' ending."

"You came back to Boston then, when your father died?"

The words came slower as Kaytra paused, trying to remember.

"Not for a while. I think Mother didn't want to come here. After Papa's debts on the ship and cargo were paid, there was no choice. I don't know if we went to Boston. I was only six. My mother was very sad. I think we went to a big house. I think we - saw someone, but-."

"It's alright, dear." Lydia placed a reassuring hand on Kaytra's shoulder, sensing the confusion in her words, the vague uncertainty. "Maybe you'll remember it someday. Did your mother marry Everette Koch before you came to Provincetown?"

There was a slight unsteadiness in Kaytra's hand.

"Yes, he met her in - New York, I think. I never liked him. He wasn't unkind, at first, but eventually the money was low. He moved us to Provincetown. We lived in a cold, dark shack. Mother worked so very hard. She wasn't the same. Everette Koch yelled a lot, at her and at me. He - beat Mother once. It was terrible. She-."

"Kaytra. Please. No more for now." Tears filled Lydia's eyes when she felt the tension building in Kaytra. "Please stop."

Kaytra shook her head and started scribbling the thoughts which fought inside her to be let out. Finally, the last words were written, more boldly and in larger letters than the rest. The anger behind them was painfully obvious.

When it was over, Lydia said nothing. Instead she gently encouraged Kaytra to stand until she could enfold the younger woman close in her arms. She was surprised to see that there were no tears in Kaytra's eyes. Perhaps bitterness held them back. "Kaytra?" Lydia stood away in order to see her face. "You do believe in God, don't you?"

Yes.

"Then you must know that your mother is in Heaven now. That she is safe and-."

No, Kaytra seemed torn as she shook her head, turning again to pick up the pen.

> *"Mother never believed. It was Papa who taught me about God. My mother never forgave God for taking Papa away from us."*

"But you can forgive, Kaytra." The chance to share her faith made Lydia's voice rich with emotion. "You can understand things. You can see what God's purposes are. He hasn't lost you, even after all these years. I'm not doubting the words you just wrote down. But you have to let go of the anger, Kaytra. You have to forgive-."

> *"NO!"*

That single word looked ugly on the paper. Kaytra let the pen fall to the table before she turned away. The unyielding set of her shoulders told Lydia not to push any further. She left Kaytra to clean up the breakfast dishes. Right now, she needed to pray. On her way from the kitchen, Lydia gathered the book, pen and ink.

Bess was in a foul mood by the time Kaytra got around to milking her. The cow refused to budge from her crossways position in the stall at the far side of the barn. Much cajoling and pushing on Kaytra's part only served to worsen the situation. She finally plunked the stool down and set the pail under Bess, intent on completing the job, but her skirt got all tangled with the stool and she landed on the floor.

Was that a gleam in Bess' eyes? Kaytra pushed herself upright to begin again. It took a full minute to get even a trickle of milk into the pail. Milking a cow was tiring work, especially when the cow kept pushing her weight around. Kaytra moved herself three times before the pail was half full.

Finally, after three-quarters of an hour and one near miss from a wicked back kick, Kaytra was close to tears. They needed the milk for supper because she planned to make clam chowder. With a deeply drawn breath, she slapped Bess' rump, pushing her over yet again. Bess reacted strongly to the insult by knocking both Kaytra and the pail over into the hay.

Had she not heard Colin's distinctly masculine chuckle from the doorway, Kaytra would have stayed put, nursing her bruised elbow. As it was, he crossed the floor to help her before she could recover even a hint of dignity. His brown eyes noted her frustration, yet lost none of their amusement. "I guess old Bess taught you a good one." The way Kaytra jerked her arms out of his hold confirmed Colin's guess about the frustration. "You should have been nice to her. Patience is a virtue, you know."

Twin flags of color rose in her pale cheeks. Kaytra pursed her mouth into a tight line.

Colin could clearly see the storm brewing in those blue-gray eyes. "What would you say to me right now, I wonder? What would your impulsive nature spew forth to try and wound me?" His challenging questions only made her breathing more rapid. In order to break his mastery over the moment, Kaytra pushed past him to get the milk pail, but he beat her to it. "Allow me." Colin looked ridiculously large sitting on the stool milking Bess, and Bess....Well, Bess just stood there, munching on a mouthful of fresh hay until he was finished.

Though the one thought in Kaytra's mind was to leave his company as quickly as she could, Colin's longer strides enabled him to easily make up the head start she had in leaving the barn. It was disconcerting to have him walk beside her. He was so tall and self-assured. And she was so....so mad!

Part way back to the house, he reached out with his free hand to slow her head-long rush. She refused to raise her eyes to see the expression on his face. Colin smiled a little at the stubborn frown creasing her brow. "You aren't going to let this spoil your birthday, are you?"

Her head snapped up in surprise. How did he know?

One side of Colin's mouth lifted in a lopsided grin. "It was in the letter you wrote yesterday, remember? Didn't you think I could add?"

Kaytra looked away from him, crossing her arms tightly over herself. He was in a teasing mood now. She almost preferred to have him angry; that she could handle.

Colin wasn't sure what the look on her face meant. "I could have sworn you wanted to lamb me back there. Why didn't you?"

Lamb him! She would have blackened both eyes given the chance!

"Maybe now that you're seventeen and all grown up, you thought it improper?" Colin asked as he started walking again. He didn't need to see her face to know his sarcastic words had only added fuel to the fire. And now that the fire was already started, why not pile on more? "Does turning seventeen mean you're going to wear your hair up all the time? It doesn't suit you. You're still too carefree on the inside to pretend to be a lady."

Pretend? Kaytra stopped firmly in her tracks. He had no right to say those things to her, to assume he knew her so well! Did he think he ruled every waking moment of her day that he could constantly tell her what to do or what not to do? She could have stayed in Provincetown and had more freedom than-.

"Kaytra." Colin was standing on the porch, confidently holding the door open. With all the pride she could muster, Kaytra swept past him and on into the kitchen.

Colin followed with a knowing smirk on his face. "Don't get going on anything, Kaytra," he said to the back of her head. "I want you to show me where you found the broken lamp."

She slammed a pan onto the stove.

In marked contrast, Colin was careful how he set the milk pail on the counter. The flush of anger on her cheeks made her look quite pretty.... "About this morning; ground seas mean there isn't any wind, just rough water and buggerish is-." He felt a smile forming, but kept it at bay. "Well, it's kind of like you, I guess."

Kaytra half turned toward him, her manner inquisitive once more.

"Buggerish is rain and strong wind and roaring seas all mixed together. Pure turmoil. Chaos-. "

She swept past him with her head held high.

And Colin grinned. "I'll just run up and tell Lydia we'll be gone for awhile."

Chapter Ten

It seemed to Colin, as he and Kaytra walked south along the bank, that she had used his brief absence to compose herself. The irritation was nowhere to be seen now. In fact, her expression seemed almost too mellow. She was watching Rex and studying the sky and acting as if nothing in the world bothered her.

But Colin knew differently. The nightmares, the crying out in her sleep had increased lately. As he studied the far-away look in her eyes, the words of her letter came back in full clarity. He wondered where it was she dreamed of being today? Tendrils of blonde hair moved against her cheeks with each touch of the breeze. More than ever he saw her as a child locked within the life of a young woman. He may have been teasing earlier, yet part of him had been serious. She was a mystery to him in more ways than he could count.

When they reached the place where bayberry bushes grew, Kaytra set her empty basket beside the bushes. "What are you going to pick them for?" Colin asked out of curiosity. "Are they good to eat?" He reached out to take one, but she immediately pushed his hand aside, shaking her head firmly. "They're not good to eat?"

No. She thought a moment, then gestured with her hands. A tall candle. Striking a spark. Lighting the wick. The glow...Colin was fascinated by the delicate movements of her hands. "You make candles from the berries?" She smiled, pleased that he guessed what she had "said".

In a short time, they picked enough berries to fill the basket and Kaytra gave Colin a look he hadn't seen from her before, her own sort of stately "thank you". "You're very welcome." He returned her playfulness with a gentlemanly bow only to be rewarded with a curtsy, an action he wouldn't have guessed she knew. Had her mother taught her or maybe -? Right now he couldn't think of any "or maybe" possibilities. "Let's go find the spot where the mooncussers have been operating."

He let Kaytra take the lead as there wasn't a path along the bank. Though she moved along easily, the going was rough in some places. Colin began to understand why she had been all out of breath earlier that morning.

His growing sense of appreciation for her stamina vanished into disbelief when they came upon the place where tracks showed that she had scrambled down the bank to the beach. He stopped to stare at the steep, twenty-foot drop. "Kaytra."

When she turned around, the curious expression in her eyes met his disapproval.

"You went down there?"

Her gaze shifted to where he was pointing in an accusing manner.

"You could have broken your fool neck!"

She shook her head defiantly.

"Don't give me that look." He wouldn't be distracted this time. "You know it was crazy! Nothing could have been so important that you had to risk your neck like that!"

Kaytra hesitated, then shrugged her shoulders indecisively. He wouldn't understand how much she wanted to see the sunsqualls. Things were either right or wrong to Colin MacRae. There was no in between. Slowly now, she turned to continue along the path. It was some time before she heard Colin's footsteps behind her. If he wanted to be upset, there was little she could do to change his mood.

Her steps in climbing the last rise were slower, more thoughtful. Rather than staying with Colin and Rex to look over the site, she wandered off to the edge of the cliff. Its rusty-yellow clay had been burrowed and curled by ageless winds, carved by the relentless hand of the sea, molded by storms far worse than yesterday's. A verse, remembered from her childhood, created an ache deep in her heart. "Thou art the Potter, I am the clay." The Potter...She let her gaze search the eastern horizon, not knowing what it was she looked for or what she hoped to find.

Colin looked over the tall posts and charred ground with distracted eyes. It wasn't that the mooncussers weren't a threat. He would need to do something about it at once, but he couldn't shrug off the sense of uneasiness which flooded through him every time he thought about Kaytra going down the bank. Didn't she care what kind of risks she took? She could have fallen this morning and lain there for hours before he found her!

Even now, he looked up to find her standing at the edge, carelessly defying the danger. No, he would not let her tempt fate! In a few long strides, he was beside her, ready to draw her away from harm. Yet, before he could reach out to pull her back, he found that the expression on her face held him captive instead.

Unaware that he stood so near, Kaytra's eyes fully reflected the lost, wondering soul inside herself. In that moment, he realized this was the real Kaytra. There were no walls to hide what he saw in her: a desperate desire to find someone who could but say they knew her. Not the town Dummy. Not the half girl - half woman, beaten and afraid, who had come to Highland to be a housekeeper, but this Kaytra.

A tern screeched overhead, dispelling the suspension of time.

Abruptly conscious now that Colin stood beside her, Kaytra swung toward him, lowering the defensive veil, closing him out from her thoughts. But the expression in his eyes showed her the truth; she was too late this time.

Color drained from her face. Something untouchable, something precious had passed between them. They both knew it. She had, in a moment of weakness, relinquished a part of her true self to him. A part of herself she could never take back.

Colin stared down at her without speaking. Neither of them found words necessary or even possible. There was a language all its own in their silence. The wind was a mere whisper. Only the faraway sighs of the ocean were carried into song around them.

Time didn't stand still in that moment - it lay open and expectant, stretching forth eagerly to see what would happen. Kaytra tilted her head to one side. Her blue-gray eyes were nearly lavender with emotion. Colin sensed, more than saw, the soft movement of Kaytra's arm. When he did look down, her hand was held palm up for him to grasp. Was she asking him to forget their differences and be her friend?

The child-like gesture had great power over him, enough to take his hand and reach it out in return until the tiny fingers were held securely inside his own. What he wanted just then confused him to the depth of his being. There was no understanding it. It was simply there to believe in or to deny. Before he could do either, Kaytra pulled upon his hand, expressing that they should leave now. She even turned to go, but Colin drew her back, expecting the question he saw in her eyes.

He hated to speak, to break the silent communication. Yet his silence was making her misunderstand. "I don't want to go back. I have something to say to you." The look in her eyes changed to one of reservation. When she would have pulled her hand away, Colin grasped it more firmly. "You keep - looking out there as if you're waiting. As if you - need something, some kind of answer."

Kaytra lowered her eyes to look at their entwined hands.

"No, Kaytra," Colin said with obvious emotion. He cupped his hand under her chin and gently persuaded her to look up again "I need to see your eyes. It's the only way I can tell what you're feeling. Don't shield your thoughts from me. Be honest, Kaytra. Open."

She watched the wind lift his hair.

"It was your father who talked to you about God," Colin spoke his thoughts aloud, wondering if his mention of Henry Lange brought those tears rushing to her eyes. Somehow, he resisted the urge to catch the single tear which slipped past the thick fringe of her brown lashes. Somehow, he checked the more rapid breaths filling his lungs. "Do I - remind you of him in some way?"

It seemed a long time before Kaytra admitted yes. Her eyes held sad confusion. Colin's intuitiveness was focused so exactly that she wanted to pull away from him. No, not from him really. Only from the way he could see into her heart.

Once again Colin tightened his hold to prevent her from moving. His eyes scanned her face, touching every curve. "God didn't die with your father, Kaytra. God isn't lost out there somewhere. He's bigger than that. All you can see, even all you can't see, is held in His hands. The earth and all that is in it are His. You are His."

When she tilted her head to one side, it was almost Colin's undoing, but he kept control. The burden in him had grown to actual pain. It had never been so hard for him to share his faith. Was the difficulty there because of him, how he felt, or because of Kaytra? He didn't know, but he had to try. "When you open your heart to God, He - He doesn't come and go. He doesn't leave you empty when you most need Him. God doesn't ever pull away from you."

Then why couldn't she find Him?

Colin read the brokenness in her eyes. "He's there, Kaytra. The closer you draw toward Him, the more you'll learn to feel Him with you." Her hands trembled so, it was natural that he bring them together between his own. "That's the secret of Highland Light; finding out that God is like the light in the tower. Constant, unchanging. He's at the center of it all and life moves around Him."

An expression of wonder sprang into her eyes as Colin put words to the feelings she had found at Highland.

"I wish-," his voice became husky with emotion. "I wish I could take those steps for you, Kaytra, but I can't. Nobody can do it for you." More tears pooled in her eyes. "I can tell you how. I can even pray with you, but the desire has to come from your own heart."

Without hesitation, Kaytra moved her hands in his until they were pressed palms together, ready for the prayer he talked about, the prayer which would bring God into her life.

Colin wanted to. Dear God how he wanted to, but a knot twisted against his throat, constricting the words. He gripped her hands so firmly his knuckles turned white around the fragile, little fingers. "It's not that easy, Kaytra. There's so much to understand about what God has done for you, how He made a way to forgive you for your sins and -."

Despite the wrenching pain it caused, Kaytra jerked her hands away from his. Her mouth was pressed into a frown. Her eyes showed despair. God would never be able to forgive her. She wasn't worthy of that much mercy.

Colin drew in a deep breath, expelling it so slowly Kaytra felt as if every nerve in her body was stretched to the breaking point. It would never work. How could it work if -.

"Kaytra, I know something happened to you." He watched her face grow very pale. Yet a new feeling made him go on. "If you ask God into your life there can't be any hate in your heart, there can't be any resentment."

Then she could never take that step. She moved past him, picked up the basket of bayberries and marched in the direction of the light without a backward glance.

As if he sensed her troubled mood, Rex followed Kaytra quietly toward home. As they got closer, he pricked up his ears. The signal alerted Kaytra to a change. Within seconds, she spied the wagon and horse near the barn. Company? Or perhaps another visit from an FLC inspector? She didn't think so. The wagon was a simple farm wagon.

"Hello, theahe!" A short, stocky man called to her from the front porch. It was too late for her to go in any other direction. Besides, his quick, rolling gait soon eliminated the distance between them.

He was an older man, with alert brown eyes, graying hair and a shrewd sense of thoughtfulness evident in the way he studied her in return. "You must be the housekeepeah Miss Lydia mentioned. Wheahe's Colin? 'Spected he'd be comin' 'long, too." Kaytra felt embarrassed that he waited for an answer she could never give. When she shifted the heavy basket, he reached out to take it from her. "I'm Seth Buckley. We'ahe neighboahs?"

She nodded a little.

Another long silence.

Kaytra chewed on her lower lip, letting her gaze fall to the ground between them.

Seth Buckley wore homespun clothes: a dull brown-colored coat and pants, a tattered hat atop his gray head and mud-spattered, leather boots. "My Anna, she thought it past time we come ta visit. Heahd Miss Lydia been ailin' lately." The words hung uncomfortably in the damp air. "You'ahe young, ain't ya? Don't look neah stuahdy 'nough ta spit 'gainst the wind!"

Kaytra's head snapped up. The smile of amusement she gave him was entirely unexpected.

In return, Seth's grin showed that he had a few teeth missing. The lines deepened around his eyes. "Could likely chahm the waves ta dance foah ya though, can't ya?"

She raised her eyebrows mischievously at that, much to Seth Buckley's delight. "You ain't so shy." Suddenly, he was looking past her, to the way she had just come. "Well, Colin! Feahed ya got lost oah somethin'!"

When Colin got close enough, the two men shook hands. "Hello, Seth." Though Colin threw a probing gaze at Kaytra, she had already averted her eyes. "It doesn't look as if either one of you would have missed me much if I had gotten lost."

Seth noticed it, too. The tension in her stance. But he chose not to say anything about it. "Glad ta see ya' got some help out heahe. Youah sistah been sick some?"

"Some." Colin agreed soberly. "Kaytra's been nursing Lydia quite well, though. There is new improvement each day."

"Must be so," Seth said cryptically. He cast another long look in the girl's direction. She hadn't even looked at Colin. "You two have a fight oah somethin'?" The outspoken question caught both young people off guard. While he had their undivided attention, Seth hurried on. "Bettah cheeah up. Don't want ta spoil nothin' what Miss Lydia got planned in theahe."

Colin frowned a little at the conspiratorial wink Seth sent his way. Of course. It was Kaytra's birthday. Lydia must be making a cake.

Still, the two guilty parties avoided looking at one another. Seth would have none of it. "Come on now. Whateveah it is, say ya foahgive one 'notheah an' have done with it."

There was a moment of awkward silence, a darkening of Colin's brown eyes. "Kaytra can't talk, Seth."

"Ohhh?" The surprised reaction from Seth was accompanied by a nod. "Well, 'couahse she cen talk! She cen talk with heah eyes! Seen it meself 'foahe you come 'long, Colin. Go on now." He encouraged them more firmly this time. " 'pologize civil like, both'n' ya."

If Seth had witnessed the look Kaytra gave Colin, he would have reconsidered the self-satisfied smile on his face. Instead, he watched her hurry away, skirts in hand. "Guess a body don't need woahds all the time, huh? She's a smaht thing, ain't she? Wheahe'd ya find heah?"

Colin sighed deeply, bringing his own reaction to Kaytra's latest unspoken barbs under control. "I found her in Provincetown, actually."

"Ahh," Seth walked beside the taller man as they started for the house. "Know some folks down that way. What be heah last name?"

"Lange. Her mother was married to Everette Koch."

As soon as he said the name, Seth stiffened. "Koch?"

"You know him, then?" Colin glanced sideways at his neighbor, trying to judge the man's initial feelings.

"Yeah, most Cape folk heahd o' him." Seth chose his words slowly, as if he was thinking about something else. "Makes sense now. The gal be who's called the 'Dummy', ain't she?" It was Colin's turn to become tense. Seth held up a calming hand. "No need foah that. You know how folks talk 'bout anyone unusual. Stoahies 'bout that gal been like a wild fiahe. Nobody what stops it 'cause they's all a'feahed o' it." There was a thoughtful shake of the older man's head. "Shamed ta say that I listened, now. Pooah gal don't deseahve folks thinkin' bad o' heah."

Knowing their conversation couldn't be carried indoors where Kaytra would easily overhear the sobering remarks, they had stopped side by side on the porch. Seth had seen enough of life to recognize the particular look in Colin's eyes. It was wisdom which bade him to leave the thought unspoken. Instead, he forced a cheery smile onto his weatherbeaten face and slapped a hand on the younger man's broad, muscled back. "How'd ya like the li'l stoahm yesteahday?"

Colin smiled, too, appreciating Seth's careful change of subject. "Little? You mean, that didn't even rate any higher than a Grandmother's Day?"

"Grandmotheah's!" Seth's rousing laughter went with them as Colin led the way into the house. Three pairs of eyes turned in their direction. "It was moahe'n that, son. Buggerish, I'd say. Wouldn' you, Ma?"

A plump gray-haired woman, dressed in the same kind of home-spun cloth as her husband, flashed a wide smile of greeting across the room. "If'n you'ahe meanin' me -." She left the rest unsaid as she began transferring the apples they brought along with them into a box Kaytra had found.

"Of course, he didn't mean you, Anna." Colin hung his coat next to Kaytra's on the pegged board beside the door. The Buckleys were a lively pair, constantly bantering back and forth - just what he needed to distract him from thinking about Kaytra. "Got any coffee ready, Lydia?"

"It was ready an hour ago," Lydia said as she moved to get two more cups, but Kaytra was there before her, reaching into the cupboard. "What took you so long? You didn't - meet them, did you?"

By mutual consent, Colin and Seth settled in the two empty chairs at the table. "No, we didn't." He could see that Seth was waiting to hear an explanation for the anxious note in Lydia's questions. "Kaytra found a place about a mile straight south where some mooncussers have been operating."

"Mooncussers?" Seth's reaction mirrored Anna's who had unconsciously reached out a hand from where she now sat beside him to touch his arm. Both of them waited, wide-eyed, for Colin to go on.

"I'm afraid so, Seth. I wonder how they fared last night when it was so 'buggerish'?" His tone lacked some of the seriousness which he had shown at first learning of the site, but he wanted to keep the others from becoming overly concerned. "Probably got soaked to the skin, wouldn't you say so, Seth? And waddled home like a pair of clean-plucked mallards!"

"Colin!" Lydia scolded him for his boldness, but couldn't help smiling at the mental picture his words brought about. She wasn't alone. Seth and Anna shared a chuckle. The tense moment passed. Really, her brother always seemed to know how to make people smile, even if his ways were a bit unrefined at times. "I guess you must be planning on charming those old mooncussers into surrendering?"

A pleasant smile turned up the corners of Colin's mouth. "I guess you could say that." He happened, just then, to catch Kaytra's gaze over Lydia's shoulder. She was too quick to hide those expressive eyes, though, and Colin had no time to guess her thoughts.

Talk soon turned away from the mooncussers. Kaytra listened as she moved restlessly about the kitchen. This day had been anything but ordinary. The surprise birthday cake on the counter, dressed in swirls of white frosting, was proof of that, and now the Buckleys were here.

She liked the older couple. Anna had talked to her so kindly when Lydia introduced them, and Seth certainly had a keen sense of humor. His comment about her being able to charm the waves had made her feel special for one fleeting moment....until Colin had come back.

As she remembered the things Colin said on the bank, Kaytra's emotions plummeted to despair. There was a slight tremble in her hands as she began washing the dirty dishes piled beside the basin.

When she was done with that task, Kaytra's eyes fell upon an empty basket beside the counter. The clams. She could hardly make chowder without them. The chance to be on her own and collect the jumble of thoughts racing around in her head made her pick up the basket. She was within reach of the back door, when Anna's cheerful voice stopped her. "Oh, Kaytra, you aren't leaving, are you?"

She didn't turn around, which caused the others to cast a wondering look at each other. Colin alone noted that Kaytra's slim shoulders had stiffened at the question. He gripped his mug between both hands, staring at the black liquid. Then, in the next instant, he was on his feet, moving toward her while the others watched. "Kaytra?" His tone was much calmer than he felt inside, especially when Kaytra lifted her chin just high enough so she could glance at him through her lashes. "You could stay and visit with us." She didn't have to run away again. She didn't have to always be isolated, with only her troubled thoughts for companionship. "Please?"

It seemed an eternity before she shook her head, before she gestured vaguely toward the ocean.

"You're going to the beach?"

Her nod was barely noticeable.

Colin wanted to touch her hands as they grasped the handle of the basket, but he didn't. Not in front of the others. He wanted to explain what he had felt out there on the bank, but he couldn't fully understand it himself. "If you need clams, I'll get some later. Stay and -." Kaytra suddenly lifted her eyes to his, showing him the reason why she couldn't stay. His heart contracted to see how her eyes were filled with pain. Colin forced himself to speak past the regret. "Don't be gone long."

Kaytra didn't breathe again until she was well away from the house. Rex tagged along behind her. She was grateful for his presence, grateful that she could let her true feelings show and he would not judge her for them. If it weren't for Lydia, she would simply keep walking and walking – away from Colin.

Why couldn't he let her thoughts be hers alone? In lifting her eyes to the place where sea and sky melded as one, she knew it was fear that made her want to pull back. A whole new way of life had opened up to her here at Highland. Different feelings. New challenges. More hope... She wasn't ready yet to let it all be taken from her in a single moment. That's what really lay behind the fear. Colin MacRae was getting too close to the truth. He was the one who held her tomorrows firmly in his grasp. He had the power to allow her to stay or to send her back.

All the while she worked, finding clams hidden in their sand covies, Kaytra's insides boiled with turmoil. At a point far away from the light, she turned back, following the faint path of her own footprints which wound aimlessly at the edge of the encroaching waves. Late afternoon offered sunshine which was softer, more gentle than the morning brightness to which she had awakened.

Step by step, she placed her feet on top of the prints she had already made in the damp sand. Doing so made her wonder - would she spend the rest of her life going forward in tiny leaps of faith only to have to retrace her steps in order to learn again the lessons of patience and contentment? There seemed a great ocean of confusion between what she could and could not hope for.

Unconsciously, her gaze swept upward until she could see the light tower. It had come to represent all that had been missing from her life since her father's death, all that she would lose if Colin sent her away. Today, she had been but a prayer away from that dream. A prayer she knew she couldn't pray. Not yet. Maybe not ever.

Chapter Eleven

Kaytra's birthday celebration that evening turned out to include more than just the cake. Tall, tapered candles of purest white graced the table. Between them bloomed a vase of wild flowers which Kaytra was very much surprised to learn Colin had provided.

She felt his curious gaze several times during their meal, but couldn't bring herself to look up and meet his eyes. She only listened quietly as Colin and Lydia talked about the Buckleys and of how unlikely it would be to find such simple friendliness in the people they knew at Boston. As in the past, Kaytra noticed a certain reservation in Colin's tone when he mentioned Boston. His words didn't hold bitterness, merely discontent.

The same wasn't true about Lydia. It seemed now as if Colin and Lydia saw the past in different ways, especially when they spoke of their parents, Shaun and Catherine MacRae. While Lydia described them with endearing terms and great understanding, Colin only spoke out of loyalty. Perhaps the difference came because Colin no longer felt the same about his parents since coming to Highland.

The thought rushed unbidden into her mind startling her so much with its insight that she actually raised her eyes to make sure he hadn't spoken it himself, but it was Lydia who was talking. The movement caught Colin's attention and he glanced at her. For the second time that day, he seized her private thoughts to make them his own.

"Well," Lydia nervously broke their silence. "Shall we have cake?...Oh, no, Kaytra." She motioned the young woman back into her seat with a quick gesture. "You just sit there and be a lady of leisure for the rest of the night."

Her choice of the word "lady" made Colin smile rather secretly at Kaytra as he stood to help Lydia get the cake and extra plates. The subtle reminder left a soft blush upon Kaytra's cheeks, one which only deepened when it was time to make a secret birthday wish.

For Colin, it was an enchanting combination; her innocent blush and the unexpected brilliance of her tears dancing with the reflection of candles atop the cake. Somehow, Kaytra's expression seemed to hold both joy and sadness. Colin added his own silent prayer as she closed her eyes to make the wish.

When they finished eating, he offered to do the dishes, something Kaytra positively wouldn't allow. Because she blocked his way to the hot water on the stove by planting herself, arms crossed, in his path, he finally conceded the argument and let her help. A sort of companionable easiness settled between them as they worked side by side. The day's earlier unrest seemed forgotten. If not entirely forgotten, at least purposely ignored.

It wasn't long afterward that Lydia added one more surprise to Kaytra's day. As Colin walked into the parlor and took his usual chair, Lydia looked over to where Kaytra was preparing to carry an armload of freshly laundered sheets upstairs. "Will you stay for our Bible time tonight, Kaytra? It's been such a wonderful evening, I hate to see it end."

So did Kaytra. But-. She stared hard at the bright, white linen.

"Come sit here by me," Lydia encouraged with a little pat on the cushion of the settee. "Colin was just going to start reading."

He was? Colin held his sister's smile a moment before reaching for the Bible which sat on the small table beside his chair. By the time he had adjusted the wick in the lamp to burn a little brighter, Kaytra was sitting beside Lydia, brushing back a tendril of hair which had fallen against her cheek. The heavy book fell open to where a marker had been placed; John, chapter fifteen. It was the next chapter they were to read. "I am the true vine," he began, "and My Father is the husbandman. Every branch in me that beareth not fruit he taketh away and-."

"Colin?" Lydia's interruption was spoken gently. Something in the look she gave him caught at his sense of expectancy. "Would you read from First Corinthians...chapter thirteen?"

His nod came with some hesitation. He knew when his sister was up to something. Now was one of those times.

Though Kaytra glanced from one of them to the other, she couldn't decipher the meaning in their expressions. It wasn't long before Colin found the passage Lydia requested. It seemed to Kaytra that he delayed reading it while he studied the page.

In fact, he was toying with the idea of going back to John fifteen. Sometime during the day, Lydia had marked parts of this new passage. Her meaning was all too clear. As soon as Colin raised his eyes, she smiled slightly in that winning way she had, causing Colin to smile in return. Before he began to read again, Colin sent a brief, probing glance in Kaytra's direction.

"Though I speak with the tongues of men and angels and have not-," here Lydia had penned across the word charity and written another word above it - Colin went on, "and have not love, I am become as sounding brass or a tinkling symbol.

"And though I have the gift of prophecy and understand all mysteries and all knowledge, and though I have all faith, so that I could move mountains, and have not - love," Lydia's word again, "I am nothing."

Colin felt something special stir within him as he read. It was a feeling he had experienced often since coming to Highland: a move of the Spirit bringing God's presence yet nearer to him. "And though I bestow all my goods to feed the poor, and though I give my body to be burned and have not love, it profiteth me nothing.

"Love suffereth long and is kind, love envieth not, love vaunteth not itself, is not puffed up, doth not behave itself unseemly, seeketh not her own, is not easily provoked, thinketh no evil, rejoiceth not in iniquity but rejoiceth in truth."

Lydia's word fit so perfectly with the others, Colin used it again. "Love beareth all things, believeth all things, hopeth all things, endureth all things. Love never faileth, but whether there be prophecies, they shall fail, whether there be tongues, they shall cease, whether there be knowledge, it shall vanish away.

"For we know in part and we prophesy in part. But when that which is perfect is come, then that which is in part shall be done away. When I was a child, I spoke as a child, I understood as a child, I thought as a child, but when I became a man, I put away childish things.

"For now we see through a glass darkly, but then face to face. Now I know in part, but then shall I know even as I am known. And now abideth faith, hope and love, these three...But the greatest of these is love."

The moment he finished reading, Colin looked at Kaytra. There was a curious light behind her eyes, a rather deep sense of wonder as if she had heard the words before, but just now had come to fully understand them.

Lydia noticed it, too, and reached out her hand to cover one of Kaytra's. When her touch failed to break the concentrated look passing between Colin and Kaytra, Lydia felt both pleased and out of place. Those feelings soon passed, however, and she smiled as if she hadn't even noticed. "I've always been fond of that chapter. Thank you, Colin."

His gaze slowly shifted to her face, letting her know he had found out her motives. "Don't you have something you want to give Kaytra?"

Kaytra turned startled eyes to Lydia, wondering what was to happen now. Excitement heightened Lydia's color as she reached behind the pillow nearest her and retrieved a simply wrapped package, tied with a white ribbon. At first, Kaytra wouldn't take it, but the quiet generosity of Lydia's expression changed her mind.

Her hands trembled in unwrapping the gift. A fact she was sure Colin would notice. Beneath the paper was a box and inside the box-. Her quickly drawn breath sounded almost painful.

"I do hope you like it, dear." Lydia spoke calmly. "My father and mother gave it to me for my seventeenth birthday. Do you remember, Colin?"

"Yes." He answered, somewhat distracted by the way Kaytra's finely shaped features had softened. Had he really told her earlier that she wasn't at all a lady? The idea disturbed him now. If she was sitting in the elegant grand salon at his parents home, she could not have looked more graceful, more beautiful.

Her small hand lifted the necklace as if it was the finest of treasures, touching lightly the single tear-drop pearl which hung as if suspended in time at the bottom of a delicate, gold chain.

"Let me help you put it on." The offer was out of Colin's mouth even before it was a clear thought.

Kaytra stood obediently, turning until her back was toward him. That she became tense at the touch of his fingers upon the sensitive skin at the nape of her neck, was obvious only to Colin. Though he had no trouble with the minute clasp, he didn't hurry to finish. "Smile," his demanding whisper was for her ears alone.

Of course...She was being unkind to Lydia by not appearing to like the gift. And Colin had misunderstood. Kaytra wanted to turn and tell him he was wrong, that she did love the necklace, but he had moved away. With a shy, lovely smile, Kaytra took a step forward, clasped Lydia's hands and guided her to her feet in order to give her a hug.

Lydia couldn't have received a warmer thank you. Diamond bright tears filled their eyes when they pulled apart. "Happy Birthday, dear. You are very special to me. The necklace is perfect. Don't you think so, Colin?"

He had gone to stand by the windows. It was dark now, not the pitch black of late night, only the deep blue of evening. At Lydia's question, he half-turned to see what his answer should be. The necklace now lying at the soft swell of Kaytra's white blouse, received but a glance before his eyes caught hers. "Yes, it is perfect...I'll go check on the light now. You should get to bed, Lydia. It's been a busy day."

The room seemed larger without his presence.

For some unspoken reason, Lydia was unusually quiet as Kaytra helped her get ready for bed. Only after she lay beneath the warm quilt, did she say anything. "Sit down, Kaytra. Please."

Kaytra automatically laid her hand over one of Lydia's. The gesture had become one of mutual comfort when one friend sensed a deep need in the other. Lydia sighed tiredly. "Did you have a special day after all, Kaytra?"

How could she answer with a mere nod? Kaytra picked up the journal she had written in earlier. Words flowed from her heart.

> *"Not a special day, Lydia. Special can mean so little - as a special pet or a special flower. Something one likes above the ordinary things in life. This day has been to me extraordinary. I thought it not possible to be at once a child and a woman, yet that is how I feel, all alight with wonder, fascinated with life again. Is it silly to want to throw my arms wide and embrace these feelings, never to let them disappear?"*

As Lydia shook her head slowly, a kind expression came over her face. "No, dear. It isn't silly at all, but the feelings aren't outside of you." Kaytra frowned slightly, tilting her head to one side. "Those feelings are inside of you, wanting to come out, to be born again. Someday - soon - I hope you'll realize you don't need an excuse to feel this happy and alive." Kaytra unconsciously touched the pearl she wore, drawing Lydia's attention to it once again. "It is perfect, you know. I'm glad you like it."

> *"I shall never wear it without being reminded of you."*

"Then it is a true gift." A momentary silence followed Lydia's words. She settled more deeply into the pillows. "Do something for me?" Kaytra nodded at once. "Go back downstairs and write out what it is you first thought when you felt the pearl, your very first thought." Again, Kaytra nodded. "Then show Colin what you wrote...Please?"

The hesitation Kaytra felt lasted but a moment. Lydia was her dearest friend and a very wise woman. Who else knew Colin so well? Kaytra smiled a yes, then replaced the journal before she kissed Lydia gently on the forehead and left the room.

Downstairs by herself, putting her thoughts into words was no effort at all. It wasn't quite as easy, though, to think of actually handing Colin a piece of paper and having him stand in front of her to read it. Kaytra was finished writing in a few minutes. Afterward, she sat at the desk, reading and rereading the page, trying to guess what Colin would think, what he would say.

So lost in thought was she, she didn't hear the fall of footsteps on the porch which preceded his opening the door. His gaze was bewildered for a moment at seeing her at the desk. Then he became curious. Kaytra looked away while he hung up his coat.

When he did speak, he was standing two steps behind her. The deep timbre of his voice caused her to jerk a little in reaction. "What are you up to now, Kaytra?" Colin reached around her to pick up the sheet of paper laying on the desk. His curiosity increased at seeing his own name at the top of the page. Her handwriting had made his name seem different somehow. He surely wasn't used to the gracious curves she had added to the familiar letters.

When Colin felt Kaytra's eyes upon him, he glanced down at her. "I'm supposed to read this?"

She raised her chin slightly. The gesture was neither a yes nor a no.

He read it anyway. To himself. Slowly. Words such as Kaytra wrote were not meant to be skimmed over, but read thoughtfully to catch each subtle meaning. Each delicate expression...

> *"Colin...When Lydia asked that I do this for her - to write these words, then give them to you, I had supposed it was for her alone that I agreed. Now, I find that I, too, desire that you understand. My first thought at seeing the gift Lydia gave to me could not be happiness. My first thought could not bring a smile. Perhaps if you had not turned away, I could have shown you why."*

A tightness formed inside his chest, making each breath shallow. Colin took the paper with him as he went to stand beside the lamp near his chair. He was unaware of how his shadow loomed upon the wall, distancing Kaytra's hopes that her words would help him to know he had misjudged her.

> *"...My thoughts just then were that I could not possibly deserve such a friend, such an unconditional acceptance. My feelings were ones of being humbled, of being brought to my knees by the simplicity of your sister's*

belief in me. I felt for a moment, that I must give back the gift until I could prove myself to her...and to you. Then you placed the chain around my neck and the weight of the pearl settled upon my heart. It was as if it meant to hold back all the uncertainties. To gather them away, like a wave returning to the sea where it is once again lost among the waters. And behind, in their place, was left this one perfect drop. This one perfect pearl. Perhaps you would think even now the gift meant so little to me that I needed you to bid me express happiness. In truth, Colin, every joy my life has ever known could fit within this single pearl, so few are they. What I needed was to feel its warmth against my heart, reminding me all has not been lost. I needed to know the sense of hope you and Lydia seem to come by so naturally. Perhaps in time my joy will surpass even this day's blessings. Can I wish for such a dream?"

Kaytra had moved into the kitchen. She felt unsettled, waiting for Colin to finish reading what she had written. Some unspoken instinct told her when he finally looked across the room to see her banking the fire in the cast iron stove. It took a great deal of self-control to resist turning, to resist studying the expression on his face. If he wanted to say anything, he would do so.

When she was finished at the stove, she went to the door to let Rex inside. He barely licked at her hand before running into the parlor to find Colin. As Kaytra followed Rex's movement with her eyes, it was impossible for her not to glance up at Colin .

Her heart all but stopped as he walked toward her with slow, deliberate steps. Did a lifetime really pass before he said anything? Or was it that something inside of her died in those seemingly endless moments? Though she tried desperately, she could not read the expression in his eyes.

"Do you want to prove yourself, Kaytra?" His voice held her to the place where she stood. If not for that power, she would surely have run upstairs to the relative safety of her room. "Do you?" He wanted an answer this time.

Her nod was given even as tears of sadness blurred her vision.

Colin clamped his jaw together so tightly a muscle worked at the corner, revealing how close he was to the edge of control.

Kaytra swallowed the rise of fear threatening her.

"If you want to prove yourself, then you should stop turning away from what she's trying to teach you. Your whole friendship with Lydia is based on what you can do for her, how you can make her more comfortable. How you can - take care of her needs."

Kaytra's reaction to his tightly spoken words was to pull into herself, wrapping her arms across her chest.

"It's a lie, Kaytra. God help me, I want to believe the things you wrote. I want to trust you." Colin threw the paper at the table, not caring that it fluttered to the floor instead. "How could you stand there and not know what she needs is for you to stop wishing for some faraway happiness when it's right here in this house, when all you have to do is open your heart and feel it?"

The accusation stung sharply, chasing the color from Kaytra's face. But he didn't know!

Colin surprised them both by suddenly reaching out to take her arms in his hands, drawing her so close she could feel the heat of his breath on her skin. "I'm tired of watching you put my sister through this, Kaytra. You don't have to live this way. You don't have to make people feel sorry for you just so-."

A strange, pitiful moan surfaced from somewhere deep inside Kaytra as she tried to free herself. Rex was beside them now, ready to defend her, even against Colin if he had to. When the dog growled, Colin commanded him to lie down. His command was heeded slowly.

Under Colin's superior strength, Kaytra soon hung her head, timidly giving up the struggle. "Look at me, Kaytra." When she wouldn't, Colin let out a heavy sigh. This wasn't easy for him, but he felt as if he didn't have a choice any more. "I'm not like Lydia. I won't let you pretend. I can't." At no other time in his life could Colin remember feeling so much raw emotion. He felt powerless against the deep flood of awareness, against the very real chaos which seemed to have been building these past weeks. "I've given you so many chances, Kaytra. Even today, out on the bank, I tried. But you keep holding onto your secrets as if they mean more to you than finally being free from the past."

Unexpectedly, Colin loosened one hand to pick up the pearl which rested upon her breast....When he looked up again, his eyes had darkened, but Kaytra could not fathom why. He sensed as much. "The words I read tonight from the Bible, you knew them, didn't you? You remembered them from a long time ago?"

Kaytra nodded, completely confused by the change in Colin's voice. He spoke almost tenderly now.

"Am I right, Kaytra, was your father the only one who has ever loved you?" He could tell by the startled look which leapt into her eyes that he had guessed the truth. Somehow he knew that Mary Elizabeth's pride and bitterness had come between them. Whatever Mary Elizabeth had felt for Kaytra the last years of her life had not been the love a mother should have for her own daughter.

Kaytra, unconsciously relaxing beneath the softness of his questions, watched as Colin ran his thumb over the pearl. "Did he read you those words when you were a little girl?" She nodded. "And now abideth faith, hope, love...Which is it that we are missing, Kaytra?"

Her blue-gray eyes scanned his face before finally meeting his gaze and silently asking how it was possible to separate such feelings.

Colin brought his other hand up alongside her face. The warmth of his skin against hers encouraged her not to pull away, even when he lowered his mouth to hers in answer to her question. His kiss was as gentle as his words had been....

Yet, if anything, Kaytra looked even more confused when Colin drew away. He shouldn't have done that, but she had looked so beautiful. All day long he had been avoiding his own feelings.

There was so little control left in him, it took every ounce of strength to say what he did next. "Go to bed, Kaytra."

Her eyes were round with an emotion hovering somewhere between panic and misery. Colin could tell she was barely breathing. For a moment, she became utterly still....Then she turned and fled up the stairs. He heard her door close solidly once she was on the other side.

Colin stood at the bottom of the stairs with one hand gripping the newel post as if it was the only thing keeping him from losing all control. He wouldn't allow himself to touch her again. He would not fall in love with her. Dear God, he would not love Kaytra Lange!

Lydia's life had nearly been destroyed by the love she felt for Sidney Kent. If there could be no foundation of trust and honesty, love would be in vain. No, he would not allow himself to feel that way for Kaytra. The prayers he said these past weeks had gone unanswered. Perhaps it was time to choose for himself which direction to turn.

His gaze fell upon the letter which lay abandoned on the wood floor near the table. Every word had burned its way into his soul. He would heal, but not without painful scars.

Chapter Twelve

Mid-October became clothed in gray fog and chill, damp breezes. The rich hues of fall gave way to a barren sameness. Even the shades of brown seemed to blend together with the coming of winter. It was time again for Colin to make a trip to Provincetown. The barrels which held the oil used in the lamps needed to be replenished and supplies for the house were low.

The long day spent alone, away from the light, gave him time to think and to pray. Written at the bottom of Lydia's list of things they needed from Provincetown he had read the words, "...And please, please bring me back the old Colin. The one who used to say, 'I love you, Sis'."

He hadn't been fair to her lately. She didn't deserve his inattentiveness. Whatever was wrong between Kaytra and himself shouldn't affect his relationship with Lydia. In fact, he very much needed her now. Maybe he could find something very special at Jolly's to get for her. Sort of an "I'm-sorry" gift.

Other thoughts occupied his mind, too. Namely the unsolved problem with the mooncussers. He had made several midnight trips to the site, but had so far failed to catch them at their unlawful deed. The weather had been poor of late, which may have kept the mooncussers away. He knew he would be tired from the long ride, but tonight, if it was clear, he would have to try again.

As Provincetown came into view, Samson responded to the slight urging for more speed. Under a colorless sky, the town appeared even more washed-out than it had before. Little eddies of dust swirled where wind touched the sand. Once again, Colin's first stop was at the General Store. Young Timmy, who was sweeping the steps, gave him a cheerful wave and a smile which Colin couldn't help but return. "Hello, Timmy! How are you?"

"'lo, Siah! I be fine, thank ye!" Timmy was pleased the light keeper remembered him by name. "Come ta get oil, did ya?" He motioned to the barrels in the bed of the wagon.

"Yes, I did." Colin swung off of the seat, grateful to stretch his cramped muscles. Samson didn't object to being tied to the post either. It had been a long trip. "I can't very well run the light without oil. Is Jolly in the store?"

"Yes, Siah! He is. An' suahe I am that he be glad ta see ya!" When Timmy opened the door with all the flourish of Carlisle, the butler at the MacRae mansion in Boston, Colin couldn't resist ruffling the boy's dark hair.

Nothing inside the crowded store seemed to have changed. Perhaps there were a few more people shopping. The potbelly stove stationed in the center of the store now sent out an inviting warmth. Colin nodded at the two men who had drawn chairs near to it. They waved back, much as Timmy had done.

"Well, Colin! An' good it is ta see ya heahe!" Jolly's voice boomed a greeting from behind the counter.

Colin shook the older man's outstretched hand, pleased to see him in good health. "Hello, Jolly."

"I haven't foahgotten ya. How's it goin' out theahe?" With his usual candidness, Jolly came directly to the point. His gaze had already taken in the changes on Colin's handsome face, not that he could have said exactly what those changes were... "Youah sister?," he asked cautiously

Colin leaned against the wood counter with an unconscious sigh. "She's doing well, Jolly. Thank you for remembering. I'll be sure and tell her you asked after her."

"And the gal?" Jolly lowered his voice. Not everyone in Provincetown needed to know how the girl had fared at Highland. The fact that she hadn't come back now with Colin was a good sign. Jolly had been expecting the pair of them to show up weeks ago.

"Kaytra is fine," Colin answered. "She's been a good worker, just like everyone said. Have you got anything special? I'd like to get my sister a gift."

Jolly scratched his head in silent surrender. If Colin didn't want to talk about Kaytra, then he wouldn't push. "Suahe, an' I got somethin' foah heah. Theahe's some nice fancies oveah by the yahd goods. Help youahself."

Colin thanked him with a preoccupied smile before going off in search of Lydia's gift.

Some time later, when the store had been cleared of customers, Jolly invited Colin to "pull up" to the stove for a plate of stew and biscuits. Timmy brought plates of food from where Jolly lived in two small rooms behind the store. The meal was nourishing, though not nearly as tasty as what Kaytra would have made. Colin could picture her lifting pans of golden brown bread from the oven, her cheeks flushed with the heat. Thinking about her brought a quick frown to Colin's brow

The expression didn't go unnoticed by Jolly. "What ya got ta be so woahied 'bout, boy? Seems ta me like you'ahe too young ta go scowlin' like that."

Colin hunched forward, resting his forearms on his knees. "You're right. I've no reason to be worried. Tell me, how are you keeping up with the growth around here? I heard talk of more people coming over from the mainland."

"Not exac'ly pouahin' in, is they. But business has been good. Gettin' kinda used ta seein' folks what I don't know in heahe." Jolly nodded to himself, as if confirming the idea in his own mind. "Most of 'um head on south. They heah the Cape has good livin' foah those willin' ta woahk hahd."

"Fishermen, I suppose?"

Jolly seemed undecided. "Some...'Couahse, theahe's always the usual followin' wheahe eveah a passle o' men go. Wished all of 'um was honest, but then I ain't the one ta stand guahd oveah who should come oah not."

There was a thoughtful silence between them. Colin hadn't meant to let Everette Koch's name slip into his mind, but it was there none the less. He glanced at the old man seated beside him, trying to gauge how much Jolly would know if he asked about Kaytra's life here.

"Got sumpthin' on youah mind, Colin?" Jolly drained what was left of the tar-black coffee in his enamel mug before wiping his mouth on his shirtsleeve. Only when the ritual was complete, did he look Colin straight in the eye.

Colin's honesty drove him to speak the truth, plain and simple. "I do have something I want to ask, but I'm not at all sure you'll answer me."

Jolly, who admired such openness in a man, nodded slightly for Colin to go on. "Is Everette Koch still around?"

"Fah as I know, he is." There was a spark of interest in his age-faded eyes. "Ya got ta see him?"

"No," Colin ground out the single word. "I'd likely knock out a few of his teeth if I came within arm's reach of him."

Jolly stood very carefully to refill his cup from the huge coffeepot sitting on the barrel stove. He poured more into Colin's cup at the same time. "What ahe ya sayin', Colin?"

"He beat her, that's what I'm saying. He beat her, Jolly." The muscles of Colin's shoulders ached with tension. He barely noticed how hot the coffee was as it touched his lips. Certainly, he hadn't meant to share how he felt with the older man.

A sad expression clouded Jolly's eyes as he sat back down. It was a while before he dared say anything. "I guess it's 'bout time I told ya a stoahy, Colin, bein' that you'ahe paht o' it now, too."

Colin's attention was entirely focused on the look which had settled over Jolly's face. Suddenly, he seemed older, more tired. There was another uncomfortable silence, while Colin wondered how Jolly could be tied into Kaytra's life.

As he stared at a far-off spot on one of the shelves, Jolly began to tell the story. "I cen 'membeah the fiahst day Ma'y 'Liz'beth an' the gal come in heahe. She had such big, lonely eyes, ya see, an' so - quiet like, Ma'y 'Liz'beth that is. Katy - I always called heah that - Katy was diffeahnt. So alive inside. So spahkly like. They looked 'lot the same. Could tell then that Ma'y 'Liz'beth was out o' place, as if she didn't belong heahe atall."

Jolly sighed, then grew quiet again, lost in his own thoughts...."Foah a while, Katy come most eveahy day. She be a shahp one. Full o' questions. Used ta be I could see hope in heah eyes. Took me a while ta know Katy's Mom. Took patience. Sumpthin' I ain't got much o'. 'Couahse, I knowed she was mahied ta Koch. Had a hahd time 'ceptin' it. Ma'y 'Liz'beth was so special. She didn' have no one ta talk to an' I had willin' eahs. Pretty soon, I had a willin' heaht, too...I fell foah heahe."

Colin caught his breath in surprise. It was the last thing he would have imagined.

Jolly smiled a sad little smile at the younger man's reaction. "I ain't so old that I cen't love a woman, son, though I don't know 'xactly what Ma'y 'Liz'beth saw in me ta feel the same way. That soaht o' knocks the wind outta ya, huh?"

"Well...I -. Yes." Colin stammered over the words. "Why didn't you tell me this before?"

"You an' I, only what met twice, boy."

The reminder brought things back into perspective. Sometimes Colin felt as if he had known Jolly all his life.

"Anyways," Jolly continued, "not but 'notheah soul knows 'bout me an Ma'y 'Liz'beth 'cept you. Not even little Katy. Guess she ain't so lil' now, but we didn' want heah knowin' the way o' things."

It was probably for the best. Colin settled against the wood chair. "Was Mary Elizabeth unhappy with Koch then?"

Jolly nodded slowly. "Moah than unhappy...She hated him. Can't say as I blamed heah none. He's a mean cuss. Mean as sin. Koch hit Ma'y 'Liz'beth - close ta killed heah once." There was a hardness in Jolly's voice now, a passionate anger.

"I neah went mad. Neah took the both of 'um, Ma'y 'Liz'beth and Katy, an' left heahe. But she wouldn' have it. I think Koch had sumpthin' oveah heah. Sumpthin' he knew could a huaht heah moahe than the beatin's."

"A secret?" Colin frowned deeply. "Maybe something about her past?"

Jolly's only answer was a tired shrug. He had never been able to get the truth from Mary Elizabeth. "Don't know, son."

"Koch didn't hurt Kaytra while her mother was alive, did he?"

"Nope. Ma'y 'Liz'beth kept him from touchin' heah. Think she had sumpthin' oveah him, too; only way a man like Koch woulda left the gal be."

Colin ran a hand through the thick waves of his hair, wanting to know more, yet, at the same time, not wanting to. He felt torn inside by the things Jolly was saying. Another question began to burn in him. "What was Kaytra like?"

"Befoahe heah mom died? She was shy, but ya could jus' see the goodness in heah wantin' ta come out. She's one o' the few people not boahn heahe I'd say belongs heahe, if that makes any sense?" Colin thought he understood. "She'd walk 'long the beach an' seem a paht o' it. Neveah played with the otheah kids. Guess that's mostly what stahted folks thinkin' she was simple."

"Didn't it bother her to be so alone all the time?"

Jolly gave Colin a long, searching look. "Was it Katy what told ya how Ma'y 'Liz'beth changed towahd the end?"

It would have been impossible to miss the note of protectiveness in Jolly's tone. Colin felt dread create a hollow pit in his stomach. When he shook his head, Jolly sighed very deeply.

"Ya should know then. 'Bout six months a'foahe she died, Ma'y 'Liz'beth stahted losin' touch with what was real an' what wasn't. She hahdly knew Katy. Hahdly left that ol' shack. Stayed 'way of eveahyone. The gal had ta do most all the woahk. Twas a buahden foah heah, but she'd not complain. Told me once, she did, that -." Jolly had to swallow hard and blink his eyes clear of tears, "that heah ma didn' love heah 'nuff ta want ta stay anymoahe. She'd stopped fightin', you see. She stopped wantin' ta live."

"But you-."

"I-," Jolly interrupted harshly, then lowered his voice to a hoarse whisper. "I had tuahned heah 'way, Colin. Had no choice. When Ma'y 'Liz'beth was beat so bad that one time, it was 'cause Koch 'spected we was close. He was just too much a cowahd ta face me 'stead o' beatin' heah. And me -...Guess I was a cowahd, too, 'cause I neveah tried hahd 'nuff ta take heah away from him. Didn' know what ta do.

"All I knowed is that I couldn' let heah go through that 'gain, so I made up my mind not ta see heah any moahe. My Ma'y didn' undeahstand it, though. I huaht heah deeply an' neveah will foahgive myself foah doin' so. I stole Katy's ma 'way from heah suahe as if I'd killed -." He cut off the words sharply, throwing a horrified glance at Colin, but the mistake was already made. He had said too much.

Colin's eyes narrowed. "Killed her? Koch killed Mary Elizabeth?"

"Now, I - I don't -." Jolly swore fiercely as he threw himself out of his chair.

Colin stood more slowly. He wasn't going to leave without knowing the truth. "Tell me, Jolly, please. It's important ."

Jolly had never meant to tell another living soul about his suspicions. Mary Elizabeth was gone. Five years now. No amount of wondering would bring her back. Pain etched itself across his face like a mask. "I think you'd betteah ask Katy ta tell ya. She be the only one know foah suahe."

"Kaytra?" Colin felt his whole body grow stiff with tension. "You mean, she saw it hap-."

"Don't mean nothin' o' the soaht!"

"She found her then? She found her mother dead?"

Jolly nodded gravely.

An agonized gasp filled Colin's lungs as he ran an unsteady hand over his eyes. A picture flashed into his mind of the day on the beach at Highland when Kaytra had panicked because of the blood stains on her apron. Had he known, perhaps he wouldn't have been so hard on her. Another thought slammed the breath out of him, forcing him to face Jolly again. "If you think Koch killed Mary Elizabeth, if you knew he beat her, why in heaven's name did you leave Kaytra any where near him?"

The young man was clearly upset. He had every right to be. Jolly had lived with his guilt for the past five years. Seeing it through Colin's eyes, made it all the more wrong. Still, he tried to justify his reasons. "An' what do ya s'pose I coulda done? Took heah inta my own house? An ol' man and she a neah lady? What do ya think folks woulda called heah then, Colin? Nobody what knows how I felt 'bout Ma'y 'Liz'beth. Not even Katy. I could no moahe have stepped in an' taken heah than the next man."

Colin walked a few steps away, struggling to absorb all Jolly was saying.

"I had no proof, Colin. I had only me own gut feelin's. Koch is a sly one. Kept the gal 'way from anyone coulda helped heah. Woulda been woahse foah heah if'n somebody done said sumpthin'"

"Worse?" The word exploded from the very pit of Colin's anger. It was the sight of Jolly's grief stricken face which made him fight for control of his emotions. Finally, Colin let out a pent-up breath. "I'm sorry. I'm sure you were in an impossible situation. I just-." He spread his arms wide in a gesture of helplessness.

"You just wished it wouldna happened," Jolly said very seriously. "No one knows moahe than I how ya feel, son."

The implication of those few words hit Colin like a ton of bricks. "Jolly, I don't-...I'm just - concerned, that's all. Kaytra has-. I'm just -. Well, I can't figure her out and it's - frustrating!"

Amazingly, a smile creased Jolly's lined face. "Can't say as if I know how ta help ya theahe, Colin, 'cept that she won't take no one's pity. Like as not, ya'll find she's stubboahn as a bob cat sometimes, soft as a kitten the next." Colin's eyebrows shot up expressively. "Now, don't go doin' that. Did ya get heah ta talk yet?"

Colin sucked in a breath. "How do you-?"

Jolly waved a hand as he bent to gather the dishes they had used. "I always figuahed she'd been scahed outta talkin', an' could just as well be scahed back inta it, too. She ain't talked since the day Ma'y 'Liz'beth died. Been moahe than hahd foah heah since then." He straightened to give Colin a suddenly sober look. "Don't give up on heah, son. She's got a heaht o' gold inside, that one. She needs someone ta love heahe, Colin." Having said that much, Jolly disappeared into the back rooms. Colin was left alone to wonder if it was more than a little possible God had this whole day planned two months earlier when Kaytra Lange had first stepped into his life.

It wasn't until late that same night that Colin had a chance to spend time alone with his sister. She looked like a little girl, snuggled in bed, opening his gift with a smile of pure delight. "Oh, Colin...You really didn't have to-."

"Hush." He scolded her playfully. "I wanted to get you some-thing. Consider it my way of making up for being so rotten to you lately."

Lydia's eyes filled with unshed tears. "Colin, I-."

He placed a finger over her mouth to seal the words. When she smiled, he bent to place a kiss upon her forehead. Everything would be all right between them now. "Open your gift, silly. I want to see what you think." He watched her tear at the plain brown paper. In-side, wrapped in tissue, was a delicate, ivory shawl woven with a pat-tern of roses and vines. He had known immediately, when he saw it in the store, that it would be perfect for her.

"Colin! It's beautiful!" Lydia reached up to give him a big hug. "Wherever did you find it?"

"It was at Jolly's. The General Store? Do you remember meeting him?"

"Of course." Lydia allowed Colin to help her wrap the shawl about her shoulders.

"He asked after you today. In fact, he and I had quite a long talk." As his tone grew serious, Lydia settled back onto the pillows, waiting for him to go on. "He used to know Mary Elizabeth, Kaytra's mother."

His special emphasis on the word "know" caused Lydia to raise her eyebrows. "You mean-."

Colin nodded. "They were intimate friends, Lydia. He loved her, and - from what Jolly said today, Mary Elizabeth returned the affec-tion." Lydia's brow creased in a thoughtful frown. "Jolly also said - actually he let it slip out - that he thinks Everette Koch killed Mary Elizabeth."

"Oh, Colin," Lydia sighed softly. "I already know."

"You know?" Colin pulled back a little. "How?"

"Kaytra told me. Well, she wrote it down actually."

"And you didn't say anything to me?"

She took one of Colin's hands in her own, gazing down at the strength of it. "I didn't feel as if I could. Not yet anyway, but I'm glad now, relieved that you know, too"

"What else has she told you?"

"Colin-."

"Okay, okay." He squeezed her hand tightly. "That's between you and Kaytra. I wouldn't want you to break a confidence." Lydia smiled her thanks. "What did you say to her when she told you about her mother's death? Was she still very upset?"

A nod preceded Lydia's answer. "When I told her that she needed to forgive him, she shook her head and wrote 'NO' in big letters at the bottom of the page. She seems so disheartened sometimes, Colin."

"And I haven't helped much." He saw her wince a little at the honesty. "It's okay to yell at me, Sis. I'm not perfect by any means. I've never pretended to be."

"You sound just like Max," Lydia said, relieved to hear him talking like his old self. "Nobody is perfect, MacRae. It's too easy to let our feelings get in the way sometimes."

For a moment, there lay a certain thoughtfulness in Colin's expression. When it cleared he did not pursue the remark she had made. "You'd better go to sleep now. You look worn out." He stood slowly, placing a goodnight kiss upon her cheek. "Have you been feeling well lately?"

Her smile was indulgent of his concern. "I'm fine, you goose. See you in the morning."

"Night, Sis. I love you."

"I love you, too."

Colin turned out her light, letting a shadowy darkness claim the room. Yet it only took a few seconds for the comforting glow from the lighthouse to settle in, softening the otherwise sharp angles.

Downstairs in the parlor, Colin sat alone at his desk to record his trip into Provincetown and give a list of the supplies they had on hand. In opening the journal, he saw that beneath his last entry at seven that morning were two neatly written paragraphs. One at noon and one at three, in keeping with the schedule.

Kaytra's handwriting was, by now, familiar to him. At noon she had written,

"A splendid white cloud is anchored due east, seemingly untouched by the slight wind which tries to push it off course. Beneath it, the sea sleeps comfortably on a silken sheet of azure blue. It is too cool to be warm, too warm to be chilly. Perhaps bracing would be a more suitable word."

Colin smiled to himself. He could picture her sitting where he was with a quaint frown upon her brow, trying to puzzle out how to describe the day. He read on...

"Three o'clock already? The day is more than half spent, yet it looks not even hours old. Could that be the secret of fall, making one think winter is ages away because of the bright blue afternoon sky and the sudden youthfulness of the sea as it plays into shore? If so, I will keep the secret and pretend the now cooling breeze is meant only to waken my senses so that I, too, might think this day perfect...until tomorrow."

Until tomorrow? She hadn't smiled in days, not that he knew anyway. What an effort it must be for her to hold such moments of wonder inside when on the outside, her life seemed anything but perfect.

Colin picked up the pen to begin writing an account of his trip. It paled in comparison to Kaytra's words, but he was too preoccupied with his own private thoughts to notice. Half-way through the list, his attention was shattered by the touch of a hand upon his shoulder.

He swung around so suddenly, it frightened Kaytra, draining some of the color from her face. It took but one glance to see she had come from her room. She wore a plain, white nightgown. Her hair was loose, falling in tangled waves past her shoulders.

Colin brought his eyes back to hers. "What is it, Kaytra? I thought you were asleep." As usual, she had disappeared shortly after eight-thirty. A look of indecision crossed her features now. "What's wrong?"

She took several unsteady breaths, shifting her eyes to the paper on the desk. No. There wasn't time! Instead, she grabbed one of Colin's hands, pulling him to his feet.

They were at the door of her room before she thought how improper her actions might seem. Her troubled eyes swung up to Colin's face. He didn't look angry though, only confused.

Kaytra led him through the door, finally stopping before the single window on the south wall. As she pointed out into the darkness, her heart pounded so hard she was sure Colin must hear it.

"What in the world?" He was staring at her instead of looking outside. "Kaytra -." More urgently, she gestured outside again.

"Kaytra, I-." Colin had no idea why she was so upset. He searched the darkness, moving out further and further from the house. Then, he saw it, too - a mere pinpoint of light, showing unsteadily through the blackness. Colin tightened his hand around Kaytra's, unaware until that moment that neither of them had let go. "The mooncussers." His tone was quiet so as not to awaken Lydia. "Did you just spot them?"

Kaytra nodded. She knew already, by the staid expression upon Colin's features, that he meant to go after them. Part of her wanted to try to stop him, but he was far too determined. Even now, he stared hard at the light as if trying to see across the distance.

All in an instant, he was turning to leave her room. Kaytra was forced to run down the steps in order to keep up with him. Their hands collided when they both reached for their jackets. Colin frowned down at her sternly. "You aren't coming, Kaytra."

Though she couldn't hide the fear stirred by his intense emotions, her chin rose slightly. Colin thrust his arms into the sleeves of his heavy jacket. "Don't say anything to Lydia. And keep Rex indoors." During the crisp recitation of orders, he had moved to a cupboard set beneath the stairs. It wasn't until he turned around that Kaytra saw the gun.

Her eyes flew to his face.

"Don't look at me like that." He shoved a leather pouch of powder into his pocket. There would be time to load it on the way. "Stay in the house."

Kaytra neither agreed nor disagreed.

"I mean it. I can't be taking care of this mess and worrying about you, too." Colin's long, urgent strides carried him past her and to the door. Rex was there already, waiting to go along. "Call him back, Kaytra." She clapped her hands together and the dog went to her, hanging his head in disappointment. Colin gave her one last search-ing look. "I'll be back as soon as I can."

Chapter Thirteen

Picking his way over the path along the bank was tricky business in the dark, demanding much of Colin's attention. He tried to remember from his other nighttime trips where the sand was loose, how the path wound around an outcrop of pitch pine. Every step required his keenest instincts.

The rest of his thoughts were spent wondering about the look he had seen in Kaytra's eyes just before he walked out the door. Why was she so afraid? Could the anxiousness in her blue eyes be for him alone? As the answers continued to elude him, he forced himself to think only about what he would face at the site. If he kept puzzling over Kaytra now, he wouldn't be ready for the mooncussers.

Since the Federal Lighthouse Commission had enacted much stricter laws against mooncussers, there hadn't been any trouble on Cape Cod. Whoever chose now to defy those laws was - in Colin's mind - a very real threat. His heart hammered anxiously inside his chest.

If men were callous enough to kill innocent people by trying to draw ships off course, what would stop them from turning that same cold-blooded attitude on Colin? At the thought, Colin paused to load the gun he carried. Once before, in Boston, he had seen how quickly a gun could end someone's life. Dear God, he prayed it wouldn't come to that tonight.

Every forward movement along the bank brought its own struggle between determination and fear, between Colin's sense of duty and his reluctance to face a potentially violent situation. He knew he had no choice. The mooncussers must be stopped at all costs.

Colin frowned slightly when he paused to catch his breath. Over the moan of the wind, he could hear voices, excited voices. His hand gripped the loaded gun tighter.

In another five minutes, he was crouched just outside the circle of light near the tall post. There were two of them, and they weren't men - they were just lads. They looked to be about fifteen, sixteen at the most. He felt sick inside to hear their words. This was a game to them, a prank to indulge their sense of adventure.

Still unnoticed, he rose to his feet, taking the necessary steps to bring himself into view. "Hello, boys." Their faces held first astonishment, and then fear. The sudden appearance of anyone would have been shock enough, but Colin's size and sober expression made them even more alarmed. The two boys glanced at one another, then back at Colin. Finally, their eyes rested on the gun he held in one hand. "Do you know who I am?" Colin asked in a demanding way.

Both boys shook their heads. Colin moved closer. "I'm the keeper at Highland Light...Colin MacRae." He raised his eyebrows as understanding showed in their frightened eyes. "I guess you know me now. You also know that what you're doing is illegal."

He motioned to the taller of the boys. "You, take down the light. Carefully. But don't put it out." The youngster was too afraid not to obey. He used a long pole to lift the oversized lantern from its perch. "Set it down right there." At least having it off the post would make it virtually impossible to see from off-shore.

Colin gestured the boy back to stand near his friend. "Okay...What are your names and where do you live?"

"T-."

"Don't say nothin'!"

The harsh words coming from behind Colin made him whirl around.

There was a third boy and he held a gun of his own pointed directly at Colin's chest. "Bettah hand oveah the gun, misteah. Easy like."

He was a year or two older than the others, dressed in the same worn clothes. But there was something different about him. Something in the steely hardness of his eyes told Colin not to try to overpower him. Slowly and smoothly, Colin bent down to lay his gun upon the ground.

"Good...You's a smaht fella." The boy's wicked grin showed a few missing teeth. His eyes ran up and down Colin, before finally coming to rest on his face. "Now, what we s'posed ta do with ya? 'Taint nice comin' heahe ta -."

"What isn't nice," Colin interrupted with a note of authority, "is that you don't care who gets hurt as long as you have your fun." Much to the boy's surprise, Colin turned and faced the other two again. "People die in shipwrecks - or had you forgotten that? What have you gained out here, anyway? The right to brag to your buddies that you're mooncussers?"

"Leave 'um be, misteah!" The boy with the gun moved around to face Colin. There was youthful pride mingled with his anger now. He was close to losing his temper...

Which was exactly what Colin wanted. "Who are you to talk? You're in the same mess as they."

"I got this heahe gun what says you'ahe in the mess. Not us."

Colin appeared unconcerned to the point of insolence. "You've only got one shot."

"Only need one." Again, that same wicked grin.

"Hank-."

"Shush up, ya idiot!" The oldest boy's shout made the other two jump in alarm. "He don't know us foah nobody. Use me name 'gain an' you'll be six feet undeah, ya heah?" He got an anxious nod for an answer.

They were an odd trio, that's for sure. Colin could have sworn there was a resemblance between the kid with the gun and the one who had clumsily let the name slip out. If they were brothers, there was a good amount of dislike between them. And a good amount of control on Hank's part.

Colin crossed both arms over his chest, sizing up the situation. The way he saw it, he had two choices. Either he talked Hank out of continuing the show of bravado or he rushed him with the hope that nobody got hurt in the process. It wasn't likely he'd succeed at either one.

The light coming from the lantern on the ground threw heavy shadows over their faces. It was a typical Cape Cod night, becoming even windier now. Clouds slipped across the half moon, hiding more often than exposing its pale gray-yellow glow.

"Hank."

Angry eyes flashed directly to Colin's face.

"You're a little jumpy, aren't you?...A real man would put the gun down and listen to my offer." He walked forward, closing the distance between them to just six feet. In doing so, he felt their combined tension rise to a dangerous level.

Hank squared his shoulders. The closer Colin was to him, the smaller he looked in comparison. And he knew it. "A smaht man would kill ya on the spot an' not blink an eye...Ain't that so boys?"

The other two remained stone silent.

"Take youah jacket off. Don't want no blood on sumpthin' I cen use lateah."

Colin jerked out of the coat and threw it away - so that it safely buried his gun should one of the other boys get any sudden ideas.

"Got any last woahds ta say, misteah?"

"Since I don't think you actually know how to use that thing," Colin said, "I wouldn't consider anything I say to be my last words. Don't you want to hear my offer?"

"If'n it'll make ya feel bettah 'bout meetin' youah Makeah, go ahead. Tell me youah offeah."

Colin smiled. "How old are you anyway, Hank? Seventeen?"

It unnerved Hank to see how relaxed Colin seemed to be. What kind of man faced a loaded gun and stood there smiling about it? "Don't matteah none!" The words were shouted. "One o' yous put the lanteahn out!"

"But-."

"Do it, I say! And you-," Hank jerked the gun toward Colin, "you get down on youah knees, light keepeah!"

Colin didn't move. Instead, he watched Hank's brother shuffle to where the lantern sat. Somehow he knew Hank wouldn't actually shoot him until the light was out. A strange sense of calm took over.

Not so with Hank. Hank's eyes were darting from Colin to the other boys and back. His hands were shaking. One slip, and the finger he held on the trigger would cause the gun to go off. One small move on Colin's part and it would be over.

Suddenly, the site was as dark as the rest of the bank. Though they were all blinded at first by the change, those few seconds were too brief for Colin to make an effort to save himself.

As it was, he didn't have to. A sharp half-cry, half-moan came from Hank's brother before the boy dropped to the ground in a dead faint. The other boy, his face chalky white in the moonlight, crossed himself in prayer to the Holy Mother Mary.

Hank, too, stiffened as his eyes became fixed on a point some-where past the site.

Colin swung around.

At the very edge of the bank, seemingly suspended between sky and sea, was an apparition. The blood red light held in the spirit's hands cast over its flowing form an appearance so ghastly it chilled their bones. It made their hearts freeze in mid-beat.

Slowly, as if emerging from thin air, the beast appeared beside her. Evil shone in its untamed, hungry eyes......

"The Widoah Stevens," Hank barely uttered the words.

The other boy suddenly turned and ran like a body possessed.

Colin glanced back, certain for an instant that Hank would run just like his mate. But Hank was made of sterner stuff. He raised the gun. "No!" Colin's warning came too late. All that prevented Hank's shot from hitting its mark was Colin himself. He felt a searing heat, then pain which took his breath away.

In the confusion, it was easy for him to wrest Hank to the ground. The boy was half-crazy with fear anyway. He didn't even struggle against Colin's strength, not until he saw that the ghost was gliding across the bank toward them, then he fought to be released. "Let go, man! She's afteah souls! She's gonna get us!"

Colin jerked Hank to his feet by a handful of the boy's coat.

All Hank wanted was to sink to his knees and beg for mercy. His face was gray. His eyes as big around as saucers. They would both die! She was coming for them! "Noooo," he moaned aloud.

"Maybe I should just let her have you!" Colin shook the boy hard enough to rattle his teeth.

"No! No, don't!"

"Shut up!" With one hand clamped about Hank's arm, Colin swung him around to face the very thing he so greatly feared. The spirit stood mere yards from them now, still bathed in the sickening pale red light. Colin's eyes met those of the Widow Stevens, hardening into severe anger. "I told you to stay home!"

Hank sucked in an agonized breath. The man was mad! Nobody in their right mind would talk to a ghost like that! Much to Hank's further horror, he found himself being dragged right up to it. And the beast - it was positively horrid. All mottled black and white. Bared teeth.

When Hank stumbled to his knees, Colin decided to let him stay there. The boy didn't seem to have a single ounce of strength left. Besides, he wanted some answers. "What do you think you're doing out here, anyway? You could have been killed!"

Kaytra's chin lifted higher in blatant defiance.

"Don't you dare argue with me! I told you to stay put!"

If Hank thought he was confused before, he was downright bewildered now. The woman - he could see now that she actually was real - hadn't uttered a single word of argument. Yet Colin MacRae spoke as if she had! He shifted his eyes from one face to the other and back again.

"You shouldn't have come here," Colin repeated.

And she again held his gaze.

When a weak moan came from Hank's brother, the only sign of life since he had collapsed like a rag doll, Kaytra seized the moment and glided to him, kneeling next to his prone body. When his eyes opened, his first vision was that of the "Widow Stevens" reaching out to touch his face. He screamed first, then as quickly begged for mercy.

"Kaytra!" Colin yelled impatiently. "You're scaring the poor kid into an early grave! Would you at least get rid of the light?"

She threw Colin a fierce look even as she whipped the red scarf from the lantern she carried.

Hank's brother wasn't one bit convinced. Somehow he scrambled upright. Kaytra raised her eyes to his and held out her hand in a gesture of friendliness, only the movement was so fluid, so completely like her, that the boy was convinced she wanted his soul.

He disappeared into the night before anyone had a chance to make him stay.

Several steps away, Hank himself was dumbstruck by the sight of the hairy beast rubbing against Colin's hand without trying to tear the man limb from limb.

"You -. He-...You-."

Colin's eyebrows rose expressively. "Well, did you suddenly run out of slick words, Hank? Cat got your tongue? Or should I say, Kaytra's got your tongue?"

As Hank's nervous gaze shifted rapidly from Colin to Rex to Kaytra, Kaytra stood again, walking back to them. Now that the light was uncovered, she could see the ugly stain marring Colin's white shirt. Her bottom lip was caught between her teeth.

Colin guessed the reason for her anxiety. "It's not that bad, Kaytra."

She met his eyes, surprised when he spoke so gently to her.

But he could see more, too, now that the light was uncovered. He could see how pale she was, how she shivered despite the heavy black cloak which was tied over her shoulders. Without saying anything, he motioned Hank to his feet. The boy was considerably subdued now. "I hope you and your friends learned a lesson tonight. If I so much as catch sight of you within a mile of here, I'll wring your necks, all of you. It's a foolish, deadly stunt you're trying to pull."

Hank nodded sheepishly. He seemed much changed by the past five minutes. In a way, Colin felt sorry for him. He felt sorry for all three boys. They got more than they bargained for tonight. Kaytra herself had paid them in full, ten times over. It wasn't likely that they would set foot on the bank again. "Go on. Go home." Colin gestured in the direction the other boys had gone. "I'll keep your gun for you as a reminder of how costly messing with authority can be. I'll also trust you to tell your brother and his friend that what they thought they saw was really a girl playing make believe. There isn't any such thing as ghosts or spirits or the like. Agreed?"

After a slight delay, Hank nodded his head. Before he left, he took one last, long look at Kaytra, still uncertain who or what she was.

It seemed only seconds before the darkness had swallowed him, too, leaving Colin and Kaytra alone on the bank.

Kaytra moved first, stepping closer to Colin in order to tie the red scarf around the wound on his shoulder. He had to grit his teeth at the way it stung. When she was finished, she bent down to get his coat and the two guns. Then she simply started off in the direction of the lighthouse. Colin grabbed up the lantern she had left for him. Rex picked up the rear.

The uneasiness grew with each step. Colin had too much time to think of all the justifiable reasons he had for being upset with her. On the other hand, Kaytra could think of only one thing; if she hadn't gone to the site, Colin would be dead right now, a fact he seemed to have overlooked in his anger.

She reached the house ahead of him, having run the last hundred yards. Its warmth and lighted interior provided a brief, few seconds' haven before Colin came through the door. Neither of them looked at the other. Kaytra hung up his coat and the wool cloak she had stealthily borrowed from Lydia's room. The guns were leaned upright in a corner.

Colin went straight into the kitchen for the things he needed to clean his arm. By now, the wound throbbed painfully. Blood had soaked the thin scarf to trickle down his sleeve. Kaytra came to take the water pot from the back of the stove. For a moment, Colin wanted to refuse to give her the bowl in his hands, but the expression of stubbornness on her face outmatched his, and he set the enamel bowl on the table before slumping into the nearest chair. They both made a conscious effort to be very quiet. The last thing they wanted was for Lydia to come downstairs.

Colin stared hard at the wall. He had already made up his mind to keep silent until he could actually stand face to face with Kaytra, when she had no excuse to look away from him. He jumped a little to feel a small hand suddenly loosen the top button of his shirt. When his head swung in her direction, she calmly motioned for him to do it himself then. In seconds, he had all but ripped his shirt off. Having her touch the bare skin of his arm as she began to wipe away the blood, added further tension.

Kaytra frowned in consternation. She was only trying to help. He didn't need to be so defensive. The bullet had gouged a deep wound, but it wasn't lodged in the muscle, which was a good thing, because she wasn't at all sure she had the strength just now to dig it out.

"It needs stitches." Colin's words drained away what little color there was in her face. She pulled back sharply. "I can't do it myself, Kaytra. Go get a needle and some heavy thread."

She went with obvious reluctance and returned in the same manner, hardly daring to breathe while she set the stitches. Colin tried not to wince or show any sign of pain. As soon as she finished, Kaytra snatched up the things she had used and would have turned away except that Colin's hand suddenly closed about one of her wrists.

"Set it down, Kaytra."

Her eyes were wary of the quietness in his voice.

"I want an explanation for what happened out there. Go sit at the desk."

It wasn't a matter of choice. Some of the bloody water splashed over onto the table when she set the bowl down. Kaytra walked stiffly to the desk and sat in Colin's chair. When he came up behind her, reaching around to get paper and pen, she noticed that he had slipped into his shirt, though he hadn't taken time to button it.

"There." He spoke close to her ear. "You can start by telling me who the Widow Stevens is - or was - I should say. And -." He turned his head in Rex's direction. The dog was sprawled out on the floor. "What did you put on Rex? Starch?"

Kaytra wrote quickly.

> *"Starch would have made him stiff. It's flour. I'll give him a bath in the morning."*

"Well?" Colin demanded that she go on, adding credence to his stance by swinging around to lean against the corner of the desk, arms crossed in front of him. Because of the dim light, his tousled hair and steady eyes appeared nearly black. "The Widow Stevens?"

In Kaytra's careless anger, drops of ink made a trail from the bottle to the paper.

> *"It's only an old story. She was the young widow of a sea captain from Truro who was lost in a terrible storm. People say she used to wander the bank every night carrying a red light in silent hopes that she could find her husband."*

"Why a red light?" Colin interrupted just as if they were carrying on a real conversation.

> *"Because she knew in her heart that her husband was dead."*

"But that doesn't make any sense! If she-."

> *"She was waiting for his spirit to come back and claim her so that they could be reunited, not in life, but in death. The red light is said to be seen by those who have died and can't go on from this world because of a true love which holds them bound."*

"That's ridiculous. You don't actually believe that, do you?"

Kaytra's eyes darkened to the color of a brewing storm.

*"I never said I believed it! But it worked and you're
alive and what more explanation do you need, anyway?"*

Colin's expression was infuriatingly calm. "What happened to
her, this Widow Stevens?"

"It's only a story, Colin."

"Tell it to me."

Tense moments passed before Kaytra began writing again.

*"She started staying out on the bank for days at a time.
People rarely saw her. When they did, she ran from them.
They said her hair was uncombed and tangled. She wore
a tattered black cloak and a white dress, her wedding
gown. Someone saw her with an animal, a wolf that
was larger than any ever seen."*

"You and Rex just fit the part then, didn't you?" Colin said it too
harshly. He set his hands on the edge of the desk, gripping the wood
tightly.

"We saved your life, MacRae!"

"I had everything under control. If somebody saved anybody's
life out there, it was me saving yours. Hank's bullet was meant for
you, Kaytra."

*"Not before it was meant for you! That means we're
even."*

Kaytra dropped the pen and pushed herself away from the desk.
But before she could get up, Colin set his hands on the arms of the
chair, imprisoning her there. His closeness was intimidating.

"It doesn't mean we're even, Kaytra. It means you could have
been killed out there and how do you think that would have made me
feel?" Two months ago, he would have used Lydia's name in place of
his own. Yet all that had changed now. His eyes captured Kaytra's,
refusing to let her look away. "I won't praise you for doing something
so utterly foolish.

"God alone knows how you got out there on the edge! You aren't
indestructible, Kaytra. You're flesh and blood! Don't you care one bit

about your life that you would risk it so unnecessarily? Couldn't you have trusted my judgment for once and waited for me to come back?"

Kaytra pushed his arm aside and leaned over the paper, scribbling words haphazardly.

"There's a verse - my father - I don't -."

Her breathing became shallow with the anxiety to express what she felt.

"I can't remember it exactly. Part of it seems lost - the important part - but.... 'that a man lay down his life for a friend'."

She looked up at Colin, desperately hoping he would know what she meant.

His eyes were still fixed upon the words she had written. Something trembled deep inside of him, very much like the feeling of the butterfly wings upon his hands those many years ago. Finally, he brought his gaze to rest upon Kaytra's face. Every part of it had become familiar to him now, but not this expectant, hope-filled light which had carried so much life to her eyes.

"Go to bed, Kaytra."

She paled as if he had slapped her.

"I am not a child!"

"No? Well, you certainly didn't prove that tonight, did you?" Colin continued to stare at her, even after she turned her head away from him. He could guess that there were tears in her eyes. Tears she didn't want him to see. "No adult would go traipsing off into the dark, dressed like this Widow Stevens. No adult would have scared three young boys half to death."

Some of the fight seemed to have gone out of the way she wrote now.

"No child would have stitched up your arm."

"And I'm supposed to be grateful for that? I'm supposed to forget that you went against my orders just because you sewed me up?"

"I wasn't aware that Highland Light was a military fort, Captain MacRae!"

Colin practically threw himself off of the desk in frustration. A hand was shoved through his disheveled hair. "You deliberately twist everything I say."

Kaytra wrote slowly,

"You deliberately misunderstand me. Does that, too, make us even?"

"No!" He shouted louder than he intended, causing Kaytra to start nervously and Rex to raise his head, instantly concerned. Colin took a deep breath to gain some sense of self-control. It didn't quite seem to work. "I won't stand here all night fighting with you, Kaytra. All I want is your promise that from now on, you will do what I tell you to do."

She sat stiffly in the chair, not answering his request.

"Kaytra?" Colin sensed something, some feeling from her which he couldn't explain. All he knew was that he suddenly remembered Lydia's warning about pushing Kaytra too far. An icy fear choked him. He moved up behind her, watching every word she wrote, growing more concerned with each one.

"Lydia is well enough now that you could send for a housekeeper to come from Boston. It was a mistake for me to come here in the first place. I will leave tomorrow."

Colin tried to get her to look at him, but she pulled away sharply. "Kaytra!"

"You hate me, Colin. I will not stay here any longer."

He was too strong not to get his way. Colin lifted her from the chair until she was facing him. His eyes searched her face, but an invisible mask hid her true feelings from him. Her beauty suddenly looked cold and hard. "You might be able to shut yourself away from me, Kaytra Lange, but you will never be able to run away from me. You will not leave tomorrow. I paid Koch six months wages for you.

Do you have the money to give back should you walk out that door before the time is up?"

Her eyes hardened.

"I didn't think so. Then you aren't free to leave."

He was suddenly conscious of the fact that she still wore only her nightgown and that she was small and vulnerable next to him. He let his hands fall away from her arms.

As soon as he released her, she lifted a hand to the neck of her gown. From beneath it, she withdrew the chain which held the pearl. Without so much as blinking, she jerked savagely, causing the chain to snap in two.

In the next moment, she had taken one of Colin's hands and dropped the necklace into his palm. She didn't need paper and pen to tell him what was so clearly expressed in her eyes. The pearl had symbolized hope to her. She had said its weight held back the uncertainties...

It was true then, all was lost, and he had been the one to take it from her.

As Kaytra turned and left him, Colin's fingers closed helplessly over the tiny pearl.

Chapter Fourteen

And Jesus answering them saith unto them, 'Have faith in God. For verily I say unto you, that whosoever shall say unto this mountain, Be thou removed and be thou cast into the sea; and shall not doubt in his heart, but shall believe that those things which he saith shall come to pass; he shall have whatsoever he saith…Therefore I say unto you 'What things soever ye desire; when ye pray, believe that ye receive them and ye shall have them.'

Lydia read the words over for the tenth time in as many days. There still seemed something untouchable about them, something far beyond her reach. She laid the Bible on her lap and gazed out at the sky visible from the windows of her bedroom. "Kaytra, do you ever wonder why life should hold so many questions for which there are no real answers?"

Kaytra's hands went still upon the sheet she was folding. Her brow puckered a little. Lydia had been quiet all morning and now, to suddenly voice such a mystery-. She, too, looked out the window, as if trying to find a clue in the unbroken, dull gray.

"I suppose," Lydia went on slowly, "that God is teaching us what faith is truly all about. If He gave us all the answers, we wouldn't need Him nearly so desperately. How much more faith it must take to keep believing, just because." She turned her head until she could see Kaytra sitting on the chair near the door.

Not for the first time, she tried to picture the young woman as Colin must see her. She kept her long hair in a tightly wound bun. Every day, she dressed in the same uniforms she had sewn: a plain gray dress and crisp white apron. Lydia doubted that anything could be done to make Kaytra appear more like a servant.

But it was more than that. Things seemed to have slipped backward in time.

Kaytra no longer smiled, not even with her eyes. She hadn't written a single word since the day Colin returned from Provincetown. She never looked at them, never reached out to communicate a thought or idea. Though Lydia had tried again and again to keep her own relationship with Kaytra open, that, too, seemed to have changed. Except for the precious journal in the top drawer of her dresser, she would not know the past months had even existed.

Resting her head upon the pillow, Lydia thought about the verses she had just read. "To move a mountain". Certainly there seemed a mountain before her now. Could it be she had allowed the beginnings of doubt to seep into her prayers? Perhaps she needed to be more patient.

No, it wasn't patience He was asking of her....

"Kaytra, have you ever wanted something so very much that you hurt inside? I remember when Sidney first took Sondra away. I ached just to have my arms around her again. Sometimes I thought I wouldn't be able to stand the loneliness, not knowing how she was, what she was doing, what she looked like."

Lydia sighed tenderly, "I prayed and prayed with all my heart to have her back in my arms, but God never answered that prayer. He kept telling me, 'Trust me, Lydia. Trust me to put My arms around her for you'. Do you know," she waited until Kaytra's hands were still and she knew that she was listening, "that was the hardest thing I've ever had to do, to trust God to take care of Sondra. I knew He could do a much better job than I could, but the letting go - that was the most difficult."

For the next few minutes, while Lydia was quietly reflecting on her own thoughts, Kaytra finished folding the sheets and clothes and put them away. She would have left then except that Lydia stopped her at the door, "Is Colin still gone, dear?"

Kaytra nodded without looking up. Colin had left a note on the table earlier, saying he would be riding Samson along the north bank to make sure no ships had run aground in yesterday's storm.

"Why don't you make some tea then, and hold dinner until he comes home. Bring two cups, won't you? Spend some time with me."

Again, Kaytra gave a slight nod. Then she slipped out the door.

Guilt chased her down the stairs. She knew what Lydia wanted to say: that she missed their old friendship. Try as she could to put such regret from her mind, it kept resurfacing. Kaytra blinked back tears as she began to set the tray for tea. Seeing two cups reminded her of the earlier kinship she had shared with Lydia. She knew it was her own doing which had made those special times mere memories.

No, not only her doing, but Colin MacRae's, too. Hadn't he forced her into pulling back? Hadn't he made it impossible to continue on here as if she could ever be more in their lives than a hired servant? Even though her position here was safer than being in Provincetown, it certainly wasn't any less painful. At first she thought it might be, but those hopes had soon faded.

Some of the hot water from the kettle splashed onto her hand, causing new tears to flood her eyes. She quickly wiped them away and finished filling the china pot. So many things made her cry lately, but none of them seemed worth the tears. Her life didn't seem worth such a strong emotion as "silent self-pity", Colin's own choice of words.

While the tea brewed, she arranged half a dozen crisp sugar cookies on a plate. Maybe they would tempt Lydia to eat something. She had barely touched her breakfast. For that matter, Colin hadn't eaten anything at all, not unless he packed something for himself. Kaytra moved the pot of stew she had made for dinner to a cooler place on the stove so that it would stay warm without burning.

The weight of the tray seemed twice as heavy today. Kaytra held more tightly to the silvered edges on her way up the stairs. She had left the door open. It swung in now with a small push from her elbow. When her entrance made the cups rattle a little in their saucers, Kaytra felt an inward cringe. Lydia's eyes were closed. What to do now? Surely she shouldn't awaken her.

Unconsciously, Kaytra bit down on her lip. How very peaceful Lydia looked in her sleep. The shawl Colin had given her made a perfect frame for her long brown hair. There were no lines of worry or concern upon her face. Peaceful. She hadn't set her Bible aside. One slim hand still lay on the open pages. Very quietly, Kaytra set the tray down on top of the dresser, then she moved to the bed to make Lydia more comfortable.

Within inches of touching the Bible, a sudden fear gripped her heart A cold, heavy hand stole her breath. Lydia?.....Only when she began to feel dizzy did Kaytra remember to breathe. Yet she still waited. Waited for some sign of life.

Oh, dear God. No! Kaytra's hands flew to Lydia's shoulders, shaking her a little, but Lydia's head rolled lifelessly to the side, her pale color becoming even more evident now that Kaytra knew she was indeed gone.

Kaytra stumbled back from the bed, unable to tear her gaze away from Lydia's face. Only minutes ago, Lydia had been talking, asking about Colin and-. Colin! Kaytra whirled around and ran from the room.

Outside, she faced a rising panic. She was completely alone! Colin was still miles away! And Lydia was dead! Dead! The word hit her so hard it drove her to an abrupt standstill at the bottom of the tower.

The bell! Wooden, halting steps brought her to it. She actually reached out and held the rope in her hand before she realized what she was about to do. No, she couldn't use it. Colin had forbidden her to use it unless he was hurt.

Each time she felt her own heart pound against her chest, it made her more aware that Lydia's heart had suddenly quit beating. Kaytra felt a sob well up from within. The tears which had been so close to the surface these past several days could no longer be held back. She pulled down on the rope...again and again and again. The sound she had once imagined would be joyful was instead an empty death knell. Sobs tore at her whole body. It was wrong that Lydia had died. Wrong! Wrong! Wrong!

It couldn't be true! But there wasn't any escaping the lifelessness-.

No, Kaytra! She heard the scream inside her head and knew she mustn't think any more. Over and over, she rang the bell. Lydia is dead. Lydia is dead. Dead....dead.....dead...

Each stroke, each deep, hollow bong repeated the word. Kaytra collapsed against one of the posts supporting the bell and continued to pull down until her hand grew raw where the rough rope rubbed her flesh. Dead...dead....dead...

Thirty long, agonizing minutes after he had first heard the sound of the bell, Colin raced within sight of the tower. Samson, lathered with sweat from being driven so hard over the loose sand, sped forward still, sensing a new urgency in his master's hands upon the reins. Finally, Colin pulled him to a stop and slid out of the saddle, running the last few yards.

Not until he jerked her away from the bell did Kaytra seem to realize he was even there. She wouldn't be standing except that he held her upright. His heart froze to see the blank devastation imbedded in the depth of her eyes. "Kaytra! What-?"

A weak moan escaped her parted lips, but no more. She wanted to tell him. Oh, how she wanted to tell him! Of their own accord, her hands dug into the material of his coat.

"Dear God." Realization swept the questions from his eyes. "Lydia." He was already racing toward the house. Already gone.

Kaytra followed him more slowly, drained to the very core of her being. She knew she would never forget the look on his face. Not as long as she lived. Inside the house again, Rex went to his usual place on the rug by Colin's chair. Kaytra weakly propelled herself up the stairs, one long step at a time, pausing just outside the open door to Lydia's room.

Colin was seated on the chair near the bed, holding one of Lydia's hands between his own larger ones. As if sensing her presence at the door, he turned his head to look at her. For the first time since the night of the mooncussers, she didn't glance away when their eyes met.

The words he spoke chilled her as much as the closed expression in his eyes. "I don't want you here."

She was too deeply in shock to hide her own grief from him; to hide the hurt his rejection brought.

Colin's eyes grew dark. "I told you to leave."

Kaytra backed away, turning at last to run down the stairs and out through the door, letting the wind slam it shut behind her.

Seth and Anna arrived a few minutes later, driving their wagon to the barn where Kaytra was trying to get Samson inside. She turned to face them in confusion, then realized that they would have heard the bell and come to help. With a quick leap, Seth was on the ground and moving toward her. "Kaytra! What's goin' on? Is it Colin"? Is he huaht?"

Kaytra struggled to shake her head.

Anna joined them, noting the white strain on the young woman's face. "It's Lydia then?" The question came softly, making Kaytra want to throw herself into the comfort of Anna's arms. Instead, she only nodded.

The older couple exchanged an anxious glance, speaking a hundred words with one look. They had expected something terrible, but surely not this. Seth gently reached out and took Samson's bridle from Kaytra's unsteady hands. "Has she - died then, lass?"

Kaytra's blue-gray eyes misted over with tears. Yes. Lydia was dead.

"Wheahe's Colin? In the house?"

Yes, but he didn't want anyone with him. Kaytra tried to spare them the pain she had just endured, but the words wouldn't come and neither Seth nor Anna quite understood what her expression meant.

Anna took charge then, gathering Kaytra close with one arm around her shoulders. "Come, deah. You shouldn' be out in this cold without a jacket. We'll be in the house, Seth. You cen take cahe o' the hoahse?"

He agreed with a sad nod. It didn't take long before he got the horse inside the barn and began unhooking the saddle and reins. What a tragedy. Lydia had been so young. Poor Kaytra seemed in shock herself. She must have been alone then. From the looks of Samson, Colin had ridden him hard and no wonder; the steady, agonized tolling of the bell had been enough to alarm anyone. The pieces started falling together to create a disturbing picture.

Though Colin was grateful for the quiet, unquestioning support which Seth and Anna gave him, there remained an emptiness in him, one he couldn't share with the Buckley's. For now, he simply reacted automatically, doing what needed to be done, making decisions.

His parents would want Lydia to be buried at the family plot in Boston. There wasn't really a choice, only the necessary arrangements to make. He would take Lydia to Provincetown and see that the coffin was safely aboard the first ship to the mainland. It was out of the question for him to accompany her all the way. There wasn't a replacement for him here.

As it stood, he might have to be gone overnight to complete the arrangements, but Kaytra knew how to keep the light going. He supposed she could handle one night. He wouldn't feel right leaving for any longer than that and he absolutely refused Seth's offer to stay. It would be a hardship for the rest of the Buckley family to be without Seth for even that short time.

While Colin and Seth worked together at making a coffin, Anna and Kaytra silently bathed Lydia and dressed her in the soft rose dress. Of necessity, Anna had laid out people many times. In stark contrast, the only other person Kaytra had even seen dead before had been her mother. Memories kept pushing in on her until she sank down into the chair Colin had occupied an hour earlier, her gaze fixed upon Lydia's face.

"I guess Lydia was like a sisteah to ya'." Anna's soft-spoken voice was like a soothing balm. "I would wish ta know heah betteah myself. She seemed so kind when we'd come ta visit, always like she was happy ta just sit an' talk. Last time we was heahe, she talked an awful lot 'bout you, Kaytra. I could tell she thought good 'bout you."

Kaytra forced her lips to stop trembling by pursing them into a tight line. Ever so gently, she swept the hair back from Lydia's forehead just as she had done so many times before. Anna was deeply touched by the gesture. "Don't grieve foah heah, child. She knowed the Loahd. Ain't no place betteah ta be than with Him."

There wasn't any kind of response from Kaytra.

"We should see ta makin' a linin' foah the casket now."

The two women left Lydia's room to go downstairs. It was a shame, Anna thought, that Kaytra couldn't speak out her feelings. What a heavy burden for one so young to bear.

Evening had moved in on the horizon by the time Seth and Anna left. Kaytra prepared a meal for Colin, though she wasn't surprised that most of it remained untouched. Shortly afterward, Colin went back outside and didn't return until Kaytra had gone to her room.

She lay in bed, listening to the sound of his restless movements. Finally, he walked up the stairs. Instead of going into his own bedroom, he went into Lydia's. A sad brokenness settled over Kaytra, causing her to pull the blankets closer.

Sleep that night, was hardly more than a constant tossing and turning away from the nightmares. When she opened her eyes, it was to find that the black patch of sky outside her window was just beginning to lighten into a gray morning. Because her thoughts were of Lydia, as she dressed, she found herself fumbling over the most ordinary tasks. Somehow, the buttons would not fit into their holes and her hair tangled painfully with the brush. Oh dear, dear Lydia. Why did God have to take her now? It seemed completely unfair.

For a long time after she went downstairs, Kaytra stood at the front door, looking out at the ocean. She did not even hear Colin come up behind her.

"Kaytra."

With one hand pressed to where her heart pounded in her chest, she turned to face him. He was dressed in his uniform. Every part of his appearance added an aloofness to the tone of his voice. Except for the dark circles beneath his eyes, he looked quite the same, acted quite in control.

He gave her brief instructions on what to do while he was gone. "Do you have any questions?" Her silence had never seemed so full before. There was nothing left to say then. Colin reached for his cape on the hook beside her.

His action seemed to release Kaytra and she moved toward the stairs on legs which betrayed the weakness she tried to hide. At Lydia's room, she took in a ragged breath before opening the door. Something inside of her collapsed at the sight of the empty bed. At once, she whirled away from the door to face Colin, who now stood at the bottom of the stairs.

"I've moved her already," he said evenly. "There wasn't any reason to wait."

Kaytra clung to the top of the railing until her hand became white. No reason! She wanted to say goodbye, to see her friend one last time.

Colin stared hard at her a moment longer before he abruptly turned and left the house.

How could he? The question sounded hollow in her ears. How could he?

This trip into Provincetown was so different from the last one. As soon as Colin walked into the store, Jolly knew something wasn't right. It was Jolly who found a ship sailing for Boston within an hour of Colin's arrival. The letter which Colin had written to his mother and father the night before was given to the captain who kindly offered to take care of the matter himself.

As the *Tremaine* pulled anchor, Colin stood on the dock beside Jolly. He had never imagined this moment, never imagined sending a stranger to tell his parents that Lydia was gone. They would be crushed. He should be on that ship. He should be there to comfort them, to help them bury her.

But he couldn't go. Not now. God knew the circumstances. The choice had not been made easily. Perhaps someday, Colin would understand God's reasons for taking Lydia home. Today, he simply felt empty.

It took very little effort for Jolly to persuade Colin that he should rest awhile before he made the return trip to Highland Light. Colin drank cup after cup of strong, black coffee, very much needing the sustenance it poured into him. Neither man talked much. There were no words to take away the loss.

By the time Colin headed Samson out of town, the clouds were thickening overhead. He would be fortunate to make it home before it started to rain. Already the air was damp. Colin drew the collar of his coat higher against his neck and urged the horse to a quicker pace.

Even though it was still afternoon, the lighthouse beam was clearly visible across the distance. He wasn't surprised Kaytra had done what he said and turned the light on when the encroaching clouds made it necessary. She always did as she was told now. He hated it. The only signs of life he had seen in her since the night of the moooncussers were yesterday's shocked disbelief and the torn anger he had caused her earlier that morning.

Colin gripped the reins tightly, refusing to be any more honest than that. He didn't wan't to examine the "why's" behind his actions. All he wanted was to be home again.

Home - it was never going to be the same again. Though he had accepted the possibility of Lydia's death years ago, dealing with it now was another matter. He was starting to hurt, starting to feel the edges of grief seep into his heart. The long ride back had given him too much time to think, time to remember every detail which yesterday had been so unclear.

Had Lydia known she was so near to death?

Yes, he could see now that she had. The long talks they shared the past few nights weren't mere chance. Her thoughts about Sondra, the way she kept asking him to talk about the wonderful times they spent together as children. She had known her time was close.

Looking back now, he could see that he had been too blind to understand any of it. A new pain was added to the others. He may not have been able to change the fact that she had died, but at least he could have been there for her when she needed him most.

He couldn't remember ever being as tired as he was when he finally climbed down from the wagon. His body was a mass of numbness and aching pain. As soon as he had Samson unharnessed, he took the horse to the barn. It struck him as odd that he could hear Rex barking from inside.

When Colin opened the door, he expected the dog to rush out at him. Instead, he found Rex chained to one of the large posts supporting the roof. The dog, who was alert and tense, only ceased his barking when Colin began talking to him. "Settle down, old boy. What are you doing in here anyway?" Rex strained at the chain, wanting to be let loose, but Colin had other things to do first.

Samson seemed glad to be in his own stall again. Colin fed him and gave him a quick rubdown. By the time he was done, Rex was pacing between Colin and the open door to the very limit of his chain. It was clear he wanted to be outside, yet Kaytra must have had a reason for chaining him there. Colin thought it best to find out from her what that reason was before he simply let Rex go.

Rex did not agree. He sent out a new din the moment Colin walked out of the barn.

Each step he took seemed to sharpen his senses, forcing away the weariness. The great light of Highland Lighthouse was on, but the house itself was dark. Kaytra had never chained Rex before, not once since bringing him here. Where was she that she wouldn't want Rex to follow?

A new uneasiness caused Colin to fling the back door of the house open as soon as he reached it. "Kaytra?"

Silence answered him. Complete, empty silence. He knew instinctively that she wasn't there. The tower? No. She wouldn't have gone there either. The truth of what she had done, where she had gone, slammed hard against him, shattering his control for a long, agonized moment. No....No!

Colin retraced his steps to the barn at a dead run, skidding to a stop next to Rex. His strong fingers made short work of the heavy clasp. "Go find her, boy!"

Rex raced first to the house, running around there in apparent confusion until Colin caught up with him. Then the dog suddenly picked up his head, listening intently.

The only sounds Colin could hear were the wind buffeting the house and the ocean roaring as it picked up strength....

South. Rex turned and ran south, following closely along the bank.

Chapter Fifteen

"Kaytra!" The wind flung her name back at him as Colin tore down the bank. Adrenalin pumped fire through his limbs. Racing half a mile along the shore wasn't the sole cause for the wild beating of his heart. "Kaytra!"

Though she must have heard him this time, she struggled out into deeper water, fighting frantically for each step, the black of her dress a stain against the angry, gray water.

While Rex stopped short of the water, Colin plunged in after her. The icy water shocked his system as much as her intent. He would not let her kill herself. Dear God! He wouldn't! Yet if she made it out to the floodtide, she would be swept away in an instant. "Kaytra!"

She glanced over her shoulder at him, eyes wild and desperate, but she didn't stop.

If it was fear which made her strong enough to resist the pull of the undercurrent, that same fear made Colin even stronger. When he lunged toward her, the weight of his body carried them both under. Colin regained his footing first, reaching for Kaytra as she struggled.

The next wave pushed them toward shore, then selfishly snatched them out again. Salt water stung Kaytra's eyes, choked her when she swallowed.

"Don't fight me," Colin yelled above the moan of the sea, dragging her behind him as he headed for safety.

But she broke away, going down again in almost the same moment.

Colin was beside her the instant she resurfaced. He grabbed Kaytra by the shoulders, digging painfully into her tender flesh. Water ran down her pale face. Her lips were blue with cold. "You - won't - win - this - time!" Even as he said the words, Colin felt her go rigid beneath his touch. He pushed her back to shore, catching her each time she stumbled.

Just a few feet from where Rex stood, with water still reaching up to her waist, she whirled around to face Colin with eyes that begged him just to let her go, to let her finish what she had begun. Colin stood solidly in her path, his hair and clothes plastered to his body. No, he *would not* let her go back.

When her begging look changed to fury, he was ready for the fists she flailed at him. Wrenching sobs robbed her attack of any real strength. Colin easily caught her wrists until she collapsed against him. Had it not been for his arms around her, the sea would yet have claimed its victim for she lost all consciousness. Her world went completely black.

By the time he carried Kaytra home and laid her on the bed in Lydia's room, she was chilled through, her temperature dangerously low. Only a thin, thready pulse beat against the fingers he placed at her wrist.

The storm surging around Highland was nothing compared to his emotions. For the next twenty-four hours, Colin fought anger and desperation and doubt to take care of her until, finally, there was nothing more to do except wait. His eyes burned with fatigue. His body ached. He sat back in the rocking chair near the bed, letting his eyes stray over her still form, then back to her face.

Color stained her cheeks, unnaturally so. The fever had begun two hours ago. Colin released a tense sigh. None of this should have happened! Surely Kaytra knew that taking her own life went against God's Word. Surely she knew -. Something twisted inside his gut. Who was he to assume what Kaytra knew about God? He, who had turned away from the responsibilities God set out for him, who had neglected her salvation these past weeks! God forgive him for standing in the way of her coming to know the truth.

As soon as she was well again, he would show her in the Bible how precious she was in God's sight. Just as soon as she was well....Colin listened to the rhythm of his rocking chair upon the wood floor for a long time before finally allowing himself to sleep.

It took Colin a few moments to realize that the voice he heard wasn't part of a dream. He shrugged off the remnants of sleep, focusing still weary eyes upon Kaytra. The obvious sign of pain on her face caused instant alarm and he moved to sit beside her on the bed. She was tossing her head restlessly from side to side.

As he had done so many times to Lydia, Colin brushed the hair away from her cheek and forehead. "Kaytra?" At once, her eyes opened, but he wasn't sure she knew him. She didn't seem focused on him. He reached over to the bedstand and dipped a cloth in the bowl of water there.

When the coolness of it touched her heated skin, she gasped, trying to pull away by pressing herself deeper into the mattress. "Shhhh." Colin spoke gently to soothe her confusion. She looked so young, so vulnerable. "It's alright, Kaytra. You're very sick. This will help."

While she drifted in and out of sleep, Colin continued to bathe her face. Would she speak again? Maybe her struggle between choosing life or death held the key. Maybe now she would be able to break free from the bond of fear. When he was certain that she would rest awhile, he went to clean the lamps in readiness for another long night.

Hours passed. Colin saw no improvement. If anything, Kaytra became worse. The fever drained her body of energy. He was sure that she knew neither who he was nor where she was.

Just when he began to pray for her, he couldn't say, but once he did, he never stopped. Beyond prayer, all he could do was watch her lying there. Sob-like moans escaped her parched lips whenever he touched the cloth to her brow. At times, she would stare wildly at him.

Other times, she was too weak to open her eyes. One heartbeat... Colin knew a single heartbeat could separate her from this life.

God alone gave him strength. It was too soon after Lydia's death for Colin to feel any strength of his own. If Kaytra died -. No, he couldn't let her die. He couldn't. God would hear his prayers. Colin knew he needed God now, perhaps in a way that he had never needed Him before.

In order to keep his body busy while his thoughts were so much on Kaytra, Colin began to pack away Lydia's clothes. The trunk he carried into the room was the same one his sister had unpacked eight short months earlier. In a way, it seemed a lifetime ago, so much had changed. Colin emptied the armoire first, carefully folding everything inside it except the towels and wash cloths.

The scent of Lydia's lilac water floated up to him when he lifted the bottle from the shelf. With some surprise, he found the simple action of handling his sister's things to be healing for him. The faith they had shared made it possible to hope. And hope in itself was stronger than any amount of grief. He would miss her dearly, but he hadn't lost her completely. Not as long as he held on to the promise of being with her again one day in heaven.

When he first discovered the journal in the top drawer, he felt a quickening in his spirit. The writing inside was Kaytra's. His eyes sought out her face upon the pillow, then slowly returned to the book in his hands. Should he read it? Why hadn't Lydia mentioned its existence to him? Colin set it on the dresser unopened. Its presence there remained a constant question as he finished cleaning out the drawers.

Once the trunk was full, he took it out onto the landing. Later, he would put it away in the attic. Below him, the clock in the parlor gently sounded eight bells - past time for supper. He made sure Kaytra was asleep before going down to the kitchen.

Throughout the day, he had kept both the cooking stove and the parlor stove blazing with fire. The weather had turned colder; winter wasn't far away. One morning soon he would awake to find snow blanketing the ground.

Rex hungrily gobbled down the leftover stew Colin placed in a dish on the floor. For himself, Colin settled on a piece of cheese and bread. It wasn't very tasty, but at least it would give him some nourishment. He was more concerned that Kaytra hadn't eaten anything.

A quick survey of the pantry produced very few options suitable for one so ill. What she needed was some broth. First thing in the morning, he would butcher one of the hens. He closed the pantry door again and had barely turned around when he heard a heart-stopping cry.

Kaytra!

Colin took the steps in great leaps, gaining the top in seconds. Inside the bedroom he found her cowering against the headboard. "Kaytra." Though he kept his tone calm, the fever had risen now, causing delirium to plague her with terrifying visions. Her hands pushed desperately at his when he reached out to touch her.

"It's alright, Kaytra. I won't hurt you."

Like a cornered animal, she knew only to seek escape.

Colin caught her before she actually tumbled off the bed, pinning her arms down with his hands. Her absolute terror at being forced into stillness stunned him, but Colin couldn't let go, not even when she slipped into unconsciousness again. What, in the name of heaven, had been done to her? He recoiled from the possibilities running through his mind. Perhaps there was a way to know for sure.

In a few strides, he was at the dresser, grabbing the journal. He fairly threw himself into the rocker then, already well into the first page. Lydia must have asked Kaytra to write about her parents, about her mother and Everette Koch. There were no surprises in the honesty with which she expressed her feelings.

The next page caught and held his complete attention. Kaytra had written it sometime on her birthday, after Lydia had given her the pearl necklace.

"I shall never wear it without being reminded of you."

He remembered then, with perfect clarity, how he had accused her that same night of disappointing Lydia. It wouldn't have mattered to his sister. Lydia wasn't the kind of person who made demands, who asked that her efforts be appreciated. What confused him most was knowing that he wasn't that kind of person either. But no one else had caused this kind of uncharacteristic change in him. Kissing Kaytra that night had proved as much.

On the pages which followed, he read how bewildered Kaytra was because of his words and actions. He was reading Kaytra's side of some very intimate, very telling conversations with Lydia...

> *"I want to understand, Lydia. I have tried to understand. But it makes no sense to me. Am I such an awful person? I suppose I must be for all that has befallen me. How can one live in a world of pain and hatred and lies and not be consumed by them? Even if I could become the person Colin wished me to be, he would be disappointed to find there are yet those things which may never be changed."*

Disappointed? He glanced at her. Of all the feelings he felt, none of them was disappointment. The pages rustled quietly, revealing more of Kaytra's thoughts to him....

> *"It scares me sometimes that I want my life to neither tumble backward nor rush forward. The moment I would choose it to be was the morning of my birthday when I walked alone along the bank. The storm was completely over. I felt the gentle breath of the wind, all of life hanging upon the promise of a new beginning. The colors were vivid, somehow touchable. The birds sang for me. The sea danced with me. The day waited for me and I wanted it all to stay that way forever....Forever is such a place, isn't it Lydia?"*

> *"He hates me!"*

The words leapt at Colin as soon as he turned the page.

*"No, Lydia. It is true. I have lived the past few years
seeing people look at me in that same way. None of them
knew me, the real me. Colin doesn't know me either.
What hurts the most is when all my pretending otherwise fails and I am forced to admit that it does matter
after all. In Provincetown, I used to wait for darkness
to come so that I could go outside and not make anyone
uncomfortable because I was near them. Here at Highland, there isn't anywhere to hide. I am so tired of merely
existing, but to live, to really live, can hurt so very
much."*

Colin wasn't sure what Lydia would have said to Kaytra after
she had written those words. It was true that he hadn't been very gentle
with Kaytra sometimes, but he had never hated her. The expressions
she may have seen on his face could in no way be compared to what
the people in Provincetown felt. For some reason, though, Kaytra had
believed there wasn't a difference and so she had called it hatred.

The next page was stained with tears. Some of the words were
blurred. Colin clenched the book more tightly as he read....

*"I'm not sure I know what that verse means, Lydia.
Strength and courage are feelings Colin would know;
for me, fear and dismay. I can imagine that your brother
is very much like this man Joshua. But it does scare me,
Lydia. Sometimes I feel as if I will never know what it
is to be loved. There is so much inside of me, so many
things I want to tell him, but he will not listen because
he believes I am unwilling to let God change my heart.
Oh, things about Highland. How it seems so perfect
that it faces the beginning of each day in the eastern
sunrise and that - when the sun sets - it is but a reflection upon the sea because all of our yesterdays are behind us. We are meant to remember the beauty they
hold while keeping our eyes fixed upon the tomorrows
ahead."*

*"I have never had a brother to care for me as Colin cares
for you. No, please do not cry. You see, now I am teary-
eyed, also. I would want to tell Colin I see something*

*precious, something wonderfully binding in the way
he takes your hand at times just to hold it in his own,
just to be that near to you. He loves you deeply, Lydia,
in a way that reminds me of how little earthly things
matter when such eternal bonds are ours.....I am not
sure."*

It ended there. Abruptly. He raised his eyes, fixing them upon the familiar curve of Kaytra's face. Colin wanted to know what question his sister had asked. He wanted to know how Kaytra could possibly have described Highland in exactly the way he saw it. But what he most wanted to know was why Kaytra had linked her heartfelt desire to be loved with the very mention of his name. What had Lydia been talking to her about?

He was able to close the book, but not to block out these new thoughts. The light needed to be checked one more time for the night. When he got back, he would finish reading the journal. There were many pages left.

Something cool and wet touched her lips. They felt tender, but she was so thirsty she didn't want to pull away. As consciousness returned, she opened her eyes. Slowly because of the daylight. No, it wasn't daylight. She tried to focus. Things were so blurry. The lamp threw shadows all about her.

It seemed as if her body was a lead weight, heavy, sinking. The thought alarmed her, causing her to stiffen against the mattress. She remembered that she had been in the water, but-. Colin, was he there, too?

He pressed the damp cloth to her lips again. "Good morning, Kaytra." There was some relief in his voice that she was awake again, that she saw him this time. Really saw him.

She parted her lips involuntarily as if she would speak, but a confused look clouded her eyes and she closed her mouth again.

"Are you thirsty?"

When Kaytra nodded slightly, he reached out to pour her a glass of water from the pitcher on the table beside the bed. As he turned back to her, he saw the tremulous movement of her hand as she brought it to rest on the slight rounding of her belly. "The baby is fine, Kaytra. It's been moving quite a bit."

Involuntarily, her eyes pooled with tears, then, just as quickly, rounded with shock. He knew! She felt a tumbling in her heart. He knew. All at once the realization swept in upon Kaytra that she was in Lydia's room. In Lydia's bed wearing one of Lydia's too-large, clean white nightgowns. She was here only because Colin had stopped her from drowning herself. He didn't let her do it, even when she fought him.

Kaytra closed her eyes tightly, wishing that the memories would stop flooding into her mind. She had been very sick and-.

Two strong hands came under her shoulders, lifting her until she was half-sitting against the pillows. Kaytra met Colin's gaze apprehensively, but he didn't say a word, didn't demand to know everything as she had imagined he would. He brought the glass to her lips so that she could drink some of the water. She winced at the raw feeling in her throat as she tried to swallow. "Take it slowly. You haven't had anything to eat or drink for a couple of days."

A couple of days? Her eyes showed a childlike bewilderment that made Colin smile. "It's November 3rd. You've been sick since the day I went to Provincetown."

Since the day after Lydia died. Kaytra shrank from the thought, turning her face away from him, but not before he saw signs of her grief. Colin set the glass back onto the table.

"Look at me, Kaytra. Please." The concern in his voice matched the gentle touch of his hand as he guided her chin upward to bring her eyes level with his again. It was as if he knew her thoughts. "I won't ask any questions. Not until I know you're stronger, until you're ready for them, but I have to say this; if you're hurting because Lydia is gone, don't turn away from me. She was my sister, my best friend. You're only hiding pain I already feel myself."

Kaytra brought a hand to her trembling lips. Ever so tenderly, Colin pulled her close into the circle of his arms. He held her there while she cried, his hand cradled against the back of her head, smoothing the soft, thickness of her hair.

She must have slept then. A feeling of hours having passed caused some confusion when she again opened her eyes. Slowly, Kaytra turned her head. The rocker near the bed was empty. Where was he now? After listening for a few lonely moments, Kaytra knew he must be downstairs, sitting at his desk, for she could hear his chair move upon the floor. What would Colin write in his journal today? She looked toward the windows, seeking the answer there.

This, then, was the view Lydia must have memorized all the months she had spent lying in bed. Oh, Lydia.... Kaytra felt a strong need to be with her again, to gain strength and peace from listening to Lydia talk. A single tear slipped down Kaytra's cheek. More blurred her impression of the tower as it stood just outside the tall windows. She could not see all of it, only the gentle white walls silhouetted against a cloudy gray sky. To think of how the lighthouse rose so far into the sky somehow made Kaytra feel incredibly small and fragile.

Beyond the lighthouse, there was a glimpse of the ocean. Today, the waves rolled into one another, becoming lost. How very far one could see from here. Perhaps Lydia was now in a place just at the edge of the horizon. Perhaps heaven wasn't really so far away after all. Certainly, Lydia had spoken of heaven as being wonderful. To Kaytra the idea held a sense of mystery, of something cloaked in gossamer to make it beautiful, but still untouchable.

A feeling of grief stole over Kaytra so suddenly then, she didn't have time to escape its pain. Anna had told her the best place to be was with the Lord. Why then had God made her stay behind in this world, in this place which held no real future for her? How much easier it would have been to slip under the deep, black water.

It seemed as if every ounce of grief she had never been able to feel for her father and mother was now combined with the emptiness left by Lydia's passing. In her weakened state, it threatened to tear Kaytra's heart in two. Why? Why was she left behind with so many uncertainties? Could she not have been happy in Heaven? Could she not have seen her father again and been with Lydia? Did she have to-.

A movement near the doorway drew Kaytra's attention. For one moment, when Colin's eyes met hers from across the room, she sensed his indecision. Whatever caused it, though, must have been thrown aside, because he quickly came to her. He sat down on the bed and gathered her hands into the warmth of his own. There was a silent searching of her eyes before he finally spoke. "You can't let her go, can you?"

Kaytra wasn't surprised any more by the way he could so exactly know her thoughts. She moved her head upon the pillow until it lay at an appealing, childlike angle.

"Is that why you tried to -." The words lodged tightly in Colin's throat, forcing him to begin again. "Is that why you wanted to die, Kaytra?"

She didn't have an answer for him. Those thoughts, those feelings still seemed all mixed-up. When Colin looked down at their hands, Kaytra did, too. One of his thumbs began to gently trace the line of veins running toward her wrist.

"Do you remember the day we went out along the bank, when we picked bayberries and found where the mooncusser's pole was set by the cliffs?"

Kaytra's eyes clouded with the memory.

"I was wrong that day," Colin said softly.

The measure of regret in his voice dazed Kaytra, took her already uneven breaths and made them catch in a painful way.

He raised his eyes to her face. "I was wrong to let you leave without explaining what God was saying to me. All this time, I was wrong to think you only had to open your eyes and you would see God, you would see Him working in your life. It's not always that easy."

As he spoke, the words calmed Kaytra's earlier sorrow. She didn't understand why he should be telling her this, but it felt right to have so much honesty between them for a change.

"There's something I've never said to anyone before. I know Lydia told you about Sidney Kent, but there's so much more, Kaytra, so many things I kept from her to protect her." He saw the slight confusion in Kaytra's eyes. "Sidney's lies affected me, too. They stole away some of my trust. They - he made it hard for me to see things as anything more than black and white. Do you understand that, Kaytra? Do you understand what I'm saying?"

One shoulder was lifted slightly off the bed, but it was more a gesture of wanting to believe, than of really understanding.

Colin tightened his hold, feeling a need to open his heart to her now. "Life can't only be black and white. It can't only be filled with definite choices and ordered emotions. There has to be room for bending and accepting, for having compassion. I was wrong about you, Kaytra. I wasn't willing to help you find the peace you've been seeking, because I couldn't see past what I thought kept you from making a commitment to God."

When he began to move from the bed, Kaytra felt a sensation of disappointment, but he only went as far as the dresser where he picked up his worn Bible before returning. This time, he sat down next to her with his back against the headboard in order that she might see the verses he wanted to show her.

"Did your father ever tell you about Jesus, Kaytra?"

The quiet question caused her emotions to tumble for a moment. She remembered bits and pieces of those childhood talks, but not enough to erase the uncertainty from her blue-gray eyes.

Colin had to swallow hard. He couldn't fail her again. He couldn't fail God again. If Kaytra noticed how his hands shook in holding the Bible, she didn't let on. Finally, he found the passage of Scripture he wanted. "One of Jesus' followers wrote this after Jesus died on the cross. 'For He is our peace, who hath made both one, and hath broken down the middle wall of partition between us.'"

Kaytra tilted her head to meet Colin's eyes.

"I want that wall between us to come down, Kaytra."

She nodded that she very much wanted the same.

The beginning of a smile crossed Colin's mouth. It felt natural somehow to Kaytra when he slipped his arm around behind her, supporting her, drawing her a little closer. "Let me show you more. Let me show you Jesus." He felt her nod against his shoulder.

Colin turned backwards to the book of John. "See here, how it says, 'And the light shineth in darkness; and the darkness comprehended it not.' It's like the lighthouse, Kaytra. Jesus came to be a light in this world, to save people who were living in darkness, but some of the people didn't know how to look for the light and let it guide them to safety. Your father knew how. I'm sure he did."

A wondering expression softened the signs of sickness upon Kaytra's face.

"But it isn't enough just to find the Light either," Colin explained gently. "You have to trust in it, too. Captain Henry Lange must have learned how to do that. He learned how to trust the light to bring him through the darkness. I was just a boy when I heard about Jesus being the Light, but it has stuck with me ever since.

"Here, this is another verse. In Psalm 119." He let her read it her-self.

> *"Thy word is a lamp unto my feet and a light unto my path."*

Just for a moment, Kaytra closed her eyes and Colin tightened his arm around her, thinking she felt too weak to go on, but when she looked up at him, her eyes were filled with new tears. "Did Lydia tell you that verse?"

She could only nod her head a little.

"It's so true, Kaytra. The path God had planned for Lydia brought her right up to heaven. He planned for her to go there. But not you. Not right now."

Kaytra trembled, sinking a little against Colin's side in remembering those awful moments down at the ocean, when she had so desperately wanted to die.

"I-. I found this while you were sleeping."Colin turned to the marker he had placed in Deuteronomy and read in a voice husky with emotion. " 'I call heaven and earth to record this day against you, that I have set before you life and death, blessing and cursing: therefore choose life, that both thou and thy seed may live: that thou mayest love the Lord thy God, and that thou mayest obey His voice and may cleave unto Him: for He is thy life.'

"The choice is yours, Kaytra, but you have to know it's more than what happened out there in the ocean. It's choosing the life God has for you. It's putting yourself in His care and knowing you have eter-nal life."

Very slowly, Kaytra laid one of her hands over one of Colin's. She wanted to know more. Colin felt her need. Had Captain Henry Lange lived, he would have been the one to lead his daughter to the Lord. The thought brought a certain awe into Colin's eyes.

He let the Bible close again. This he would do with the words hidden in his heart. "Jesus loves you, Kaytra. More than anything, you have to know that. He came to be your Light."

In her eyes, Colin could see the question, "But I am the town Dummy, how could he love even me?"

"Christ looks upon the heart, Kaytra, at the inward person. He died on the cross that all who reach out in genuine faith might be changed by His sacrifice."

With what little strength she had, Kaytra sat upright until she was facing him. Her eyes held an expectancy which tugged at his heart more powerfully than anything he had felt before. Yet Colin waited a moment, praying for the right words to say. "We can't even begin to comprehend that kind of love, Kaytra, but it is very, very real. If it's what you want, all you have to do is ask and He will give it to you. All you have to do is believe in the Light. You have to choose life, Kaytra."

Her lower lip was caught between her teeth in a gesture which made Colin want to touch the softness there and make her stop, but he didn't. He only continued watching her eyes. And she was watching him, saying to him somehow that she couldn't take the next step without him.

Colin laid the Bible on the quilt, then gently helped Kaytra to kneel down on the rug beside the bed. Her tiny hands were lost when he placed his own around them. Side by side, they knelt before the Lord and asked that Jesus would come into Kaytra's heart, that he take away her sins and fill all the empty places, that He would make her whole again. The dividing wall was broken. It lay in ruins beneath the powerful love God sent into that bedroom at Highland Light.

As the minutes passed, the room began to lighten with morning sunshine. When he finally felt the tension easing out of Kaytra's tired body, Colin drew back a little. Enough so that he could look down and see her face. "I have to go. The light."

She nodded in understanding.

With the same display of gentleness, Colin helped her back into bed and covered her with blankets. "Will you be alright by yourself for a few minutes?"

Yes. She set her hand against his in the smallest affirmation that they had just shared an unforgettable experience.

Colin nodded in understanding. "I don't want you getting up yet. Try to sleep."

Kaytra watched him move out of the room.

After only half an hour, his absence disturbed her. She reasoned the feeling to her state of weakness. Perhaps everything would be different for a while. At least until she gained strength again. The emotions which had driven her to attempt to take her own life were gone now. But there still seemed so much for her to learn about trusting the Lord.

With so many thoughts running through her mind, it was easy to dismiss her dizziness as confusion when she swung her legs off the bed and stood up. Each step made her more aware of how her body ached, but she was determined. She wasn't going to lie down and let Colin take care of her. His compassion in the past hour changed things somehow, but it scared her, too. She wasn't going to be a burden to him, to give him a reason to feel even one moment of responsibility for her.

Hand over hand, she moved around the big bed, then stumbled to the doorway, clinging to its steadiness once she was there. A few more steps and she would-. Suddenly, without warning, Colin appeared at the bottom of the stairs. The look on his face spoke volumes, as did the way he crossed his arms over his chest. Kaytra raised her chin a little, refusing to tear her eyes away from his. One of his eyebrows arched upward. "Maybe I should have prayed that you would become a cooperative patient."

Kaytra's long lashes shielded her eyes from his knowing look.

To her further embarrassment, he moved up the steps, swept her into his arms and carried her back inside the room. After he laid her on Lydia's bed, he kept an arm on either side of her so that she was trapped there. "Will you listen, *really* listen to me for a minute?"

When Kaytra's eyes met his probing gaze, their looks collided with an almost physical shock. Colin drew back, inhaling deeply as he went to one of the windows and looked out at the ocean. "The FLC won't allow men without a family to operate a lighthouse," he spoke in an even tone. "Until now, Lydia was my family. I need someone here at Highland or I'll lose my position. You need someone to be a father to your child....We could be married, Kaytra."

She felt her heart stop completely at his quiet proposal. What he said next, started it pounding painfully.

"But it won't be a marriage of convenience. You will be my wife, Kaytra, in every sense of the word." Still Colin didn't turn to look at her. "When do you expect the child to be born?"

The abrupt question startled her from the state of numbness into which she had fallen. Kaytra stared at him blankly for a moment, then rubbed one hand across her forehead.

"How many months until the baby will be born?" Colin repeated the question with a quick glance over his shoulder.

Kaytra held up four fingers, but as quickly laid her hand on the blanket again. When he wasn't looking, her hand closed into a fist around the soft material.

Four months, Colin thought as he watched a sea gull land on the edge of the bank. It was sooner than he expected. The baby must be very small. Of course, Kaytra had been half-starving herself, probably in hopes that he wouldn't guess. Looking back, Colin remembered that she had worn the big apron constantly the past couple of weeks. He also remembered some of the careless things he had seen her do. That particular discussion would have to wait for another time.

He counted backward. Kaytra had been here since late August, which was just three and a half months. It didn't quite add up. Perhaps he could think of some explanation. In moving away from the window, he glimpsed an openly exhausted look upon Kaytra's face. She needed time to adjust to everything he had said. Colin walked over to the door. "I'll leave you alone to make your decision. Don't get out of bed again." It wasn't a statement this time, but a command. He set a hand on the door frame as he looked back. "When you're ready to eat, let me know. Otherwise, I'll check on you in a few hours."

All she could do was nod her head before he left the room.

Many long minutes later, she finally escaped into the oblivion of sleep. Her mind was made up. Perhaps, after all, the choice hadn't ever really been hers to make.

It was nearly a week before Kaytra felt strong enough to make the trip. Despite the warmth of Lydia's thick, black woolen cloak about her shoulders, she could not control the shivering of her body. It was a cold November day, but that had little to do with her discomfort. While the sky overhead lay crisp blue and cloudless, Kaytra's thoughts were on things not so clear, such as the reason why Colin had barely said anything to her since the day she had written her decision on paper.

She managed a quick glance at his face now as Provincetown came into view. His expression revealed nothing. He had made a point lately to show no emotion whatsoever. No surprise. No patience or impatience. No concern. No anger. Perhaps because she had written no explanations, he felt that his response should be indifference.

For whatever reason, Kaytra sensed he was as anxious as she for this day to be over. If only the people wouldn't stare at her! She held more tightly to the edge of the wagon.

As if he guessed her silent thought, Colin took his eyes off the road to look at the people they passed. Their expressions went beyond curiosity to rudeness. He didn't have to look at Kaytra to know that she would be staring straight ahead, eyes fixed inward rather than outward.

At Colin's urging, Samson picked up his gait slightly. The sooner this was done, the better for all of them. When they drove by Jolly's store, Colin saw young Timmy peeking out through one of the dust-smudged windows. So much for a quiet arrival.

The closer they got to Shank-Painter Swamp, the more attention they drew. Colin clenched his jaw so tightly his teeth hurt. He kept his eyes focused straight forward, his thoughts intent on only one purpose.

When they reached Everette Koch's shack, Colin pulled Samson to a stop. Before he could get down and around the wagon, Kaytra was climbing out herself. Colin made no move to help her, even when it seemed her legs were unsteady and she clung with one hand to the security of the wagon a moment longer than was necessary.

After drawing in a deep breath, she left Colin standing by the wagon and walked up to the door. It felt awkward to knock as she did, but she really didn't belong here anymore. Old memories washed over her unpleasantly until her heart clamored out a warning to run. Perhaps she would have done so if Colin wasn't behind her, if Koch hadn't swung the door open just then.

For those first few seconds, Kaytra had the advantage over her step-father. His black, beady eyes rounded out wide in a waxen face. A hissing breath was sucked in through his thin lips. "What ya' doin' heahe?," he growled.

Kaytra clasped both hands together in front of herself, waiting the moment longer it took for Koch to look past her and see Colin by the wagon. A clear warning bell sounded inside of her this time. The look on Everette Koch's face meant trouble. With a quick side-step, she moved once again into line with his eyes, forcing his attention back to her.

Koch spit at her feet in disgust. "Don't wantcha heahe! Cen't come back anyways 'til youah six month is up at Highland. He paid ya fer the woahk! Cen't come back!" His eyes shifted to a spot just over her right shoulder, but Kaytra had already sensed that Colin stood there now. "Told ya when ya took heah that she was ta woahk fer six month!"

"There was a lot you didn't tell me, Koch." Colin kept his voice low, making Kaytra fearful because she knew how close he was to losing patience.

"Don't owe you nothin', light keepeah!"

"No," Colin spat out the word. "You don't!" With that, he shoved Kaytra's worn carpetbag in the general direction of her hand, not bothering to see that she took it firmly before he let go and turned away. His angry strides had carried him halfway back to the wagon before Koch recovered enough to speak.

"But ya - ya cen't jus' give heah back!" Everette carelessly pushed past Kaytra to get out the door. She felt a sharp sting where her shoulder hit the wooden jamb. "Light keepeah!"

Colin kept walking. The muscles in his arms felt knotted in a dozen places. It took every ounce of self-control in him to ignore the other man.

"You done swoahe ta take heah foah six month! Got witnesses ta say so. You'ahe goin' 'gainst youah woahd!" Koch hurried after Colin, right on his heels, badgering him in a tone the whole neighborhood could hear. Kaytra recognized the edge of desperation beneath his words. "What, ya think you's too high an' mighty ta keep youah woahd on the Cape jus' 'cause you's a Boston man? Ya won't get no money back!," he shouted carelessly. "Ain't gonna give you no money back!"

Colin stopped dead in his tracks then, causing Everette Koch to stumble into him. The smaller man righted himself by the time Colin swung around. A look passed between them which sent an icy chill through Kaytra. If Koch had any sense at all he would back down - right now. But Koch was beyond seeing reason. He stared at Colin, oblivious to the small crowd of onlookers who gathered in scattered groups. "How come you all the sudden want ta get rid o' heah, light keepeah? What'd ya do ta heah that you-."

"Stop it, Koch," Colin cut him off in a threatening way. His hands were balled into tight fists at his sides. "Don't say another word or I'll-."

"You'll what, light keepeah?" Koch taunted with an evil grin. "Gonna buy yer way outta these folks knowin' -? "

He got no further. Colin's hand closed around his collar, twisting it until he effectively cut off the possibility of speech.

A collective murmur of surprise rose from the people who watched. There were even more exclamations when Colin literally dragged Koch toward the old shack, his face a mask of stone. Kaytra moved aside as he got nearer. Without meeting her eyes, Colin ordered her inside.

She practically fell into the dark interior of the dirt-floor shanty which had been her home for the past five years. Smells - all too familiar smells - assaulted her. Nothing had changed.

When Colin and Koch were inside, too, Colin slammed the door shut with the flat of one hand. It rocked precariously into place, sealing out much of the daylight. "Light a lamp, Kaytra." Colin gave the command without taking his eyes from Koch. He was too wary of the other man now not to watch every move.

In mere seconds, Kaytra located a lamp, lit the wick and set it on the crude table in the middle of the room. While she watched Colin look over every single detail about the room, Kaytra wished she could be anywhere but here.

His eyes missed nothing. The stacked crates used as cupboards for cracked dishes, bent pots, and a handful of foodstuffs. The poor, crumbling fireplace over which she had cooked meals. A half-hearted fire smoldered there now, barely sending out enough heat to change the temperature inside from what it was outside.

He saw the broken liquor bottles that lay next to a chair where stuffing oozed out of mice-bitten holes. Scraps of cloth were tossed upon a wooden pallet against the far wall. Did he guess that she had slept there? There was an open door to the shack's one other room, a space which held a bed, a table and nothing else. Dirty dishes littered the floor. Everette's clothes had been thrown carelessly across the chairs. Home? No, she could never think of this place as being a home. It was a prison.

Colin's shadow moved across the wall behind him as he stepped closer to Koch. Kaytra held her breath. "Let's get one thing straight right from the start, Koch."

Everette swallowed hard, remembering what it felt like to have one of those strong hands wrapped around his throat.

Colin deliberately knotted both arms over his chest. It was either that or slam a fist into the other man's face. "I'll do the talking, you do the listening."

Koch didn't actually agree, but neither did he have the courage for outright defiance.

"I've never wanted to kill a man before, and I never thought I would - until now. You're one word away from getting that scrawny neck of yours snapped in two."

Each threat hung heavily over the room. Koch's little game of deception was done. He knew as much by the expression in Colin's eyes. A look of pure loathing was laced with the rage.

"After what you did to Kaytra, I ought to string you up from the nearest tree and tell all of Provincetown what scum you are! You don't even de-."

A strangled moan from Kaytra drew both men's eyes in her direction. She still clutched the handle of her bag, holding it in front of her like a shield from their combined anger.

Koch, who took a half-step toward her, was aware that Colin watched him warily. "What'd you say?" Everette's face paled in asking her the question.

With their full attention on her now, Kaytra felt a dryness in her mouth which made it more difficult. "No-o-o. Do-n't." Each syllable seemed painful for her, a great effort which left her entirely drained. Her gaze slowly shifted to Colin. "P-le-as-e."

The quiet, labored plea tore at him; made him feel her anguish until it became his, too. That shared anguish twisted the tension between them even tighter. She had spoken. Not in delirium this time, but in fear. It struck Colin at once that she had no reason to believe he wouldn't indeed do what he had just threatened. Fear - and not any amount of willing it on his part - is what finally broke through the locked door. Fear that he would destroy himself right along with Koch. Colin snapped his eyes away from hers, away from the secret which yet lay unspoken and unrealized between them.

In those moments of charged silence, Everette Koch regained a wicked composure. With Colin suitably distracted by his own thoughts, Koch slid over to Kaytra, stopping a foot away. "Got yer voice back? Ain't that convenient."

She recoiled from the smooth menace in his low, whispered tone.

"Did ya tell him how ya brung me a good price?"

Kaytra closed her eyes.

Though he couldn't exactly hear what Koch said, Kaytra's anguished reaction was enough. Colin warned him to back off. "Leave her alone, Koch."

Koch whirled on him like a man possessed. "S'pose you think it's me got heah with child! Well, it weren't me!"

An even more troubled look flashed into Colin's eyes. What had happened then? In his heart, he knew it was not possible that Kaytra gave herself to any man, not like that. His chest heaved with the painful breath he drew into his lungs.

To witness the depth of Colin's emotions gave Koch more confidence than he should have felt, for the truth spilled forth without thought for how much worse it would sound. "Happened one night when she was out walkin' like she does. Some smaht, young buck foahced heah, he did. Pulled heah way off where nobody would know. She come back the next moahnin' in bad shape. But I didn't tuahn heah away like I coulda done. Coulda thrown heah out, but no." Everette shook his head, filled with his own twisted sense of self-righteousness. "Me, I listened good round heahe, found out who done it and then I made 'im pay. Made 'im pay foah damagin' heah like that!"

Somewhere in the middle of the story, Kaytra started backing away from him until she was mostly hidden in shadow near the back of the room. Still, Colin felt the shame she must have felt. He felt the horror and the ugliness of what that other man had done to her. His hands balled into fists at his sides in an effort to block out the very real images in his mind.

Koch swung his head in Kaytra's direction, sneering at her lack of courage to face up to what had happened. "S'pose you come back ta rob me from that money by tellin' folks who it was so's the whole town know what scum the councilman's son is? Well ya' ain't sayin' a woahd! They'd have me run outta heahe fast. An' I ain't goin'. Not cause of you!"

"She'll leave if she wants to leave, Koch." Colin took a deliberate step toward him.

Koch reacted by placing himself between Colin and Kaytra. "You ain't got no say oveah heah, light keepeah!"

"That's not what you just said out there in front of all those people."

"You want ta throw youah money 'way? Fine! Make quite a stoahy how she come back 'spectin' a child an' you jus' dumped heah down like yesteahday's garbage! That's what I'll tell folks 'bout you, light keepeah!" Koch spat onto the ground at his feet. "Don't want you in my house. You ain't welcome heahe no moahe. Get out!"

Suddenly the tide had turned against him. Colin felt more than uncomfortable. He had never been forced to hate before. It welled up inside of him now like a terrible, burning flame.

In seeking Kaytra's eyes, he found only a blank expression, one he could not fathom. All he knew was that she had refused to marry him.

Colin stared hard at Everette Koch for one long moment before he turned and left. The door closed quietly behind him. He would stop at Jolly's to mail the letter which was tucked into his breast pocket, the letter resigning his position... Then he would go back to Highland and wait.

Chapter Sixteen

A blast of January's icy breath stole across the floor as the door was opened. Jolly finished placing cans of tobacco on the shelf before turning to see who was out this late in the afternoon on a day that was far from friendly. A smile of greeting automatically deepened the wrinkles around his eyes and mouth. "Colin! Didn't least ways 'spect you taday!" He wiped his hands on baggy brown pants.

"Hello, Jolly." Colin set his small trunk down near the door.

Jolly had moved around the counter now and was walking over to him, his eyes bright with curiosity, his right hand extended. "Who's that ya got? Looks like Kaytra's old dawg."

"It is. Do you mind?"

"Naw!" Jolly waved a hand. "I'd foahgotten 'bout him. Didn't want ta stay out at Highland with the new folks?"

Colin rubbed a hand over Rex's silken head. "I'm sure he would have. He really liked the Davis children. Truth is, I didn't want to leave him." Rex, who seemed to know he was being talked about, lifted large eyes to Colin's face. "I've grown quite attached to him, I guess." The slightly melancholy note in Colin's words drew Jolly's thick, white eyebrows together in a definite frown. Seeing it, Colin immediately smiled and clapped his friend on the shoulder. "Take heart, Jolly. You'll be rid of us soon enough. I just booked passage for Boston. I've got about an hour to spare if you have the coffee pot on?"

"Coffee's always on." Jolly went to get the cups. Since the store was empty, he would have a good chance to talk with Colin before he left. "What'd ya think o' the Davis family? They seemed nice 'nuff folks when they come in last month."

"They are." Colin agreed as he stretched his long frame into one of the chairs by the store's barrel stove. "Mr. Davis has quite a few years' experience with lighthouses. I didn't really need to stay the extra month to show him about Highland, but those are regulations."

"Couldn' believe theys had half-dozen kids an' one on the way. Mrs. Davis looked plum woahn out, an' heah still a young woman yet." Jolly handed Colin a cup of his steaming, strong black coffee, then sat down himself.

Colin welcomed the warmth of coffee. It had been a cold ride into town on Samson. He had boarded the horse at the livery until he decided whether to keep him or sell him. So much depended on what the next few days brought. "Have you seen Kaytra lately, Jolly?" The question came out as a surprise to Colin. He hadn't meant to ask after her.

When Jolly didn't answer right away, Colin looked away, concentrating on the smudge of ashes fallen to the wooden floor beneath the stove. Kaytra had been in his thoughts more often than he cared to admit.

But Jolly didn't need any admission to that fact. He hooked the thumb of his free hand through the suspender at his waist. "I ain't seen heah since the day afteah she come back with you."

There was a visible tensing of the muscles along Colin's arms. "Do you know if she's alright? Does anybody ever talk to her?"

Another long silence preceded Jolly's response. His tone became pensive. "She ain't heahe, Colin."

The younger man's head snapped around like whipcord.

"She left on the fiahst ship out."

"She - left?"

Jolly nodded solemnly. "Had to. I made heah."

Colin sat up straighter in his chair, studying the look on Jolly's expressive face. "Why?"

"Koch beat heah 'gain. I knowd if she stayed, she'd end up like heah Ma."

Hearing the sober words forced Colin to his feet. A low curse tore from him. The worst he'd imagined these past weeks had come true. He moved to the counter, leaning against it as something solid when the rest of the world seemed suddenly tumbled upside down. "I didn't want her to come back here, Jolly. I offered her a home at Highland. I offered to marry her, to give her child my name." Colin slammed a fist onto the countertop before swinging around to face the other man. "I never wanted her to come back! She could have stayed at Highland."

"No, Colin." Jolly stood slowly, shaking his head in a very wise way. "She couldn't stay at Highland. The life you offeahed heah would've been neah as bad as what she come back to."

Colin stared at Jolly with growing disbelief.

"I talked ta heah foah a long time. She come ta me afteah he hit heah. She was scahed, Colin. Almost lost the baby."

Colin expelled a heavy sigh, closing his eyes briefly against the thought.

The fact that he felt sorry for Colin still didn't stop Jolly from speaking his mind. "Colin, if I've eveah met a moah stubboahn man, I don't 'membeah him. You coulda stopped heah from eveah wantin' ta leave Highland, jus' by admittin' youah own feelin's."

"You're wrong Jolly." Colin spoke with quiet respect. He knew Jolly meant well. But he was, after all, looking at this from a different perspective. "Kaytra wasn't running away from me, she was running away from herself. She wouldn't have accepted what I feel for her. She's not ready for that yet."

"So you jus' - gave up?"

"I gave her what she wanted."

Both men were silent awhile. Their judgment differed on this one. The only common ground between them was that they both cared very much for Kaytra. Jolly walked around to the other side of the counter, setting his coffee cup down near Colin's at the same time. "She went ta Boston if'n ya want ta know."

"Boston?" Colin faced him slowly, a look of perplexity creasing his brow. "Why would she go there? How-?"

"Ma'y 'Liz'beth's folks is theahe. I gave heah what money I had an' told heah she should try an' find 'um."

"Who are they?"

Jolly shrugged his shoulders. "Don't know. Ma'y 'Liz'beth neveah talked 'bout 'um much 'cept ta say they lived in Boston."

It was a fool thing to go chasing after someone you didn't know. They could just as well be dead by now. The idea of Kaytra all alone in that big city was unsettling to Colin. A customer came into the store then, giving him a chance to collect his thoughts while Jolly was otherwise occupied.

Rex was getting restless now. He still sat next to Colin's trunk by the door, but his eyes kept shifting from one window to the next. Colin knew he wanted to be outside again.

After Jolly had recorded the new purchases, he met Colin in the center of the store. An emotion akin to regret saddened the older man's eyes. "Think you'll be back some time, Colin?"

"Not to run Highland." There was regret in Colin's tone, too. He would miss Jolly and the Buckleys, miss the life he had begun to know here on the Cape. "The Davis' don't deserve to be switched around from one light to the next. They're a family. They need a home."

"And what 'bout you, Colin? Don't you need a home?" The question stung a little, though it wasn't meant to. When he realized Colin wouldn't answer, Jolly went on. "Hope you'll come visit, anyway."

"I will, Jolly." Colin held out his hand, feeling some comfort to know this friendship at least would not be finished when he walked out the door. "You know, I never did hear what your real name is. Your parents couldn't have named you 'Jolly'."

A wide grin split Jolly's face. "Long as I knows yer leavin', guess it's okay ta tell ya. My Ma named me Zebulon afteah a son of Jacob's in the Bible. Had so many boys in ouah family, you see."

"Zebulon is a proud name."

"Stuffy if'n ya asked me. You take cahe now."

"I will," Colin promised with a parting smile. "Good bye, Jolly."

The older man saw him out the door, raising a hand in farewell when Colin glanced back.

Life was strange sometimes, allowing such brief acquaintances to have a lasting impact. Who could explain why God brought people together, gave them an understanding, then separated their paths? One could only accept God's will.

Colin stood on deck for a long time after the other passengers had gone below where it was warmer and out of the biting wind. Though his eyes were trained on the receding outline of Cape Cod's western shore, he was seeing something else all together.

In his mind, he was back at Highland, looking out from the windows at the top of the tower. He had stood there alone that morning, willing the scene before him to become etched in his memory: A steel gray sea churned by swelling rises of white as the wind lashed its power. The gray sky seemingly void of color, so endless, so empty of any expression. Distant sails sliding like ghosts in their journey northward. Gulls flying low, trying to defy the greater force against them. At moments, they appeared to be suspended, standing still between sky and sea.

There were sounds, too. Kaytra's silence had made him more aware of how the ocean beat a rhythm upon the shore, of how the wind could swirl its voice, rising and falling like a lonely song. He heard the sharp, throaty cries of the bank swallows. The more distant wail of the gulls. The icy rustle of the beach grass not yet hidden by the snow. Even the fires in the lamps had their own sound now, a barely detectable slow hiss as the oil burned to create life-saving light.

He had never wanted to leave.

Colin turned now and leaned his back against the ship's railing. Absentmindedly, his hand sought out the warm comfort of Rex's thick coat. Boston was only a few hours away. It seemed strange to be going back, strange to think of how quickly life had changed. His gaze traveled upward into the tall masts with their tangle of ropes and straining billow of sailcloth.

It had shocked him to learn Kaytra was in Boston. Somehow he couldn't picture her there. She had seemed so much a part of what he was leaving behind. He wondered now if she had found her grandparents. If they had welcomed her. If she and the baby were safe.

A weathered sailor, passing in front of them on his way aft, gave Colin a curious look, one which reminded Colin that anyone else in their right mind would be below. He pushed himself upright. "Come on, boy. It's a while before we make port." Rex followed him across the deck with steps unused to the rolling pitch. Neither of them would find the trip a pleasure.

Boston's harbor was busy, even at such a late hour. Ships were being loaded and unloaded all along Griffin's Wharf. In the frozen darkness, shadows blended easily with moving objects. The usual dock riffraff slid from one shadow to the next. Worn sailors and hardened captains moved about in relative silence. Muted sounds came from horses hooves on the cobblestones, more unpleasant sounds from the drinking establishments which lined the streets in this part of the city.

Colin sent a young boy off to get him a cab. By the time it arrived, he felt a definite weariness spreading across his shoulders. After giving the driver his address, he settled back in the seat, thankful for once that his station in life meant he could afford such a luxury. Sights familiar to him faded into the blackened background as he rode through streets leading away from the harbor. He had traveled this route so many times before that he could have closed his eyes and described exactly where he was.

Rex, on the other hand, sat alert and watchful, taking in this new environment somewhat warily. If not for the way he trusted Colin, he would surely have stayed near the sea where things seemed more familiar to him.

The steady clip-clop gait of the horses carried them into the wealthy section of town, a place where fences separated street and home. Where life moved at a more stately pace. Where there were front gates for those deemed worthy and service gates for those who weren't.

The MacRae Mansion stood atop Copp's Hill on a richly groomed square of land, surrounded by other stately mansions, all vying for attention. Somehow, though, it seemed much larger and grander than its counterparts. On this winter night, it gleamed silver and gold as moonlight fought to outshine the lamplight streaming from the front windows.

Colin hesitated just outside the door, drawing in a whispered prayer for what was to come. Maybe he should have told them he would be arriving. It was too late now. The wide, marble-tiled foyer stood empty as he and Rex stepped inside. Warmth enveloped him. He set the trunk near the foot of the sweeping staircase. Nothing had changed. Not one piece of bric-a-brac was moved. A dozen red roses graced the cherrywood table, their scent mingled with that of the beeswax Beatrice used daily to bring a shine to the banister. His father's hat, the same gray one, lay beside the vase. Nothing had changed.

"Colin?"

He turned toward the double doors which led into the library. "Mother." An ache pierced him to a surprising depth and, though he smiled at her, he couldn't deny the sudden pain. She moved forward as he did, walking into the arms he held open for her.

Catherine MacRae was not a small woman. She was taller than most, willowy and graceful. Yet next to her son, she seemed delicate and as frail as a swallow. The paleness of her finely chiseled features was accentuated by the black dress she wore in mourning. Her hair, a crown of rich gray, was soft beneath the hand Colin laid upon her head as she rested her forehead against his chest. "Oh, Colin, I have wished desperately that you would come home."

Her broken words twisted the already present ache inside of him. He felt guilty now for his selfish anger at being forced to leave the Cape. "I'm sorry, Mother, that I couldn't be here for you when - Lydia died."

There were tears in Catherine's brown eyes when she pulled away to look at him. Losing her only daughter had been tremendously painful. Some of that sorrow showed in the way she had aged since he had last seen her. Colin laid a tender hand alongside her face. At fifty years of age, she was still a beautiful woman in his eyes.

"Is father here?"

Catherine nodded, slipping her arm through Colin's in a possessive way as they both turned to the doors from which she had emerged a moment earlier. Not to be forgotten, Rex rose to follow them. Catherine gave the huge dog a startled look before deciding he was probably harmless or her son wouldn't have allowed him indoors.

"I know this is a bit of a shock, my just showing up like this."

"You always did rather enjoy shocking people, Colin."

He smiled down at her, relieved to hear the faint, teasing lilt in her words.

Once they entered the library, however, Colin's smile was gone. After the warmth of his mother's welcome, he had secretly hoped - ...But no, Shaun MacRae's expression was not welcoming. "Hello, Father."

"Colin." The crisp reply could have been spoken to a stranger. Shaun MacRae sat back in the leather-upholstered chair behind his desk, setting his elbows firmly on the arms of the chair before bringing his hands together into a single, tight fist upon which he then rested his chin.

The gesture was one Colin remembered from his earliest childhood. It had somehow always served to set his father aloof from those around him. The same was true now. Nothing had changed.

"What brings you back to Boston?"

"I was replaced at Highland." Colin felt his mother's hand upon his arm, silently cautioning him to soften his tone.

Shaun MacRae narrowed his eyes slightly, eyes which were the same as Colin's, tending to grow darker with anger. "Replaced... Because you were alone, I suppose. Now that you've seen your sister into the grave, Highland Light no longer holds any interest for you?"

"Shaun!" Catherine rushed forward, putting herself between her husband and her son. It was a familiar scene. All too familiar. "Please, we don't need to discuss-."

"Maybe you should ask Beatrice to see that a room is made ready." Shaun interrupted her smoothly, though his voice held an edge of authority. "Is that your beast?"

Colin glanced over his shoulder to where Rex had stopped just outside the door, almost as if he had sensed beforehand that he would need to earn his right to be invited in. "Yes. He's my dog. His name is Rex. Lydia named him actually." This last was added as a barb in return for the one which had just been struck him.

An expression of sadness dulled Catherine's eyes. She swung her gaze between them, not knowing how she could right all the wrongs, if indeed that were even possible. "Excuse me then," she said. "I think I will retire after speaking with Beatrice." She gave Colin a long look. "I'll see you in the morning?"

He nodded woodenly.

Once Catherine left the room, Shaun slowly rose, moving around the desk to stand just a few feet from Colin. People had always said they were alike. The same height. The same muscular build and strong, masculine features. The same temperament. Except for a few lines of age and the gray hair of a distinguished sixty-year-old, Shaun admitted he and his son were quite the same. "Didn't I tell you it would end this way?"

Colin deliberately turned and walked to the tall fireplace, shrugging out of his coat as he went, throwing it over the back of the nearest chair. "I'm sure you did, Father." It wasn't a quiet agreement, but a cool rebuke. Colin took up the poker in the andiron to shove it at the burning logs, sending up a burst of orange and yellow sparks. He sensed when his father came to stand behind him.

"You shouldn't have taken her there."

"Lydia wanted to go, Father." Colin reminded him firmly. "She was sick for a time, but she had gained strength the past few months. Her death was completely unexpected."

"Unexpected!" Shaun's anger exploded. Yet it was no release for what had been building inside him since the day Lydia's body was buried in the graveyard of King's Chapel. His face was flushed and set when Colin turned toward him. "What did you think would happen to her when you took her to that God-forsaken place? Have some sense, son. Or is it too late for that?"

The muscles in Colin's jaw worked aggressively as he ground his teeth together. "I should have had more sense than to think you would understand. I'm hurting, too. She was my sister."

Shaun expelled a disbelieving grunt. "You wouldn't know the kind of pain you put your mother and me through."

"I wasn't the one who decided Lydia should die. God-."

"God! You can't stand there and tell me you're going to place the blame on God for your own foolish actions!"

"No! I'm not!" Colin replaced the poker with a noisy clatter, then turned to leave. He was all the way across the room before a voice inside pulled him up short, urging him to explain. His father seemed surprised to see him stop. Their eyes met in silence for a long time before Colin felt calm enough to speak. "Nobody needs to be blamed. When you know God, death isn't some kind of dreadful punishment. Lydia didn't see it that way. She didn't die because I took her to Highland. It was just her time to go. I've accepted that and, even though I still hurt sometimes, I won't cheapen her life by pretending it was cut short. Nobody cheated her. Not me and not God."

Shaun stared down into the fire, his face starkly sober in the weak light it gave. "If you're asking me to forgive you, Colin, that day will never come."

The words rang with enough finality to drive Colin from the room. His long, frustrated strides carried him up the stairs. Rex followed behind, sniffing at smells which were strange to him. When Colin's steps slowed outside the first door of the left wing, Rex stopped, expecting that they would go in. Instead, Colin gave the closed door a brooding, pensive look, then continued down the richly carpeted hallway. Further along, the door to another room was already open. The sound of a woman humming a merry tune met them before they entered.

Rex immediately liked the jolly, round face which turned in their direction. Such kind eyes could only mean this woman would be an ally.

"Well, lookee there! Yer Mom said you done brought a dog home. From the sight of him, I'd say it's time Cook stocked up on some meaty beef bones!"

"Hello." Colin offered a distracted greeting before setting his trunk on the floor. His old room should have been inviting. Somehow, tonight, it wasn't.

Beatrice clucked a sorry look, causing the starched bonnet atop her head to tip precariously over the disarray of white curls. Nobody knew exactly how old she was. "That's a fine 'nice-ta-see-ya' for an old friend."

He sighed deeply, sinking into the big chair by the fireplace. The fire had only recently been started and emitted little heat, but the flames were giving it a brave try. "I'm sorry, Beany."

She grinned like a schoolgirl at his use of her pet name. Both he and Lydia had found it easier to say than Beatrice and the name somehow suited her.

"It is nice to see you. I hope I'm not putting you out by having you do up my room so late."

"Putting me out?" She sounded distressed, then laughed with contagious good humor. "As if I'd refuse you anything at all, Colin MacRae. This is a pleasure. Gets my heart pumping good to have a bit of excitement 'round here!"

"I don't think my father would agree with you."

Beany frowned slightly as she straightened fresh sheets over the bed. Not home half an hour and the two MacRae men were fighting again. "You're probably sore tired, Colin."

"And what's my father's excuse?"

The retort earned him a mildly censoring look. "No matter if you disagree with him, Colin, he is still your father and you should respect him as such."

Colin silently conceded the argument, leaning his head back against the chair and closing his eyes. By concentrating very hard on listening to Beany move about the room, he was able to forget the things his father had said to him. After a few minutes, she came up to lay a calloused hand over his. This time, when he looked at her, there was a genuine smile in his eyes.

"That's more like it." Beany patted his hand just as she had done twenty years earlier. "You get yourself some sleep now, Colin. Life always seems clearer in the morning."

"Thank you, Beany."

Her eyes suddenly filled with tears. She was too late in moving away to hide them from him.

Colin stood slowly. There were maybe half a dozen times in his whole life that Beany had displayed any sadness in front of him. He had a good idea now what was bothering her. "Beany." She was pretending great interest in petting Rex. "Lydia was happy out at Highland. Both of us were."

The older woman unconsciously wrapped both arms around her ample waist in a gesture of self-will before she looked up at him. Beany had a strength in her which Colin had often admired. Her eyes displayed that strength now. "Never thought I'd live ta see the day when you two were separated."

Colin moved forward, taking her hands in his very gently. Beany was like a second mother to him.

"I've missed you, Colin."

His smile charmed an answering one onto her face. "And I you, Beany."

"You've changed somehow." Her cloudy, green eyes studied him in the subdued lighting. The change had been apparent to her right from the start. Measured against the familiar, darkly-paneled room with its gold and red furnishings, Colin seemed not at all the same man who had left last spring.

He squeezed her hands a moment before letting them go. "Life wouldn't be worth living if we always remained the same, now would it Beany?"

"Depends on what changes you." Her sharply perceptive answer was followed by a long silence. He had changed. There was a time when he would have shared his thoughts with her. "Will you go see Patricia now that you've come back?"

Colin's eyebrows rose in amusement. "Still match-making, are you, Beany? I suppose you've managed to marry off Stephen while I was gone."

"Stephen Kemp is as stubborn as you are when it comes to women." Beany began to walk toward the door. "You and your friend shall likely become frustrated, lonely old bachelors together if left to yourselves. Goodnight, Colin."

"Night, Beany." He followed her, closing the door after she was gone.

For a while, he busied himself with unpacking part of his trunk. The rest of the things he had wanted from Highland - Lydia's trunk and some of their books - would be sent later. Besides his clothes and Bible, the only other thing he had packed into his trunk had been Kaytra's journal.

Colin settled into the massive, four-poster bed, taking the journal with him. He had read it many times. Especially the last few pages. It wasn't Stephen or Patricia or even his parents who occupied his last thoughts before sleep, but Kaytra.

Chapter Seventeen

Colin dressed in gray breeches, a white shirt and a darker gray coat the next morning before going down to breakfast. He felt rested, though a bit unsettled. The adjustments between Highland and Boston would take some time. On his way to the dining room, he met Carlisle, the young butler who had been with the MacRaes for a little over a year now. Carlisle said he would see to it that Rex was settled in the kitchen and that the carriage Colin requested would be ready at the front door in half an hour.

There were some things Colin wanted to do right away. Besides, it was Friday and most of the businesses would be closed for the weekend. He walked into the elegant cream and gold dining room with his usual confidence. Shaun and Catherine were already seated at the long table. Their conversation ceased immediately at seeing him.

Catherine flushed a bit beneath the questioning glance he gave her. He knew, of course, that they had been discussing him. "Good morning, Colin. Did you sleep well last night?"

"Very well, thank you, Mother," Colin said in a loving tone. He stopped by her chair to place a kiss on her cheek before going to the sideboard to serve himself. Cook had thoughtfully prepared all his favorites: scrambled eggs, caramel biscuits, savory pork sausage. He would have to remember to thank her later. "I'll be using the pair of bays this morning," he paused for a moment, "if that's not a problem?"

Catherine exchanged a quick glance with her husband.

Shaun was the one who answered. "It isn't a problem, of course. You'll find I've made some changes in the stable."

The brief look Colin gave him held some curiosity, but none of the possessive alarm Shaun had expected. The horses had been Colin's expertise, his responsibility by mutual consent.

"I sold some of the older horses." Shaun watched his son intently. "The new stock has proved a good investment."

"I'll look forward to seeing them," Colin said as he sat opposite his mother.

His purposely calm reaction brought a rise of resentment in Shaun MacRae, causing him to blurt out the inevitable. "I sold Glory Morn."

Colin met his eyes. The realization that his father meant to gain some hold over him by the act was only too clear. For that reason alone, Colin kept his voice void of any expression. "Did you get a good price for her?"

"Hawkers don't pay top dollar."

No, he refused to take the bait this time. Colin bowed his head to say a quick blessing, then began eating his food.

It was left to Catherine to break the troubled silence. "So - you have plans for this morning, Colin?"

The new serving maid came at that moment to pour fresh coffee for them. She was a plain-looking young girl with an intelligent light in her blue eyes. As she moved about the table, she seemed to miss nothing. Colin caught her curious gaze once, smiled in a friendly way, then answered his mother's question. "I was going to go see Preston Napp."

Shaun frowned slightly at hearing his son mention the family's lawyer.

"Then I plan to stop in at Stephen Kemp's. He is still around, isn't he?"

"Of course, he is." Catherine readjusted the linen napkin across her lap. "We saw him just last weekend at a small dinner party given by the Henrys'. Speaking of which," she tried to judge Colin's reaction before mentioning her idea, "there is to be a cotillion tomorrow evening. We wouldn't go except that there will be quite a few of the banking executives there. I'm sure you would be welcome to come along, Colin. Some of your old friends will want to see you now that you're home."

"I'll think about it, Mother." He wasn't ready to jump right into the old way of life. Colin quickly finished his coffee and rose to his feet. "You can expect me home around noon."

Two pairs of eyes watched him leave the room - his mother's and Maggie O'Brien's, the young maid. Shaun MacRae just kept eating.

The office of Preston Napp was situated among some very prestigious buildings along Boston's main street, one was the MacRae Bank. As Colin reined the bays to a stop, he looked up at the impressive facade of Napp and Cambridge, Attorneys at Law. The forest green building with wide windows and fancy gold lettering bespoke distinguished service. Colin knew it to be true. Preston Napp had earned the younger man's respect a number of times.

The man who sat behind the secretary's desk looked up when Colin entered. "Good day, sir."

"Hello." Colin worked the leather gloves from his hands. "Is Mr. Napp available?"

"Who shall I say is here?"

"Colin MacRae, and tell him I won't keep him long." After receiving a nod in reply, he was left to await the secretary's return. Those few minutes gave him a chance to form what he would say. It was going to be a delicate matter, one requiring discretion.

Preston Napp greeted Colin with a mixture of surprise and reserve. The two of them shook hands before being seated on their respective sides of the desk in Napp's office. "Colin, I understood you were still on the Cape."

"I was, until yesterday." Colin eased some of the other man's concerns with an unexpected grin. "No doubt news will travel fast now that I've been seen in public. The wandering son returned home."

Preston leaned his arms upon the desk as he sat forward. "That's hardly the case, Colin. And those who think so have given ear to too much gossip."

Colin's eyes took on an interested expression. Then people had been gossiping about him.

"Now, now," Preston was quick to add. "It's not as bad as it sounds, son. The rumors are harmless."

"All rumors are, Mr. Napp. It's the truth which can do the most damage or correct it for that matter." Colin wasn't really concerned. "I've got a proposal for you. Something I can't take care of myself. It would mean a good deal of your time, which can't really be avoided, I'm afraid. I would, of course, reimburse you well for your trouble."

"You know money is not my primary objective, Colin." The mild rebuke settled the last of Preston's initial reservations. "Now, how can I help you?"

Colin spent the next half hour with Preston Napp. By the time he left, it was well past ten o'clock.

The drive to Stephen Kemp's led him into an impressive neighborhood. Stephen lived in a towering row house built of sturdy red brick with formal lines and crisp white shutters. The two of them had been friends since grammar school, though Stephen was a year younger and much different in character.

Memories of their times together accompanied Colin up the short flight of stairs to the door. A uniformed butler answered the bell. Since Colin had never met him, it took some explaining before he got a foot inside. Finally, the butler showed him to a well-appointed drawing room where he was asked to wait for Mr. Kemp.

The wait wasn't a long one. Once Stephen heard who had come, he raced into the room full speed. "Colin! Colin MacRae!"

"Hello, Stephen. Surprised you, did I?" Colin laughed heartily at his friend's half-dressed state.

Stephen didn't care that his tie was undone, his shirt tails untucked or that his left boot was in his left hand instead of on his left foot. He clasped Colin's outstretched hand, pumping it with enthusiasm. "By George, Colin! What are you doing back? Not that I mind, of course. But it is a shock. When you left, you meant to stay at Highland forever and now you -."

"Stephen." Colin good-naturedly interrupted the rambling words. "I could use a cup of coffee."

"Sure. Just a minute." Stephen pulled on his boot as he hobbled to the door. "Make yourself comfortable. I'll be right back."

Once they had settled with steaming cups of coffee into chairs near the drawing room fireplace, Colin was ready to answer some of Stephen's questions. Their old camaraderie returned as they talked. It was easy for Colin to recount all that had happened during the months at Highland, until it came time for him to tell Stephen about Kaytra. Her part in his life was difficult to explain.

Stephen sensed Colin's turmoil right from the first mention of the girl's name. He sat forward a little. "You say she couldn't talk? How did you communicate with her then? Or wasn't she there very long?"

Colin wrapped both hands around the china cup he held. "She stayed until after Lydia died. It's a long story, Stephen."

"Which means you'd rather not talk about her?"

The silence, which stretched out far too long, made Colin uncomfortable. "It means she and I communicated only too well. Sometimes, all I had to do was look at her to know what she was feeling."

"What was she like?," Stephen asked quietly. "Young? Pretty?"

"Very." Colin stared into the fire, seeing the image of her face against its glow. "Golden hair. Expressive blue-gray eyes. She's small. I felt like a giant next to her. Her father was French; a sea captain who died when she was a little girl. Her mother was from Boston."

Stephen paused in refilling his cup from the silver pot at his elbow. "Was?"

"She was killed a few years ago....by Kaytra's step-father." The look on Stephen's face was much as Colin had expected it to be. Dismay. Disbelief. "He was quite the character. I met him a couple of times. He beat Kaytra, too."

"Colin!"

"It's true. When she came to Highland, she was covered with bruises." Colin described what those first days had been like, finding that Stephen hung on every word. The story was so far removed from their lives here in Boston, it seemed incredible that such a fate could come to an innocent, young woman.

Stephen ran a hand over his wavy, blonde hair. By nature he was a shy man, and his lean handsomeness and glasses added to the impression. What Colin saw in Stephen's blue eyes now was a man trying to grasp at the raw truths he heard. "I don't know what to say," Stephen let out a sigh. "No wonder you wanted to protect her."

"But I made so many mistakes, Stephen." Colin's admission was even more sobering. "I need to talk to somebody about it."

"Of course." They had shared confidences before. Yet this moment seemed different from those other times. Before Stephen could encourage his friend to go on, Colin glanced up at the grandfather clock across the room.

"I told Mother I'd be back around noon and I'd still like to visit King's Chapel." The thought of seeing Lydia's grave had been heavy upon his heart all morning.

"Would you like me to come along, Colin?"

He accepted Stephen's offer, grateful for this true friendship that was willing to share the burdens as well as the joys.

They were on their way in just a few minutes. Stephen filled in Colin's silence with news of the Kemp family and some of their mutual friends. He, too, extended an invitation that Colin attend the cotillion, but Colin was still undecided. He just wasn't ready to step into that whole scene again.

King's Chapel was a mammoth church built with Gothic turrets and heavy lines. Colin had never much appreciated its tradition. For him, it was a symbol of that unseen hand dividing "religion" from real faith.

Massive oak and maple trees stretched naked limbs over the graveyard. A wrought iron fence separated life from death. Though Colin hadn't been here in years, he knew that the family plot was in a secluded corner of the old cemetery. He guided the bays slowly down a narrow track between the grave sites. Gray stones stood in stark reality against winter's soft blanket of snow. Stephen gave him an encouraging pat on the shoulder as they parked the carriage and climbed down. Lydia's headstone was different from the others nearby. Not only was it unweathered and set apart by the sites reserved for the rest of the family, but strangely it had been brushed clean of the powdery snow which had fallen overnight.

Colin moved toward it, stepping atop the footprints already leading there. His eyes weren't fixed on the name and dates carved into the marble stone. Instead, he stared at the single rose lying upon the snow at its base, the yellow-gold color of it like a drop of faded sunshine fallen to earth. He squatted down, taking the flower in his hand. Though it was slightly wilted and limp, the delicate petals were not frozen. It had been placed there not long ago.

"Who do you think would bring flowers out here?" Stephen's wondering question took Colin by surprise a little.

He had almost forgotten that he wasn't alone. Still holding the rose, Colin stood upright and faced his friend. "Kaytra."

"But-."

"She's here in Boston, Stephen. There's quite a bit left to the story." Colin's eyes wandered about the graveyard and beyond, as if he would yet see her hiding somewhere nearby, watching him. Finally, his gaze came back to rest on Lydia's grave. Knowing that Kaytra had come here, probably more than this one time, stirred an emotion in him which seemed impossible to identify.

Was his sister still to be the only link between their lives? Even in death, would Lydia pull them into meeting once again? The passage from First Corinthians leapt into his thoughts. *And now abideth faith, hope and love. These three, but the "greatest of these-."*

"What's that?"

Colin didn't realize he had whispered the words aloud until Stephen interrupted him. He shook his head distractedly, then leaned down to place the rose back where it had lain. "Let's go. Mother is probably waiting lunch."

Stephen walked beside him to the carriage, wondering at the contemplative frown upon his friend's face.

The rest of that day was interminably long for Colin. Though he kept busy getting the last things in his trunk put away and looking over the new horses in the stable, it wasn't the same as being out at Highland where every action had a definite purpose.

He talked with his mother awhile that afternoon. Some of her openness from the night before seemed stifled now. Colin thought he knew why; it was because of the strain between him and his father. Catherine loved her husband very much. That she would feel torn by loyalties was only natural.

Neither Catherine nor Shaun shared the deep Christian faith of their children. For that reason, Colin thought it best not to press his own belief. If they would only let go of their grief, God would heal their hurt, their sense of loss. The longer he talked to his mother, the more he could see how strong his father's influence was upon her life.

Saturday morning, Colin again visited King's Chapel, not to go inside, but to see if Kaytra was there. She wasn't. No one moved within the confines of the black iron fence. He drove past, suddenly deciding that he didn't want to go back home just yet.

The day was warm for mid-January. A bright sun radiated warmth to the world below. The slight saltiness to the breeze reminded Colin of Highland. The presence of people crowding around him increased his yearning to be on the Cape again.

He took the Brighton Road, knowing full well where he was headed. Within twenty minutes, he was standing in the foyer of Michaels Hall, removing his cape and gloves.

"Right this way, Mr. MacRae." The downstairs maid walked a short distance to a set of double doors opening into a glass-walled conservatory. A smile crossed Colin's face. He might have known she would be in this room. The maid left him to announce his own arrival.

At first, she didn't realize he was there and Colin had the chance to observe her unaware. Her coiffure was perfect, not one lock of raven black hair escaped. The ivory smoothness of her complexion hadn't changed. It was, in fact, as perfect as he remembered, set off by the rich deep blue of her dress. He was immediately aware of the sadness in her dark eyes as she stared out the window. The last time he had seen her, when he had said good bye before leaving for the Cape, she had given him such a look.

"Tricia?"

She swung her head around slowly at the sound of his voice. For a moment, she simply clutched tightly to the arms of the chair in which she was sitting. Then she was on her feet, hurrying forward. She slipped her hands into his with a familiar gesture.

To see that her eyes were filled with unshed tears, was rare. "A penny for your thoughts," Colin teased. They had played the game before, a long time ago. Patricia tried to smile, but failed miserably. "Come on. It can't be all that bad. I could leave again if-."

"Oh, Colin. Don't be ridiculous." She drew in a deep breath which only revealed how shaky she was. Colin's hands tightened in a comforting way. "How is it that you seem always to show up just when I need someone to talk with?"

"From the looks of things, I should say I'm too late for that."

Patricia gently pulled her hands from his and walked a few steps away, turning her back to him.

Colin was convinced now that something was very wrong. He moved up behind her. "Is it your parents? Is one of them ill?"

"No, Colin. They are both perfectly fine." Patricia managed a weak smile this time as she looked at him. She held her hands clasped tightly together in front of her. "How are you? You look very tan and fit." Another expression suddenly filled her eyes as she remembered. "Oh, Colin. I was sorry to hear a-about - Lydia."

"Thank you."

"It must have been very hard."

Colin frowned down at her. "Not 'have been', Tricia. It's still very hard." One of the tears quivering upon her lashes slipped down her cheek, but he didn't wipe it away. "What is it that you want to talk about? I am willing to listen, you know."

Her hand sought his again. She led him to one of the benches set among the array of hot-house plants which formed an indoor garden. "Perhaps later...Tell me how you happen to be back in Boston? I thought you wouldn't have leave until this summer."

Colin settled onto the bench beside her, not taken in by her attempt to make him forget her earlier distress. "I'm back for good, Tricia. After Lydia died, it was impossible for me to stay."

"Then.....you'll be here for a long time?"

"Is there some reason I shouldn't be?"

Her back stiffened at his counter question. "Of course not, Colin."

"Tricia, I know you too well to take that answer as the truth. What's going on?" When she would have pulled completely away, Colin set his hand on her arm. "It is your parents, isn't it?"

She stared at his hand for a long time before she said anything. This was Colin, after all. He had shared her dreams and sorrows for many years. He knew her better than anyone. "You know how they feel about you, Colin."

"About 'us' you mean."

Patricia raised her eyes to his, finding an amused understanding in the way he looked at her. "Papa was very angry when you left."

"I know that, too."

"You aren't making this any easier, Colin." She sent him a pleading look, very near to tears again. "I shall not tell you unless you promise to be serious." Some of her pampered, only-child upbringing could be heard in the tone of her voice.

Colin's gaze grew serious then as he waited for her to continue. Patricia had confided in him many times before, but never with this much honesty. It was there for him to see in her eyes.

She started out slowly, cautiously as if she was forming the thoughts for the very first time. Colin listened with a growing uneasiness, feeling more and more as if he shouldn't be hearing the things she was saying. Had he not been so taken by surprise, he might have offered her some much-needed advice. Instead, he found himself feeling rather sorry for her and asking if he could escort her to the cotillion later that night.

Tricia gratefully accepted. Colin always had been able to solve her problems.

Among those amazed to see Patricia walk into the ballroom on Colin's arm were John Michaels and Shaun MacRae. They had been in a far corner discussing politics when their children arrived. The certain breathless hush which rippled over the entire room of guests was not to be unexpected. Boston had long ago desired a marriage between these two of its most prominent families, the Michaels' and MacRaes. Colin's departure several months ago had dashed all such hopes. Until now.

"Shaun," John Michaels continued to stare proudly at his lovely daughter dressed in a becoming pale lavender gown deeply set with lace and ribbon, "you didn't tell me Colin was back." The young couple took the floor, gliding with the other dancers in time to the waltz being played by the orchestra. Not an eye in the room missed the fact that it seemed as if they were enjoying one another's company. John turned to look at Shaun MacRae. "Did you know they were coming tonight?"

"Are you disapproving?" Shaun asked suavely. He knew the answer already.

"Certainly not."

"Neither am I. Why then don't we look as if we expected this and no one will be the wiser."

Colin was whispering much the same thing to Patricia just then on their second circuit past the refreshment table where all the eligible young bachelors had gathered. "You're very good at pretending, Tricia." His brown eyes held amusement in watching a smile light her face. She had been as nervous as a cat just a few minutes ago. "Then again, everyone would expect you to be happy, wouldn't they?"

"I'd forgotten what a wonderful dancer you are, Colin." Patricia's eyes had widened ever so slightly, challenging him not to let her change the subject. Anyone looking on would have guessed she was merely responding to what he said.

"You are a vixen, Tricia."

"Do you mind terribly?"

He had almost forgotten how good she was at this verbal sparring. The months at Highland had been blessedly free of such nonsensical games. Now he could admit that Highland had been a place of honesty. Brutal honesty at times...

"Colin MacRae, you are frowning at me." Patricia's hand tightened inside of his, jolting him back to the present. "Does that mean you really do mind?"

A smile crossed his face which was half regret, half apology. "Perhaps I was simply assuming you might have grown up some since I've been gone." Patricia's angry look was hooded by artfully coy lashes. "You're what - twenty-one now?"

"Not nearly." She sounded slightly offended. "Not until the end of the summer."

"You aren't officially an old maid yet?" Colin deliberately whirled her around at a breathtaking pace, slowing only when he felt some of the fight go out of her body.

"I would have married you years ago, Colin." Her reminder carried much self-pity.

"Except that I've never asked you to marry me." His reminder carried much gentleness. Tricia had enough problems without his being cold toward her. "Ten years from now, you'll have half a dozen children, a big house and a husband who will dance much better than I can. I'm sure you'll look back and wonder why you ever worried about-."

Patricia interrupted smoothly. "You sound like you're getting ready to quote some appropriate Bible verse and give me a sermon. I don't want either one, Colin." For a while, during his silence, she thought she had made him terribly angry. Either that wasn't the case, or Colin was still a master at controlling his emotions, for he only continued to lead with strong, graceful movements.

She really would have married him. In fact, she had tried to bring about a proposal on numerous occasions. Over the years, their acquaintance had held its moments of ardor, but never in that fully committed way she had hoped. The only person Patricia could say Colin MacRae was committed to was Lydia.

Now that she was gone, if there was room in Colin's life for marriage, the woman he chose would have to learn to take second place - if not third - behind God and lighthouses, in that order. Certainly, Colin had said he was back in Boston for good. But Patricia hadn't believed him for a moment.

The rise of jealousy against whatever hold such things as endless expanses of sea and sky had over him left her as quickly as she chased it away. She couldn't allow herself to be distracted by old feelings. Colin had promised to help her now. Perhaps afterward he would-.

"Tricia?" Colin whispered so that only she would hear. "Isn't that Clifton Montgomery standing next to the Henrys?"

Immediately, her attention was focused on the middle-aged man whose bronzed skin stood out in contrast to the others around him. It was Monsieur Montgomery. "Please, Colin. Come with me. I'd like you to meet my new mentor." She had already stopped dancing. Despite his misgivings, Colin tucked her hand into the crook of his arm and led her across the room.

Much as Colin expected, Clifton Montgomery and Patricia greeted one another as strangers meeting for the first time. They showed only mild interest as the introductions were made. If anyone felt uncomfortable now, it certainly wasn't Patricia. Mr. Henry's properly English tone hastened a brief explanation of Montgomery's somewhat gilded reputation as Boston's latest big-money investor. If not for the way Montgomery had chosen to invest, he would surely have been welcomed with open arms. Instead, he was in an awkward position where people didn't dare spurn him, yet neither did they completely accept him.

Colin was aware of the saber-sharp look which Clifton Montgomery pressed on him: a momentary "sizing-up" as it were, then guarded observation. Colin's first impression became crystal clear; Montgomery was a dangerous man. Beneath the fancy clothing and paunchy build wasn't a gentleman, but a breed of man set on survival at any cost. Any cost at all.

As they had all presumed he would, Clifton Montgomery asked Patricia to dance. Colin watched the two of them from a distance, forming a hundred arguments in his mind, all of which he intended to lay on Patricia later that evening when he took her home. Yet, as he sipped punch from a ridiculously small glass cup, he knew in all likelihood that she wouldn't listen to anything he said. She was caught in a web that was more tangled than he had suspected.

Stephen separated himself from some friends and walked over to where he had seen Colin standing, watching Patricia. "Here you are. I had my doubts you were even going to show up tonight."

Colin smiled, beginning to relax a little. "I'm just full of surprises lately."

"Not the least of which was arriving with Patricia Michaels."

The two of them looked at one another with their usual frank honesty. Colin knew exactly what his friend was thinking. "She needed help, Stephen."

"She always needs help, Colin."

A true statement. Colin shifted so that he could scan the room. His father and mother were dancing together. They were a handsome couple. Several older gentlemen in the huge ballroom nodded at him as they met his eye. Colin nodded back, politely. A group of young women - girls mostly - tittered behind their fans when he gave them a long glance. "Have you danced with any of them yet, Stephen?"

Stephen followed his gaze. "Are you kidding? I'm still working on getting up the nerve to talk to them."

"Come on then." Colin started out, leaving Stephen no choice but to follow.

"Patricia won't like it." Stephen's warning was muttered quickly, before they reached the girls.

Colin shrugged his broad shoulders. The jacket he wore was cut perfectly. Black, like most of the others in the room. He knew that

Stephen was right, but Patricia was dancing with Montgomery just now. "Good evening, ladies," Colin said as he and Stephen stopped the proper distance away from the girls. They responded in kind. Proper. Life in Boston was meant to be that way. Stiff. Formal. Binding in a way he hated.

For the next hour, he and Stephen danced with several of the women. Colin charmed them out of their shyness, while Stephen's shyness charmed them in itself. By the time Patricia rejoined them between sets, she had plenty to say. "I thought maybe I could have the next dance, if it isn't too much trouble, of course?"

Her eyes hadn't lost that adoring look. Yet Colin knew her well enough to see the flashes of irritation lurking beneath those lashes. Stephen retreated with a hastily mumbled excuse, leaving Colin to face her alone. "Actually, we should talk to our parents first. They're all coming this way." Patricia's smile froze on her face. "Now, now." Colin brought his hand up to her cheek in a gesture anyone watching would consider endearing. "Don't be that way, Tricia. You can put on a better act than that. Your father will expect to see stars in your eyes." He looked over her shoulder then. "Hello, Mother. Father. Mr. and Mrs. Michaels."

"Colin!" John Michaels shook hands with him. "It's good to see you."

"Thank you, sir...Mrs. Michaels," Colin's gaze shifted to the short, round, bejeweled woman. "I hope you don't mind that I stole Tricia off without your permission." In another convincing motion, he brought Tricia's hand to his arm, keeping it covered as if he didn't want to let her go. Tricia played her part by giving him a shy, utterly happy look.

"We don't mind at all." Mrs. Michaels piped in her falsely high voice. "You must join us for dinner some evening soon, Colin. We've missed seeing you at Michaels Hall."

"I should enjoy that immensely." Colin turned to meet the curiosity in his own mother's eyes. His father's look was more one of suspicion. Suspicion wasn't quite as easily disarmed with words, but it was worth a try. "Tricia helped me decide that tonight would be a good opportunity to get reacquainted with a few people. She also graciously agreed to come with me so that I didn't feel so out of place."

Tricia's eyes widened. "Colin! You make it sound as if you had to drag me here. You know perfectly well, Mr. and Mrs. MacRae, that your son is being too modest. Any girl here would dearly love to have Colin as an escort tonight. I just happened to be the lucky one he asked."

"And why not?" John Michaels exclaimed heartily. The pride in his voice was unmistakable. "You two make a comely pair. I've always said as much, haven't I, Shaun?"

Shaun MacRae agreed with a slow, calculated nod. "Yes, John. I seem to remember hearing that statement a few times. Colin, I'd like to talk with you for a moment. If you will excuse us?"

Father and son strode with matched steps from the others.

Neither of them spoke until they were in the nearly deserted outer hall. "How did your appointment with Preston Napp go?"

The suddenness of the query set Colin on guard. He took a moment to answer, doing so only after he had studied the equally guarded expression in his father's eyes. "It went well."

"What was it about?"

Colin sucked in a deep breath. "That's my business."

"It's my business when you withdraw that amount of money in notes from the bank."

It hadn't escaped his attention then. His father had probably been watching him like a hawk. "I withdrew the money from my personal account...just as any other individual customer at the bank. Do you question them, too?"

Shaun's face became a chiseled mask. "What are you up to, Colin? I can go to Napp if I must."

"And pay him more so he'll tell you? That's not the way Preston Napp works. He's not about to compromise his integrity just so you can satisfy your own distrust." Colin consciously lowered his voice to keep their conversation private. "What I asked him to do is very important to me. I thought it over carefully. I'm doing what I think is right. When I feel that I can tell you what it is, I will. Until then, I'm sorry you don't approve." From Shaun's angry silence, Colin guessed he had said enough. "Excuse me, I owe Tricia some of my time, too."

Chapter Eighteen

Tuesday arrived before Preston Napp finally sent a note to the MacRae Mansion. The information it contained was hardly encouraging, but at least it was not a dead end. So far, the entire afternoon had been dismally gray, shutting Colin indoors until he thought he would go crazy. After reading Preston's note, his mind refused to be at rest. Too many questions remained unanswered.

Colin pulled on a heavy wool coat and called Rex to his side. They would both be better after a long walk. Instinctively, Colin headed toward the wharf. The cool, salt-misted breeze whipped color into his cheeks. He kept both hands sunk deeply into his jacket pockets. Each step became more anxious.

Rex, too, seemed restless. Though he had outwardly adjusted to the confinement of being in Boston, Colin thought he noted times when the dog clearly wanted his old freedoms. He was not the only one.

A covered carriage passed by, giving a brief glimpse of feminine bonnets. Tonight, he was to take Tricia to the Travois. Ever since Saturday's dance, he had wanted to tell her that he wouldn't be part of her scheme. Yet, he knew if he didn't go, she would attempt it on her own. The possibilities disturbed him enough to carry through with his promise. Really, Tricia needed to do this. She needed to see what it would be like to be thrown into such an atmosphere.

Part of his concern was that she would find it suited her only too well. Tricia was not the person she let other people think she was. Deep down inside was a reckless, almost desperate young woman. When she entered that other world, that unexplored side of life at the Travois, he wasn't at all sure what her reaction would be. There seemed only this one way to find out.

Colin's first glimpse of the sea afforded a sense of release for some of the tension which had been building in him since his return to Boston. The slate blue water, visible beyond a forest of ship's masts, riggings and sails, reminded him that he wasn't as far from the Cape as he felt at times. He was still unhappy about being forced to leave. So much of what he wanted from life was out there. So many of his dreams......

His hand closed around the paper in his pocket. Preston Napp's note had been repeatedly crumpled in his fist on the long walk down to the wharf. Colin pulled it out, not needing to see the words again to know what they said. He stared instead at the swirling eddies beneath the wooden dock where he was standing.

It had been several days since Colin last spent any time in communion with God and he felt a hunger to do so now. This restlessness in him was not an emotion he cared for. Surely his time at Highland had taught him how to seek the one Presence which could bring peace. A verse formed in his thoughts, reminding him that God was not the one who had moved away. "Draw near to God, and He will draw near to you."

Perhaps he would have to give up his desire to be back at Highland. Maybe that was the only way to find any contentment in his life again. But that choice seemed utterly impossible. How could he set aside his yearning to be wholly free? How could he give up what he had set out to find at Highland? Why did it seem as if God was taking so many things away from his life just now? For the first time since coming to know the Lord, Colin felt stripped of everything but Him. Could this be God's will - that he have nowhere else to turn?

Another thought stabbed through his consciousness. Even though she had come to a saving knowledge of Christ, Colin felt he had somehow failed with Kaytra. At the very root of his restlessness lay this one condemnation. He had failed. If he didn't find her again, he would feel that sense of guilt forever.

Colin had tried time and again to ask forgiveness. Dear God, but he wished he could go back in time and change so many moments when the unspoken words had come between them. He would search deeper for the gentleness which she needed. Where there should have been a strength in him, instead there had been too much hesitation. Someday, maybe God's forgiveness would take away the guilt. Still, Colin wasn't at all sure he would ever forgive himself.

Minutes later, his thoughts were broken by the sound of Rex's barking. It took Colin a moment to determine in which direction the dog had disappeared. Some seamen stood in a tight group a couple of hundred yards distant. The piercing whistle Colin gave failed to bring Rex to him, though several of the men swung their heads his way. Colin had a feeling that Rex wasn't barking a warning, but that he had only found something much more interesting to do on the docks than watch Colin stare at the water.

"What's he got in there?"

"Don't know."

"Cen ya see anythin'? Let me see!"

Gruff voices rang round the knot of men. Colin tried to push through them, but made little headway. He couldn't see what Rex was doing. Some of the men laughed, so it couldn't be all bad.

"Ain't never seen such a dog."

"Ain't no dog, man. He's part wolf if'n ya asked me."

"Naw. Look at him waggin' his tail like a wee puppy."

"Excuse me, please." Colin raised his voice, adding just the right amount of authority to it until the sailors began to part, letting him get closer. Rex wasn't barking anymore. Half of his body was wedged into a space between two large crates. "Rex! Come here!"

"He your dog?," someone asked.

"Yes." Colin answered as he stepped over a roll of heavy rope and around a few barrels. "Rex!" The dog broke free long enough to glance up before he resumed barking and plunged back into the crates, knocking over empty ones stacked on top.

A rumble of male laughter surfaced from the onlookers. "Must got some fair sized rat in there. Fixin' on havin' hisself a good supper."

"Naw. It's a rabbit. Off the ships from England. Get a pair on board when ya' start out an' ya have a hold full by the time ya dock!" More raucous guffaws rose at that joke.

Colin reached Rex, grabbing the leather collar around his neck to pull him away from whatever poor animal was cowering in the shadows of the boxes. "Come on, boy. You're not that starved." It was a test of strength to get him from the crates. Rex seemed determined to go on standing guard.

The sailors watched with growing interest as Colin literally lifted the dog over the jumble of ropes. They were well matched, this man and his beast. Colin spoke several stern commands, finally making Rex stand in obedience at his side. Without saying another word, the dog knew to follow when Colin started away from the scene. Several approving looks marked their steps.

"Did ya see 'im pick that guy up?"

"Thought he'd get 'is arm chewed off gettin' that close. No wolf woulda let me take 'im 'way from his lunch."

"Say, Turk! Whatcha doin'?!"

"Gonna see what he was after!" The last handful of curious men made short work of the pile of crates. "Hey!" Mouths opened wide in astonishment at what they found.

One of them finally recovered enough to reach out a hand and offer assistance to the pathetic creature huddled against the rough boards.

Had Colin known what Rex found beneath those boxes, he wouldn't have simply walked away. Not one of the sailors thought to make any connection between the well-dressed gentleman and the tattered, very obviously pregnant girl.

Kaytra shook in reaction to what had nearly happened. She pulled her torn, dirty cloak more tightly around her shoulders and slipped away from the bombardment of questions the group of men threw at her. While her frantic steps carried her in exactly the opposite direction from Colin, another reason for fear waited just a discreet few paces away, watching all that had happened, following her every move. She had tried before to lose him and had succeeded. Today, she was too tired - too upset to do any more than seek out the relative safety of the room in which she had been staying since she arrived in Boston.

As soon as they walked through the doors of the Travois that night, Colin knew he would regret bringing Tricia there. The atmosphere was charged with an excitement that made him uncomfortable. It was crowded. Nearly every table was filled, right up to the wide stage set across the far wall. Heavy blue velvet curtains hung from the ceiling.

A quick glance around the room showed Colin he was among strangers. He did not recognize even one face. Drinks flowed freely, no doubt creating much of the uncensored talking and loud laughter he heard. "Tricia, I don't think-."

"Look!" Her hand tightened upon his arm. "Mr. Montgomery is coming."

Too late now. Colin bit back his first response as he watched Montgomery stride across the room, oblivious to the pungent haze of smoke from the pipes and cigars. He was dressed more conservatively tonight in a black suit and white shirt. His only concession to flamboyance was the red brocade vest he wore. In Colin's book, he was considered a "dandy", but Tricia was too blind to see it.

Somehow, she was also able to overlook the fact that the Travois was the epitome of everything the name Montgomery stood for: grandeur without respect, loose money and low morals.

Colin was careful while they were there to keep himself detached, to view things with a question in his mind. It troubled him a great deal to think there was a part of Tricia which was reckless and daring enough to step over the lines separating her from this kind of world.

When Stephen came to see him the next afternoon, Colin told him exactly where he and Tricia had gone and why. Stephen echoed Colin's concerns. "You aren't going to let this go on, are you? If her father ever found out, he'd-."

"I'm beginning to wonder if that isn't what she wants." Colin stood next to the windows in the drawing room, gazing at the patterns of frost which jeweled the panes of glass.

"Tell him then."

"I can't, Stephen." The two friends met one another's eyes. "John Michaels would never believe me. Even if he did, he'd likely make life so miserable for Tricia that she'd simply run away some day."

"She'll probably do that anyway," Stephen pointed out gravely. He suspected Colin might be feeling some of his old attraction toward Tricia, letting what they had once shared overshadow his judgment. "She's changed, Colin. Ever since you left for Highland she's been - well, different. I don't know quite how to put it." He spread his hands wide in a frustrated gesture.

Colin crossed his arms over his chest, stretching the fabric of his white shirt over his shoulders. "Are you trying to make me feel guilty for leaving?"

"No!" Stephen dropped his hands immediately. "I'm trying to say, 'Be careful'. Patricia is cold inside. She's just using you, Colin."

"But she needs my help."

A sad look came into Stephen's blue eyes. "Maybe what she really needs, my friend, is someone who will tell her she's wrong."

There came a sharp knock on the door before it opened. Somehow, young Maggie O'Brien managed to carry a full tray through the narrow opening with one arm and close the door again with the other while still taking in every detail about the two men. It was this unusual feat which had both Colin and Stephen raising their eyebrows.

Their reactions brought a silly grin to her face. "Don't believe I've grown a second nose, have I?," she asked with much amusement, crossing the room to set her tray on a low table near two chairs by the Italian marble fireplace.

Colin chuckled at her boldness. He hadn't seen much of her since coming back, but she certainly was proving to be a surprise. "No, Maggie. You haven't grown a second nose."

When she smiled, twin dimples appeared at the corners of her mouth, giving an appealing, child-like quality to her petite features. There were freckles upon her nose, made visible by the sunlight coming through the windows. "Good. 'Cause the one I have suits me just fine. I don't suppose I need a second one." Her gaze moved to Stephen.

The long pause made Colin feel as if he should introduce the two of them, though he had never before introduced a household servant to any of his friends, with the possible exception of Beany, of course.

"Stephen, this is Maggie O'Brien. Maggie - my oldest friend, Stephen Kemp."

To Colin's utter astonishment and - it appeared, Stephen's, too - Maggie walked forward and held out her hand. "Good day, Mr. Kemp."

Stephen took her hand lightly in his own, not quite expecting the firmness of her grip. "Miss O'Brien."

"You may as well call me Maggie right from the start. I was raised in a house with ten children, more than half of them girls. I learned early that I'd get lost in the shuffle unless I made myself a name instead of being plain old third from the oldest." She chuckled at Stephen's expression. Only when she pointedly looked down at their still joined hands did he release hers. Maggie glanced over at Colin then. "I know you didn't ask for coffee, Mr. MacRae, but I figured it was the only way for me to have an excuse to come in here."

It was Colin's turn to look at her with a puzzled expression. "And why exactly is it you felt you needed to come?" His mother had gotten more than she bargained for in hiring this young girl. In a very good sense of the meaning, of course.

Maggie O'Brien, all five feet-four inches of her, took in a slow breath, letting it out again as a whisper-soft sigh. "If I may speak freely, sir?"

"I think you've already done that, Maggie."

She smiled along with them at Colin's teasing. "Well, rules are rules, you know."

"Only when needed." Colin felt comfortable with her, and so did Stephen, judging by the amused look on his face. "What is it you need, Maggie?"

"Oh! It wouldn't be me needing anything. It's your mother."

"My mother?"

Maggie gave a quick nod and suddenly busied herself with pouring coffee for the men. "Mrs. MacRae has been very much improved since your return. In some ways, that is." She handed Stephen the first cup. "But she is still grieving over your sister's death. Now, I never knew Lydia, but from what Beany has said about her, she was a wonderful person."

Colin agreed with an interested nod as Maggie served him also.

It seemed only natural that she sit down on the sofa while the men sat in the chairs. "I'm worried that Mrs. MacRae should still be so torn over Lydia's death. When my own mother died, it hurt a great deal, but the pain eventually got less and less. Some days, I still miss her and it's been five years now. Mrs. MacRae -. Well, sometimes I'll find her just crying and crying as if her heart was broke, almost as if she was feeling some weight of guilt that was keepin' the grief pressed in like." To see the depth of compassion in Maggie's eyes, one wouldn't remember she was but a servant girl talking about her mistress.

A frown of concern had gathered on Colin's features. Maggie was a very perceptive girl, and a brave one at that. Not even Beany had come to him with this problem. "Do you think I should talk to her then, Maggie?"

"Well," she considered her words carefully now. "No, Mr. MacRae. I think she needs to have some distraction. Some reason to look out of herself and see that life is still going on all around her. Talking to her would only make her think about the grief more. Distracting her would give her time to heal."

Stephen met her gaze thoughtfully once she was done speaking. He had been silent all along, listening. Maggie's expression now somehow made him think she was seeking his approval for what she had just done. He gave it to her with a slight tilting of his head.

The sound of the doorbell ringing could be heard through the closed door and Maggie jumped to her feet. "I must get that. Excuse me." She was only gone a few minutes, but instead of returning to finish their discussion, as Stephen expected, she handed Colin a thick envelope. "For you. A boy brought it by."

Immediately curious, Colin set his coffee down and tore open the seal. His hands stilled. Both Stephen and Maggie sensed a tensing within him. Behind the bank notes there was a worn, yellowed scrap of paper. He recognized the handwriting at once,

"Please keep the money. I neither need it nor want it."

Stephen couldn't take the silence any longer. "What is it, Colin?"

Characteristically, Colin shared the note without a second thought, though he directed an urgent question at Maggie. "A boy brought this? Did he leave?"

"Well, yes sir. He-."

Colin pushed past her, intent on stopping the boy. A cold blast of air met him as he jerked open the front door. The churning of emotion he felt carried him outside without a coat or hat. He raced down the steps toward the gate.

There was only one boy in sight on the entire street. "Wait! You, boy, wait a minute!" Colin's loud voice frightened the young boy, but he wasn't sure that was the sole reason why the lad took off running. It was easy enough for Colin to catch up to him. His hand closed about the worn collar, pulling the boy to a skidding halt. Wild, green eyes in a dirty face looked up at him. "I won't hurt you. I only need to ask you some questions."

The boy fought to free himself, but he was no more than nine years old and on the wiry side. "Le'me go! Le'me go, I say!"

"Not until you tell me who sent you here!"

"Can't!"

"Do it anyway! I need to find the woman who gave you the envelope. Tell me where she is!" Colin didn't wonder why the boy was looking at him as if he was crazy. He made an effort to keep his own anxiety under control.

Caution made the boy cease his struggling. "She paid me only ta d'liver it here."

"Okay." Colin knew the game well. "I'll pay you to show me where she lives."

"How much?," the boy asked with eager suspicion.

"Enough. Come on. We'll take a carriage." Colin kept a firm hold on him as they started back up the drive. He wasn't at all surprised to see Stephen and Maggie in the doorway, waiting for him to return. When Stephen found out what Colin was going to do, he knew he needed to go along.

The boy sat between them on the seat, tightly grasping the silver coins Colin had given him for fear they would bounce out of his hand the way the horses were being driven so recklessly.

When they reached the area near the wharfs, Colin was forced to go slower. With the boy giving him directions, they traveled past rows of warehouses and taverns. People stared at them because they were so out of place - a fine carriage and two gentlemen in the midst of Boston's lowest slums. Little children, playing in the street, dressed in thin, ragged clothes ran to hide from them. Old men, some not quite sober, eyed them with uncertainty.

Finally, they pulled up where the boy directed, a shabby, three-story building. It was a narrow building, seemingly squeezed between two others just like it. "Are you sure this is it?," Colin asked, partly because he could already guess the conditions he would find inside. He didn't want to believe she had been living in such a place.

"I'm sure. Top floor." The boy climbed down after Stephen and would have bolted out of sight except that Colin called him back.

"Wait! I'll pay you to stay and watch the horses." He didn't trust anyone in this kind of neighborhood. The boy received another coin in promise not to let a soul take the carriage before Colin and Stephen returned.

Inside, the building was dark. It smelled of tobacco and cooked cabbage, mildew and urine. Colin's stomach turned at the stench, but he took the lead and they hurried up two flights of narrow, creaking stairs. At least half a dozen closed doors stared back at them. Short of knocking on each one of them, Stephen didn't know how they would find the right room.

Before he could ask, Colin was striding forward again, raising his hand at the second door on the left. There wasn't an answer. He knocked again.

"Maybe it's not her room." Stephen felt self-conscious standing in the middle of the hallway.

"It is. It's the only one that's been cleaned." Colin repeated his knock while Stephen looked around and realized his friend wasn't mistaken, though how he had determined so much at a mere glance was a mystery.

"Kaytra! Open the door...I won't leave until I see you."

Stephen had never seen Colin quite so doggedly determined before. As soon as he had a chance, he was going to make Colin tell him the rest of the story about Kaytra Lange. For now, he watched the door shudder beneath Colin's impatient summons.

"Kaytra!...I won't-."

The door was suddenly flung open from the inside and Colin found himself standing face to face with the woman who had occupied his thoughts so many times since they had last seen one another over two months ago.

Only Kaytra, the Kaytra who stared back at him now, seemed pitifully shrunken and pale, reminding him of how she had looked the first time she came to Highland, except that now the child had grown within her. As they stood there, staring at one another in silence, an expression darkened her eyes which Colin couldn't, at first, identify.

When he did speak, it was with more gentleness than he intended. "Did you really think I'd believe you didn't need the money?"

Kaytra glanced over his shoulder, embarrassed that Colin had brought someone else. The other man held her gaze for only a moment, long enough for her to determine that he was uncomfortable. She moved her eyes back to Colin's. "No, I thought you would call off your henchmen."

It was the longest sentence she had ever spoken to him. Colin was momentarily taken back by the heavily-accented quality to her voice. Her French heritage was still very much evident in her words.

"How was I supposed to find you without hiring someone?"

"You didn't need to find me." Though she tried hard to keep her voice even, it became impossible. Colin's eyes narrowed immediately. She had to get rid of him. "Go away, Colin. Please, just leave me alone."

"That's not possible, Kaytra. How can I let you change my life forever, then forget all about you?" His voice was still calm, but it also held a measure of growing impatience. Colin felt Stephen's hand on his arm, cautioning him, but he was already praying that God would help him remain in control.

A few doors opened along the hallway as curious tenants poked their heads out to see the unusual exchange. Colin ignored their stares.

"Jolly said you came to find your grandparents. He gave you money to find them, but you haven't yet or-."

Though Kaytra used her last reserve of energy to push the door closed, Colin was too quick for her. He blocked it with his forearm, using superior strength to force it wide open again. Maybe if another spasm hadn't come just then, she could have won. Maybe she could have made him leave. Instead, she suddenly let go, staggering around until she could grip the edge of the dresser.

For a long time, she knew only the pain which tore through her chest at each gasp for air. She closed her eyes, seeking that one pin-point of light which had been her concentration for the past weeks. When it was over, she weakly raised her head to find Colin and his friend in the room, staring at her. Tears pricked hotly at the backs of her eyes. "Please, just - just leave." Already another rise of pain came. It must be the turmoil, having to face Colin again.

Colin began removing his coat. "Stephen, go get Dr. Graham."

"But-." Stephen's worried expression made him look pale. "He - he won't come here, Colin." His hands indicated the whole room in one sweep. It was clean, but hardly bigger than a water closet and so cold it was a wonder she hadn't frozen to death. "She can't have the baby here!

"She's not having the baby." Colin swung his coat around Kaytra's shoulders, making another decision which he knew she would welcome even less. "Pack up her things then. We'll take her home."

"No!" Kaytra jerked away. "I - won't - go."

Incredibly, Colin smiled down at her stubborn expression. "You know, I think I liked it better when you couldn't talk!"

"Th-at can - be - arranged!"

Sometime during the carriage ride through Boston, Kaytra fell asleep. When she awoke again, it was to find herself in a strange room, a beautiful peach and cream room. She felt warm again and -. The sound which had awakened her came again. Glass clinking. She turned her head toward the sound to find an elderly man measuring something into a glass of water.

As soon as she moved, she realized the heaviness in her chest all over again. A fit of coughing drew the man's attention. He was odd looking, a stranger. Kaytra automatically shrank from him when he came near her to help her sit up. "It's alright," he said in a low, gravely voice. "You have no reason to be afraid."

But she was afraid. She didn't want him to be there, to touch her. She curled up into a tight ball, still unable to control the coughing which ripped through her chest.

"Go get Colin then." The man spoke urgently to a woman Kaytra noticed next to the doorway.

By the time Colin hurried into the room, Kaytra had worked herself into a panic, making it even harder to regain her breath. Her color matched the whiteness of his evening shirt, except for the evidence of fever staining a flush upon her cheeks. Colin slid onto the edge of the bed. "So, you finally woke up." He lifted her until she was sitting.

Doctor Graham and Beany exchanged a startled glance when Kaytra sank into the comfort of Colin's arms. They had, of course, privately wondered about the relationship between the two young people, but they had not felt it was their place to ask.

Colin smoothed Kaytra's hair with a tender hand. He was a little surprised himself that Kaytra clung to him so desperately, but she was sick and - if he knew her at all - more than a bit overwhelmed at being in a room full of people she had never seen before. "Doctor Graham is our family doctor, Kaytra. I asked him to help take care of you."

Gradually, her breathing became more normal. Colin could feel the heat of her body penetrating his shirt. Even so, she had begun to shiver. "Let's get you covered up." He spoke in gentle tones, being careful as he laid her upon the bed.

"Here, Colin." Dr. Graham moved forward, handing Colin the glass of water. He seemed satisfied when Kaytra drank it thirstily. "She has a lung condition. It's rather serious, I'm afraid."

Colin gave him back the empty glass. "She'll be fine. How is the baby?"

Dr. Graham tilted his head at a thoughtful angle. To say the least, young Colin's manner had been strange right from the start; summoning him to the MacRae Mansion in all haste, presenting a girl who was soon to have a child herself. But whose child? And where had she come from, anyway?

Colin read the questions in the older man's eyes and chose to prod him on. "Well? Is the baby alright?"

"As near as I can tell, yes, but she needs to rest. She needs to eat. She needs-."

"Kaytra will get everything she needs, Dr. Graham." At the sound of Colin saying her name, Kaytra opened her eyes, searching out his face. Though he smiled reassurance, that expression vanished. He recognized the empty, distant expression in her eyes only too well. He turned on the doctor in anger. "What was in that water?"

"Colin, she-."

"No more," Colin said it in absolute firmness. "She won't be kept drugged as you did with Lydia. Is that clear?"

Dr. Graham, a musty, white-haired, bespectacled man nearing the age of retirement, stiffened in judgmental pride. "That young lady will die, if you must know."

"She won't die."

"She will if she gets overly excited. If she fights against those who try to help her!"

Colin relaxed a little. Obviously, the doctor's pride had been injured. There weren't many patients who weren't in awe around "the" Dr. Henry Graham. "Give her some time to get used to being here." Colin's gaze included Beany, who was holding herself strangely aloof from the scene. "She'll be just fine, really. And without the powders."

"But-."

Colin cut off the doctor's arguments with a crisp "no". After seeing what the medicine had done to his sister, he wouldn't allow Kaytra to be caught up in that numb, unemotional fantasy world.

In a few minutes, Dr. Graham left the room, promising to return the next morning, or sooner "if the need should arise", meaning none of Colin's words had convinced him that Kaytra would survive.

But she would. Colin touched the hollow of her cheek with the back of his hand.

"I'll be downstairs." Beany's abrupt announcement drew his attention, yet she made no move toward the door. Her eyes shifted uncomfortably between Colin's face and Kaytra's. "Yer parents will be wantin' an explanation. For your sake, and hers, I hope you'll have one."

"You don't approve of my bringing her here, Beany?"

"'Tain't my place to 'prove or not. It's them you'll have ta convince." Beany picked up the pile of Kaytra's old clothes which Colin had asked to have washed. In her opinion, they should have gone right in the trash. "God help you, boy, what ever you done."

"I'm sure He will, Beany. I'm sure He will," Colin repeated as she left the room.

All was quiet then. They were alone. Colin pressed a fingertip to Kaytra's slightly parted lips. He had discovered with Lydia that it was the one place not desensitized by the drugs, the one way he would draw her back to reality. Kaytra opened her eyes. "They're gone now. I'll stay with you." He guessed that Dr. Graham hadn't given her much of the drug after all for she tried to speak to him. When she found out she couldn't, tears filled her eyes. "Shhhh." Colin soothed her fear. "It will be gone in a few hours, then you can talk. I won't let anyone give you the medicine again. I promise."

Kaytra seemed to understand and blinked her eyes very slowly.

"I brought you to my home. This is Lydia's room. I thought you would be comfortable here. Dr. Graham is a good doctor, Kaytra. You should be nice to him." Colin smiled, feeling rather foolish for having to defend a sixty-year-old paragon from this mere slip of a young woman. "The other person who was here is Beany. Her real name is Beatrice. She's been around since Lydia and I were young. You'll have to be nice to her, too, or she'll hold it over my head forever that I never told her about you."

Though Kaytra's eyes had closed again, Colin sensed she wasn't sleeping. "That's not the real world, Kaytra. I know it doesn't hurt and it's peaceful, but it isn't real. Lydia told me how easy it is to get lost there, to feel - released, I guess. But it's a prison in itself. This world is real. I'm real." He resisted the urge to gather her into his arms. Instead, he laid his hand over the place where the baby moved. In a way, he felt disappointed that she hadn't had the baby today, as Stephen first thought. Perhaps, though, they needed more time.

Colin moved his hand to Kaytra's face in a gesture which was so tender it caught at Catherine's heart as she stood transfixed in the doorway, watching, wondering. How many times had she come upon Colin talking so with Lydia? The breath seemed driven from her with painful force.

Though she had made no sound, Colin finally sensed that she was there and turned his head in her direction, weighing her reaction in a single glance. "Mother, come in."

Catherine moved forward only far enough to gain a clearer look at the woman in Lydia's bed. Before she could form her jumble of questions into coherent words, Shaun, too, entered the room. They had heard rumors of the day's events upon arriving home. Seeing the evidence which gave truth to what the servants were saying caused a myriad of emotions.

"Who is she?," Shaun asked in a strangely subdued voice. He had ventured a few steps further than his wife, but was no less stiff and cautious.

Colin felt Kaytra's body grow tense, something very unusual under the influence of Dr. Graham's powders, except perhaps that she sensed they were no longer alone. "Her name is Kaytra. She was the housekeeper at Highland Light."

That didn't explain much, he knew. But it still didn't give Shaun leave to run his eyes over her as if she was someone less than worthy to be in his house. Catherine, too, appeared to recoil from Kaytra's obviously pregnant state. Especially since she had seen her son's af-fection for the girl.

Their disdain brought Colin to a decision, making it easier for him to speak his next words. "Kaytra is my wife. She is to have my child. Your grandchild. "

Catherine reached for the back of the chair nearest her, lifting a hand to her face, but not quite hiding the horror she felt.

Shaun's hands clenched into fists at his sides. "You're lying."

"Prove it." Colin knew his challenge would drive a wedge into their already unstable relationship, but he refused to back down. "Before you do anything, though, you should know that Kaytra was the one who nursed Lydia. She was your daughter's friend. Kaytra cared for Lydia with more love than she ever received before. If you want to go proving something, prove that you can look into Kaytra's eyes and say her kindness to Lydia doesn't mean a thing to you."

A brief silence spanned the room. Somehow, Colin knew he had hit hard against his father's defense. Yet he also guessed Shaun wouldn't give in.

He was right. "I'll expect you in my office within the hour." The ultimatum was delivered with icy calm before Shaun turned and left the room.

Catherine had recovered enough to lower herself into the chair. She shook her head every once in a while as if to clear away thoughts she found too difficult to comprehend. Colin's heart softened toward her. "I'm sorry you feel that I've done something to hurt you, Mother. I never intended for either of you to learn about Kaytra this way."

"You didn't have to p- put her in - this room!"

Colin studied the pinched expression on her face. "She'll be comfortable here."

"Never mind what my feelings might be!"

"Mother-."

Catherine gave him no chance. "I won't have a perfect stranger in your sister's room!"

"Kaytra isn't a stranger. I-."

"If she must stay here," Catherine's voice sounded pitifully shaken, "I won't have her in Lydia's room."

If she must stay? Colin hadn't expected his mother to resent Kaytra. She was usually so passionate when it came to doing what was right. He watched her get up and move from the room on wooden limbs.

It seemed now as if Beany hadn't been far wrong when she muttered, "God help you, boy."

Chapter Nineteen

It was at Colin's insistence the next morning that Maggie took care of Kaytra. Beany, still unsure of her own feelings, relinquished the role of nursemaid with a stern warning to the younger girl not to get too involved. But Maggie was involved. She had spent a few minutes the day before talking with both Colin and Stephen, learning the truth about Kaytra, promising to do all she could in order to protect her.

Now, Maggie stood next to the bed in Lydia's room. Her eyes took in every detail, feeling at once a sense of pity and a curious expectation. She set down the breakfast tray quietly, not wanting to awaken the girl who, she had learned, was two years younger than herself. But Kaytra did stir upon the bed, slowly opening her eyes to the daylight seeping through the heavy draperies. Maggie smiled kindly. "Good morning." Kaytra focused on her, saying nothing. "I brought you something to eat. Or would you care to bathe first?"

The question went unanswered as Kaytra took slow account of her surroundings. Bits and pieces of the previous night clashed with the softness of day. This was Lydia's room, someone - Colin had told her so.

She returned her gaze to the maid, though, for some reason, that word seemed unsuitable. Despite the gray dress and white apron, there wasn't an attitude of servanthood about the woman, almost as if she was proud of the work she did and meant to make everyone respect her for it. Kaytra hesitantly pushed herself upright against the pillows. The slight dizziness she experienced didn't go unnoticed.

"Here now." Maggie moved forward to help, unprepared for the way Kaytra jerked away. "I'm sorry." The apology was an injured one.

Yet, by the time Kaytra glanced back up at her, Maggie had recovered her easy smile. "I should introduce myself, I suppose. I'm Maggie. Colin asked me to sit with you this morning until he returns."

Was it her imagination or was there a fleeting moment of panic in Kaytra's eyes? Maggie hurried on. "I'm sure he won't be gone very long. In a way, I'm glad we can spend some time alone. Just the two of us." Kaytra's eyes widened a little. Colin had been right. Those striking blue-gray eyes could tell their own story. Gaining confidence now that she wouldn't pull away again, Maggie set the tray before Kaytra. "Eat up now. You must be near starved after yesterday's excitement. What do you think of your room? I've always thought it very romantic and feminine. Colin said you were close friends with Lydia?" Maggie kept talking as she moved to open the heavy drapes, letting sunshine overcome the shadowy room.

Kaytra was staring down at the food on the tray. A tiny china tea pot with a cup and saucer to match. A single, soft-boiled egg. Some thin oatmeal made deliciously brown with maple syrup. Toast. She hadn't seen so much food all in one place since - since leaving Highland. Yes, she and Lydia had been close friends. The silent thought brought hot tears to her eyes. She tried to blink them away as Maggie poured her a cup of tea, placing a lump of sugar in it for good measure.

"As soon as you are strong enough, you shall get to see all of the mansion. I can remember when I first came here. I stood out front staring for the longest time. But now I've learned to see it as a home like any other. It's the people inside who make it exciting or sad or happy." There was something soothing about the way Maggie kept on. Her voice was pleasant, carefully correct, but with a hint of youthful laughter behind the words.

Because her hands shook around the cup of tea, Kaytra was unsure whether she could get even one drop of it to her lips. When she did, it tasted mellow and warm, subduing the empty hunger.

"I'm sure," Maggie went on cheerfully, "that you'll come to meet everyone soon. Of course, you've met Beany. She is fiercely protective of Colin. She's able to put up a hard front unless you get on her good side. Though Colin seems to be able to charm her quite easily, I'm not sure yet that she likes me. Perhaps because she believes in things being very old fashioned.

"Carlisle is the butler. He's rather - oh, I don't know - dashing, I suppose. At least Trudy, the other maid, thinks so. In my opinion, he has his nose stuck up so far into the air it's a wonder he doesn't get the vapors! Here." Maggie helped Kaytra with the cereal, pleased to see that she was eating even a little of the food. "Cook is simply delightful. She and I get along very well indeed. She's a big woman, fond of all the delicate fancies she makes. But if you ever need a favor, Cook is the one to ask.

"There are stable boys and a groomsman, of course. Sometimes, for extra gatherings, Mrs. MacRae will have temporary help come in. Have you met them yet? Mr. and Mrs. MacRae, I mean."

Kaytra set down her spoon very slowly, shaking her head in an uncertain way. Surely she hadn't met them and yet-.

"I'm sure Colin will tell you all about them. If you're done eating-?" Maggie asked. Kaytra nodded. "We can give you a nice warm bath then. The tub is full already, by the fire there. You get up real careful now. I'll help you."

Maggie talked on and on so that by the time the bath was done and Kaytra, in a clean nightgown with freshly washed hair, was seated near the warmth of the fire, there seemed nothing about the young woman she didn't know. No one had ever had to assist her with a bath before, but just this one time it didn't matter. If felt wonderful to be truly clean again.

Kaytra brushed weakly at the tangle of curls, spreading them across her back to dry. She envied Maggie the energy to flit about the room, opening the draperies, changing the sheets on the bed, straightening this and that upon the dressers. Maybe after the baby was born, she would begin to feel better, too. Her hand lay for a moment upon the swell of her belly. Not long now. It kicked against her ribs, causing her to gasp in pain.

Concern brought a frown to Maggie's face, but Kaytra managed a smile in return. "Do you hope for a boy or a girl?," Maggie asked. "I should like my first to be twins, I think. One of each. If I ever do get married, that is. I'm not sure that I shall ever find someone willing to put up with me...why, Kaytra! What is it?" Maggie hurried to her, this time concerned for the tears which were escaping Kaytra's tremendously sad eyes.

Those eyes were locked helplessly on an oval, gilt-edged frame which rested next to a small book on the table beside Kaytra's chair. Just as Maggie despaired of knowing what to do, there was a knock on the door.

Doctor Graham couldn't have chosen a worse time to appear. His gruff mannerism spoke disapproval at finding Kaytra not only out of bed, but in such a "state of weakness" that she was crying besides.

He ordered Maggie to see the patient back into bed, then she was to leave the room entirely, sending either Beatrice or Mrs. MacRae to him at once. Because Beany was nowhere to be found just then, it was Catherine who arrived a few minutes later. "You asked to see me, Dr. Graham?"

"Yes. Please." Dr. Graham straightened from listening to Kaytra's lungs, giving both women their first full look at one anther - or so Kaytra thought. Except that - something-? She had heard that voice before.

"Do come in Mrs. MacRae." The older man thought it rather odd that she hovered in the doorway. "I must discuss this case with some-one who understands such things."

Catherine found little to be threatened by in Kaytra's eyes. Yet she felt odd being in the same room with her. She clasped both hands together before the black lace front of her dress. The action set her shoulders into a stiff line. "Doctor Graham, if you need to discuss treat-ment, I am hardly the one to-."

Dr. Graham interrupted as if he hadn't even heard one word. "That young maid, the one who was here - ?"

"Maggie?"

"She upset the patient dreadfully. She's too - flighty to take care of anyone so critically ill. See that she isn't allowed in here again. There should be no food on this tray. Only clear liquids. And all of this sun-shine!" He immediately pulled the heavy draperies closed, plunging the room into gray shadowed lifelessness.

The orders went on and on with Catherine absorbing what was said, agreeing with him simply to be done and quit the room, to leave sight of those penetrating, blue-gray eyes. In half an hour, she walked Dr. Graham to the front door, offering the customary "thank you" be-fore she could escape to be alone with her own thoughts.

Maggie was nearly in tears by the time she heard Colin arrive. He had already reached the top of the stairs before she caught up to him. "Colin!" He turned at once, his smile disappearing at her distress. Maggie ran up the last few steps to clutch the sleeve of his coat and practically pull him along the hall. She feared being overheard. "You were gone so long!"

"What's happened?" Colin demanded.

"Doctor Graham came. He threw me out! I-."

"Kaytra?"

They had reached the bedroom. Maggie opened the door, slipping inside ahead of him. "She was like this when I found her."

Even before he sank down onto the bed, Colin dreaded what he knew must have happened.

"She was crying when Doctor Graham got here. Something about that picture on the table. He insisted on talking to your mother...I couldn't do anything, Colin. I'm sorry."

"It's not your fault, Maggie. I'll stay with her now." In a few moments, he heard the soft click of the latch. Kaytra wasn't sleeping, yet she failed to respond to his touch. Colin sat by her for a long time before rising and walking to the table which held the picture he wanted to see.

The frame felt warmed by the fire. Dear, little Sondra...Kaytra must have known who the child was. An artist had come to the house to do the portrait on Sondra's third birthday, painting such joy and softness into the portrait that one could almost hear the little girl laugh.

Colin set the frame in its place and picked up a leather-bound book. The page most worn was one Lydia had written herself, lines copied from a poem.

"How fading are the joys we dote upon!

Like apparitions seen and gone;

But those which soonest take their flight

Are the most exquisite and strong;

Like angels' visits, short and bright

Mortality's too weak to bear them long.

John Norris - The Parting

He sat down in the chair, finding little to rest his weary thoughts except prayer. And pray he did. For hours. Undisturbed by sound or movement. Only his heart moved, between its earthly worries and heaven's strength, seeking the wisdom of One who could see a whole, complete picture.

Finally, he knew what he had to do.

This time when he touched Kaytra's lips, she opened her eyes to him. Though the effects of the drug could still be seen, Colin sensed she was aware enough to hear him. He took her hand in his, willing her to stay in the real world. "Kaytra, I needed to be gone earlier. I had some important things to do." She started to let her eyes close again, but Colin pressed her hand more firmly. "No, Kaytra, listen to me. I'm doing this to protect you and the baby."

He took his other hand from his pocket, feeling the tiny circle of gold warm against his flesh. "I hope you'll remember this later. I wanted this to be special for you." Very slowly, he slipped the ring onto the third finger of her left hand. "It's the only way. Nobody would understand otherwise. The baby needs a father. I should never have let you leave Highland Light." Colin laid her hand flat against his.

"Kaytra, you need to do something for me. Don't let anyone give you the medicine again. It won't make you better." He tried to keep the anger from his voice for he knew she would pick up on it. "Lydia became addicted to the powder. It was hard to bring her back. I don't know if I could do it again. Tell them no. Fight them - anything - but don't take the medicine."

There was so much he needed to talk to her about, yet now wasn't the time. He rang the bell, waiting out the minutes before Trudy came. He told her to bring him something to eat and also to show Stephen upstairs when he arrived.

Kaytra woke fully to find that much of the day had been lost to her. The draperies were still drawn, but this time against night's chill darkness. She stirred cautiously, feeling life come into her limbs after long inactivity. A lamp glowed beside the bed. Several more stood around the room. Colin was there, and the man she had seen - when? Was it really only yesterday? She felt more confused. The two men were sitting across the room, talking in low tones.

For a while, she simply listened to the murmur of their deep voices. It comforted her to hear them, though why should she need to be comforted? So many questions... "Colin?"

He stood as soon as she said his name, walking toward her with a smile that held relief. "Hello." He leaned over, placing an arm on either side of her. She thought he looked tired, too. A shadow of a beard roughened his face. Kaytra wondered why she felt the need to reach up as she did to know that he was real.

Strangely, Colin seemed to understand. "You're really awake. Are you hungry?"

She nodded.

"I'll get it." Stephen volunteered, jumping up to ring the bell pull. Both men were dressed casually. He turned back with a rather sheepish look on his face. "Do you want me to go now, Colin? I could -."

"Not at all," Colin objected even as he lifted Kaytra into a sitting position on the bed and rearranged her covers. "Come over here. I've yet to introduce you two properly. Kaytra, this is a friend of mine, Stephen Kemp. He was with me yesterday, do you remember?"

Of course, she remembered! Why wouldn't she? Kaytra's expression puzzled over Colin's choice of words, then became truly shocked as he completed the introduction. "Stephen - my wife, Kaytra."

"Hello, Kaytra." Stephen nodded politely, very much aware that she wasn't even looking at him, but was instead staring at Colin.

Colin's eyebrows rose. "You'll have to get over being so shy, Kaytra. What is it you want to say?"

"I-," she stumbled over the words, "I'm - not your - wife!"

"Shhh." He pressed a finger over her mouth, quieting the next outburst to a frantic whisper.

"Colin! I'm not -. I -. We -." She shook her head, wanting to pull back when he lifted her hand, except that the glimmer of a gold band caught her eye, holding her captive by its mere presence. Some vague sense of feeling that she should know when it had been placed there failed to form into coherent memories.

A brief knock preceded Kaytra's tray into the room. Maggie was the one who carried it.

"You're just in time," Colin told her with another of his easy smiles. "My wife gets rather cranky when she's hungry."

Maggie eyed all three people, not certain whether to take him seriously. One look at Kaytra told her she had indeed arrived "just in time". Not in the way Colin meant, but to spare Kaytra the quick wit of these two male friends. "And what have you done now, Colin MacRae?" She practically pushed him aside in setting the tray across Kaytra's lap. "Oh my, Kaytra. They've upset you again."

"I'm not his - his wife!" Kaytra blurted out, ashamed of the tears which pooled in her eyes. She remembered Maggie. Remembered her kindness and found herself clinging to it now.

At once, Maggie took the small hand in her own, kneeling next to the bed in earnest. "But you must be his wife, Kaytra," she said calmly. "Colin has it all figured out. How to keep you safe and-."

"Safe? From what? Who?"

"Well...," Maggie looked to Colin and Stephen for help.

It was Colin, now leaning against the end post of the bed, arms crossed, who answered. "Anyone would think by listening to you that I'm the absolute worst match you could think of. You know, you should just have said 'yes' when I asked you at Highland. It would have saved us a lot of trouble."

Stephen and Maggie had the same rather dismayed light in their eyes as they looked at each other. Colin had proposed before? Somehow that part of the story hadn't been told yesterday.

"I couldn't say 'yes'," Kaytra protested, practically upsetting the china on the tray because she was shaking so much.

"You very well could have, Kaytra." Colin spoke evenly, keeping his eyes locked with hers so that she couldn't look away. "It made no sense at all for me to take you back to Provincetown. Koch only beat you again. We both knew that would happen."

"I don't care!"

A charged silence split the room then. Stephen sensed it was time that he leave and not alone either. "Maggie?"

She raised her eyes, understanding his slight nod toward the door and stood with an apologetic look at Kaytra.

Stephen closed the door softly. Neither he nor Maggie spoke until they paused at the head of the stairs.

"Do you think they will be all right?" Maggie asked with such grave concern, Stephen felt sorry for her.

He tilted his head to the side, a gesture Maggie was beginning to recognize as a habit with him. "Knowing Colin, they will. But not before Kaytra is willing to admit that he's right."

"Right?" Maggie lowered her voice. "I don't exactly see him being completely without fault here, sir - Stephen." Her quick amendment sounded as if she had suddenly beknighted him and they both smiled in amusement.

"My lady." Stephen bowed gallantly, offering his arm to lead her down the stairs. Maggie played along, feeling all aflutter inside. "Do you pray, Maggie?"

The unexpected switch to a more serious subject surprised her. "Some."

"Then you shall have to pray for Colin and Kaytra. As I shall pray, too." Stephen glanced across at her, noting features which were becoming exceedingly familiar to him. "I'm sure God has a way of working these things out to completion."

The completion of whatever Colin had begun was hardly the most pressing thing on Kaytra's mind just then. She was, in fact, finding it difficult to accept that he had begun the lie at all. "I don't see how you could do this, Colin!"

His broad shoulders lifted in an unassuming shrug. "Think about it. How else was I supposed to explain bringing you here?"

"You didn't need to bring me here!"

He pushed himself away from the post and took two steps to sit in the chair beside the bed. "I was supposed to let you stay in that room then. Let you have the baby all alone. How did you plan to support yourselves? Selling bait bags?"

Kaytra flushed at the sarcasm in his tone. Obviously, he had found some of the net bags in her room, but that still didn't give him the right to ridicule her. She tore her gaze from his, covering her expression with a downward sweep of long eyelashes.

"Aren't you going to fight back?"

"I'm tired."

Colin didn't accept her excuse. "You aren't tired. In fact, you feel so well, you think you can get up and run around this room."

Kaytra's head snapped up. How had he known?

"Lydia told me." He answered the unspoken question. "It's a side-effect to the drug. A very dangerous one. When you come out of it, you feel a surge of energy. It won't last long, though, and you shouldn't give in to it. You'll only end up feeling terribly weakened."

"I don't understand any of this." A despairing hollowness took over her voice. Kaytra absently picked up the silver fork beside her plate, thinking that it didn't shine as much as the new gold ring on her finger. "There are so many lies, Colin. Lies only hurt people." She didn't see the darkening of his eyes. "Your parents, your mother - she was here before, I think."

"Maggie said she was. Did you say anything to her?"

Kaytra shook her head, remembering the woman she had met, remembering her sad, rather indescribable expression.

"I told my parents we were married, Kaytra." Colin leaned forward until his forearms rested on his knees. "I've got a marriage certificate and-."

"No." Kaytra let the fork drop back onto the tray. When she moved, swinging her legs over the side of the bed, Colin had to rescue the tray before it fell from her lap. He knocked over a glass in pushing it onto the bedstand. "I won't let you do this, Colin. I won't let you lie to them."

He blocked her by placing one leg on either side of her, making her feel small and frail compared to his strength. His hands came up to grip her arms. "I also told them the child is mine." Kaytra pressed an unsteady hand to her mouth. "They'll believe it if you make them think it's true. You owe me that much."

"I - owe - you?" She stared wide-eyed at him. "I don't owe you anything!"

"Not even for ruining my life? For making me leave Highland?" The single-minded hardness which leapt into his eyes made Kaytra want to pull away, but he wouldn't let her go. "There was nothing to keep you from marrying me back then, Kaytra. There's nothing preventing it now. If you don't convince my parents and everyone else that you are Mrs. Colin MacRae, I won't be there the next time you try to throw your life away." He released her so abruptly, Kaytra had to steady herself to keep from falling.

She watched as Colin stood and moved across the room, but he didn't leave. She wished he would so that she could be alone to think without his very presence distracting her. After a few moments, she rose to her feet, taking some experimental steps only to find that what Colin said was true. Her first sense of well-being was already fading. Colin turned to watch her come toward him. All at once, she found she couldn't meet his eyes and walked to the table where she reached out to lightly touch the picture which had caused her such sorrow earlier that day. "This is Sondra?"

"Yes," Colin said as he moved to stand beside her. "She's a beautiful girl."

"I wonder what she looks like now?" Kaytra had tried many times at Highland to imagine what Lydia's daughter would be like. How would it feel to have to let go of a child? Her own child had become so precious to her these past months of loneliness and uncertainty.

"Kaytra?" By placing a hand on her shoulder, Colin swung her away from her private thoughts. A curious expression crossed his face. "You were angry a moment ago, and now you're sad."

"You were angry, too." She set the frame down carefully.

"I only want to do what I can to help you."His words sounded strange after some of the things he had said moments ago.

They were close enough that Kaytra could see the new lines at the corners of his eyes, etched there since she had last seen him on the Cape. "You shouldn't have tried to find me, Colin. I never wanted you to."

"Why Boston then?"

"So that - so that I could find my - my mother's - family." When Kaytra faltered, it was only natural for Colin to reach out. The thin material of her nightgown did not keep her from feeling his familiar strength, his compelling vitality.

"Did you find them?"

She hesitated too long. "Yes."

"But you didn't meet them, did you?"

"I - couldn't."

"You wouldn't. There's a big difference between the two." He felt her start nervously at the sudden knock at the door. Even as he said, "Come in", Colin glimpsed the anguish in Kaytra's eyes. He didn't let go of her before looking around to see who came through the door.

Their closeness held a certain hushed, intimate quality that was immediately disturbing to Catherine. "Excuse me, I-."

"You may come in, Mother." Colin would give her no reason to retreat. "Kaytra is feeling better tonight."

Catherine was sure he expected her to be grateful. Instead, she tried not to feel anything at all. "This letter was delivered for you. I thought it might be important." She held the envelope out to him, but remained half in and half out of the room, forcing him to come the distance to her. After he had taken the letter, Colin returned to Kaytra's side, where there was a lamp burning, so that he could read it more easily.

During those long, silent moments, Kaytra lifted her eyes to meet Catherine's. How was a daughter-in-law supposed to act? What to say? Or didn't that matter? Would she go along with Colin's lie? Pretend to be his wife? Pretend the child she carried was his? Kaytra felt so overwhelmed, she didn't realize that she actually reached out to

Colin until his arms were suddenly supporting her. He even said something to her, though his voice sounded as if it came from very far away.

"Kaytra? Kaytra, hang on. I'll get you back into bed." It felt safe again to have him lift her and carry her across the room. "Would you get me a damp cloth, Mother? Over there on the stand." Colin laid her down gently, very much relieved to see she hadn't fainted after all. He brushed the blond hair away from her cheek. "You were on your feet too long. Next time, you can only stay up for a few minutes, alright?"

Her nod of agreement was placidly tired. Catherine brought the cloth then, handing it to her son without taking her eyes from Kaytra's pale face. So much held her back from revealing any sympathy. Colin set the cloth on Kaytra's forehead as he had done many times before with Lydia. It wasn't just that this girl had taken her daughter's place in Colin's life. There was more to it than that.

When Colin spoke again, his tone rippled with necessity. "I must leave for an hour or so, Kaytra." The disappointment in her eyes was very convincing. "A friend needs my help, but I'll come back as soon as I can. I'm sure Mother would sit with you."

"I-."

"Yes. Please." Kaytra's answer interrupted Catherine's. Catherine could hardly refuse then.

Though Colin wondered what Kaytra's agreement might mean, he couldn't ask her in front of his mother. Besides, he really did need to hurry.

"Try to sleep."

When she nodded quietly, he leaned down and kissed her - as any husband would do in leaving his wife.

Chapter Twenty

All the next morning, while Maggie helped her with breakfast and Doctor Graham came to visit and Beany ministered a nauseating mustard plaster to her chest, Kaytra's mind was set on only one thing - Colin. In the middle of the night, when she couldn't sleep, she had found his letter half-hidden beneath one of the chairs by the fireplace. After reading it, sleep had further eluded her.

She stared at the leaden gray sky visible from the windows, absently twisting the wedding ring around and around on her finger. Last night with Catherine had made it clear to Kaytra that she wasn't to be welcomed by Colin's parents. Not that Catherine had said anything. She had, in fact, only paced about the room until Kaytra had fallen asleep.

Reading the letter helped Kaytra understand Catherine's resentment. Yet what was she to do about it? If Colin hadn't accidentally forgotten it during her weakness, she would never have known. Knowing made it hurt more. Finally, when Kaytra was alone again, she got out of bed and moved about the room, learning its treasures, but even that could not distract her for long.

When the room became too confining, Kaytra pulled on the robe someone had left on the bed. It was made of silk with long, puffy sleeves tied at the cuffs with ribbons. The blue color reminded her of a spring day. No one was about in the hallway when she opened the door. She listened for a moment, venturing out only when she didn't hear anything.

Directly across from her was an open door. Peeking inside, Kaytra found it decorated in cool greens. Not a thing was out of place. She suspected that it must be for guests. The next room down the hallway was open, too. It reflected a strictly masculine taste: heavy furnishings, thick Persian rugs, touches of gold amidst the deeper mahogany. Could it be Colin's room? No, it must be Shaun MacRae's. Discovering an adjoining room decorated in feminine cream colors confirmed her suspicions. These two rooms belonged to Catherine and Shaun.

Kaytra turned back across the hallway, suddenly curious to find Colin's room, to see where he had grown up. The door she went to was closed. Instead of turning away, she twisted the knob. A closed-in smell discouraged her entrance. But the curtains allowed enough gentle light into the room for Kaytra to make out what waited inside. She moved forward slowly, leaving the door open.

It was cooler here, so she wrapped both arms around herself. Years must have gone by since anyone spent time here, except to clean every now and then. The once pleasing baby colors had faded like a rainbow about to leave the sky. The crib and cradle were bare. Kaytra wandered to a shelf and picked up a toy clown, smiling at the silly face with its big nose and half-open eyes.

She set it down again to lift a doll whose head and hands were made of finest porcelain. The dress it wore was a beautiful shade of lilac edged in ruffles and lace. Perhaps it had been Sondra's doll, set here for a day when she could play with it and not break it. Had she thought of it since leaving? Of course not. Sondra would have been too young to remember this part of her life. Kaytra put the doll back on the shelf.

There was an old rocking chair near the windows. Kaytra gave it a little push just to hear the sound of it swishing upon the floor in an ever slowing rhythm. She walked to the cradle, too. It swung in a smooth, gentle tempo. Her mother had sung a lullaby. Somehow she could remember the haunting tune, but not exactly the words. She tried to hum the music filling her mind. It faded as the cradle stopped rocking.

Kaytra hugged a blanket she found folded on the window seat. It smelled faintly of rosewater. Because it soothed her, she carried it to the rocker and sat down. Only when a shadow fell across the floor from the doorway, did she realize she wasn't alone.

Shaun MacRae had been watching her, assessing each movement as if trying to see inside her soul with his intense study. "What are you doing in this room?"

His demand caused Kaytra to raise a defense, though she wasn't aware that her chin rose a fraction or that her eyes suddenly glowed with life. "I was - looking for Colin."

"He isn't here." Shaun entered the room, seeming to tower over her as she sat in the rocker. "As long as you are well enough to wander about the house, you will be moved to one of the guest bedrooms...in the east wing. Neither my wife nor I approved of your being in Lydia's room."

Kaytra took a long time to respond. "Very well, one of the other rooms will be fine."

For a moment, it looked as if he hadn't expected her to agree so easily. However, Shaun MacRae was a man of self-control. He hooked his thumbs in the pockets of the vest he wore beneath his black business suit, and Kaytra thought how alike he and Colin were. "My son has said very little about you. Where are you from?"

Finding herself pressed in such a manner wasn't exactly a comfortable position. Besides, Colin might have said something different and her answers could expose too much. Kaytra felt a first twinge of fear. "I'm sure it doesn't matter where I'm from as long as I love your son and will be the best wife that I can be. Today is what matters the most, Mr. MacRae."

"Not entirely." He looked down at her through narrowed eyes. "Not when Colin stands to inherit my fortune."

"If you knew your son at all, Mr. MacRae, you would realize money means very little to him."

"We're not talking about my son. We're talking about you." Shaun's voice had risen and Kaytra knew he was becoming angry with her.

She stood very slowly, still clutching the blanket as a shield. "I'm - not - feeling well." In fact, she was exhausted. Her pale face helped convince Shaun she was telling the truth. "Would you show me to the - to the room you wish me to have?

He led the way to the hall and began walking with determination toward the east wing. Once they passed the stairs, Kaytra fell farther and farther behind. She felt foolish when Shaun had to come back for her, placing a firm hand beneath her elbow. He took her to the last door on the left, the back side of the house. "It has been cleaned in preparation."

So, he had planned on her moving. The room smelled strongly of lye soap and polish. Kaytra barely noted any other features. What did it matter anyway?

With one savage pull, Shaun turned back the covers on the bed. "Lie down." There wasn't strength in her to protest. Kaytra let her eyes close as soon as her head met the pillow. The cool hand he placed on her cheek didn't remain there long. "You've got a fever."

"I'm - sorry." Kaytra murmured, but Shaun was already leaving. She must have dozed then, waking only when a woman came. It wasn't Maggie this time, but another maid. She brought food and something to drink, watched Kaytra finish both, then left without saying a word. Really, Kaytra was too tired to talk to anyone. The brief, yet intense conversation with Colin's father had drained her.

She knew the truth now. Shaun MacRae hated her. Catherine did, too. They didn't want her here. Suddenly, though, Kaytra felt no pain for their rejection. All she wanted was to see Colin again. His name echoed in the empty room. When he didn't come, she gave up the struggle and let the peaceful feeling capture her again. This time, it pulled her further away than before.

Colin tried again, with measurably less patience than he had the first time. "No, Tricia. I won't. You can't expect me to - coddle your every whim at a moment's notice."

"Oh, Colin." Tricia turned away with a heavy swish of green satin skirts, knowing full well that she should give in. Instead, she slumped her shoulders as a child would. She even managed a few tears. "This is not a whim!"

"After the stunt you pulled last night, it certainly is!"

"I only wanted to be with him," she protested for the hundredth time. Colin was silent for so long, she couldn't resist looking over her shoulder at him. He really was angry. He had never lost patience with her like this. What would he be like if he knew the entire truth, the things she had been too afraid to tell him yet? "Please, Colin?"

A disappointed scowl crossed his brow. Last night, he had been awake until midnight, covering for her escapade. This morning he had wakened early in hopes of preventing Tricia from making the biggest mistake of her life. But she wouldn't listen. It was time to go home. Kaytra needed him, too.

Tricia gave a little gasp when she saw Colin pick up his coat and gloves. "You aren't leaving?"

"Yes," he said dryly. "I am."

"But - Colin!"

"Good-bye, Tricia....When you come to your senses, you may find me at home." Colin walked out of the conservatory with firm determination. The drive back into Boston gave him time to know that he had done the right thing. Somehow Tricia had to learn the difference between right and wrong.

The house was quiet when he let himself in the front door. He knew that his parents were gone, Shaun to the bank and Catherine to tea at the Henrys'. Neither Maggie nor Carlisle worked Thursday afternoons. Perhaps he should check on Kaytra before getting something to eat.

Colin took the stairs with renewed energy. When he left earlier that morning, Kaytra had been asleep. It seemed now like too much time had passed since he last spoke with her. The door to Lydia's room was open, letting cheerful light into the hallway. Beany looked up as soon as he walked in, her expression guarded at seeing his confusion to find the bed empty.

"Who moved her?," he demanded soberly.

"Now, Colin...It won't do any good to get upset."

"Beany." Never once had he used that intimidating tone with her.

She left her task of remaking the bed and walked up to him, tilting her head far back to look him straight in the eye. "It's no concern who moved her or why. If you love her at all, you'll go get her right now and put her in your room. Then, Colin, make sure -," Beany grasped his arm tightly, "make sure what happened to Lydia doesn't happen to Kaytra."

It was the first time Colin could see that she had accepted Kaytra, the first time he saw Beany's eyes express affection toward her. "Where is she?"

"The last room in the east wing. I've already taken her few things to your bedroom."

"Thank you, Beany." Colin squeezed her hand briefly. "Kaytra is very special."

"I know that, son." She gave him a push toward the door, anxious for him to have Kaytra safe.

Colin had been furious to find Kaytra drugged again. After demanding the truth from Trudy and reducing her to tears, he had literally smashed the offensive brown bottle against the kitchen wall. White powder had scattered in a hundred directions, but Colin's anger could not be scattered.

It wasn't until after supper that he confronted his father. Colin entered the library unperturbed by the penetrating, cool look his father gave him. "I want to talk with you."

"I'm busy." Shaun took up one of the papers on his desk, concentrating solely on what it said. He was aware that Colin continued across the room, but completely unprepared when his son ripped the paper out of his hands. "Leave this room at once!"

"I'm not ten years old anymore!" Colin spat out. "You have no right to treat Kaytra as you did today! The amount of powder you gave her could have killed her or the baby!"

Shaun's expression remained impassive. "She agreed to be moved."

"Of course she did. What else was she supposed to say to you?"

"You are the one who has placed her in such a compromising position. If -."

"There's nothing compromising about being married and expecting a child." Colin leaned forward, placing his hands flat against the desk. The level of tension between them had never been this high before. Neither would it get any better unless Shaun changed his ways. "I don't mind it when you hate me, father. I've come to live with that. But trying to destroy Kaytra will only push me into hating you back. Is that what you want?"

The silence was too long, expressed too much. Colin rose to his full height, feeling as if he hadn't won at all; nor had he been defeated, because the battle wasn't over yet.

Shaun stopped him just before he reached the doorway. "I visited with several colleagues today."

Colin turned to look at his father, quite unsure where this was leading. He only knew by the cold glint in Shaun's eyes that it would be unpleasant.

"You were seen at the Travois last night." The words hung in mid-air, somehow failing to crash down on Colin as Shaun expected. He added a note of stern disapproval to his tone. "Is that where the money went?"

"No."

"No? That's it?" Shaun started around the desk. "Associating with a man like Montgomery is hardly a wise choice, Colin."

"I'm not 'associating' with Montgomery." Colin's hand found the doorknob. He wasn't ready yet to explain last night to anyone, let alone his father.

"Colin!"

"I'll be upstairs!" He practically slammed the door shut behind him.

Coming out of her peaceful world was more difficult this time. Kaytra awoke feeling a tremendous loss, as if someone had taken her parents from her all over again. If only she could go back and stay forever in that place. She moaned in protest, thrashing at the weight which bound her. The shock of opening her eyes to complete darkness after such golden warmth frightened her.

When she tried to sit up, the heavy weight tightened. "Kaytra. It's alright." A voice sounded very near her ear. "There's nothing to be afraid of."

"Colin?"

"Who else could it be?," he asked in gentle amusement.

Kaytra realized then that the weight she felt over her shoulders was his arm, that she was lying beside him, sheltered in the circle of his protection. They were in the same bed, although he was fully clothed and she wore a nightgown beneath layers of soft blankets. Her confusion wouldn't allow her to form any one thought. "Where-?"

"You're in my room. It's very late at night."

She rolled onto her side away from him, staring at the shapes which began to separate themselves from the darkness. "It can't be night. I can't have slept all day. Not again. I - I don't need to sleep so much. I want - I want to go home... I want-."

"Kaytra." Colin had risen on one elbow and took firm hold of her arm to steady the shaking he felt in her. "Slow down. You'll make yourself sick."

"I'm not sick!" Kaytra pushed him away, sliding off her edge of the big bed at the same time. In the darkness, she stumbled sideways into a chair and then into a table before Colin managed to light a lamp. "I want to go home now. It's too - cold here. I want to - be - outside." The need pushed her forward to where draperies were pulled across the windows.

Colin reached her just as a cold blast of January air found its way through. He put an arm around her, pinning her body against his while he closed the latch on the window. He had gone through this same experience with Lydia before, but now, because it was Kaytra, the desperation he felt was much more intense.

In the next instant, Kaytra had twisted around until she could see his face, until she could clutch at his arms with shaking hands. "You don't understand!"

"I do understand. I told you it would be like this, remember?"

She tore herself away from him again. Her hair was tangled and her face white in the pale lamplight.

Colin was suddenly reminded of the night she had pretended to be the Widow Stevens. Only now, the haunted look in her eyes was real. She moved around the room restlessly. "You should be back in bed," he told her as he followed her to the middle of the room.

"I'm not sick."

"You are, Kaytra." It was difficult for him to remain patient at three-o'clock in the morning. He watched as she moved to a door set into the paneled wall beside the fireplace. It squeaked a protest when she opened it. She moved through too quickly for Colin to stop her. "Kaytra." He swung the door open wide, letting light from his room follow her, then he simply stood and watched. Incredibly, she didn't seem afraid of the dark room.

With strangely graceful movements, she moved to the dusty, old cradle and then to the crib. "I was in here before...this morning."

"Yesterday, you mean."

"But you were gone." She turned her eyes to look at his silhouette outlined by the light behind him. "You said you would come back in an hour."

"That was yesterday, too." The confusion of lost time had been just as difficult for Lydia to grasp.

Kaytra abruptly whirled away. "I want to go home."

"You don't have a home." Her prolonged silence told him she was trying to disconnect certain feelings, trying to rearrange thoughts so that they would fit into this world. It was a crucial time, one he hadn't reached with Lydia for months.

Colin walked into the old nursery which connected his room and Lydia's. Though he came up behind her as gently as he could, she still jumped when he placed his hands on her shoulders. "Home can't be where you're all alone, Kaytra." There was a hint of tears trembling upon her lashes as he turned her to face him.

"He hates me."

"Who?"

"Your father." She drew back a sob. Colin's hands came up to rest alongside her face. Kaytra rushed on, each word, each breath labored with anxiety. "Your mother doesn't want me here. I can't lie any more. You don't need me here. I've ruined your life. You - you shouldn't have found me." Her hands dug into his forearms. "You should forget about me. I'll just - go away. I'll tell them the truth. Then they can hate me and not you. They can -."

"Kaytra."

"They-."

"Kaytra, listen to me." He over-powered her determination. "You need to come back to bed. It's all too hard to explain right now."

"No, it's simple. I can't be here." She tried to free herself by pressing her hands against his chest. "You can't make me stay!"

"Shhh." He didn't want his parents to be awakened. Short of letting her lose all control, Colin had no choice but to bodily pick her up and return her to bed. She squirmed against him. "Keep still. You'll have the whole house awake."

"Even - Tricia?"

The reply was influenced by drugs. Colin knew that, but he also knew she was lucid enough to have deliberately chosen her words. "Tricia doesn't live here."

"You want her to live here." Kaytra wasn't asking a question this time. Her eyes locked with Colin's as he laid her on the bed. "Is she - beautiful?" He pulled the blankets up to her chin, then sat down beside her. Kaytra didn't like the feeling of confinement beneath the blankets, and immediately freed her arms. "Is she?"

When he didn't answer right away, Kaytra twisted onto her side, willing herself to be lost in the big bed. She drew up into a tight ball, her heart pounding a rhythm too loud and too fast. He had no right to treat her like a child. She wouldn't stay. As soon as it was dawn, she would get dressed and leave. It would be for the best. Tomorrow she would leave....

Colin patiently waited out her silence.

After a few minutes, he reached out, turning her onto her back again. Even though the action was a gentle one, his eyes remained unreadable. "Is it over yet?"

Kaytra blinked back tears. He must have been with Lydia a great deal during her breakdown to know how the drug worked, to know what signs to look for. She nodded her head and looked away.

"Who told you about Tricia?" His voice was so carefully controlled, Kaytra wasn't sure what he was feeling.

"I -. The letter. I - found - it," she stammered.

Colin tried to remember what the letter had said, why it seemed to have upset her so much.

"Is - she - beautiful?"

"Yes." He watched her expression as he answered. The sudden weakness had left her very vulnerable.

"Do - you -."

"I care for her, Kaytra, but that's not the same as loving someone."

"You -." Kaytra moved uncomfortably until she was sitting against the pillows. "You should marry her."

Colin thought her worried state would lead up to this. "I'm already married...to you."

Kaytra's head fell back, her eyes closed. She was weary of trying to make him understand. "We aren't married. I can't marry you. I don't belong here."

"Where do you belong?"

She shrugged her shoulders rather helplessly at his question.

"You never told me who your grandparents are."

There was an instantly guarded look in her eyes when she opened them. "You never told me who Tricia was."

"I would have if I thought you needed to know." Colin sensed that she drew back. "Why were you afraid to meet your grandparents?"

"It's not important."

Colin unexpectedly reached out and brushed the back of his hand along her cheek. "If it's not important, why do you have tears in your eyes?"

Kaytra self-consciously tried to blink them away. "I'm - tired."

He couldn't argue with that. "Will you tell me someday?"

A sigh of resignation preceded her answer. "I won't be here," she said quietly. "I'm leaving tomorrow."

"Today, you mean." Colin sounded quite calm and accepting of the choice she had made. Kaytra nodded. "Have you prayed about it?"

How could she have? He knew she had been asleep most of the day. Kaytra turned the uncomfortable question back on him. "Have you prayed about me staying?"

"Yes," he said smoothly. "Quite often."

"And...?"

"And I believe you're supposed to be here." He wasn't surprised when she looked away from him, staring long and hard at the lamp on the table. Colin finally stood and moved around to the other side of the bed. It would have been impossible not to feel her flinch when he laid down, but he pretended otherwise, as if this was something not at all unusual. Without saying anything, he extinguished the lamp, settled onto his own pillow and....waited.....

"We - aren't married, Colin," she said at last, very quietly.

Colin smiled to himself. "Go to sleep, Kaytra."

Chapter Twenty-One

Morning came late to Colin's room. When he opened his eyes, a full measure of sunshine was playing at the windows. Someone had already thrown open the curtains. But the "someone" he thought to find lying beside him was gone.

Colin lost no time in changing his clothes. He didn't even care that a day's growth of beard shadowed his face.

Carlisle cast him a rather surprised look as he hurried down the steps, asking if anyone had seen Kaytra. "No, sir...I haven't. Perhaps-." He let the suggestion fade as Colin continued down the hallway past him.

The kitchen smelled deliciously of gingerbread and fried potatoes. "Cook?" Colin's voice boomed loud enough for half of Boston to hear. The woman he called for nearly dropped a plateful of sugar cookies and gave him a chastising look which Colin, of course, ignored all together. "Kaytra isn't-."

"Land sakes, boy!" Cook shook her head. "She ain't run off if that's what yer thinkin'."

"Where is she?," he demanded.

"She and Maggie are in the sewing room...and that beast, too!" Cook hadn't really warmed up to Rex yet. But she didn't completely dislike him either, for big, juicy meat bones always managed to be found for him. "He ain't left her side for a second."

So, Colin had Rex to thank for keeping Kaytra from running away. He was sure she had planned to leave. She must have seen Rex - or he must have seen her - and then the severing, the breaking away again couldn't be done.

"Thank you, Cook. You're a dear." Colin kissed her cheek, stealing a handful of cookies at the same time.

"Oh, be gone with you, Colin MacRae!" Cook shooed him away with a chuckle, feeling happy just to have him home again.

The sewing room was really part of the servant's quarters, a whole room set aside solely for the making of clothes. Colin had hungrily eaten half of his cookies by the time he came to the open door. His noiseless arrival would have gone unnoticed except for Rex, who pricked up his ears and ran toward him in great excitement.

Both Maggie and Kaytra turned to the door. Maggie's expression held a friendly welcome, Kaytra's an anxious uncertainty. "Good morning," he said as he walked slowly into the room.

"Hello, Colin." Maggie filled in for Kaytra's silence.

Rex smelled the cookies and practically knocked Colin over to get one. He ate the first in one great gulp. Colin smiled. "Good boy!"

Maggie laughed at that. "He acts like he expected you. Don't you think so, Kaytra?" When Maggie turned to her, she found that Kaytra was staring out the window with a decidedly stubborn set to her shoulders.

The second cookie disappeared in an instant. "This is your reward, isn't it boy?" Colin rubbed the dog's head vigorously.

Maggie would have asked why, but she felt somehow that she shouldn't. Instead, she felt as if she should leave. "Excuse me."

"Just a minute, Maggie." Colin gave the last treat to Rex before walking across the room to stand in front of the shelves of material. "What colors do you think would look good on Kaytra?" He was aware that he was putting her in an awkward situation. His smile in her direction asked that she please understand. "How about this?"

Maggie took down the bolt of rose silk. "It's very pretty...The ivory would be nice, too. Or that blue."

"Have Trudy start some dresses for Kaytra. I'm sure you could show her what would be best."Colin caught sight of several pale-colored flannels. "And we should start on things for the baby. Do you know what babies need?"

"I should, " she laughed good-naturedly. "I helped raise all the little ones who came after me."

"Good." He glanced at Kaytra then. She still hadn't moved. Maggie put down the material she had been holding and quietly slipped from the room.

Colin waited awhile before crossing the room to her. He wondered if this morning had been very hard on her. Not only emotionally, but physically, as well. Despite her every protest the night before, she was ill and needed to take care of herself.

He stepped up to the window beside her. It was a gentle winter day, one in which everything seemed softened by sunshine. The bare-limbed trees in the garden looked like happy children reaching eager arms skyward.

"Do you feel like going for a walk this morning? Just a short way?" Colin turned his head to see what she thought of his idea. She refused to look at him. "Who are you angry with. Me or Rex?" Still no response. "How did you sleep?" A knot of frustration began to tighten within him, though he tried to ignore it. "Okay, if you don't want to talk, you'll have to put up with listening, but not here."

She could not tear her arm out of his grasp, especially since his determined steps soon carried them into the kitchen, past Cook and Beany who exchanged startled glances. Once in the hallway, Colin purposely headed to one of the doors, throwing it open until Kaytra found that they were in a deserted salon.

"Sit down," Colin told her as he closed the double doors, sealing them inside the gold and cream room. "Over there by the windows."

Kaytra walked to the grouping of chairs, feeling self-conscious in such elegant surroundings. She was grateful for the chance to sit down, yet restless, especially when Colin remained standing.

"Am I right, you were actually going to try to leave?" His abrupt question pushed her further into the chair. "And you would have except that you found out Rex was here?"

"I knew he was-." Though the words were clipped off, it was too late. Her mistake was already made.

Colin frowned. "How did you know?"

"That day - at the docks."

"He was after you? You deliberately hid yourself from me?"

"After being deliberately hunted, yes!" Kaytra threw out the words, then, in the next moment, stared down at her clasped hands. "Did you ever wonder what it would be like for me, Colin? To have men follow me, to have them knock on my door in the middle of the night?"

Colin could hear the fear in her voice now. But the guilt it caused was not as strong as the need he had felt to find her again. "Is it because you don't trust me that you tried to leave this morning?"

"Trust is a luxury which was stolen from me a long time ago."

"That doesn't answer my question, Kaytra." He moved to stand in front of her, arms over his chest. "You could learn to trust again. Didn't you listen to a thing I said last night about praying?"

"I'm trying to listen to what I feel!" She gasped when he leaned down and took her hands, pulling her to her feet.

"I don't think you know what you feel." His brown eyes studied every part of her face. "Remember your journal? The things you wrote for Lydia? I've read them, Kaytra."

She was ashamed of the tears which sprang into her eyes, blurring her vision. "I've read every single one of them, more than once. I read them again, last night in fact, while I sat there, watching you sleep in my bed. You could trust me, Kaytra. Trust isn't very far from what you wrote. Trust is part of those feelings."

"I -." It was barely a whisper. Her face had gone white.

"You could trust me," he insisted. "If you -."

Chapter Twenty-One

The doors suddenly burst inward, shattering his words. "Colin! Oh, Colin!"

Afterward, even though she tried, Kaytra couldn't remember seeing the look on Colin's face as he turned and caught the young woman who ran across the room, throwing herself into his arms. Instinctively, she knew it was Tricia. And yes, she was beautiful. She was more than beautiful.

From her dark hair spilling out of the mink-trimmed bonnet, to her doe-eyed, ivory-skinned elegance and the costume of blue velvet beneath a hastily tied, matching-mink cape, she was exquisite. When Kaytra's heart tumbled inside her chest, she pressed both hands over the ache, watching as Colin led Tricia to the settee in the middle of the room.

She sobbed incoherent words against his shoulder. He tried to comfort her. And Kaytra...Kaytra took a few hesitant steps, feeling a numbness invade her body. Before Colin noticed her again, she was moving past them and through the double doors. He called out for her to wait. Part of her wanted to. Part of her knew she couldn't.

Earlier that morning, she had left her cape and bag on a chair in the foyer. Now they were gone. She stood in indecision.

"May I help you?"

A voice from behind, startled her. It was Carlisle. Kaytra hadn't met him yet. But he was dressed like a servant and he fit Maggie's description. "My - things? I left them here."

"Of course." He moved to the closet where they had been placed. "Do you wish to have a carriage made ready, Mrs. MacRae?"

Kaytra wasn't sure that she liked the way he looked at her. "No, just my cape and bag please." He found them and held the cape for her as she prepared to leave. "And - keep the dog here. He isn't to follow me."

Carlisle nodded slightly.

Could he tell she was totally unused to giving orders? His disparagement said that he could. Kaytra opened the front door herself and left without saying anything else. Somehow the day had become even more discouraging for her. She pulled the edges of her cape closer, trying to hold in some warmth.

The stone pillars which marked the beginning of the driveway became her first goal. One step at a time. After that, it was the corner of the block and then the tall, graystone building visible above the trees. Gradually, she began to recognize where she was in the city. A few more turns and she could see ahead to the place where she now knew she wanted to go.

Her muscles ached terribly. So did her chest. But that alone wasn't the reason for her tears as she stood by herself in the cemetery beside Lydia's grave. She desperately wished she could talk to her friend.

The words of the letter Tricia had sent to Colin kept flashing in front of her eyes when all Kaytra wanted to do was forget it completely...

> *"Colin, please come. You are the only one. My dream can have no beginning without you.   Love as always, Tricia."*

Kaytra wiped away the presence of tears on her cheeks. What right had she to prevent Colin from marrying Tricia? None at all. She had carried out her promise to Lydia. It wasn't supposed to have happened that Colin would find her again.

She bunched up her cape to sit down for a moment on the snow. With the sun beaming softly through the trees, she wasn't cold any longer. She had come here often during the past few months. Strangely, it wasn't thoughts of death which occupied her mind at those times, but thoughts of life. The happier moments at Highland....

Many times she had stood on the wharfs, gazing at the lighthouse which served Boston's harbor. But it wasn't the same. Lydia had told her life was never supposed to remain the same. Life itself meant change. But couldn't there, for once, be some good changes? Changes that didn't have to hurt? Or was that being selfish? Was she not willing to accept God's ways?

There had to be answers. Somehow, Colin always seemed to have the answers for his problems. He seemed to, and yet, there was still that part of him which she had never understood.

Kaytra felt chilled now and rose to her feet, taking one last long look at Lydia's name engraved in stone before she walked back to the street.

Her thoughts were so turned inward that she forgot to be careful. Perhaps it was weariness, too. When the carriage came racing around the corner, Kaytra was directly in its path. The next moments were a blur of sound and fear. She had an impression of black: Black horses, a black carriage, black cape and hat...someone shouting.

The horses reared in alarm, straining their harnesses and throwing snow into the air with their powerful hooves. The carriage skidded sideways, nearly colliding with another. Kaytra felt a whoosh of heated air from the horse that stopped nearest her. Its eyes were rolled back in alarm. So close was it to her, that Kaytra could have reached out her hand to touch it. But no part of her body would move.

The driver jumped to the ground, shaken to the core at the near tragedy, yet not at all fearful for Kaytra. He went to the pair of horses, ignoring Kaytra's white silence. Another man climbed from the carriage, demanding to know what had happened. He seemed in a wicked temper at the interruption. "Solmes!....Solmes!"

"Here, sir." The driver stood at attention.

"What the devil are you doing?"

"Checking the horses, sir. This girl -." He pointed an accusing finger at Kaytra now that it suited his purpose to recognize her. After all, she was the one who had stepped onto the street without looking. He caught the bridle, trying to calm his horses, without a care that one was yet within striking distance of Kaytra.

"Who are you?" The man from the coach strode toward her, noting her slow reaction, as if everything else was going by too quickly for her to grasp. "Well?" He stood directly in front of her then. Kaytra frowned a little. "Are you hurt?"

"We didn't touch her!" The driver defended, though his comment was suitably ignored by his employer.

Somehow, Kaytra sensed she was being evaluated by the sophisticated man. His blue eyes held hers. "I want to know if you are hurt," he asked again.

She was about to answer when the carriage door opened again, drawing her attention to the child who jumped down into the snow. Again, a pair of blue eyes were trained upon her face. But these blue eyes-. Kaytra blinked slowly, trying to clear her thoughts, trying to hold back - what? She wasn't sure...But she knew-.

"You are hurt." The man's gloved hand touched her arm, his accented voice suddenly more concerned than angry.

When she finally stopped staring at the girl and brought her dazed eyes back to him, she found he was looking at her rather curiously.

The child took a few steps forward, sensing something serious. "Papa?"

"One moment," he answered. His grip on Kaytra tightened. "Who are you? Do you know your name?"

She tried to say yes, but the world suddenly became all harsh sounds again. Too loud. People talking. The horses ....Carriages rolling by....Too loud.....She reached out weakly to grasp and hold the man's hand. Then all was black.....

Chapter Twenty-Two

Nobody could simply disappear from the face of the earth, not unless they wanted to. Even Napp's men, the ones who had tracked Kaytra before, couldn't locate her. After a week of exhaustive searching, Colin found it difficult now to concentrate on anything else. He studied the whole world with suspicion. It was like that every time he stepped out of the house. Every person on the street, every carriage which rolled past, every image of a young woman seen through the windows of a shop.

Just that morning, his father had cruelly told him to give up any hope of finding Kaytra. Should he? Could he endure losing her all over again? Perhaps the choice was out of his hands.

He had so far stubbornly refused to tell his parents the truth about his so-called marriage. Some part of him wasn't ready to give up yet. He saw a mother walking toward him, carrying her child...Had Kaytra's baby been born yet? Didn't she realize how he felt, not knowing? How he hadn't once slept more than a couple of hours at a time because thoughts of her would awaken him?

With a tired sigh, he pulled himself back to the task at hand and entered a jewelry store. He needed to find a birthday gift for his mother. Just as he had done in the clothing store and book shop, Colin spent a half-hour looking for the right gift. But his mother already had so many jewels. One more would hold little significance for her.

Catherine had been withdrawn since the day Kaytra left, speaking little to anyone. Colin wasn't sure why. He stepped onto the snow-covered sidewalk, pausing there to look down the crowded street. A simple sign above the florist's shop caught his eye.

Last year, he and Lydia had given their mother a beautiful silk shawl and some roses. Perhaps they would mean more to her than anything just now. He crossed the street quickly, dodging a few carriages as he went. The man attending the shop looked up as Colin came through the door. Now that he had decided upon a gift, Colin was able to give him a semblance of a smile. "Good afternoon."

"Evening."

Whether it was a crisp greeting or a pointed reminder, Colin wasn't sure. The hour was late. Nearly time for business to cease for the day. "I won't keep you long." Colin walked directly to the counter. The heady scent of hot-house hyacinth and lilies permeated the small space. "I wish to order some flowers to be delivered tomorrow." He waited until the man had picked up his pen. "White roses. For Catherine MacRae. Two or three dozen. The add-."

"Wait." The man looked up with a puzzled frown. "Haven't these been ordered already?"

"No. I'm sure-."

"Here it is." He produced a paper from among those neatly stacked to one side, then set a pair of glasses on the bridge of his nose. "White roses. February 2nd. Mrs. Shaun MacRae. That is Catherine?"

"Yes, but..." Colin was no less confused when the florist handed him the paper to see for himself. His father hadn't ordered them. The billing address belonged neither to their home nor to the bank. One of his mother's friends? He was almost positive they didn't know anyone from the village of Chester.

"Do you still wish to order the roses?"

Colin answered without raising his eyes from the paper. "Yes...Please."

"I can't promise you three dozen then. Maybe one or two. White roses are very unusual, you realize. Most customers order red or even yellow, but white-."

The rest of the explanation was left dangling. Colin let the paper in his hands fall back onto the counter. "Do whatever you can." He absentmindedly threw too many coins down between them and was gone before the man could protest.

It was a tradition in the MacRae house that birthdays be celebrated with gay parties, many friends, extravagant food, singing and dancing. This year was different. Lydia's death was still too recent for Catherine to want anything more than a gathering of some of their closest friends for a simple dinner.

Patricia and her parents would be arriving soon. The Henrys, always fashionably late, would ring the bell at precisely a half hour after the appointed seven o'clock. Colin had invited Stephen to come, too, but he had been otherwise engaged, something very unusual indeed. Or perhaps not. It was Maggie's night off. The thought brought a contemplative frown to Colin's brow as he faced his reflection in the mirror above his bureau.

Stephen and Maggie had made no secret of the fact that they very much enjoyed one another's company, at least in front of him. What would Stephen's parents say if their son chose to marry Maggie? Probably much the same reaction that Colin had received. Disapproval. Whatever happened, though, Stephen would seek God's will for his and Maggie's future.

Colin himself had tried to seek God's will. Over the past week, he had struggled with wanting to believe God was still in control, yet feeling as if his faith had come to an abrupt standstill. He expertly knotted his ascot before picking up the gold cufflinks for his shirt. Instinct told him that it was time to make changes. He only wished that the churnings of emotion he felt toward Kaytra would allow him clearer judgment, clear enough to accept the fact that she might possibly never be part of his life again. He pulled on the deep brown coat which had lain in readiness upon his bed. It was time to go downstairs.

The bell rang just as he stepped onto the floor in the foyer. Carlisle suddenly appeared from somewhere or Colin would have answered it himself. A huge bouquet of white roses occupied fully half the doorway and a pint-sized boy the other half. "Delivery for MacRae - Mrs. that is."

Carlisle took the flowers in one hand. "It's rather late, isn't it boy?"

"Well 'um..." The wide-eyed boy peered around the imposing butler at Colin. "They's had trouble gettin' so many, you see."

"Very well." Carlisle started to close the door.

"Wait." Colin moved forward, digging some coins from his vest pocket. The boy smiled gratefully. "You'd best be getting home now."

"I will, sir. Thank you, sir!"

After the door had been closed, Colin turned back to Carlisle. There had been a level of strain between them since the day Kaytra left. Colin wasn't quite sure yet if he would forgive the younger man for letting her out the door unescorted. And Carlisle had firmly taken the stand that he was "a butler and not a prison guard". "I'll take the flowers," Colin said now. "See that the Michaels' are shown to the grand salon."

Carlisle only nodded.

On his way down the hall, Colin removed the layer of tissue which had protected the roses. Their rich fragrance, stirred by passing from one room into the next, had Catherine looking up from her chair in wonder before he had even stepped through the doorway of the salon.

"Oh, Colin." Her breathless whisper told him how touched she was. He laid the roses in her arms as tenderly as he placed a kiss upon her cheek. "They are - beautiful." Catherine's eyes filled with tears, making her look young again. The flowers stood out against the deep green of her evening gown. "Thank you, dear. What a thoughtful gift."

"I'm sorry to say I wasn't the only one who thought of them."

Catherine looked up at him as he straightened to his full height. Her puzzled expression was answered easily enough.

"I think you'll find a card in there somewhere. And it's not mine. The florist was being very diplomatic sending the two orders all in one big bouquet like that."

She did find a card, half buried in the blossoms. It was addressed simply to "Catherine" and on the reverse side, in careful handwriting "May you have a blessed day...and thank you."

"Who is your other admirer?"

"I-." Catherine flushed a little. "Just an old - acquaintance. You wouldn't remember. Please, won't you have Beatrice arrange these on the table?"

"Of course." He accepted the bouquet. "I'll be back in a minute...Happy Birthday, Mother."

She smiled tremulously and reached out for one of his hands. There was something unsure about her grasp. "Thank you, Colin. Hurry now, before our guests get here."

As soon as he was gone, Catherine rose and walked to the fire-place, staring at the flames long after the card had been reduced to ashes.

At dinner, Colin thought Tricia was a bit too preoccupied with buttering her roll, and pushing morsels of food around her plate. He shifted his gaze down the table to see that he wasn't the only one to have noticed. John Michaels sent his daughter a probing look which spoke volumes to Colin. He hadn't expected Tricia's secret to remain hidden for long. Throughout the rest of the meal, he planned a way of drawing her aside to learn just what was going on.

His plan, however, didn't work out until much later than he would have liked.

As was the custom after dinner, the men retired for brandies in the library and the women went on to the salon. Colin rather astounded his father by accepting a drink when it was offered to him. The fiery liquid did little to suppress the emptiness he had been denying all week, nor did it keep his thoughts from returning to Kaytra.

By the time the men rejoined the women, he felt too restless to endure another two hours of idle visiting. Had it not been his mother's birthday, he would have made some excuse to leave. Instead, he paced about the room, drink in hand, half listening to the others talk.

Quite often, he found himself at the windows, staring out into the night-cloaked garden. He wanted her back...but why if she had deliberately walked away from him? Perhaps because his mind kept going back to the last page of her journal and the words she had written in her own hand. "Yes, Lydia. I do love him."

Yet how could she love him and still leave as she had? Colin's eyes were drawn to his own reflection in the glass. Had the brandy loosened him enough to admit the truth? A cold, hard image stared back, seeming to scream "yes". He resented her leaving. It would be easy just now to say he didn't love her. It would be easy to let the time he had spent at Highland perish beneath the resentment he felt. Perhaps he should just bury himself in life here.

The last of the liquor slid down his throat, burning its evil path straight to that final remnant of belief. He had strived for an answer from God only to find that every door remained closed. There were no answers, no sense of direction. Since he could have neither Highland nor Kaytra, Colin decided he would choose his own path. He would go on without them. He would even go on without God, if he had to. He caught sight of Tricia moving up behind him and turned, perfectly in control of the movement despite the liquor he had consumed. Her eyes searched his before she spoke, but he gave away no secrets. "I've never seen you take a drink before."

"I'm not exactly a saint, Tricia." His smile appeared natural. "Do you think we can convince them to give us some time alone?"

Her gaze narrowed, though only for a moment before she nodded her agreement. Colin made the necessary request before leading her from the room. He had thought briefly about going outside, but it was late and dark and Tricia didn't especially like to be outdoors. There was a little sitting room at the front of the house. He would take her there.

Tricia walked clear to the far wall, noting every unchanged detail about the room.

"Your father knows, doesn't he?" Colin saw her go completely rigid before she swung around and faced him.

"Colin-."

"It's alright. No one will hear us." He moved toward her with a reckless ease unusual to his nature. Tricia clasped her hands into tight fists. "I told you he would find out. It really wasn't worth the risk, was it?"

"You're being terribly cruel, Colin."

"I'm being terribly honest. You should never have started this whole charade. Those few stolen moments of satisfaction are going to cost you. Whatever Montgomery has promised you is never going to happen."

Her color had risen, though in anger rather than embarrassment. "I'm going to marry him!" She blurted it out in a challenging tone, defying him to tell her she couldn't.

"He's twice your age, Tricia."

"So?"

Colin took the last steps to her, speaking now with little emotion. "Are you doing all this only to get me to marry you?" She looked away too quickly. His hand came up to touch her skin, the warmth of her cheek. "Do you remember the first time I kissed you, Tricia?"

When he forced her head back, she had no choice but to look at him. "No...I don't." Her attempt to hurt in return failed.

"You're good at lying." Colin swept his mouth over hers. He wanted to know if she was really serious about marrying Clifton Montgomery. But Colin realized he was testing himself, too.

They both failed. She pushed him away after a few moments, staring up at him as if she had never seen him before.

"You won't marry Montgomery - you're smarter than that, Tricia."

"But he promised me a music career. You know I've always wanted to sing."

Colin shrugged his shoulders, insensitive to her plea. "Does it really matter?"

Some of the color was chased from her face. "What happened to you at Highland?"

He let go of her completely.

"You changed out there."

"Maybe so." Colin knew it wasn't Highland which had changed him as much as it was Kaytra. "Maybe I should have married you, Tricia."

"You don't love me."

His eyes, usually warm and expressive, were cold now. "You don't love me either." He turned and walked away. "Love demands too high a price."

"How would you-?" She cut off the question suddenly as she realized the answer. He had fallen in love sometime during his months away. Her anger began to ebb. For once, it was not dissipated by jealousy, but by concern. She walked up to him, placing her hand on his tensed arm. "Colin?"

He refused to look at her.

"I'm sorry."

"I don't want your pity." His tone was even, but harsh.

"And you don't want my companionship either? We could marry, Colin. We could be happy together."

He turned his head in her direction. There wasn't a legal reason why they couldn't marry. His parents would have to be told the truth about Kaytra, but perhaps their shattered trust in him would be somewhat nullified because he had chosen Tricia after all. "I wouldn't let you go to the Travois again...ever."

"I have a contract to-."

"You won't sing there again. I'll pay Montgomery to give up the contract."

"But-."

"No, Tricia." He moved his arm until he was gripping her hand. The alcohol made him forget his strength. "You won't go there again."

She nodded, feeling that the slight pain caused by his hand could be no worse than the pain she felt because of the emptiness in his eyes.

Yet, as suddenly as he had shown anger, his touch relaxed and he slipped his arms around her waist, pulling her close. "She isn't like you at all."

Somehow Tricia knew about whom he was talking. The stab she felt caused her to feel weak.

Colin kissed her again, harder this time, with even less emotion. His eyes snapped with frustration when he finally raised his head. They stood there, locked in his own misguided purpose, until a voice spoke from the open doorway.

"Colin?"

He faced his mother with neither apology nor explanation.

"You can't - do this."

Tricia pulled away from Colin, trying not to reveal her earlier misgivings. "Oh, Catherine....Colin and I are to be married."

"No! No, I won't let you!"

Colin froze. The brandy hadn't so dulled his senses that he could mistake the meaning behind her words.

Catherine's troubled eyes moved from Tricia's face to his. For one prolonged moment she looked at him. Then she fled the room, forgetting the very reason she had come to find them.

The sitting room was uncomfortably silent after she left. Tricia felt very much like weeping. "I - thought she would be - pleased. They've always wanted us to be married." From beneath her lashes, she could see that Colin still stared at the place where his mother had stood. "You will - talk to her, Colin?"

He took a long time to answer her. "Yes."

"Is it - too soon after Lydia perhaps?" She waited but he said nothing. Just at that moment, he was so lost in his own thoughts, she doubted he had even heard the question. Tricia let the tears in her eyes roll down her cheeks. Only when she slipped her hands into Colin's did he look at her.

Her tears were deliberately quickened in order to keep him there for the next half-hour.

By then, the Michaels and Henrys were leaving. In the activity of parting, Colin was able to steal several glances at his mother's face. She smiled her "thank yous", and said the appropriate things. Yet there was a tension in her. As soon as the door was closed, she pleaded exhaustion. Shaun accompanied her up the stairs.

Colin watched awhile before he said anything. "Mother?"

She stopped to look down at him.

"I'd like to speak with you."

"Perhaps tomorrow, Colin."

"I'll come to your room in ten minutes."

Shaun would have objected to his son's terseness, but Catherine laid a hand on his arm. "Very well, Colin." Her eyes didn't falter from his now. "Let me change first. Why don't you and your father wait for me in the library."

Shaun MacRae was nothing if not a perceptive man. The undercurrents racing around him were not to be ignored. He needed no second urging from his wife to move back down the stairs. Even Colin's silent look of disapproval wasn't enough to make him stop.

Father and son walked into the dimly lit library together. Shaun sank down in the chair by the fireplace, eyeing Colin, who stretched his frame onto the small sofa. "I'd offer you another brandy, but I don't think you need one."

"You're probably right."

Agreement? Shaun folded his hands beneath his chin, letting the silence sink in. All evening long, his son had been acting quite out of character. Could this be a measure of the walls he was building around himself? "Patricia seemed in a different mood just now," Shaun observed calmly.

Colin leaned his head back. "She should be. I told her I would marry her." His half-closed eyes noted Shaun's sudden stillness.

"What about your wife?"

"Kaytra and I were never married. The child isn't mine either." He had envisioned it being hard to tell the truth. Instead, he felt rather numb.

The rest of the story was poured out in similar abruptness. Shaun listened intently without interruption. Near the end, when he heard an edge of hardness in his son's voice, he got up and poured them each a long drink of brandy. Colin accepted the glass. "You aren't angry? I thought you would be ready to disinherit me."

"Why should I?" Shaun resettled in his chair.

"Because I lied to you."

"You've never lied to me before," he answered the obvious as Colin stared at the dark amber liquid in his glass. "You've also never been as willing to admit to me that you've made a mistake."

They both took a drink of their brandy. Colin looked across at his father. "We're too much alike. That's why we're always fighting. We both think only our way is right and the other is wrong. I thought I could help her."

"She didn't want to be helped."

"No." Colin couldn't feel any pain now.

"Maybe you thought I was being stubborn when I wouldn't accept her kind here, but you can see now how wrong it was."

"And that means I shouldn't love her?" His words were slurred together now. "Don't worry. I've decided that on my own tonight. I won't love Kaytra." He drained his glass carelessly, setting it down on the table near his elbow. "I won't love Patricia either, but she already knows that. You and Mother - where is she anyway?"

It was taking some time for her to change. Longer than usual. Shaun shifted uncomfortably. "She'll be here soon." He had been around drinking men long enough to recognize the usual effects. Colin wasn't drunk. Not yet. But the brandy had unleashed its share of emotions, most obviously, impatience. He was secretly surprised when Colin rose and paced the room so steadily.

"You've always wanted me to marry Tricia. John has, too. He needs money to back his political ambitions.... Is it a smart move for us, financially I mean?"

"Yes, I sup-"

"We'll have to draw up some kind of agreement," Colin interrupted without thought.

"An agreement won't be necessary."

"You trust them, then?"

Shaun leaned forward to hold his half-empty glass with both hands. "I trust you."

The abrupt change from antagonists to allies, from being chosen strangers to being father and son, took a moment to register in Colin's mind. In the process, he looked away from Shaun.

"Colin, it's time I told you."

Told him why there was this unforgivable anger between them? Slowly, Colin moved to one of the windows and brushed the heavy drape aside to stare out at the black world.

Shaun stood behind him, unwilling to speak such difficult things unless he had some measure of self-control over his actions. He cleared his throat before speaking again. "Over the years, you and I-. We've grown apart. We've let - things come between us. I know when it started, exactly when it started." A definite resentment edged the words. "Do you remember when you first met Max?"

Colin's expression deepened to a confused frown. "I was about thirteen, fourteen maybe."

"An impressionable age." Shaun walked a few steps to the middle of the large room, then back to the same spot again. "It seemed as if Max stole you away overnight. He gave you all the attention I didn't take time for. He fed you fantastic stories and wisdom and-...You no longer needed me as a father, Colin. Not when you had Max."

It wasn't true. Colin let the curtain fall into place again before turning around, before he met the wounds his father's words had exposed. But Shaun wasn't the only one who bore scars. "Max never stepped into your place in my life. It's simply been empty. An empty, unfillable void. I'm sure I could come up with as many excuses for being with Max as you can for being gone, but none of it matters any more."

"Doesn't it, Colin?" Shaun refused to give up. "Are we going to tear the wall down now or leave it in place and keep throwing the anger and resentment from one side to-."

Shaun's words were dramatically cut off when the door, which had been only half closed, was suddenly flung inward. Shaun and Colin were both caught off guard by what they saw when they looked up.

"Colin, you're - all right?" Kaytra reached for the door, very much needing its support. In her anxious flight, she had merely thrown a cloak over her shoulders and left her hair down. It rested in tangles upon her shoulders, brushing her pale face. She fought to breathe evenly. "I thought -. She said you were hurt."

"Who said?" Colin demanded in a tone not yet void of shock.

"I said." Catherine came into view just behind Kaytra, drawing all eyes in the room toward her for explanation. It dumbfounded the men to see her put a protective arm around Kaytra's shoulders and lead her further into the room. "I'm sorry, Kaytra. I knew my note would alarm you, but you needed to come."

"Catherine-."

"No." She held up a hand to dispel any forthcoming argument. "Please, do come and sit down. You're very pale."

Kaytra sat heavily in the same spot Colin had vacated earlier. One hand rested on her swollen belly, the other gripped the arm of the sofa for support. Her eyes rose slowly to where Colin was standing. He seemed different. The way he looked at her seemed different, as if he could pierce straight through to her heart.

Shaun was the one to break their awkward silence and he did so with little regard for the young woman who had suddenly reappeared. His question mirrored the unwelcome look in Colin's eyes. "What are you doing here?"

Kaytra's fear became all too real. "I - I want to speak with Colin - alone."

"No. You-."

"Yes," Colin broke in with bitter control. "I think that's a good idea." He walked a few steps closer to where she sat, pinning her to the uncomfortable sofa with a harsh stare.

Catherine, trying to weigh the wisdom of her hasty summons of Kaytra and finding none, lifted a hand to her troubled brow. Her rash decision to send Carlisle to deliver the note seemed utterly wrong now.

Seeing the waves of guilt wash over her features, Shaun knew it would be up to him to get her from the room. No doubt, she would spill out the story to him upstairs. He took her firmly by the elbow. "Come, Catherine." The door closed with a certain finality, sealing Colin and Kaytra alone in the library.

With some effort, Kaytra pushed herself to her feet. "If you're going to yell at me-."

"Who's yelling?" He took another slow, measured step closer, taking in every detail of her appearance. Beneath the cloak, she wore a very elegant gown. If not for her pale face, she would have looked very much improved from when he had last seen her. "How did my mother know where to find you?"

Kaytra moved closer to Colin, but did not touch him. Instead, she clasped her hands together so tightly the fingers became white. "She's known all week...I've written to her several times."

"To her...and not to me."

She refused to step away. "You've been - drinking. You never drank before."

A cold smile showed on his face. "My wife has never left me before either."

"We aren't married."

Colin abruptly turned away. "Where have you been?" He received only silence, forcing him to look at her again.

"I can't tell you."

His eyes went as hard as steel. "Can't or won't?"

"Does it matter which? You're in no mood to believe anything I say."

Colin agreed. His thoughts were too scattered to listen to any explanations. If she had written to his mother - but why would she? It made no sense. Though how else would Catherine know the marriage was false, or where to find her?

He ran an impatient hand through his hair as he went to stand in front of the nearly dead fire in the fireplace. His forearm rested along the mantle. Someone had bought her new clothes and nursed her back to health. Someone had sheltered her this past week. Her grandparents? But she had seemed so against facing them...

The sound of the doorknob clicking open made him whirl around. "Kaytra!"

When she looked back, it was with a saddened expression.

Something clenched the very breath from him. "You're going again?"

"I have to." They stared at one another from across the room. "I'll come back tomorrow. In the evening. I promise."

"What if I don't want you to come back?"

Her quiet answer was nearly lost in the empty room. "Pray about it, Colin."

"Pray? Dear God in Heaven, Kaytra! You left of your own free will without so much as a good-bye!" His steps toward her were accomplished before she could even think of turning to leave. "I looked for you! Other people did, too! Pray about it? No!" He threw the words at her like daggers. "I won't pray! I prayed before that you would stay and look what happened!"

"God had a reason-." She gasped with pain when he grabbed her arm.

"Do you really think I want you to come back after what you did?"

"Let go of me, Colin." Her voice was unsteady. "You're hurting me."

He ignored her plea and blurted the words he knew would accomplish his goal. "My mother sent for you because I'm going to marry Patricia." He didn't feel satisfied when she cringed. "I decided tonight that you aren't worth it, Kaytra. Not you or the baby. I told my father everything. He agreed with me."

For once, she didn't care that he saw the tears clouding her eyes. "But you said you read the journal -."

"They were only words."

"When you say you don't want me to come back, those are only words, too."

"Are you sure about that?" he asked coldly.

A long, tense silence stood between them. It scared Kaytra to see how the past week had hardened him.

Finally, Colin let go of her arm. "Well, what are you going to do now?"

She lifted her chin, though the hurt remained poignantly readable in her eyes. "I'm going to pray about it."

Colin's reaction was to reach behind her and push open the door, sending a clear message that he didn't care in the least whether she prayed or not.

She walked from the room, but stopped in the middle of the foyer when she saw Shaun. He stopped, too, halfway down the stairs. Something in his face was more clear, more open than before.

In the brief moment he looked at her, Kaytra dared to hope again. She turned at the door before opening it, knowing she would find Colin watching her. "I'll be back tomorrow."

Chapter Twenty-Three

Whether by chance or by design, both Shaun and Catherine were away the next evening when Kaytra was shown into the dining room where Colin was having his dinner. He looked up at her in silence. Only after Carlisle closed the door again did he speak. "I didn't expect you this early."

Kaytra stood a few feet from him, trying to guess his mood from that one nearly toneless sentence. "I was able to get away sooner than I thought."

He slowly sat back in his chair, letting one hand remain around the slender stem of his water goblet. Though he appeared to be at ease in her presence, Kaytra knew differently. She tilted her head to the side a little in a gesture which was achingly familiar to him. "Have you eaten yet?" She shook her head. "Maggie!" The loudness of his voice carried through to the kitchen.

Maggie, who came at once, was rendered speechless at the sight Kaytra. Yet only her tear-filled eyes revealed the secret joy. Kaytra smiled back, longing to both give and receive a warm hug, but Colin shattered the brief moment. "Bring a place setting for her." Maggie agreed with a nod and turned to go. "Keep Rex in the kitchen, too."

The harshness of his command was lost to anyone other than Kaytra. He lifted his eyes, waiting for her objection. When none came, he motioned her with an impatient gesture into the chair opposite his where Catherine usually sat. Kaytra moved to it, grateful for the chance to sit down.

Tonight she wore a pale blue dress, as fashionable and expensive as the other. Her hair had been twisted into an elegant chignon, though some tendrils had escaped in childish abandon. The way candlelight played with the brightness of her eyes was very distracting. Colin chose to think instead about the sleepless night he had endured.

In a moment, Maggie came with plates and silverware. Common sense told her that now wasn't the time for happy reunions. She did her duties and was quickly gone from the room. Stephen had been teaching her to pray and pray she did, in earnest.

Very little of the food on Kaytra's plate actually found its way to her mouth. As the minutes ticked by, Colin's impenetrable silence made her more and more uncomfortable. She could feel his eyes upon her several times. Yet each time she looked up, he was engrossed in himself again. Kaytra finally gave up the pretense of eating. Her gaze moved to the arrangement of roses gracing the center of the long, lace-covered table. Their fragrance had faded during the day, but they were still very lovely.

"Were you the one who ordered them?"

Kaytra nodded and met his eyes. Did he resent that, too?

"Where did you get the money to buy them?"

"I - had some."

"From whom?"

"Colin, I-."

"You won't tell me that, either?"

She pressed her lips together, unwilling to strike back against his rising anger. Perhaps if she let him get it all out, he would then listen to her.

"Are you through?" He suddenly shoved his chair back and stood up.

Kaytra realized for the first time that he had lost weight since she had been gone. There were lines of strain around his eyes, too. She stood more slowly than he had.

Anyone looking on would have taken them for strangers by the way Colin led her from the dining room, down the hall and into the library. The room was less than inviting. A single lamp burned on the desk. Fire sputtered weakly on the grate. Kaytra tried to ignore the disappointment which threatened to overwhelm her by reminding herself that she had been praying, all day long.

Colin turned toward her. "Sit down."

"No, thank you." She would rather stand, even if he did tower over her.

"I want an explanation. What happened after you left the cemetery that day?" He saw her surprise. "Rex tracked you that far. You must have gotten into someone's carriage after that. Whose?"

"I can't tell you."

"No, you *won't* tell me. There's a big difference between can't and won't. Isn't that true?"

"Alright," she conceded smoothly. "I won't tell you. You'll just have to trust me, I guess."

"You guess wrong!" Restlessness drove him to stand behind his father's desk, one hand shoved into his pants pocket, the other flat against the smooth top. "I won't ever trust you. I don't think I really did to begin with."

Kaytra shrugged her shoulders expressively. "Maybe not. But trust can be learned. Isn't that what you told me the morning I - left?" His stony silence failed now to unnerve her. "You'll have to start trusting me sometime, Colin."

"What makes you so sure?"

It seemed a long time before she pulled an envelope from the reticule which hung on her wrist. "This makes me sure. I think you should read it. You might find it rather interesting." As she spoke, she walked across the room. The white paper envelope slid easily over the desk.

Colin grabbed it up as if it offended him. He cared little that he tore the corner of the single page inside when he opened the envelope. The sudden tensing of his body was expected.

Kaytra watched his face as he skimmed the words. He threw it down between them so quickly she wondered if he really comprehended what it said. "The FLC was very interested to learn that you are married now." She saw his brown eyes darken. "And the Davis' have found it impossible to stay on at Highland. Mrs. Davis is especially unhappy there. Naturally, the FLC would offer the position to you and your wife."

"Naturally."

Kaytra drew in a deep breath. "It says in the letter that you must let them know by the 21st. That's-."

"I know what day tomorrow is."

"Well, good!" Her control finally snapped and she swung away, moving to what small warmth the fire offered. Tears stung her eyes, blurring the fire's orange-gold glow. The only sound in the room was the monotonous "click-click" of the pendulum in the mantle clock. Kaytra tried to slow her racing heartbeats to match its sound.

She lost count of how many clicks she heard before Colin came up behind her. Still, she didn't turn around. He spoke so close to her, she could feel his breath stir her hair. "You planned all along to come back in time for me to answer that letter?"

She nodded, breathless again to have him so near. When his hand came up to touch the tender skin at the nape of her neck, she unconsciously swayed toward him, seeking the gentleness she knew he possessed.

"Did you miss me, Kaytra?"

Her eyes closed. Yes, she had missed him - very much.

His hand cradled the back of her head. Even before he looked down at her, Colin could feel her longing. He could see for himself that she had admitted the truth.

As his hold on her slowly tightened, her eyes flew open. This time, he didn't spare her one ounce of his anger. "You had no right to contact the FLC!"

"But-."

"No!" He slid his hand to her neck, forcing her head back until fear entered her eyes. "Your tricks won't work. The wife I take to Highland will be Tricia. Not you!"

"She - won't - go."

The strangled words robbed his threat of any real harm. It was true. Colin released her, but didn't move away.

Kaytra trembled beneath his gaze. "Tricia won't go anywhere near the Cape. If you want Highland back, you'll have to take me."

"And if I don't want Highland back?"

She paused. "You can't be happy anywhere else - not really."

"Why couldn't you have seen that before? Why put us both through hell by forcing me to leave there?"

"I -." She bit back the words with a gasp.

Colin was instantly wary. His eyes narrowed. "You what, Kaytra?"

"I - have to - to leave now."

He blocked her way. "And when will you conveniently come back? Next week? Next month?"

"Tomorrow."

"Ohhh?" How decisively his doubt cut through her. "Why tomorrow?"

Kaytra bit down on the inside of her cheek. "Because, I can come back tomorrow. For good."

He studied her closely. "Will you tell me then where you've been and why?.... No, I can see for myself that you won't. I'm simply supposed to 'trust you', right?" She was visibly hurting now. "I could make Mother tell me where you are. I could even follow you there now ."

This threat she couldn't disarm with words. She could only look up at him helplessly, waiting for him to say he wouldn't.

Colin felt stabbed by the expression in her blue-gray eyes. How could his feelings betray him this way? What was this confusion he felt? He wished she would leave, yet willed her to stay. "And what time tomorrow will you come?"

"I - I'm not - sure." When she moved to get past him, he let her go.

Tonight, he didn't follow her from the room. Instead, he lowered himself into the chair near the fireplace and sat there for hours, thinking past tomorrow, but always coming up against the same blank wall. A wall built by Kaytra's secrets.

He had a choice of going back to Highland or staying here. He had a choice of marrying Kaytra or Patricia. He had a choice of scaling those blank walls or walking away from them. What it all came down to was trust.

And he wasn't going to trust her. He couldn't.

Colin was awakened the next morning by a vague sense of uneasiness. After trying several times to ignore it by falling back to sleep, he finally got out of bed. The overcast sky promised snow before long. He turned from the window.

Nothing he did that morning relieved his restlessness. He spent hours exercising the horses, throwing himself into caring for their needs. At noon, he sat at the dining room table alone again, not eating the food Cook had prepared to tempt his appetite. In his mind, he kept picturing Kaytra across from him as she had been last night, bathed in candlelight....

What he had failed to notice then stood out now as significant to him. He remembered that she still wore the wedding band he had given her. He remembered how it caught the light several times.

Finally, he gave up sitting there and went up to his room, only to find its confinement stifled him even more. Where was she now? Why, after deciding last night that it was over, did his thoughts seem constantly occupied with her today?

That a man lay down his life for a friend. The thought came unbidden, sweeping over him so completely he checked it at once, stopped it cold.

Colin felt his hands ball into fists. Why should these words come so strongly into his mind now? He tried to set them aside, only to discover that a deep feeling of concern was growing in his heart. It had been months since Kaytra wrote those words on paper and turned to him, desperately seeking some explanation, some meaning for them other than childhood wonder. And he had not told her what that meaning was. But he knew....

When he moved to stand by the window, the feeling of concern pursued him.

She needs you, Colin.

"No." He spoke aloud, arguing against the thought.

But it came back more insistently. *Kaytra needs you.*

To feel the Spirit of God touch him with such clarity now, struck deep in Colin's heart. He didn't welcome the guidance. He didn't want God to remind him that he should lay his life down for Kaytra's sake. Colin ran a hand over his eyes.

Hurry, Colin.

He swore beneath his breath.

Now, Colin. She needs you now!

The heavy snow falling from the sky received his undivided attention...Until the story of Jacob wrestling with God's angel crashed into his mind. It would cripple him for the rest of his life to fight against the Spirit of God.

Hurry, Colin. He heard the same voice again. *She needs you.*

Catherine was just coming in the door as Colin raced down the steps with Rex close on his heels. She frowned deeply to see her son pull a coat from the closet. "Where are you going?"

"Chester." He shoved his arms into the sleeves, repeating the name of the village on the florist's bill.

"Colin-."

"I'm going to get Kaytra."

"But, Colin. She isn't in Chester." Catherine, who reached out her hand to stop him from leaving, also searched his face for a long, tense moment. "She's *at* the Chester's. They've gone to Europe and rented out the house."

Four-nineteen Chester. He saw the address again, mentally berating himself for not understanding sooner. The Chester house, not the village of Chester. Four-nineteen wasn't half a dozen blocks away. How else could she have come so quickly the other night?

"Colin, you can't go there. She-."

"I have to go." He pulled away.

Catherine could only stand there, staring at the closed door.

All this time, Kaytra had been within walking distance. Colin swung aside the wrought iron gate and strode up to the front door of the Chester's house with Rex at his heels. The Chesters were clients of his father's. He had met them before. The brass knocker sounded as impatient as he felt.

No one came to answer. Colin pounded on the door with his fist. Still no answer. When he turned the knob and found that the door was locked, he moved back, looking up at the second story windows. Then he stepped back onto the walk and rounded the house. The servants entrance was unlocked.

Upon reaching the foyer, Colin stood a moment to question the closed-up emptiness about the house. Nobody was there. He raised his eyes to the top of the stairs. "Kaytra?" Her name echoed back. Then he heard a sound, so faintly he could have imagined it.... "Kaytra?"

Rex suddenly bounded past him. Colin took the steps two at a time. There was only one door open along the hallway.

His heart stopped when he reached it. Kaytra was lying on the bed in a tight ball, fully clothed and very obviously in pain. He crossed the thickly carpeted floor, watching the dog nudge at her and whine for some response.

"Kaytra? Kaytra look at me." He wasn't sure that she heard him. She moaned when he reached out and rolled her onto her back. Her face was damp with perspiration. Colin smoothed the hair from her frightened eyes. He had seen her afraid before, but never like this.

"The - baby."

"It's alright. I'll get you - home." His words faded apart as he noted the intensity of her pains. She wasn't going home. She wasn't going anywhere. "It's coming now?" All she could do was nod her head. Colin swallowed hard. "Right now?" His answer came as she arched her back, trying to fight against the unending waves. He stripped his jacket off in one motion and began rolling up his sleeves. "You'll have to tell me what to do, Kaytra. I've never delivered a baby before."

Though her eyes were large and darkened by pain, she attempted a slight smile. "Neither have - I."

"Kaytra." His tone held concern as she was gripped by another contraction already. He had helped Glory Morn foal a colt before. How much different could this be? Kaytra moaned fitfully as he lifted her and tore the blankets down, exposing the clean sheets beneath.

Glory Morn hadn't moaned.

Her eyes flew open. "Oh, Colin, it - hurts!"

Colin ignored her and looked at the long row of buttons on the front of her dress.

When Kaytra was seized by another, more urgent contraction, he set his hands at the collar of her dress and tore it from neckline to hem in one instant. He did away with all but her camisole in the same manner before throwing a sheet over her. Then he was gone.

There came a tearing inside. She fought off the blackness which wanted to claim her. But it was so hard. Ever since she had left Colin last night, and through the morning hours until the house was empty, she had hoped the baby wouldn't come this day. In denying the possibility, she had lain down on the bed, waking every few minutes to increasingly hard contractions. Waiting and waiting all alone....

But she couldn't do it anymore. A half-cry, half-sob escaped her parched lips. "Kaytra?" Colin's cool hands were suddenly holding hers.

She opened her eyes, seeing that he frowned down at her in concern. "Please - st-ay.."

"Of course, I'll stay," he smiled . "I think you're supposed to push with the pains, alright?"

She nodded. Her body had told her as much, but it didn't seem to work somehow.

"No, don't arch like that." He pushed her flat onto the bed. "Push now, Kaytra."

When he moved away, she reached for him. "Colin?"

"It's alright." He talked her through the next few pains, trying carefully to keep some encouragement in his voice. She looked as white as the sheets and was growing almost too weak to push. Finally, the baby's head crowned. "Push again, Kaytra."

She went limp instead.

He didn't mean to shake her as hard as he did. "Kaytra! Push or the baby will die!"

"I - can't!"

"You can!" He shouted back.

By the time he held the baby in his hands, Kaytra was nearly unconscious. "It's a boy, Kaytra. A tiny boy. He's perfect." Colin wrapped the child in one of the towels he had found. It stared up at him quite contentedly.

"Colin."

His head snapped around at Kaytra's weak, anxious cry.

"Some-thing - is - wrong."

He set the baby safely in the middle of the big bed while Kaytra, worn by the ordeal, writhed again in pain. Colin placed his hands on her shoulders. "Kaytra, don't. Just lie still."

"Colin!"

"What?!"

She jerked as if he had slapped her. "There's - another baby!"

"What? You can't...You-." Of course she could have twins! But not now!

Chapter Twenty-Three

"It - hurts!" She tried to sit up again, but found she couldn't.

The next moments were only blackness and tearing pain. Blackness and pain...She thought she heard a baby crying. She knew she heard Colin telling her to push. For a while, she did try, but something really was wrong. She felt a rush of warmth. "Co-l-in...."

"Shhh. It - it's alright."

The pain was suddenly too much and she screamed against it. Then it was gone, and there wasn't blackness anymore, but a blinding white and she became so cold. All the warmth was draining from her.

"Kaytra!" Colin lifted her shoulders from the bed.

She tried to say good-bye....but the words came too late.

Chapter Twenty-Four

Colin sat in the chair near the window in his room. His arms had begun to ache from holding the baby so long. In the hours that the baby had slept, Colin had been watching him, strengthening the bond between them.

From the first moment the boy had stared up at him, Colin had claimed him as his own son. And he could easily have been. He had thick, dark hair and he had dark blue eyes, which Beany said would turn to brown in time. He could be Colin's son...He was Colin's son now.

The baby stirred, causing Colin to tighten his hold. Beany had found some clothing upstairs in the attic. Maggie had given him a bath. He smelled faintly of soap and talc. Colin smiled at the way the baby's lips were slightly open, moving now and then with little sucking sounds.

It was only moments before those eyes opened wide with wonder. "Hello, there." Colin said softly as he shifted the baby up to his shoulder just as Beany had shown him. "I suppose you're getting hungry." A small, warm fist pushed against his neck, somehow defining the loss Colin felt.

He sighed deeply. Life and death walked so closely together. What God had chosen to do didn't seem fair, but there was no changing what had happened. The baby nestled against him and started to whimper. "Shhhh. It's all right." Colin stood slowly, remembering that he had said those same words to Kaytra. He brought one hand up to rest on the boy's head.

Now that he was wide awake, the baby had one thought in mind. Eating. The whimpers became full-fledged crying.

"Shhh, baby." Beany hadn't told him what to do now. Colin carried the baby out into the hallway in search of some womanly advice.

When it was Shaun who appeared at the top of the stairs with a bewildered frown, Colin was hardly prepared to offer any lengthy explanations. Shaun moved forward all in one rush. "Whose baby is that?"

"Kaytra's. Where's Mother?"

"I just got home." Shaun stopped to peer at the baby more closely. The sound of a child crying hadn't been heard in the MacRae house since Colin was that size. "What are you doing with her baby?"

"It's kind of - hard to - explain right now," Colin said as he awkwardly shifted the baby to his other shoulder.

The door to Catherine's bedroom opened. "Colin, whatever is wrong?"

"I think he's hungry or wet or - something."

Catherine rubbed the child's back.

"Will someone tell me what's going on?" Shaun demanded

"Shhhh!" Both Colin and Catherine shushed him, but too late.

The door immediately to Colin's right was already opening. Kaytra looked around their circle of faces, ending with Colin and the baby. The moment Colin saw her sway faintly, he pressed the baby into his mother's arms and reached for Kaytra. Though Colin was very gentle about how he carried her back into Lydia's room and laid her on the bed, there was still a moan of pain. "You shouldn't get up again, Kaytra."

"Where - is - the - baby?"

"He's right here." Colin motioned his mother forward.

Shaun followed, taken back by the younger woman's pallor. She seemed barely able to focus on the child in Catherine's arms.

"No." Kaytra shook her head weakly from side to side. "Where's the - other baby?" When Colin didn't answer, her breathing became short, anxious. "It - died?"

He nodded slowly, wishing to have kept the pain from her awhile longer. She turned her head away from him, growing so still it reminded him of those terrible moments in the other house when she had slipped into unconsciousness, when she had been so close to dying herself.

During their silence, Catherine gave the baby back to Colin and indicated with a nod of her head that she and Shaun would be downstairs. He waited until they were gone before sitting next to Kaytra. "Your son is hungry. You have to feed him."

She didn't respond.

Colin laid the child in her arms so that she could feel its soft warmth moving against her as he had, but she shrank away. The baby found its fist and sucked at it vigorously for a moment. "Feed him, Kaytra."

"I want to - to be alone with him."

"Kaytra-."

"Please!" She didn't ask as calmly the second time.

"I can't leave you. Not like this." Colin set a hand alongside her face.

Her first tear slipped over his fingers. Then her eyes lifted to his, silently begging him to leave.

"No, Kaytra. You've been through a great deal with the delivery and then moving you here from the Chester's." Mention of where he had found her raised the level of tension between them. They were both thinking of the secret which she had kept from him. Colin felt it burn deep inside himself until he had to ask. "Who rented the house, Kaytra?"

"I - won't tell you," she murmured. A flush of color stained her pale cheeks. Colin had every right to be angry, yet he was holding back his own emotions because of her grief. The baby gave up his fist and started to cry. He was a beautiful baby, healthy and strong. She ran her fingertips over his cheek, then his hair.

It startled her when Colin set his hands beneath her shoulders to lift her upright against the pillows. "He needs to be fed." The reminder was spoken quietly.

Kaytra leaned her head back against the pillow, but still didn't meet Colin's eyes. The baby began crying harder. If only Colin would leave, then she -. Tears stung her eyes. She wanted to hold the other baby, too. Somehow, she was able to undo the top of her nightgown. When the baby began to nurse, she knew a deeper sadness.

The moment she trembled, Colin reached out to support the baby with one hand. "What will you name him?"

"I - don't know."

"Haven't you thought about it before?"

Of course she had. But it wasn't that easy. Again, the silence overtook them, chasing away what had to be spoken between them. Kaytra felt another tear escape. This time, Colin did not offer comfort.

She switched the baby to her other breast. The truth lodged in her throat, constricted by unshed tears. Yet she had to tell him. She had to have faith. Kaytra brought her eyes level with Colin's. "I - can't name him until...until I know if you want to - marry me or not."

Colin stiffened, a frown creased his brow. "That hasn't got anything to do with naming him."

"You - you told me before that - that you would give him your name."

"Before you left the first time, you mean? What about now - after you've done it again?"

She lowered her gaze to the baby. He was almost asleep. The prayer she said in her heart brought little relief for the depth of emotions rioting between Colin and herself. It nearly broke her to see how Colin touched the baby's tiny hand with a gentle finger. "If you won't trust me, Colin, trust God."

When he drew back, Kaytra moved the baby to straighten her gown. Before she could guess his intentions, Colin was lifting the child into his own arms. He stood then, doubling the loss she felt.

"Get some sleep."

"Colin-."

He didn't even look back.

Kaytra recovered slowly from the birth. Emotionally as well as physically. For three full days, she spent the hours between feeding the baby, sleeping, or reading. After that, she forced herself to walk around her room and the nursery, though never once did she approach Colin's bedroom door. It had remained firmly closed. She hadn't even seen him since the day the baby had been born.

The women of the house were her companions. Catherine, loving and wise; Maggie, encouraging; and Beany, the one who was praying for her. She grew to appreciate them, but she still felt terribly lonely.

Quite unexpectedly, Shaun came one night to visit her. It was late, nearly nine o'clock. He apologized for the interruption, but the baby had finished nursing and Kaytra, though she was nervous, welcomed the chance to speak with him. He sat in the chair opposite her, watching her as she held the child. "You love your son very much, despite what happened to you?"

The question took Kaytra aback for a moment. Colin must have told him everything about her past. She raised her chin a little. "Yes, I do love him. He's something - precious, something good and innocent out of all the bad."

Shaun pressed his hands together beneath his chin. The expression in his eyes was a thoughtful one. "You have the whole household wondering what you will name him."

Kaytra wet her lips, feeling his disapproval. The way she pushed a strand of hair away from her face revealed her unwillingness to tell him.

"Does it have anything to do with my son's foul mood lately?" Shaun asked.

She looked away then, feeling a heated blush rise to her cheeks. "Yes, I suppose it does." She could think of nothing else to say.

But Shaun, with his own insight, knew what lay behind the simple answer. "I didn't just come here to see the baby. Colin is downstairs in the salon...with Patricia." Their eyes locked.

It had been a definite choice on his part to come here, to tell her about Patricia. Kaytra's heart beat an anxious rhythm.

"I think it's time you met her, Kaytra." Shaun stood and rather awkwardly took the baby. "Put on a pretty robe and go down."

Kaytra rose, too, still unsure. "But he-."

"He's a storm ready to blow. Perhaps someone needs to take the wind out of his sails a little. Hurry now. Wear the blue satin robe. It matches your eyes."

Shaun's prompting carried her right up to the closed doors of the salon with little indecision. But once there, she stood perfectly still, weak with apprehension and doubt and a hundred other emotions at war within her. She tightened the belt of her robe, wishing she had taken the time to dress.

Her hand trembled on the knob as she turned it slowly. She saw them at once. Patricia, with her back toward the door, was standing before Colin, her hands on his arms in a close, intimate way. Colin's eyes hardened the instant he saw Kaytra enter the room. In confusion, Tricia turned to search out the reason for his tension.

Kaytra stepped only far enough into the room to close the door again. She was sure the others could hear her heart pounding against the wall of her chest, especially Colin. He wore black pants and boots and a white shirt. His coat lay discarded over the back of a chair.

"What do you want?," he demanded tersely.

"I wanted to meet Patricia." Kaytra surprised herself by speaking evenly. She let her gaze move to the other woman. Patricia was already measuring her, noting every single detail. It was an old game. Kaytra knew it well and felt hurt by the easy dismissal she received as being no real threat. She squared her shoulders. "Colin told me you were beautiful, Tricia. He's right."

Her unexpected compliment rather upset Tricia. "Well, considering he wouldn't even tell me your name, Miss-"

"Kaytra, please."

"Kaytra? That is an odd name."

Colin suddenly had enough of their civil conversation. "Now that you two have met, you may leave, Kaytra." He moved around Tricia, closing the distance to the doors with long, angry strides. After he flung them both open, he stood aside, clearly intending Kaytra to do as he asked.

She defied him by moving to where Patricia stood. There were highlights of interest in her tone when she spoke again. "Have you known Colin long?"

"Longer than you," Tricia shot back, but subtly so as not to reveal her agitation.

Kaytra smiled. "I'm sure that is true. Lasting friendships such as yours take time to develop."

"Friendship?"

The doors were suddenly slammed shut again, breaking the women's intense exchange. They both turned to look at Colin, who was facing them with unspoken fury, both arms knotted over his broad chest.

Again, it was Kaytra who recovered first. "Colin, perhaps you would get us some tea? Surely Cook could-."

"No! I will not 'get you some tea'!"

"Very well." Kaytra lifted one shoulder, unconcerned, then shifted her eyes back to Tricia. "Tell me about yourself, Tricia. I hear you have a lovely singing voice. What is your stage name again? Bonnie-"

"Colin!" Tricia turned on him accusingly.

But he was too busy studying Kaytra through narrowed eyes to care. "How did you know?"

She smiled sweetly again, preparing to apologize now that she had made her point. "Oh, I am sorry." A consoling hand reached out to touch Tricia's arm, though Tricia was in no mood to be consoled and shrugged away violently. "I didn't mean to upset you, Tricia. I'm sure your father won't even notice that you poured thousands of dollars into the Travois. After all, he trusted you would use it for charitable purposes. Part ownership in the Travois should qualify. Somehow."

The tears which appeared in the other woman's eyes seemed too convenient. She whirled and ran to Colin, sobbing into his shoulder. "I want to go home! Take me home!"

He had no choice but to agree. "Of course." His hands on her shoulders pushed her away enough so that he could throw Kaytra the full force of his annoyance. "You... will wait right here until I return, is that understood?"

"Of course." Kaytra nodded. "Good-bye, Tricia. Do come back tomorrow. We could have a nice chat together."

Tricia swung around with the agility of a cat, all tears forgotten. "Come back? Don't expect to be here that long!"

"Ohhh?," she responded calmly.

"Yes, 'ohhh'!"

"Tricia." Colin's tone warned Tricia to quit the petty argument as he firmly took her arm and pushed her toward the doors.

Once they were gone, Kaytra sat down in the nearest chair. She was shaking from head to foot and utterly exhausted. This was the first time she had been downstairs. It really hadn't been such a good idea to pick a fight, or to reveal as much as she had.

Now Colin would come back and demand answers to his questions. At least she had a little time to prepare. She leaned her head back and closed her eyes. There must be some way to tell enough of the truth to satisfy him, yet not jeopardize anyone in the process. There must be some way....

Colin stood in the doorway of the salon. Even though Tricia's hysterics had kept him away twice as long as he expected, he didn't think Kaytra would feel so comfortable and self-assured that she could fall fast asleep waiting for him.

He walked into the room. The rest of the house was quiet. Everyone else had retired for the night. Still, he closed the door behind him. For some reason, the sight of her curled into the corner of that big chair made him approach quietly rather than with the scolding he had envisioned during the ride home.

He sat down on one of the sofas some ten feet from her, but his eyes never left her face. Having her under the same roof again had not improved his sleepless nights as he had supposed. With a slow hand, he unknotted the ascot at his collar, then rolled back the sleeves of his shirt.

After what Kaytra said tonight, he couldn't believe she was the one who had rented the Chester's house. When he questioned his mother earlier, she implied that Kaytra stayed there alone, but that wasn't true. The two of them were hiding something.

It didn't set well with him, all her secretiveness. Yet he sensed she wasn't being vindictive. Patricia would act vindictively, but not Kaytra. He leaned forward, resting both arms across his knees. The single lamp, still burning on the table next to her chair, sputtered and finally went out, leaving only moonlight coming in from the windows.

It was a long while later that the clock in the library sent out its deep musical chimes. Though the sound was distantly muffled, Kaytra must have heard for she stirred. When she saw his figure in the darkness, a startled gasp escaped into the silence.

"It's only me," Colin said quietly, disrupting the twelfth bong.

Kaytra sat up rather stiffly, disoriented by the darkened room. "I - fell asleep."

"Quite soundly it would seem." He watched her pull into herself defensively.

"I was - tired."

"Then it's time you went upstairs." He stood slowly, waiting for her to do the same. There was an unsteadiness about the way she rose which drew him near enough to keep her from falling when she actually lost strength.

Almost as soon as he caught her, she was pushing herself away. "I'm sorry. I -...Colin, no." She protested when he lifted her into his arms.

"Just be still."

He carried her across the room, leaning down easily to open the door, allowing them to pass through. All the way upstairs and into Lydia's room, he never looked down at her or spoke a word. Kaytra could feel his heart beating against her arm. It was rock steady, while hers raced anxiously.

Rather than laying her down on the bed, he set her on her feet near to it. His continued silence made her words sound nervous and disjointed. "I'm sorry I-, that I fell asleep, but you - you did take a long time. You wanted to speak with me?"

"Get some rest."

"But-."

"Kaytra."

His warning was ignored. "Tell me what you -."

He covered her mouth with one hand too swiftly for her to avoid. "Since you have effectively ruined any chance I had of marrying Tricia and the FLC is expecting my wife and me within a week - during which time I could hardly convince a stranger to marry me - I am left with no choice but you. Tomorrow morning at ten a.m., you will be dressed and ready. There must be some judge I can buy off to come here and perform the ceremony. You will also have your son's name picked out so the necessary papers can be signed. No one outside this house will know he isn't mine."

As he dropped his hand from touching her, Kaytra drew in a shaky breath. "Colin-."

"Just be ready." He turned from her and left the room.

It was hardly the way she had wanted it to come about. He made marrying her sound like a cup of bitter dregs he was being forced to swallow because it was the only way he could get back to Highland. He made it sound as if....as if he hated her.

Chapter Twenty-Five

There was no music or flowers. The judge Colin found was a seedy old man, impatient to the point of rudeness. Maggie and Stephen were the only two people allowed into the library, and that only because law required witnesses. Kaytra's wedding gown was a simple white blouse and black skirt. She made a desperate effort not to let Colin see how deeply hurt she felt, but she wondered if he sensed it anyway when he held her hand to place the ring on her finger a second time.

His hands were cool and calm, his eyes void of emotion. If ever he seemed a stranger to her, it was the moment when she heard him repeat the vow uniting them as man and wife. When he didn't kiss her afterward, Kaytra dropped her head and pulled away, reaching for the baby Maggie was holding.

The judge was paid well to fill out the birth certificate so that it recorded Colin and Kaytra MacRae as parents. MacRae was added to the baby's christened name....Michael Logan.

Colin looked at Kaytra sharply when she gave the name. They both knew it was the name Lydia had chosen for the son she had never been able to have. Somehow, Kaytra had hoped Colin would be pleased, but he wasn't. If anything, he seemed to further distance himself.

Determination forced Kaytra to walk from her room through the nursery to knock on Colin's door that night. Her mouth went dry standing there waiting for him to open it. When he did, she was grateful to have prepared her speech. "I need to know exactly when we are leaving for Highland so that I may finish my business here and also pack for both Michael and myself."

Colin stared at her a moment and then, without answering, turned and walked away. Kaytra wasn't sure if she should leave. He removed his jacket, throwing it carelessly at the end of the bed. When he did look at her, it was with a sarcastic smile. "Are you so afraid of me that you stand there like a child?"

"I am not afraid of you. Not - entirely," she finished in a whisper.

"Come here." He noticed that she considered not doing it. "I prefer carrying on a conversation with someone in the same room, Kaytra."

She lifted her chin and practically marched across the room to fling herself into the chair in front of his fireplace. It wasn't lost to him that she hadn't actually changed the distance between them, rather only the direction he was forced to look.

"What is this - 'business' you need to finish?"

"It's no concern of yours."

His eyebrows rose. "Really? Now that you are my wife, I would consider anything you do to be my concern."

"Really?" She mimicked his tone to perfection, bringing a sudden darkening to his mood. "You would be that interested in me to know?"

"Interested, no. Not in the slightest." He sat on the bed, pulling his boots off with a few savage tugs. "But you do have a reputation for - mysteriously disappearing, shall we say."

"That's not fair."

"Isn't it?" Colin dropped the boots to the floor with a thud.

"No. You've never been fair to me. Not even after-." Her voice broke a little. She looked away so that he couldn't gloat over her tears.

Colin crossed the room to her. "After the other baby died?" His hard words caused a convulsive sob, but he kept on. "It was a girl. She was dead before she was born. She was so tiny she fit into the palm of my hand. I had her buried next to Lydia at the cemetery. I even named her for you so they could put something more than just the word 'baby' on her headstone."

He leaned over her, placing one hand on either arm of the chair. "Mary Elizabeth - MacRae." Kaytra felt the tears sliding down her cheeks as she turned her eyes up to his. "Now tell me I've never been fair to you."

"Did she - did she look like Michael?"

Colin flung himself upright in frustration. Why did she have to ask such a thing? He ran his right hand through his hair, leaving it disheveled in the fight to regain self-control. The deep breath he drew into himself didn't work either. "We're going back to Highland on Friday. Until then, you aren't to leave the house without me." As soon as he said it, he walked away.

She was dismissed. The journey from her chair to the door of the nursery seemed endless.

Michael's longest nap during the day came late in the morning. Ten o'clock wasn't the ideal time to go calling on anyone, but Kaytra didn't want to take him along. She didn't want to take Colin along either, but she had no choice.

She learned from Carlisle that Colin was in the stables, so she donned her cloak and a measure of courage. March had come without her really being aware of its arrival. During her days of confinement, the snow had retreated into thin patches beneath the trees. A breeze washed warm sunshine over her uncovered head. It looked to be a beautiful day, too beautiful to deliberately invite the sorrow she knew awaited.

The groom she met at the stable door directed her to the last box stall on the right. Colin wasn't aware at first that she was there. He was instructing a boy on how to rub down one of the big bay mares.

"No, Tommy. Go with the contour of the muscle. It massages them."

"Yes, sir." Tommy stretched and tried again. "Like this, sir?"

"That's good. You need to grow a few inches more, though." Colin's smile was the first genuine one Kaytra had seen from him in a long time. He even reached out to rumple Tommy's hair. "Keep it up and you'll make a master stablemate someday."

"Yes, sir."

Colin turned then, catching Kaytra's unguarded stare.

She blushed furiously. "I - I was - looking for you." He made her feel like a fool letting her stumble on. "My - business."

"Now?"

She nodded. "Michael is - sleeping."

"Very well... Tommy-." The boy stood at attention. "Tell the groom to have a team and carriage made ready."

Kaytra watched Tommy run from the stall eager to do Colin's bidding. Colin pulled on a pair of gloves as he stepped out beside her. "Where are we going?"

"It's not far."

For whatever reason, he didn't ask her any more than that. Throughout the ride, Kaytra kept her eyes straight ahead. Her thoughts focused on what she would say. "Hello. I'm you're granddaughter...Hello, Grandfather." Nothing seemed right. "Hello, I'm Kaytra. You don't know me, but-."

"Kaytra?"

She started nervously as Colin's voice intruded into her thoughts.

"I need some kind of directions."

"Oh." It took a moment for her to recognize where they were. "Another block. It's a big, red house. Brick. On the left."

He gave her a curious look, but said no more.

As many times as she had walked by the house, it still mesmerized her. Colin pulled the carriage into the semi-circular drive, stopping the horses just outside the huge door.

"Kaytra?" Colin was on her side of the carriage, waiting to help her down. His hands lingered at her waist a moment longer than necessary, his eyes probing her too-pale features.

She walked to the door on stiff legs. The knocker, shaped like a lion's head, felt heavy in her hand. When the door was opened, Kaytra fumbled for her voice. "I - I'm-."

"Good morning, Millie," Colin said pleasantly, even as his hand gripped Kaytra's arm beneath her cape. "Is Mr. Wainwright in?"

"Yes, Mr. MacRae." The ancient housekeeper, an imposing figure in black even to the bonnet on her head, let the door open wider. "We haven't seen much of you lately, Mr. MacRae."

Colin guided Kaytra in ahead of him. "No, Millie. I've been gone awhile. Shall we wait in the library?"

Millie nodded, recognizing the concerned looks Colin kept throwing at the woman next to him. The girl did seem rather anxious. She led them to the appropriate door, promising to tell her employer immediately that he had guests waiting.

Unlike the library at the MacRae's, the room they entered wasn't a work place, but a space in which to relax. The furnishings were worn and comfortable. Books lay about, taking up nearly every bit of table space. There were pictures throughout the room. Pictures of ships at sea. Ships being built. Coastlines with busy harbors. A dozen miniature vessels, sails fully billowed, sat atop the shelves.

Kaytra had only a brief glimpse of it all before Colin was swinging her around to face him. "You're as white as a ghost," he accused. "You could have at least told me why we were coming here."

She was still shocked that he not only seemed to know the housekeeper, but obviously her grandfather as well. The dryness of her mouth made it impossible to speak.

Colin's grip tightened. "Don't you dare faint, Kaytra."

That was easy for him to say. He wasn't meeting his grandfather for the -

"Kaytra!"

She forced her eyes open.

"Maybe you should sit down."

Yes. Maybe she should. She sank into the chair with a slight push from Colin. The room stopped spinning. Colin had squatted down beside her. "Does he know you're coming?"

No.

"This isn't the most brilliant idea you've ever had!"

No. She quite agreed.

He undid the clasp of her cloak, sliding it off her shoulders. Beneath it, she wore a new dress, the blue satin he had picked out the day she had disappeared. He had forgotten about it until now. It fit her perfectly.

Footsteps came nearer the door. Colin rose as it opened.

"Colin!"

"Hello, Max."

"Well and it's been ages since-." Maximilian Wainwright stopped in mid-sentence, in mid-stride as he caught sight of Kaytra. He was older than Colin's father by a good fifteen years. Age and arthritis had withered his spare frame to five feet eight inches. He walked with a cane and carried himself carefully so that even the well-tailored, brown tweed clothes he wore didn't quite fit him properly.

"Max -." Colin moved forward a step.

But the older man held up the cane to stop him. The silence was laced with tension. Max's shrewd eyes, gray as the sea, watched Kaytra slowly stand. His expression changed from initial confusion to shocked disbelief - and then became unreadable as if he drew a veil over his face in the same way that he lowered the cane again.

He moved to the side of the room opposite from her and stopped there to stare at one of the paintings. A magnificent ship, riding a stormy sea... "Why did you come here?"

"I - wanted to - to see you." Kaytra saw him cringe. "I - wanted to meet you."

Max whirled around, eyes ablaze. "You talk like him, but you look like her." He stared hard at her. "His eyes, but her face. Her way of standing. Her hair. I was told about you, after she brought you here.

I was glad when Elizabeth sent you both away. Glad to - live out my days without ever, ever seeing you."

Colin, who heard Kaytra's painfully drawn breath, forcibly pushed Kaytra into the chair again before she fell down on her own. Her face was as white as before.

"What's wrong with her?" Max moved a few steps closer.

"She's scared," Colin told him quite honestly. "She also had a baby a few days ago."

"A - baby?"

"And she shouldn't have come here in the first place!"

"That I'll agree with!" Max snapped out only to have Kaytra give him a pale, wounded look. Colin noticed it, too, and sent his old friend a silent warning to ease up. "Alright. Alright." Max grumbled, moving around the room. "Go get her some smelling salts or - something. Millie will know what to do."

Colin hesitated. "Is it safe?"

"I'm not that cold-hearted, boy."

After Colin left, Kaytra tried to seek refuge in her weakness, but her grandfather had other ideas. "What is your name?"

He didn't even know that? "Kaytra. After my father's mother."

"Kaytra." Max tried it for himself. "I don't like it."

"Well, I'm sorry!" She opened her eyes, not caring if he saw her tears.

"No need for hysterics."

"I'm not hysterical, only a little - disappointed."

"What did you have?"

She frowned in confusion.

"The baby?" Max hit his cane on the back of a nearby sofa. "A boy or a girl?"

"Both." She tried to hold back the ache. "M- Michael and Mary Elizabeth. The - girl - died." Max cleared his throat, obviously uncomfortable by the display of emotion. Kaytra closed her eyes again.

"What is young Colin to you?"

"My husband."

"Hmmm." He took a few more steps, then stopped again. "Where did he find you?" Before she could say anything, he answered his own question. "On the Cape. Highland. Is - she still there?"

Kaytra hadn't expected this to be so difficult. She stood again, wanting to face him. He didn't make it any easier by retaining his bitter expression as she braved a half-dozen steps toward him. He looked old to her. Old and - lonely. "My mother died when I was twelve."

Max tightened his grip on the handle of the cane, leaning into it more than he had before. "She died alone?"

"No." Kaytra unconsciously strengthened her voice. "I was with her."

"I mean did she marry again?"

Having heard their raised voices, Colin practically ran back into the room, stopping beside Kaytra. She had more color in her face. Her eyes held new determination. Max, on the other hand, looked a little - stunned. Colin held out the bottle of smelling salts for him to take. "I think you need this more than she does."

Max lifted the cane and brushed aside Colin's hand with it. "What I need is answers."

"She did marry again." Kaytra said as she moved between the two men, not willing that Colin should interfere. She knew what she wanted to say. "My mother married a man she met in New York. We moved to the Cape several years ago. She got sick. Nobody could help her."

"Well, I hope to high heaven she picked a better man the second time around!"

"My father *was* a good man!"

"He wasn't!"

"That's enough!" Colin drew Kaytra back against himself, not sure which one he was really trying to protect. "I think maybe it's time for us to leave." Kaytra turned toward him, ready to protest, but Colin silenced her firmly. "No, Kaytra. Neither of you is ready for this." He looked past her to Max. "I'll bring her back tomorrow. Or can you come for supper tonight?"

"Tomorrow is too soon if you ask me," Max grumbled moodily.

"Ten o'clock tomorrow morning then. We'll bring Michael with us."

"I don't want children in my house!"

Colin smiled charmingly. "You let me visit when I was a child."

"You didn't wear nappies either!" Max reluctantly smiled back. His tone began to soften. "Ohh, alright then. Bring him along. But I don't appreciate your being the one to make me a great-grandfather, Colin. Hope to high heaven he doesn't look like you!"

"He does," Colin answered quickly before Kaytra's honesty drove her to spew out the truth about Michael's parentage. He moved to get her cloak. "Come on, Kaytra."

She gave Max one last piercing look, then turned to leave, snatching her cloak from Colin's hands on the way. She was already out the door when Max stopped Colin with a tone suddenly serious again. "Colin?"

The younger man half-turned to face him. It had been years since he had seen that look of absolute uncertainty in Max's eyes. Not since Elizabeth had died. Colin felt sorry for him.

"I never told you the truth - about Mary Elizabeth. Never told you I had a daughter." Max stared at the floor.

"There are two sides to every story, Max. Nobody is ever perfect. You took time to teach me about the sea. To share that part of your life with me until I wanted it for myself." Colin saw the old Max when their eyes met again. "Trust me. Not only with our friendship, but with Kaytra, too. She needs you, Max."

"I'm an old man, Colin. I haven't got anything to give her."

"Give her what you gave me....part of yourself."

The drive home was a silent one. As soon as Colin stopped the carriage, Kaytra climbed down to the ground. She was grateful that he didn't follow her. Grateful that no one was around to witness her stumbling, teary-eyed ascent up the stairs.

Holding Michael was her solace. He stirred as she lifted him from the cradle. The deep blue innocence of his eyes gazing at her began to soothe the jumble of emotion inside. Kaytra sat down in the rocker near the window, unbuttoning the bodice of her dress so that Michael could nurse. The room was quiet. Peaceful.

After a time, the rhythm of the rocker calmed the worst of her tension and she was able to release her tight hold on the baby. She stroked his cheek, marveling at how soft he was.

To Colin, who stood in the doorway of his own room watching them, it was a touching scene: the way her hair fell over her shoulder with sunshine from the window flaming it into pure gold, the age-old beauty of a child nursing at its mother's breast, the fluid movement of her hand ministering love. He hadn't allowed himself to be with Kaytra enough to see how deeply she had bonded with her son.

If he could only forget the past few months. If he could have them back at Highland without all the lies and the secrets following them. If she could only -. But it wasn't possible to deny the past, to change what had already taken place. He left without her knowing he had even been there.

Visiting Max wasn't any easier the second time. Kaytra had made a vow not to let him upset her. Having Michael along stabilized her a little more, until Max walked into the library fully prepared to ignore his great-grandson.

"Well." He sat down in the middle of a sofa far from them, holding himself stiffly, gripping the cane as a soldier would his sword during battle. "You came back."

Colin moved into his line of vision directly behind Kaytra's chair. "Ten o'clock. You taught me never to be late, remember?"

Max gave an indecisive "humph", switching his eyes back to Kaytra. "What have you got to say?"

Chapter Twenty-Five

She tried counting to ten.

"Well? Speak up! I've got another appointment."

Five. Six. - "I appreciate your taking time to-."

"You should," he interrupted crossly. "But that's not what I asked you."

"Max." Colin received a firm gesture from the cane to be silent. He bit back a retort and moved away, still intending to listen to everything that was said.

Kaytra felt flushed with nervous energy. "I haven't got anything to say. I only wanted to know more about my parents."

"No." Max pounded the tip of the cane onto the floor, as if his denial was answer enough.

It wasn't. "Why not?"

He shrugged his shoulders slightly. Unemotionally. "Because it's over and done with. They're both dead."

"But I'm not."

One didn't have to know Max very well, as Colin did, to recognize when he was truly unbendable.

Kaytra shifted Michael to her shoulder, trying not to let the disappointment be heard in her voice. "I wasn't very old when my father died. I barely remember him. My mother brought me back here...to Boston. I don't - I can picture this house, but vaguely, as if it was a long-ago dream. I remember mother weeping brokenly. I remember feeling sad, but I don't know why. Grandmother - Elizabeth wore a soft blue dress. She smelled good - like flowers, roses just before the petals fall."

Colin saw Max's expression change as Kaytra kept talking. The older man listened, captivated just as Colin had been by the beautiful way Kaytra could put words together.

"She was wearing a necklace that made rainbows and her voice-. She sounded sad to me. Sad like my mother was, but different, too. Someone took me away from them, only my mother came to get me. We left. It was raining then, because the raindrops melted with my tears. I wanted to - stay - here. To see my grandmother again. Mama said no. That we could never - come back."

Kaytra laid her cheek against Michael's, drawing comfort for the rest of her story. "Mama said - no one here would - love - me, and - I wanted to know...why?" She lifted her head only enough to look at Max. "I came back because - I wanted to know - why?"

There was a long silence. Kaytra held his gaze awhile, but gradually looked away. Not at anyone or anything, just away. Her whole heart had been poured into making him understand, yet she felt as if she had failed.

"How old are you?"

Kaytra jerked at the suddenness of Max's question.

"Fifteen? Sixteen?"

"Seventeen."

"Oh, all of that, huh?" He had noticed then the proud tilt to her chin. His eyes moved to Colin. "She's a bit young to be married and a mother besides."

Colin's eyes widened perceptibly. "She's old enough, Max....and you're very smoothly trying to dodge her question."

Max threw him an ungrateful look. "Since when did you get so smart for your britches?"

"Since I had a very good teacher. Namely one Maximilian Wainwright." Colin shoved his hands into his pants pockets, walking a few steps closer to the two of them. "She deserves to know the truth, Max. All she knows are those childhood impressions and what Mary Elizabeth told her."

"Mary Elizabeth never understood how we felt."

"That doesn't mean Kaytra wouldn't try." The wisdom of what Colin said brought its own silence.

Michael, sensing some of the tension in the way his mother held him, began to whimper discontentedly. Kaytra stood at once, hoping to walk him back to sleep, but it was unnerving to have Max follow her every move and still not say anything. He was a decidedly stubborn man. She could well see how he and Colin had gotten on so famously.

Nothing she said had made even the slightest dent in his armor. She might as well be any other stranger to him. She might as well have not come at all. Her cloak was out in the hallway....

"Kaytra." Colin stopped her a few feet from the door. "You aren't running away from this one."

She heard him come up behind her. "I'm not running away. I only want to - go home." From somewhere in her mind came the memory of the night she had said the same thing to him and his stabbing answer. "You don't have a home."

He stepped in front of her now, searching her face.

"Please, Colin?"

It was easy for him to take Michael from her suddenly limp arms. "No, Kaytra."

"Why don't you let her go." Max made his opinion known rather gruffly.

"Because." Colin countered, holding Michael in one arm while steering Kaytra back to the middle of the room with the other. "It won't help either one of you.

Yesterday was different. You both needed time to get used to the idea. Today you need to start acting like you're family instead of strangers."

"Well, we are strangers!" Max set both hands atop his cane.

"Strangers would have been more forgiving of one another."

Max actually smiled, shaking a finger at Colin. "I think you missed your calling, boy. You should have been a preacher."

Kaytra looked up in time to see Colin smiling, too. None of this was amusing to her! "Perhaps the two of you should have been court jesters!," she said haughtily with both arms crossed over herself.

"Did you teach her that?" Max gestured to his granddaughter's unwomanly stance.

"I'm afraid so," Colin admitted with another broad grin.

In those brief moments, something had changed within Max. He looked at Kaytra in a different way. "She's very pretty when she's angry. Sit down, girl."

Colin gave her a little push toward the couch on which Max was sitting. She went reluctantly.

"Colin, take the boy for a walk or something."

It was Colin's turn to hesitate. The look on Kaytra's face begged him not to leave her alone.

But Max was insistent. "Go on...I'm an old man. Haven't got forever, you know."

A sense of expectation settled over the room after Colin left. Kaytra's eyes were focused on her hands. So much for her vow not to get upset. But it was partly Max's fault, too. He was simply being-.

"What do you know about your father?"

The question startled her into looking at him. There was a grave expression on his lined face. Kaytra bit down on her lip a little. "He - was captain of a ship. He was very handsome and...and kind. He died during a terrible storm. I was only five years old. He..." Her words trailed away. How very little it was to know about one's own father.

Max picked up her silence, crashing it as fine china falling to the floor. "Henry Lange was first officer on one of my ships which traveled between Boston and France. He never had the discipline to be a captain. He was very handsome. Your mother met him at some sort of dinner." He waved his hand to show it was of no significance. "She raved on and on about him. How he had such grand ideas of owning his own ship some day and becoming very rich."

"No." Kaytra shook her head in disbelief and would have gotten to her feet except that Max shot out a hand to keep her there.

"I made it a point to talk with him myself. Lange assured me that he loved Mary Elizabeth enough never to see her again if I felt it for the best. Well, I did forbid them to be together. Not a week later, your mother disappeared. We were crazy with worry. A month went by. We received a letter from her saying that she and Lange were married. That he was taking her to France."

Max hadn't let go of her hand while he talked. Through his touch, Kaytra could feel the rise and fall of his emotions. Even his pain. She watched his face carefully as he went on.

"My Elizabeth - your grandmother - was devastated. We had planned such good things for our daughter. A stable marriage. Having her live close to us. She was our only child. Henry Lange - stole her from us. He lied to us. And she lied, too."

"They were in love," Kaytra said quietly.

"Mary Elizabeth was in love with love. Not with Henry Lange." Max looked across at her, easing the frown from her brow with a squeeze of his hand. "What I'm to say will not be easy for you to hear, Kaytra, but I want you to understand. I wrote a long letter to your father, offering him a position here in Boston if he would bring Mary Elizabeth back. You see, after much prayer and searching of my heart, I had accepted the marriage.

"There wasn't any answer. Many months went by. Then, one day, he suddenly walked into my office. We ended up talking for hours. He-." Max shook his head. "He was several years older than your mother. She had - demanded things he knew better than to give her. She had, in fact, forced him into the marriage. When he came to me that day, you were already expected, but he brokenly told me he couldn't be sure you were his child."

Kaytra sucked in a sharp breath, feeling stunned by the words.

Her grandfather held onto her hand more tightly. "There were many - stories he told me. They aren't important any more. Henry - your father - said that he could never leave Mary Elizabeth. He shared with me how the trials had brought him to a deep trust in God. I respected him. Respected his loyalty to my daughter.

"After you were born, he wrote again to say it didn't matter to him anymore. He didn't need to know for sure. You were that precious to him. I think you became central in their lives. They both loved you and therefore loved one another, in their own way. Elizabeth longed to see you. We planned a trip about a year and a half after your birth. Our - daughter wrote back, refusing to see us."

Kaytra pressed a shaking hand over her mouth, unable to keep her tears from flooding over. Her sobs moved Max to pull her into the circle of his arm until she rested her head on his shoulder. He felt hot tears sting his own eyes, but there was more to tell.

"The strain was unbearable. Elizabeth became ill. Worry. Heartache. She was never the same after that. Her bitterness seeped into my life, too. I received several letters from your father over the years. I burned them all without reading a single word. I knew, of course, when the ship went down. I knew that he had died. Elizabeth suddenly began to hope that Mary Elizabeth would come home to us.

"She sank into a depression as the months went by. I - told her the truth then, all the things that had happened. When your mother brought you here - it was to leave you with us, not to stay herself. Elizabeth refused. Sent you both away. She couldn't accept who our daughter had become."

Max looked down at Kaytra. He could see only part of her face and brushed aside the curtain of blonde hair which had fallen forward. There was something comforting in the way she had curled against him. "You are his daughter, Kaytra. I know it by your eyes. By the way you carry yourself and how you think." Max sighed deeply, feeling somehow more complete now that the difficult things were past them.

He caught a movement by the door and looked up to meet Colin's eyes. The expression there told him exactly how much the younger man had heard. Max silently bade him not make his presence known yet to Kaytra. Colin nodded.

When Max spoke again, it was with great gentleness and wisdom. "What I said yesterday...about your father - in my heart I know he was a good man, but he should have fought back. He shouldn't have let Mary Elizabeth do the things she did. It's too easy to sit back and let life take its own course...like I did. I could have looked for you after Elizabeth sent you away. Not seeing you made it easier to justify my bitterness."

Kaytra pushed herself upright until she could look into his face. She was pale, her eyes swollen from crying. "My - mother didn't want me."

"No, child. Don't think that." Max rubbed his hand over her shoulder. "What she wanted was something better than she could give you herself. She had no money. All the money was gone. She didn't have a home for you."

"Then, I still don't really - belong - anywhere." The anguish was out before she could stop it and Max, in confusion, threw a questioning look in Colin's direction which only alerted Kaytra to his being there. She sat fully upright, wiping at her eyes with shaky hands. "Where's - Michael?"

"With Millie...He needs to be fed."

She stood slowly, trying to regain her composure. Yet, with both men watching her walk from the room, any kind of calmness was impossible.

"Colin..." She heard Max say very seriously. "I want to talk with you."

Kaytra closed the door behind her, too upset to wonder what Max would say. She could only guess at how much of the tragic story Colin would know by the time they left.

Chapter Twenty-Six

Despite pacing back and forth within the confined space of their cabin aboard the ship, Kaytra could not get Michael to stop crying. Her arms grew weary from holding him. Tears stung her eyes. She had been uncertain until the wee hours of dawn that she could do what was before her. When she wrote to the FLC, she imagined returning to Highland Light stronger than when she left, but that wasn't true.

Colin had completely withdrawn from her. Even now, he chose to be away from her and the baby. In many ways, she felt as if she had failed in her promise to Lydia. But she wouldn't allow herself to think that way. Perhaps there was more that needed to be healed inside of her, more giving things completely into God's care.

She paused by the porthole, wiping frost from the edges of the glass in order to see the ocean and the calm, March skies. Suddenly she wanted to race back to Boston. It had been difficult to say good-bye to Max, to Catherine and Beany. Maggie had given her a hug, promising to visit soon, whispering that Stephen had asked her to become his wife. Kaytra's pleasure for them was mixed with a certain sadness to think that she and Colin might never know such an unconditional love.

Even with Shaun MacRae, saying good-bye had been painful. Earlier that morning, as all of them waited on the dock, he said very little to her, but she noticed him looking at her several times. Then, just before boarding the ship, Shaun had clasped Colin's hand for a moment. Their eyes met and held for a long time, before they moved to embrace one another.

Kaytra knew it was the first step for them, just like this journey to Highland Light was her first step toward a deeper trust in the Lord.

In Provincetown, Colin went immediately from the General Store to the livery, while Kaytra and the baby stayed behind to visit. Now that he was on solid ground again, Michael had fallen fast asleep. It took little persuading on Kaytra's part to get Jolly to hold him. The older man beamed down at his bundle. "He's a han'some lad. Betcha he's good as gold, huh?"

"Very good." Kaytra smiled in return. "I missed you, Jolly."

"Me, too."

"It's - okay that we came back?"

His eyes rose to meet hers, guessing at what she asked. "Koch ain't gone. Don't think he had money ta go."

"Is he still in the same place?"

Jolly's gaze narrowed. "What's on youah mind?"

"I - I have to see him, Jolly. You'll keep Michael for me, won't you?" She had already turned toward the door. "I won't be gone but a few minutes. I promise. Come on, Rex."

"Wait!"

The door banged shut after her, leaving Jolly staring from it to the baby and back again, feeling as if his hands were effectively tied in doing anything to stop her.

After twenty minutes of babysitting, Jolly had worked himself into a fine panic. Michael didn't wake up, but Jolly didn't dare move either. He barely breathed the whole time. Finally he heard a step outside the door and turned expectant eyes in that direction.

It was Colin who calmly walked toward him, pleased to see that Jolly and Michael were getting acquainted. "Well Jolly, how did Kaytra talk you into it?" Even as he asked, his gaze swung around the room.

When he didn't see her, Colin felt his heart pump faster. The look he leveled at Jolly spoke volumes. "Where is she? Where did -."

"Went ta talk ta Koch!" Jolly blurted out in a high-pitched whisper so as not to awaken the baby.

"What?"

"Handed me the baby an' said she was goin' easy as that an' I fell foah it!"

Colin retraced his steps, banged the door open with the flat of his hand and was beside Samson before Jolly had time to remember he was still left holding a baby he had no idea what to do with if it woke up!

Obviously, Kaytra didn't expect to see Colin come riding up on Samson because some of the color left her face. She stopped in the middle of the road as he slid to the ground, walking the last few feet toward her. "What in heaven's name do you think you're trying to prove?"

Her stomach tightened. "I'm not proving anything."

"Except that you're-." He bit it off.

"What?" Kaytra challenged him, moving closer for the benefit of those who stood nearby, thinking that they were having a normal, everyday conversation. "A fool? A dim-witted female, begging for punishment? A-."

"Get on the horse," Colin said through clenched teeth.

"How? Shall I fly?" Her sauciness only got her into more trouble.

Unlike Kaytra, Colin didn't care what the people of Provincetown saw or heard. In one easy movement, he swung her over his shoulder. She had a choice of either being thrown onto the horse like a sack of feed or begging for mercy.

"Colin, please!"

He twisted her up onto Samson in a semi-dignified position, then mounted behind her. His arms held her there like bands of steel as

Samson swung around. "You are a fool," Colin said harshly into her ear.

Kaytra tilted her head back enough to see his face. "And you couldn't wait to prove it just now!"

"You didn't need any help doing that!"

"I didn't need any help period." She stared straight ahead again, trying to hold herself distant from Colin's hard body.

"I suppose you think it was very brave of you to go there by yourself?" His words were sarcastic.

Kaytra jerked away when Samson's gait threw them together. If not that Colin clamped his arms tighter, she would have been thrown off.

"Sit still!"

"I didn't go there to prove bravery. Far from it."

He reined Samson in beside the wagon. "No? Then suppose you tell me why you went...or is that to be another of your secrets?" Colin dismounted and reached up to haul her down beside him.

Kaytra's blue-gray eyes were the color of a storm-tossed sea. She would rather die right now than tell him how she had gone to Everette and asked forgiveness. The thought had been part of her sleepless nights lately. Only in telling him that she had been wrong to hate him, only in forgiving Everette's part in everything that had happened, would she find a sense of peace. The Bible repeatedly said one should forgive a wrongdoing. But perhaps Colin hadn't read those verses in a long while.

"Be careful," he taunted. "You might let something slip, say the wrong thing."

She pushed herself away from him and rushed up the steps into the store. If not for finding Jolly in a state of dire emergency, she would have broken down and cried. Instead, she hurried forward to rescue her son.

Jolly was holding a very-much-awake, very-loud Michael at arms length. "He's got a good stink goin'! Glad you'ahe back, gal. Heahe! Take 'im! I'll help Colin get things loaded up! Suahe an' he'll want ta go soon like."

There were a hundred things to do once they reached Highland. Colin helped the Davis' gather their belongings. They were anxious to make it back to Provincetown in time to sail for Boston on the next ship. Life on the Cape had not been easy for them. None of them looked back as Mr. Davis drove their horse and wagon away.

At six o'clock, while Colin sat down at the desk in the parlor to make a journal entry, Kaytra was in the kitchen giving Michael a bath. It was distracting for him to hear the hushed, pleasing tone of her voice as she talked to the baby. Max's solution had seemed simple back in Boston, but actually applying it now was a different matter. Patience had never been one of Colin's strengths.

He scrawled out the briefest of entries, then closed the book with a heavy hand, making Rex look up from his place on the parlor rug. Time stretched before him like an endless wait. The light was on already. His part of the supplies had been put away. They had eaten supper earlier. When he ran out of accomplishments to list, he looked askance at the small pile of luggage waiting to be dispersed.

Michael's cradle. The trunks containing their clothes. He moved over to them. "Shall I take these up?" he asked, meeting Kaytra's gaze after she glanced at the trunks. Curiously, she blushed a little before nodding her head. Colin shouldered one of the trunks.

He had gained the top of the stairs before realizing the reason for her embarrassment. One large bedroom. Two smaller ones. And who would sleep where? He gave the door to Lydia's old room a slight push. Nothing had changed. Not even the curtains or the quilt on the brass bed. He set the trunk down just inside the doorway and turned back for more.

As he reached the bottom of the stairs, Kaytra looked up from dressing Michael. "I - I'd like my old room again, for Michael and myself."

The tremor in her voice brought a frown to his brow. "You should have the big room. It's-."

"No," she rushed on. "I don't - want it. Please."

"But-."

"Please."

Colin's frown deepened. She simply had to be the most stubborn person he had ever met! He refused to argue with her. If she wanted to be cramped into that small space, then fine. As if recognizing his decision by the look on his face, Kaytra went back to her business, and Colin went back to his. He would take the corner room and be grateful to have a big bed all to himself.

For all his good intentions, Colin didn't sleep well that night. Nor any night during the week which followed. His body was exhausted from the rigorous schedule he set for himself. But his mind, his thoughts, seemed only to intensify in those long hours of lying there, watching the lighthouse beam play out through the darkness.

Their existence here at Highland - and that is what he came to realize it was, merely an existence - was robbed of any joy, void of laughter or fun or smiles. The seriousness which greeted him every-day stifled so much of what had made this place special to him. There seemed no real freedom, no purpose beyond keeping the light.

That phrase began to repeat itself often in his mind. At the oddest moments, it would simply be there, just as if he read it on a page. "Keeping the light....Keeping the light." It was his job, his duty to be the keeper of this lighthouse. But there was more, too. Something he had lost along the way.

Exactly why had he come back? Simply to prove to Kaytra that she had been wrong by forcing him to leave in the first place? He had to be honest with himself and admit that was his initial reaction, to prove her wrong. But he had also accepted the offer knowing, in the back of his mind, that it would be Kaytra whom he brought here as his wife.

As much as he was trying to prove her wrong, he was trying to prove his way as right. And the question of God's will had never entered his thoughts. Everywhere he turned here at Highland, he was reminded of the relationship he once had with God, how dependent he had been on knowing God's Word, on seeking guidance when he needed it. Lately, he had relied only upon himself.

Keeping the light.....The Light he needed to keep most of all, he had slowly neglected until now a very real darkness was surrounding him. It was a darkness much the same as the mid-March storm he watched this morning as it overpowered both sky and ocean. Perhaps because of his thoughts, this storm bespoke more evil. There weren't huge clouds, only a potent wind to sweep down on them, churning the sea with icy whitecaps.

He stood on the ocean side of the tower, feeling its force press in on him. Something uncontrollable would come as this storm reached peak power. He knew, because the same was happening in his own life. Even as he turned to leave, he could hear the storm breaking around the sturdy tower. The door had to be forced closed again.

Colin ran against the wind to reach the house, crashing inside so suddenly that Kaytra almost dropped the bowl of potatoes she was setting on the table. After a quick, startled glance, she was moving back to the stove. Colin hung his coat on a hook. "Is Michael asleep?"

"Yes."

"The storm is going to be a bad one." He watched for some kind of a reaction from her, but there wasn't one. She set a pot of beans and a plate of bread between their plates as he sat down. They didn't usually eat a big meal at noon. Colin guessed she was planning ahead. He might not get time later to eat much. When she was seated opposite him, he looked at her again.

The strain between them was showing on her, too. She had lost weight. She didn't sleep well. She barely said more than two words at a time. "Were you able to get all the shutters closed?," Colin asked in as near normal a voice as he could. Kaytra nodded. "We'll fill the coal bins and water buckets. I don't want you going out later unless it's absolutely necessary."

She wrapped both hands around a steaming cup of black coffee, but said nothing.

Their meal was finished in the same silence. Finally, Colin pushed his chair away from the table. "I brought along an extra telescope. Do you know where it is?"

"I'll get it."

He watched her go up the stairs, feeling a sudden burden inside, one he couldn't explain.

When she was gone longer than he expected, Colin went to find her. She was in his room, kneeling before his small trunk. "Kaytra?" Sadness flashed into her eyes when she looked up, but it was as soon gone.

The telescope lay on the rug next to her. In her hands, she held his Bible. Colin stood just inside the doorway. He hadn't touched that trunk since coming here. Kaytra laid the Bible atop the journal and, once again, closed the lid before she rose slowly to hand him the leather-encased scope.

"Thank you." Colin took it from her. In their mutual silence, they could hear the wind buffeting the house, rattling window panes and roaring up beneath the eaves. The thunder which had been distant before now cracked nearby. Kaytra started at the unexpected close-ness of it, her gaze flying to the windows.

"Are you afraid?" At first, he didn't think she would answer his question.

Then she brought her eyes to his face again. "Yes, I am."

The look she gave him changed until he knew they were no longer talking about the storm. His hand tightened around the scope. "I need to go north along the coast. I'll be gone about thirty minutes." She lowered her head. If ever she appeared to him a woman, it was now. Sometime in the past few months, she had lost the innocent abandon within to become steadier, more mature.

Part of him grieved for what she had lost, what they had both lost. He surprised her by reaching out a hand to lift the tendril of hair touching her cheek. In her eyes, he witnessed the indecision, whether to pull away or to release the tears.

He made the choice for her by turning to leave.

Colin never knew how long it was that she stood there, not dar-ing to move.

Chapter Twenty-Seven

The tasks Colin asked her to do occupied the half hour he said he would be gone. After that, Kaytra spent her time between cleaning the house and walking out to the edge of the bank. She looked in often on Michael's peaceful sleep. Another hour passed. The storm worsened.

Her trips to the bank became more frequent. Something had happened. She could feel it. Fear stung her as sharply as the wind-driven rain. How helpless waiting was, not knowing for sure, but certain enough to be afraid.

Colin had taken Rex with him. If Colin was hurt, Rex would come for her. Yet it was so dark and wild. What if they were both lost? Kaytra searched the darkness, but couldn't see beyond a hundred yards. Concern pulled her away from the lighthouse in the direction Colin had gone. She gripped her coat tighter, feeling the cold seep through to her skin. Where were they?

Wind and rain cut across the edge of the bank in sheets, threatening to lift Kaytra off her feet. She heard a continual, deafening roar as the waves swept in to crash upon shore. Still, she moved north.

All those months ago, when she had tried to kill herself, the depth of her emotions had never reached what she felt now. That storm could not equal this, nor those feelings compare to the anguish she felt at thinking Colin was out there somewhere, possibly hurt....perhaps even dead. Kaytra stumbled at the thought, then stopped abruptly, bracing herself against the onslaught. Dead? He couldn't be.

She wouldn't let herself imagine that possibility again. Colin was going to come back to her. He was going to survive this storm somehow and come back. The thoughts became a desperate prayer. Her tears became mingled with the icy rain washing over her face. Finally, the responsibility she had for Michael overruled her desire to find Colin and she went back, but only as far as the tower.

Colin couldn't possibly have heard her calls. Only the bell would be able to send its sound through the storm. She rang it again and again, forcing herself not to think about Lydia. Not to lose hope. After fifteen minutes, she returned to the house, gasping as the warmth inside met her near frozen flesh. Michael still slept. His calm, sweet face made it all right to cry.

Before he woke, she made one more journey to tend the light and to ring the bell. What more could she do...except pray.

The waiting slowly turned from anxiety to fear to nightmare. Every hour that went by became an agony of thoughts and feelings. That in itself would have worn her out. But there was Michael to take care of. A racing trip out to the barn to see that the animals were fed. Fires to be kept going. And the light.

Colin hadn't told her that the fierce wind would somehow keep finding its way inside the tower room to put out a lamp or two or three. She made countless trips up and down the steep, winding stairs, refilling the oil. Relighting. Cleaning. Working as quickly as she could in order to get back to Michael.

She became numb to the aching muscles and burned fingers. Numb to the storm which seemed not to have a beginning or end anymore. At ten o'clock that night, Michael went to sleep in her arms. Kaytra rocked him still, loath to face going back out, but she knew she must. She placed a kiss on his cheek before laying him down and covering him with blankets. One more time, then maybe Colin and Rex would come home.

Bracing herself with a whispered prayer, she stepped out onto the porch only to be hit - with a sense of confusion. The wind did not assault her this time. It was calm, completely still. She searched skyward, taken aback by the sight of clear darkness, even a few stars. How could it be over so suddenly as if - as if God himself had wiped the storm out of existence?

She looked north then and could see farther, but not far enough. Not far enough to see any reason for hope. In the years she had lived on the Cape, she had only seen one other storm like this. Many people had been killed. Many had disappeared never to be seen again.

Kaytra pushed one foot before the other to get to the light tower. Every movement in replenishing the fuel was automatic. The heat in the glass room had risen throughout the day, but she barely noticed. She still felt cold inside. Trim the wick. Polish the chimney. Light...Then the next one. Fill. Trim. Polish. Light....When it was done this time, she didn't stand at the windows. She simply left.

Alone in the kitchen, she drank a cup of re-warmed, over-brewed coffee. The bitterness stung her throat. She couldn't sleep. She didn't want to face the horrible dreams and wake up to find they were real. Standing at the desk, she looked down on the open page of Colin's journal. His last entry had been at noon... "Light will be kept on. Storm riding over - huge in proportion if judged by strength of the wind. Temperature dropping. Waves three to four feet, swelling far above that. Will make a visual check of coast; esp. North along bars."

There were no more entries. She had forgotten to make them. The pen she picked up shook with the trembling of her hand. "Eleven p.m.," she wrote. "The storm which has lasted all day is calm now, though I fear more will come. Colin and Rex have not returned. The light continues to burn...for whose benefit, I am not sure. No one could have survived the strong jaws of this storm. Perhaps I keep the light burning for me alone. The simple act of doing so will carry me through the night ahead. I will find purpose in it somehow. If tomorrow I look back through eyes of gratefulness, I will know it was the Light which brought me thus far and - if through eyes of sorrow - find the same. No matter the storm. The purpose remains....to keep the Light alive."

Kaytra re-read the words, wondering where she had found such hope. She shouldn't have written so much. The page was quickly torn out. She began to recopy Colin's earlier entries, carefully so as to keep the words the same. Then she wrote down eleven p.m. again. "Storm calm for now. The light is refueled and cleaned. Temperature seems somewhat warmer, though still below normal."

Colin is gone...No, she couldn't write that. The hand she pressed to her mouth shook more than before. Her heart ached unbearably. If she let herself cry, there would be no end to the tears. No stopping the flood of despair. No, she couldn't cry...She couldn't-.

A footstep? Kaytra caught back her breath seconds before the door opened. A man - but not Colin - limped inside, swinging his gaze around the unfamiliar room until he saw her. She pushed herself to her feet, one hand still clutching the edge of the desk, not taking her gaze from him.

He stared back through weary eyes, then swallowed hard before he broke the silence, "Got to - to bring the body in, ma'am."

Body? Dear Lord, no!

More footsteps sounded past the silent scream in her head. Two men came, one supporting the other. Neither of them was Colin. Kaytra's eyes flew wildly to the doorway, past these new strangers. A fourth man, whom she hadn't noticed lingering on the porch steps moved with the others inside the house and closed the door behind him, until the latch clicked with a dreadful hollowness, echoing over and over again in Kaytra's heart.

A pain tore through her. Not Colin. Dear God in Heaven, not Colin! She looked at all of them again, feeling very weak when they stared back as they did. The man with the limp struggled closer to her, his expression shadowed by grief. He, like the others, was soaked through, pale, but not as pale as Kaytra just then. She took a faltering step away from the desk. Colin-. But he had to be alive!

The men were completely startled when she rushed through their midst, intent on reaching the door and, once there, tore it open again. It seemed her heart raced ahead of her down the slippery steps, only to be abruptly slammed back in her chest, stealing her breath away.

Rex emerged from the darkness. Seconds later, an eternity later, Kaytra saw him. He was carrying the body in his arms. There didn't seem strength enough left in her to move. Not even when he reached the porch and they stood less than a foot apart. She bit down on her lower lip to keep it from trembling, to keep from crying out.

"I need to get in."

An unnatural flush colored her cheeks and Kaytra turned from the door as quickly as she had flown there moments before. Two of the men, the younger ones, came forward to help Colin. Because she still felt so numb, so deeply shocked by their sudden appearance, Kaytra only watched as Colin carried the dead man's limp form up the stairs. She heard when he moved into the spare bedroom, when he came back down a minute later. She heard him stop at the bottom of the stairs, but couldn't move.

Again, their eyes met. "We'll need the medical kit, Kaytra, hot water and clean clothes.....How is Michael? The light?"

"He -. It's - fine." Was that her own voice sounding so distant? She looked around at the men, seeing for the first time their cuts and bruises, the torn state of their clothes. The one man who had needed support looked - awful.

"Kaytra?"

She swung back toward Colin.

"As soon as you can, please. And some food. They haven't eaten since breakfast." He was so matter-of-fact, so in control.

Kaytra stared at him, feeling her own erratic emotions still spinning around inside. Not a minute ago, she thought he was dead, thought he wasn't coming back - ever.

Colin straightened from setting down his load to catch her eye. "The medical kit?"

And hot water. And clean clothes....She had heard the list.

Then he shouldn't need to ask again.

Kaytra whirled away from their silent exchange of thoughts. Eleven hours of uncertainty ended without either of them saying what they needed to say.

Bits and pieces of the story began falling into place as she helped tend to the men's needs. They were fishermen from Truro. The storm had caught them unaware, still miles from port. As it worsened, their boat was taken up the riptide which flowed solidly north along the coast. Sometime around noon, they had abandoned the bigger vessel in hopes of making it to shore in their yawl boat.

Three crew members hadn't survived the attempt. The yawl boat was smashed onto shore a mile north of the light where Colin had found them. There wasn't a one of the five who hadn't been injured. In the crowded kitchen, Kaytra sought out Colin, finding his expression grave, strained with all that had happened. They had stayed together, trying to help Colin save the young man's life. Their shelter had been a three-sided furrow in the clay bank. A meager fire had kept them from exposure.

As soon as the calm began, Colin had gotten them on their feet, moving south to the light. They had pushed hard and were exhausted. Travis and Jim, the younger of the men were about the same age as Colin, and brothers to the man who had died. Kaytra could see grief edging in as their physical needs were met. They ate in silence while she helped Colin wrap Ed's broken ribs and bandage his other cuts.

All of them were very polite, quiet men. Tan and robust, fishermen bred with years of determination and acceptance. They talked long about the storm, drinking as much black coffee as Kaytra could set before them. She made a simple but nourishing meal, serving them in silence. She hung up their clothes as they changed into the things Colin got for them. Soon one corner of the kitchen was strung with lines of sagging, wet clothing.

At one o'clock, Michael awakened. The sound of a baby crying brought the first smiles. "S'pose that's the boy you been tellin' us about, Colin." Norman said with a side-long glance at Kaytra as she went upstairs. "Bring 'im down. Let's see if'n he's as han'some as his fatheah says he is."

Kaytra went, realizing the men could use a distraction. She fed and changed Michael as quickly as she could. Four pairs of eyes looked up when she reappeared. Colin was gone.

"Left ta check the light, " Ed explained. "How old is the baby?"

"A month." She scooted Michael up a little so they could all see him. Michael was very content with the extra attention and rewarded the men with a smile.

It was encouraging to see Travis and Jim pull out of their sadness. Jim even asked to hold the baby so Kaytra could clean the dishes. "Weahen't ya' scahed heahe by youahself, just you an' the baby?"

She nodded slightly.

"'Couahse she was, Jim." Norman mildly rebuked him for asking. "Could neah swahe she'd faint when we come in an' she thought Colin wasn't with us."

"Don't blame ya none." Travis told her. "Theahe's but a lot o' nothin' heahe ta town. Whole lot o' nothin'."

"Figures me why folks don't go crazy bein' a lighthouse keepeah." Norman shook his head tiredly, getting agreement from all around the table. "Glad Colin did what he did taday, but it beats me what bade him go out an' look foah us when he says he didn' even know why he was out theahe."

"Told us somethin' 'bout a - a voice tellin' him ta go." Travis half-swung around to look at Kaytra who had stopped what she was doing to listen. "You know what that means?"

She wiped her hands on her apron. "Yes, I do. It mean's that he heard the Spirit of God telling him someone was in trouble. Someone needed his help."

Jim nodded. "Like when Michael was boahn? Colin said he heahed the voice then, too."

"Yup." Travis remembered now. "Neveah met a man what admits ta heahin' voices in his head."

All four men laughed at that, but in an understanding way, a way that said they were pleased to know Colin. He came in to the sound of their laughter, smiling to himself to find them more relaxed.

"You've got a fine son heahe, Colin." Ed congratulated him. "Ain't made a peep. Just stahes at Jim theahe."

Colin hung up his coat slowly. "Well then, I hate to break up his audience, but it is late. The storm has picked up again."

"Know'd it was a comin' back."

"Sometimes they do that, Norman." Colin walked over to the table, taking Michael as Jim held the baby out to him. "There's a spare room upstairs with a single bed. And there's a sofa down here."

"I don't mind sleepin' on the flooah none." Jim volunteered. "Should let Ed take the bed. Come on Norman, you cen have the couch. Trav will sleep on the flooah by me."

"I'll get extra blankets then." Colin took Ed upstairs, still carrying Michael in his arms.

Kaytra was grateful to be in the kitchen by herself. A spare room? Well, certainly Colin had no choice but to give away her room, but in doing so, he had managed to salvage his pride! Of course, he couldn't let the men know the truth. She wiped imaginary crumbs from the table, feeling guilty for her thoughts. The men had endured a traumatic experience and here she was complaining about the sleeping arrangements.

Colin came back minus Michael. His arms were loaded with pillows and blankets. It wasn't long before the other men were bedded down, too. They said quiet "thank you's" to Colin. Words suddenly seemed inadequate, though, and they closed their eyes, inviting sleep.

While Colin banked the fires for the night, Kaytra fed Rex, petting him for a long time - even after Colin extinguished all but the light he would take with them. "Kaytra?" She stood slowly, but didn't meet his eyes as she walked past him.

The cradle had been moved to the big corner room. Michael lay inside, still awake, watching the gentle play of light on the ceiling. Kaytra noticed, too, that one of her nightgowns was lying on the bed. She heard Colin close the door. "You don't like having to sleep in here." He didn't ask it as a question, because they both knew the answer.

"I wasn't - expecting it." Kaytra rocked the cradle back and forth, unnecessarily straightening the blankets.

Colin watched her for a moment, then put out the lamp, leaving only a smaller light burning on the table next to the bed. "I wouldn't ha-."

"It's alright, Colin." She interrupted in a whisper, knowing she would only feel worse to hear him say that he liked the idea even less than she did.

He pulled his boots off, setting them near the door before moving over to the bed. When the small lamp went out, the room was plunged into darkness...and silence, except for the sound of the cradle on the floor. Colin undressed wearily and crawled into bed.

It was many minutes later before Kaytra even moved. He heard the rustle of clothes as she changed. Then nothing. By flipping onto his back, Colin could see that she stood beside the bed.

"I -." Her whisper was shaken. "The day - Michael was born."

Colin sat up. "What about it?"

"You told them...you came - because -."

"Because God told me you needed help. Yes."

"After - Michael...When the other baby -." Kaytra took an anxious step closer. "What happened?"

"Kaytra-."

"Tell me. Please," she pleaded with him.

"Not until you sit down." He rolled back the covers on the other side of the bed. Kaytra hesitated, but finally slid onto the mattress. "Now, lie down." She obeyed slowly. He could feel her tension. Colin pulled the blankets over her, lying on his side, facing her. "What do you want to know?"

"Everything. There's - more than you told me before."

He propped his head up in his palm. "Do you remember when she was born?" Kaytra nodded. "You were in a lot of pain. Barely conscious. You started hemorrhaging." She twisted her head to look at him. Colin heard her draw in a shaky breath. "I couldn't stop the bleeding. You drifted in and out....You were-."

"Dying?"

"Yes," he answered quietly.

Kaytra felt the truth sink in. There had always been questions about that day, things she didn't want to remember because the other baby had died. Now that she allowed herself to remember, it came rushing back. "I -. You -."

"I held you and prayed that God would let you live."

"Why?"

He went still. "Did you want to die?"

"No, but-."

"God is the one who healed you, Kaytra."

There was a long time of silence. Colin eventually laid his head on the pillow. Outside, the storm was raging again. He could see the light's beam through the windows. Though he felt sad because four men had died that day, four others were safe beneath this roof, waiting to go back to their families.

He remembered being in the storm, hearing the bell ring. Its sound had been comforting, for then he had known Kaytra was safe. When they had been able to move, the light had been their guide. For the very first time, he had known what it was to be the other person; to be the one who sought the light rather than the one who saw it go out into the darkness. It had taken this storm for him to realize Kaytra's feelings all those months ago when she was seeking God. Weariness seeped into his very bones and at last he fell asleep.

Beside him, Kaytra listened to the evenness of his breathing. If he hadn't prayed for her, she would have died. She knew it now. She remembered wanting to say good-bye to him, hearing him say her name. God had asked him to be there that day, yet still Colin had to choose. He had to choose to hear God's voice.

She awoke at the first tentative knock. Colin stirred beside her. Neither of them felt as if they had slept more than a few minutes. The knock came again. "Colin?" It was Travis, sounding very upset even through the thickness of the door.

Colin was up at once, pulling on his clothes. He opened the door still buttoning his shirt. "What's wrong?"

Travis sounded embarrassed and scared at the same time. He caught sight of Kaytra in the dim, just-before-dawn gray of the room, but quickly looked back at Colin. "It's Jim. He's havin' a hahd time 'bout -," there was a poignant pause, " 'bout losin' ouah brotheah. Nightmahes like. Could - could ya come calm 'im down? Won't listen ta me none an' - I - well -."

"Of course. " Colin joined him on the landing, closing the door as they left. Kaytra heard their hushed tones and matched footsteps going down the stairs. After a few minutes; she got up, too, unable to go back to sleep because she knew the grief Jim must be feeling.

Michael was still sound asleep. She dressed in the same clothes she had worn the day before and combed her hair, braiding it down her back. Standing at the window, looking out, she could see a faint tinge of color on the horizon where yesterday there had been only angry clouds.

Her gaze traveled to the top of the tower where the light still burned. Was Colin sharing his faith with Jim? Praying with him? She felt so confused now. If someone had asked her before last night about Colin's relationship with God, she would have said he didn't seem to care anymore.

Today, she had to wonder herself what was going on inside of him. What was he thinking? She looked over her shoulder at the trunk where yesterday she had found his Bible. She had seen him read it so many times before Lydia's death, but lately he hadn't even touched it.

Kaytra peered at the light again. If Colin was busy downstairs, she should go and turn it off. The baby would sleep awhile yet. She left the room as quietly as she could. In the parlor, Colin was sitting in his usual chair at the desk with Travis beside Jim on the settee and Norman slumped tiredly in the rocker. They were engrossed in what Colin was saying. Jim's eyes looked red from crying.

Kaytra decided it was best not to disturb them by starting coffee as she would usually have done. Instead, she walked to the door, pausing long enough to wrap a shawl about her shoulders. The air was cool outside, but up in the tower it would be quite warm. Rex came to meet her, running circles around her as if yesterday's ordeal had never happened.

From the oceanside windows, Kaytra could see the remnants of the storm far to the north. A distant dulling of the sky. And, though the day didn't promise sunshine, it would be free from turmoil, at least any that nature could bring forth.

She began to extinguish the lamps, cleaning each one thoroughly before moving on to the next. The shawl was soon laid aside as she knelt before the wheel. Though she had done this many times the day before, it seemed different somehow today and she knew the difference was inside herself.

Yesterday she had done it wondering all the while where Colin was. Why he wasn't back. If he was even alive. She stared at the glass chimney in her hands. The sight of it blurred with the tears that crept into her eyes.

Yesterday she had kept the light going, but with little trust and faith. Not as much as she should have had. Shame poured over her as she realized the weakness her fears had revealed. How very little she knew about having complete trust in God.

She wiped a hand across her cheek. God must be so disappointed in her. More tears followed those she had just wiped away.

Only a slight sound on the stairs warned her to conceal her emotion in time. When she looked up, Colin was there. It was a long time before he said anything. Kaytra knew he was trying to read her thoughts. "You didn't need to do this."

She went back to cleaning the chimney. "That's alright...How is Jim?"

"He'll be fine," Colin said closer beside her. "You look as if you could use a few more hours of sleep."

"So do you."

He frowned sightly at hearing the forced evenness she applied to the words.

"Will you take them to Truro today?"

"After I get back." He was ready for her curious look. "I have to find the other bodies first. Travis is going with me."

Of course, she hadn't thought. Kaytra replaced the chimney, turned the wheel and put out the next lamp, her movements once again perfectly efficient.

Colin watched her awhile. There would be time later to talk with her...when they were both better rested. He said nothing before he left. In his pocket, he carried the page she had torn from the journal. She had never meant for him to find it, but God had.

Chapter Twenty-Eight

Colin was gone much longer than he expected that day. Besides stopping in at Seth and Anna's to make sure they were all right, he spent some time with Jim and Travis' family. Then rain on the way home had slowed his travel.

Night was fast edging out evening by the time he saw the familiar silhouette of Highland again. He urged Samson faster, eager to be somewhere warm and dry again. Rex was soon barking a welcome. Colin saw a shaft of light as the kitchen door was opened to let him out. But it didn't stay open long. Michael was probably awake.

He pulled up to the barn, climbing down from the wagon with a weary sigh. Two days had never seemed so long as these just past. Though Samson anxiously pushed his way into the barn when Colin opened the door, the big horse stopped just inside, ears pricked. Colin could see why immediately.

There was another horse in the barn. It took only a minute for Colin to light the lamp on a high shelf near the door. The other horse, a grey-spotted mare, stared back at them from the stall next to Samson's. Obviously, company had arrived while he was away. Colin vaguely remembered seeing the mare at the livery in Provincetown. He took hold of Samson's reins, leading him forward.

In another fifteen minutes, the horse was settled for the night. Colin took the light with him to the house, curious now to know who was there. Maybe someone checking on them just as he had stopped at the Buckley's. Rex trotted along two steps ahead.

Colin used the kitchen door, smelling fresh coffee and the lingering aroma of bread baked that day. But Kaytra wasn't there. His eyes automatically moved to the parlor, even as he pushed the door closed behind him.

"Hello, Colin."

Every muscle in him went perfectly still, except for the one which worked at the corner of his jaw as his teeth clenched together. He stared at the other man, not willing to show the slightest emotion. They hadn't seen one another in over five years, years which had not been used to breed forgiveness. Quite the opposite in fact.

Colin moved first, walking to the table where he set down the lamp he carried. Then he jerked his arms from his coat, throwing it over the back of the nearest chair. A thousand thoughts raced through his mind, most of them not pleasant.

Light, hurrying footsteps sounded on the stairs. But only for a moment because Kaytra froze part way down to see that Colin already stood in the kitchen. Her face went white beneath the furious look in his eyes.

He turned fully toward her as she continued down the stairs, not missing the long glance which passed between her and the one man in the world he could truly say he had never wanted to see again......Sidney Kent.

Kaytra stopped at the bottom of the stairs, poised between the two men.

"You have some - explanation for this, I suppose?" The sheer harshness of Colin's question opened deep wounds.

"She does." Sidney took a few steps closer, carrying himself with the same studied grace Colin had come to loathe all those years ago. His blue eyes waxed cold in light of Colin's anger. "May I - suggest you listen to her before you strike out again?"

"You may," Colin ground out, "but that's the last time you talk until I hear what she says." His gaze flew back to Kaytra. "She lies quite well on her own without any help from an expert."

Just as Sidney started to move forward, Kaytra's hand shot out, touching his arm to keep him back. A look passed between Kaytra and Sidney which sickened Colin. He swung away from them both, forcing Kaytra to speak to his back. "Sidney and I met in Boston - the day I went to the cemetery. There was an - accident, nearly and - I was still so weak. I - didn't know who he was until I saw - Sondra."

The muscles of Colin's back flexed rigid.

Kaytra took a couple of hesitant steps closer. "I fainted. Sidney took me to the house where he was staying. The Chester's." She couldn't read his face at all when he slowly turned their way again. "I - didn't tell him at first who I was."

"Of course not. Why would you?"

"You aren't being fair, Colin."

"Fair!"

"Please." She rushed forward. "The children."

His eyes moved to the landing. So...Sondra was here, too?

"Please, Colin. Don't raise your voice again. It would only frighten her."

Colin looked back to her pale, anxious face and then past her to where Sidney stood. "Let me guess, you became friends. You're very good at - charming young women, right Sidney?"

"No, Colin," he answered with his own barely controlled anger. "In all truth, I disliked Kaytra when she finally told me who she was. Except for the fact that she and Sondra became so close, I would have brought her back to you and gladly so.....but she can be very - persuasive."

"Really?" Colin chided with little regard for how it would hurt her. She was making a valiant effort not to cry. "What else? There must be a 'happy-ever-after' to your fairy tale, Kaytra? An ending that is so touching I'll forget all the lies?"

Kaytra's anguish was complete with those final blows. She whirled around, blinded by tears. Sidney caught her in his arms as she attempted to escape upstairs. With her face buried against his shoulder, she didn't see as he did the murderous look Colin threw at him.

"Let - go - of - my - wife."

"Your wife?" Sidney raised his eyebrows expressively. "You don't deserve her as your wife."

"How would you know, after what you did to Lydia?"

An old battle, a battle which yet needed to be fought. Perhaps it was time. Sidney held Kaytra away from him enough so that he could see her face. "Go upstairs, Kaytra. You're tired."

"But-."

"Go on." He encouraged her, without care for Colin's disapproval. "Tomorrow we will decide." She nodded like a little girl and walked unsteadily up the stairs without looking at Colin until she was on the landing. He saw so much raw emotion in her eyes it stunned him to the core.

After she was gone, Sidney was the one who broke the silence. "There's coffee. Kaytra made it not long ago."

Something hot and strong....Colin needed it. The night was going to be a long one. He had a whole gut-full of anger to vent on his former brother-in-law in defense of the wrongs done to his sister. Then, he would learn just why Kaytra had kept it a secret that she had met Sidney Kent.

Colin moved uncomfortably in the chair where he had slept for little more than two hours. When he felt again the tapping on his shoulder which had begun to pull him from slumber, he forced his eyes open.

"Are you Colin MacRae?"

There was no mistaking her. Sondra had changed little from the picture except that she was taller and her hair longer. She had become a very lovely eight year old. Colin sat up. "Yes...I am."

"Kaytra said you're my uncle. She said you were handsome."

An involuntary smile crossed his face.

Sondra peered more closely at him. "Do you always sleep in a chair?"

His chuckle had her smiling, too. "No, I don't."

Sondra nodded in very adult fashion. "I like you."

"Well, that's good." He looked through the windows. Sunrise was breaking over the horizon in glorious colors. "You're up early, Sondra."

"How did you know my name?" Her frown was half-disappointed, half-pleased as she crossed her arms over her cornflower blue dress.

"Because I only have one niece." Colin reached up to touch the curl of blonde hair that bounced on her shoulder. A feeling of contentment came in seeing her again, knowing she was all right.

"Everybody else is sleeping. Kaytra said you could see miles and miles from the tower. I was going to sneak up there alone, but you may come along."

She certainly had a charm about her. Colin pushed himself to his feet. "If *you* come with *me*, young Sondra, I'll be putting you to work."

"I'm a good worker." Her eyes sparkled with excitement at the adventure ahead and she suddenly stuck out her hand. Colin looked down at her rather puzzled. "We haven't shaken hands yet. Isn't that what people do when they meet one another?"

"Not uncles and nieces," he said quickly. "They give one another a hug." As Sondra enthusiastically threw herself into his arms, hugging his waist with every ounce of strength in her, Colin's heart contracted with emotion. The things Sidney had said last night became very clear to him now. "Go get your coat." Sondra flew to the door, grabbing her wool cape from the hook with all the careless abandon of a child who loved life.

They were up in the tower for a long time. Colin soon found that Sondra was never at a loss for something to say. More often than not, her sentences began exactly the same way, "Kaytra said..." Obviously their week together in Boston had left quite an impression.

When it was time to go down, she made a game of counting the number of steps. Colin laughed as the number got higher and she kept missing her place on purpose in order to go back a few steps and pick up the game all over again.

They walked into the house, deep in a discussion about taking Samson for "a gallop on the beach." Kaytra and Sidney both looked up from their places at the table. Sidney with curiosity. Kaytra with apprehension. She simply couldn't sit still any longer and got up to check on Michael who lay in his cradle which Sidney had carried down to the kitchen.

"Papa!" Sondra hurried to him. "I saw the whole world!"

"Really?" Sidney gently rumpled her hair .

"No," she smiled coyly. "Not the whole world really, but I did see very far. Colin let me help him. We had a grand time, didn't we Colin?"

"Yes, we did." He joined them, taking his usual seat. Sidney gave him a questioning look, which Colin wasn't ready yet to answer.

Sondra went to see the baby, jabbering at him and Kaytra in turn. It was obvious she adored Michael, too.

Colin looked back at Sidney. The years had changed him. Added lines to his face. Given him maturity. Last night's honesty had surprised Colin. He still couldn't believe Sidney actually wanted to give up Sondra for reasons which were entirely unselfish. Yet Colin believed Sidney loved his daughter enough to see that she finally had a real home and not the constant moving from place to place as their life had been lived the past five years.

In the time Colin had spent with Sondra, he knew that he would say "yes" to keeping her. Her personality was so like Lydia's. So vibrant. He had loved her all these years. Now that love would only deepen.

Sidney finished the coffee in the cup he held in his hand. "I need to leave within an hour to make the ship back to Boston," he said it quietly, for Colin alone to hear.

"Does she know?"

"Yes, I told her on the way here....She loves Kaytra very much, Colin. Like she would a mother."

Colin sensed a certain amount of apology in those words. It was as close to admitting he had been wrong as Sidney had come. There had been some changes in Sidney over the years. Colin could see that now. Maybe they had both changed. Maybe God had done a work in both their lives ... "If she stays, it will be for good. I won't have you taking her away again." There was a slow nod of agreement to Colin's condition. "We will keep her, then."

"And Kaytra?"

The ultimatum hadn't, by any means, been forgotten. Late last night, Sidney had demanded a condition of his own. Colin must set things right with Kaytra, this half -life they had been living must be stopped and steps taken toward making it a real marriage. Colin leaned both arms on the table, feeling the tension in his muscles. "It will be taken care of."

Sidney gave him a searching look.

"I'm hungry," Sondra's cheerful voice cut the silence. "What's for breakfast, Kaytra? May we have eggs?"

"Are you very hungry?" Kaytra asked, while moving to the stove.

"Very, very. Uncle Colin is, too. He didn't have any supper last night!" She said it in a shocked voice, unable to believe someone could actually survive without supper! "Do I get to milk Bessie today? And feed the chickens?"

"After you eat breakfast, of course."

Sondra giggled. "Of course. I can set the table for you."

Kaytra got plates and silverware, trying all the while not to let her anxiety show. Colin and Sidney had been talking so seriously. Despite Sidney's earlier assurances, she felt far from confident that Colin didn't still hate her for the secret.

Shortly after breakfast, Sidney announced it was time for him to leave. Colin was quick to offer to get the horse and buggy ready. Once he was gone, Sondra made her way into her father's arms, cuddling on his lap. "Can't you stay, too, Papa? I shall miss you."

"I'll come back to see you often, Sondra. And you may write to me."

"But - it won't be the same."

"Life is always changing." Sidney hugged her close. "That's half the fun of it, don't you think? You'll enjoy living here. Having one home instead of traveling from place to place. Having Michael to take care of. And Kaytra and Colin."

Sondra nodded, stretching up to place a kiss on his cheek that brought tears to Kaytra's eyes as she watched them. The little-girl smile had returned when Sondra pulled away. "Good-bye, Papa."

"Bye, Sondra." Sidney stood to get his coat and the satchel. Then slowly, he looked across at Kaytra. "Take care of her." Kaytra nodded.

Her steps toward him were slow and hesitant until Sidney reached for her hand. "Everything will work out. I remember your telling me that not long ago. Good-bye." He placed a light kiss on her cheek, waved to Sondra once again and went out the door.

Incredibly, it was Sondra who offered comfort to Kaytra instead of the other way around. She slipped her arm through Kaytra's. "You like my father?"

"Yes. He's a good man." Kaytra smiled down at her.

"Is it time for Michael's bath yet?"

"Not until tonight, but you may help me in lots of other ways. We need to get your room set up and there is Bessie and the chickens and laundry-."

"And a gallop on the beach." Sondra added firmly. "Colin said we could. I suppose it is too cold yet to go for a swim in the ocean?"

The day flew by swiftly. There were many things to be done which the storm had postponed. Sondra spent much of her time with Colin, shadowing his every move until late in the afternoon when she began to talk less and a sad, lonely look came into her blue eyes.

Colin tried to distract her by showing her the journal. "I have to write in this every day. Four times. What shall we say about the weather now?" She moved up to him, leaning into his shoulder. "Is it raining?"

"No."

"Then it is sunny." He picked up the pen, writing as he spoke. "Sondra says it is sunny outside. And the wind-." He looked to her for the words.

"The wind is - being lazy."

Colin's eyebrows rose expressively, but he wrote it down anyway. "Now the sea. What is it doing?"

Sondra thought about that. "It looks - sleepy after the storm. All tired out from playing so hard." She waited until those words were entered, too, then laid her head on his shoulder once more. "I miss my father, Colin."

He wasn't surprised. "You probably will for a while. But every day the missing gets less and less."

"Like Kaytra said when she misses my mother?"

Colin looked over her head to where Kaytra sat in the rocking chair by the windows, nursing Michael. Their eyes met and held. "Yes. Just like that. Only your father will come and visit you sometimes. But you can't stay sad all that time, can you?" She shrugged. "I was thinking," Colin set her back a little so he could see her face. "How about if we have a party tonight to celebrate your coming to stay at Highland. Would you like that?"

Her eyes brightened. "Really? A party? I could wear my fancy dress and we could have candles and everything?"

"And everything." Colin's smile broadened. He looked back at Kaytra in time to see a shimmer of tears before she lowered her lashes to hide them from him. Maybe all three of them needed a reason to celebrate.

Sondra twirled around in the small space of her room, watching the skirt of her dress flair out as Kaytra finished getting dressed. "What will Colin wear tonight? Do you think my dress is pretty enough?"

"Yes, honey. It's very pretty."

"Not as pretty as yours." Sondra turned to look at Kaytra again, admiring the graceful beauty of the rose silk with its delicate lace. Kaytra was putting a last pin into the chignon at the back of her head. "Will I look like you when I'm big? And have a husband just like Colin? And wear beautiful pink dresses to parties and-?"

"Sondra." Kaytra laughed quietly. "I can't keep up with so many questions. Besides, we need to hurry and see how our dinner is coming along." She turned to her, thinking what a lovely child she was. She gave Sondra a quick hug. "Come on now, quietly, so Michael doesn't wake up."

Michael was sleeping contentedly in his cradle. Kaytra was hoping the nap would last a few hours so that she could give Sondra some extra attention. They walked down the stairs hand in hand.

"Colin?" Sondra caught his attention as soon as she saw him standing at the windows in the parlor. He turned with a ready smile, though his expression slowly changed when he saw Kaytra.

Sondra let go of Kaytra's hand to hurry down the last few steps and run up to Colin, catching his hands in hers. "Do you like my dress? Kaytra said it's very pretty. She brushed my hair, too, and we found a ribbon. You look nice. That's your uniform, isn't it? I like it."

"Thank you." He tried to concentrate on her words, but was more than a little distracted by Kaytra. That same sense of expectation lasted throughout their meal and the quiet time with Sondra which came afterward. She climbed up into Colin's lap, snuggling against him as if she had done so many times before. They talked of Boston and horses, of Paris and pretty clothes.

Eventually, she drifted off to sleep, looking to Colin just like a fairy princess tired from her long day of playing. While the silence wrapped itself around the room, Colin found his thoughts and feelings more focused on the other beautiful princess in the room.

"Shall I take her upstairs?" Kaytra asked in a hushed tone.

"No." Colin stood slowly, lifting Sondra with him. "I'll be down in a few minutes.

Kaytra watched them leave. The party had been a good idea to help Sondra get beyond that first loneliness. Tomorrow would be easier. There were still a few dishes to be done. She cleared off the table, stacking them beside the basin, though she hadn't yet poured the water when she heard Colin come up behind her. There was something very serious in his quiet approach, enough to lift Kaytra's eyes up to his.

"Will you leave those? I think we should talk." He didn't wait for an answer, but went to where their coats hung on the pegs by the door. She moved forward slowly, allowing him to place a cape over her shoulders.

Outside, the night was fresh and still. A golden path of moonlight traced its way across the ocean, rippling with the gentle waves. They walked side by side to the edge of the bank. It seemed an eternity before Colin found the right words to say.

"Last night, Sidney explained some things to me. He told me how Sondra was before you met them. Did you ever wonder if God had it in mind all along to bring you into their lives?"

Kaytra tilted her head back so that she could see him. "Yes, I wondered about it all the time I had to be away from you."

Colin paused under the weight of her honesty. "You helped her to be happy again, to reach out and take hold of life, just-."

"Just as Lydia helped me," Kaytra finished the thought for him, feeling the depth of his gaze.

"Why did you leave here instead of staying? You wrote in the journal that you loved me."

She caught her breath. "I - loved you enough to promise Lydia that - that I wouldn't be the one to give you the excuse to stay."

His brow furrowed with a frown. "I don't understand."

Though Kaytra looked away, he could still hear the remembered pain in her voice. "She wanted you to go back to Boston. She wanted you to really get to know your father. It hurt her to think that you would never let yourself get close to him."

"Then...you promised her I would go back, no matter what it cost." He drew in a deep breath. All this time he had accused her of ruining his life. Yet now, he knew that she had been trying to strengthen it. She had been willing to refuse a future at Highland as his wife, to risk going back to Koch and all the uncertainties of Boston in order to keep her promise to Lydia. "What if I hadn't tried to find you again?"

"I don't know, Colin." Moonlight picked up the presence of her tears, turning them diamond bright as she lifted her eyes to his.

He brought his hands up to her arms, feeling her tremble, but finding no resistance to his touch. "My father and I, we've decided to start over." Kaytra reached up to touch the buttons of his coat. He could feel the tension give way in her. "Somehow, you've managed to get two very stubborn Scotsmen to change their ways. Plus you became a dear friend to my mother. You've won her over, too, Kaytra...She knows about Sondra coming to live with us, doesn't she? That's what all the letters were about."

Kaytra nodded quietly. "And about what I felt for you." She whispered the words, shielding her eyes from his self-consciously.

"No wonder she was so upset when I told her I was going to marry Tricia." Colin felt Kaytra stiffen a little beneath his touch. He moved one hand to her face, guiding her chin upward until he could read her expression again. "I wouldn't have really, but you did make me very angry, Kaytra."

"I'm - sorry."

His smile took the seriousness out of his tone. "How did you know about Tricia and the Travois, about her giving so much money to Montgomery?"

"Through Sidney. He went there a couple of times, I guess." Kaytra shrugged her shoulders.

"Did he tell you what she's doing now?" He could see by the flash of guilt in her eyes that the answer was yes, that she was blaming herself for Tricia running off with Montgomery and leaving the Michaels' devastated. "Right or wrong, we all make our own choices, Kaytra. You had to make one where Sidney was concerned. He thinks a great deal of you for having the courage - and the faith to stand up to him." Colin slid his hand to the tender nape of her neck. "So do I."

Kaytra's eyes filled with more tears.

"Are you looking at me through 'eyes of gratefulness'?"

She parted her lips, unable to form a word. He had found the page, then. He had read her heart-felt words. The pain and worry. The love...Colin's eyes suddenly showed her what she wanted to know. His features were content and at peace as she remembered him when she first came to Highland. Only even more so...

"The Light carried us both through, Kaytra....It was wrong of me to turn from God. To hurt you as I did. I'm sorry for that." She tried to speak, but his thumb pressed against her lips. "Will you stay with me here....as my wife? Help me in keeping the Light?"

She nodded.

"I have something for you," Colin said, reaching one hand into the pocket of his coat. "Turn around." When she did, he brought his arms around her, then back to her neck until she felt the weight of the pearl upon her breast.

Her hands touched it softly as Colin fastened the clasp, feeling the warm hope it symbolized.

Chapter Twenty-Eight

"I love you, Kaytra," Colin whispered in her ear.

Just beyond them, a wave was leaving shore, spreading a thousand golden pearls in its wake. Colin moved until he was facing her again, until he could trace the outline of her lips. Their softness and the love he saw in her eyes drew him to replace his thumb with a kiss which held apology and promise all at once.

As he slowly pulled away, her eyes rose to the top of the tower to see the light as it shone there. Colin followed her gaze, pulling her close against him. Even if one day they moved from Highland, they would always be close to the Source of Light which had guided them through the darkness. They would always be keepers of the Light.